I0818283

TROUBLE WEIGHS A TON

MARK ATLEY

TROUBLE WEIGHS A TON

TULSA UNDERWORLD BOOK 2

4 Horsemen Publications, Inc.

Trouble Weighs a Ton
Tulsa Underworld Book 2

4 Horsemen Publications, Inc.
1497 Main St. Suite 169
Dunedin, FL 34698
4horsemenpublications.com
info@4horsemenpublications.com

Cover by Jenn Kotic
Typesetting by S. Wilder
Editor Laura Mita

Library of Congress Control Number: 2021951211

Print ISBN: 978-1-64450-473-4
Hardcover ISBN: 978-1-64450-743-8
Audio ISBN: 978-1-64450-471-0
E-Book ISBN: 978-1-64450-472-7

DEDICATION:

To my father ...
and as always, my wife and children.

ACKNOWLEDGMENT:

I WANT TO THANK THE FOLKS (GIRLS) AT 4 HORSEMEN for taking a chance on me, and I hope to make it very worth their while. I want to thank those of you who follow me on Twitter and offer encouragement, including Martine, Craig, Gareth, J. Todd, Scott, J.B., Stephen, Eric (Beetner—Long live Writer Types), Max, Neil, Alec, and many more who I've interacted with over the years.

To my coworkers and family who have put up with me during many story breakdown sessions. A very special thanks to my wife—for putting up with me.

And always, thank you to each and every one who reads this novel. Without you, this would not be possible.

TABLE OF CONTENTS

PROLOGUE: JIM DIMAGGIO

JIM DIMAGGIO STEPS INSIDE MAYFIELD'S GAS STATION.

"Welcome back, Jim," old man Mayfield says from behind the counter. He is positioned to the left and perched atop his stool with his shoulders slumped forward and elbows on the counter, reading the newspaper. Mayfield licks his finger and turns a page. "Not working today?"

Jim glances around and sees a kid in a black sweatshirt using the phone off to the side. The kid is opposite Mayfield and turned away from Jim. He's never seen the kid before. Figures, Tulsa's a growing metropolis, the second-largest city in the state. Jim shakes his head as he grabs a styrofoam cup and begins to fill it with thick black coffee from the burners near Mayfield's counter. "Boy's playin' in a tournament. I thought I'd stop by and grab some coffee while they're warming up. Discount still good even if I'm not working?"

"For you, always," Mayfield says. "In uniform or out of it, coffee's always free for you. How's the kiddo doing? He decide on a position yet?"

"He doesn't know," Jim says. "Like Willie Mays, he thinks he can play everywhere, and to be honest, he can. So I'm not sure if he wants to stay a centerfielder or switch to pitcher. He's one helluva pitcher, but I don't know about him being in a rotation and not playin' every day. He's leaning toward playin' every day, like Willie, 'cuz he is one helluva hitter.

Can't be both a hitter and pitcher. Babe Ruth had that problem, and we don't remember him as a pitcher."

"His school win last night?" Mayfield asks without waiting for an answer. "I've not worked my way through to the Sports section yet. I have to start at the beginning and go all the way through to the end, every word, never skim. My wife hates it, but that's how my granddaddy taught me to read. He used to say 'don't know what you might miss if you start skipping over things.' Can tell a lot about a man by how he reads. Of course, people don't read no more.

"My wife says I'm particular. I tell her, she could work the store from time to time, and then she'd find out just how slow it gets around here. When it's busy, it's busy, but when it's slow, it's slow. And I have a way of doing things to make time go by; I have to stay in a routine or I get all out of whack. I don't like things out of whack. She asks 'Aren't you worried about someone taking something when you're not looking?' And I say, 'Why would I stop them? With all that free coffee and donuts I offer Jim, we're good. If you're going to rob me or shoplift from me, that'd be pretty damn bold.' I tell her that's why I do it, to make sure nothing like that happens, insurance, see?" Mayfield pauses and removes an envelope from under the counter. "Which reminds me, here you go." He slides the envelope across the counter toward Jim, who accepts it, hesitantly. "Look, I know how you are about this; buy your boy some new cleats or something."

"You don't have to—"

"—I want to. It keeps you around. I like you. I'll pay for you to come in here because, if I have any problems, I know you'll handle them."

"That's extortion."

"Not when I *choose* to do it, it ain't. I'm lucky you're flexible enough to take it and see it for what it is."

"And what's that?"

"Me helping others; warms my heart to help out this way. Only way I can. Consider this me giving back to my community."

Jim shoves the envelope into his inner jacket pocket. "You mind watching the coffee while I take a leak?"

Mayfield says, "No problem," and Jim goes to the restroom next to the coolers, leaving his cup in Mayfield's care. He steps inside, shuts the door, and does his business. After, he opens the door to find the kid, probably twenty, if that—the same one with the phone—pointing a big, shiny, silver handgun at Mayfield, who has one hand up in the air while using the other to drop some bills into a plastic bag—cash register open.

Jim pats the envelope in his breast pocket.

If he gets paid to come around and protect the place then he can't let the old man get robbed or shot, can he?

Money comes at a price.

Even if he sometimes takes a step sideways, doing little things, like slipping a twenty out of a guy's wallet or coming in here to get an envelope full of cash, he's sworn to do the right thing. As Mayfield said, he's insured; Jim's his insurance. It's his choice to pay Jim. It's not like Jim's ever threatened him for the money.

But now someone is threatening Mayfield.

Jim unbuttons his jacket and lets it hang loosely. "Hey kid," he says, keeping his hands from the .38 holstered at his side, which isn't a bright move, but he doesn't want to surprise the kid and make him lose it and pull the trigger. "Easy now, no one hasta act hastily; we can work this out. You keep doin' what you're doin' and take the money and go. Don't do something we both'll regret."

"Stay back!" the kid yells, voice cracking with fear, attention on Jim. "Back!"

"It's alright." Jim steps closer. "Look, I've done the draw and fire in under a second. All I need is one second, maybe one and a half, and I can clear this holster and have my muzzle on target."

"Mister, I'm warning you!" the kid yells, desperation in his voice. "Back!"

"Kid," Jim states sharply. "I'm saying, I'm a sheriff's deputy. If I wanted you dead, you'd be dead. I'm not sayin' you can do what you're doin'. I'm not condoning this, but today, I'll let it go. That's a friend of mine right there. I don't like you pointing that thing at him. Put it away and finish doin' what you're doin', and we'll all go our way."

The kid squares with Jim. "Yeah, well, I have friends too."

Jim starts the draw, throws his jacket back, and drives his hand down on the gun in the holster, pulling the .38 clear, all in less than a second. But then he feels the movement off to his right: the whoosh of something in his peripheral, cold rising up to his ear, and a voice saying, "Wrong move."

Jim thinks of his boy and how he'll never find out which position—

CHAPTER ONE: SONNY ROWAN

"LET ME GO ON SABBATICAL," SONNY SAYS, FOLlowing Jimmy into his corner office, arguing his point some more.

Jimmy half turns to speak over his shoulder. "Are those even real things?" he says, taking a seat behind his desk, ignoring Sonny's actual point, and leaving Sonny standing in the doorway. "I mean do people actually leave their job for an unspecified, or specified time—seeing you're always hearing about some teacher or overworked pansy leaving for a year to quote-unquote find themselves—and their employers actually let them? Would you do that?"

Sonny stays quiet.

"Who would do that? I know who would, a coconut; that's who," Jimmy adds, tapping his temple with his left hand. "If you're working for me, you're working for me, not off, jerkin' around on nothing, following some misguided attempt to manage a mid-life crisis. I'm not a coconut."

"So is that a yes?" Sonny asks.

"You know very damn well that's a no," Jimmy says dryly, relaxing in his chair behind the desk, hands together across his stomach, a big window behind him. Through the window, downtown is on display as if it were a matte painting, picturesque, almost perfect. It's late evening, and the Oklahoma sky is painted in shades of oranges and purples. It's the only elegant thing in Jimmy's office and the only benefit to being the boss, as he puts it. Everything else is a cluttered mess of papers, books, and magazines, crammed in every nook and cranny. And that's saying something because the office is the size and color of a horse's stall, which means it's barely big enough for Sonny to stand there trying to convince his boss to give him a couple of days off, and in the mess, hay wouldn't look out of place. "This is a paper, Sonny. We have deadlines to meet. I can't just let one of my highest paid journalists—I know you disdain the word. 'Writer,' is that better?"

"'Reporter' is fine."

"Well, I can't let one of those have a couple of days off at the drop of a hat or when the wind blows. And it gets hard when he's already a week behind on his column and missed the last two weeks of football, for what—you going to tell me?"

"I know it's a paper." Sonny shrugs. "You don't have to tell me what I already know. But Jimmy, what I know is we are friends, long-time friends, and as a friend, I'm asking you nicely to let me go out to LA."

Jimmy massages his chin. "Well then, you should know, as a paper, we have certain obligations—"

"—to our readers."

"I was going to say to our advertisers and the people who sign our checks," Jimmy says sarcastically, "but sure, 'readers,' that sounds better."

"Don't be like that."

"Be like what?" Jimmy leans forward, picks up today's paper, and motions for Sonny to sit. "You're the one who interrupted me, has been giving me a hard time, and has been pestering me since I walked off the elevator. I could be in the car going home; you know, home, where there's food, beer, and relaxation. Are you going to sit down or look like a creep lingering in the doorway?" Sonny doesn't move and remains silent. Jimmy doesn't move either; he just holds Sonny's gaze until Sonny sighs and gives up. "Look, you're right. You and I, we came up together, go back a long time. You—writing for the Sports section—did some great things—"

"—I'm not dead yet."

Jimmy concedes, letting the paper fall back on the desk, abandoning his attempts at hospitality. "No, you're not dead, but what I'm saying is, you stayed in Sports—you're still in Sports. Hell, you're the best sportswriter in the Midwest—*literary* novelists should write books about you—I think there might already be some, with the way you think you can swing that weight around, but you know what weight is in this business..."

"...ego," they say together, a motto hammered into them by the old guard, who've gone on to greater things—and the greater beyond.

Playing with him some, Sonny asks, "Are we in the Midwest?"

"Are you going to bust my balls while trying to convince me to give you some time off?"

Sonny grins. "You were saying."

"What was I saying?" Jimmy ponders, rubbing the dark bags under his eyes, where the skin has grown slack with his recent weight loss. Two heart attacks can do it to you. "Oh, yeah, that's right, this is the Midwest, you stupid fuck, not the South." Pointing at Sonny with the same finger, he adds, "We aren't yelling about the Confederacy's great return or moaning about cotton fields—however, I'll entertain arguments for the Southwest."

"My grandparents had a cotton farm out toward the river on the other side of Coweta."

"That's nice for them," Jimmy continues, dismissing him. "But what I'm sayin' is that you're good, really good. You get those giants of industry like *Sports Illustrated*, *Rolling Stone*, *ESPN* to reprint your column, and it's a good column, 'Where Are You Now,'" Jimmy says, spreading his hands apart in front of his face in a grand motion as if the sun's dawning on him for the first time. "A great freakin' column, I mean you were in *Playboy* when it was good to be in *Playboy*, that freaking Jimmy Carter issue blew my mind—you weren't in that—but it's hard to stay good when your output's already slacking and you're getting old here. I can't just let you zoom off at a moment's notice—for what?"

Sonny doesn't say, which grates on Jimmy. Jimmy's a man used to getting the facts, so he hates not knowing things. Sonny knows this about him; they're friends, and he's using it against him—building suspense. Sonny asks, "So what's the problem?"

"The problem is that's where you've stayed," Jimmy says. "We started together, and yes, we're friends, but you know where I started? I wasn't lucky like you, I didn't get to just fall into my dream gig—you had Sports. No, I had to work, scrape by, do the proverbial this and that to get where I'm at. I started by workin' midnights and chasin' ambulances and police cars—otherwise known to Joe Blow as the Crime Desk—but I wasn't even getting the sexy pieces. You know those things that people remember, not the pieces—the crimes—like those two jerk-offs who murdered their entire family and tried to slit their sister's throat but didn't touch the baby. Those types of pieces. No one remembers us, you know? I mean, some do, but you're not freaking Gay Talese—he dressed a helluva lot better than you do. It doesn't matter how good you are; there's always someone better and bigger, and most importantly, they know someone more important. You know no one, but yet I'll say, you still get out there, grind out a story now and then, and let's be honest, with the quality of your work, these high school pieces, although important to us—because well it's Friday Night Lights out here—mean jack shit to anyone else in any other market. You're not even in the City with the Thunder, you're here, where the best thing we could manage was a half-assed woman's basketball team, which is gone now by the way, and some minor league teams. Now, yes, the Dodgers own the Drillers. And that's all nice and dandy. I like the Drillers, don't like their beer prices, but I like watching some major players, humbled and in-town. And the hockey team makes for good copy when nothing else is happening, but let's be real, people would rather read those crime pieces than about someone slapping a puck." Jimmy mocks a shiver. "It sounds so dirty when you say it out loud."

Sonny expected Jimmy's response. "Well, then, I have an idea for a story. I've already made some phone calls."

"What sort of story?" Jimmy asks, intrigued but playing like he's not.

"For the column—a retrospective piece on Kobe Bryant."

Jimmy's eyes thicken stale, and his body stiffens. "He's dead."

"That's why it's a retrospective piece."

"No one likes reading about dead people."

"Sure they do. Weren't you just pontificating on crime?"

"I was trying to make a point."

"You never got there," Sonny says, motioning to him behind the desk, "and you're the editor."

Jimmy frowns. "That's hurtful, you know. That's hurtful. You're trying to make me feel bad. That strikes deep."

"I'm just saying, I've thought of a couple of options here," Sonny continues. "I thought of some ways to play it. You won't give me the time off. Well then, fine. I'll make it worth the paper's time."

"You have a great thing going with that column, but I don't think you understand. No one's going to want to read a piece written by *you* about a dead guy. That's not *you*. That's not what *you* do. Next, you're going to say you want time off to write a book—not to go to LA, for whatever it is you want to do because you haven't said that yet."

"I do want to write a book."

"Jesus." Jimmy drops his head into his hands. "What's gotten into you? Why do you need to go out there all of a sudden, screw me and everything else? That's not like you."

Sonny deflects. "I have an appointment with the widow."

"What widow?"

"Kobe's widow."

"Are you talking about the retrospective?"

"I'm talking about the story."

"The retrospective—she's going to talk to you?" Jimmy asks, pointing a finger at him again, not hiding the disbelief. "Why would she go and do something stupid like that?"

"Her husband's dead," Sonny says and then adds, "Something we share, something I can relate with."

"What, you have a dead husband too?" Jimmy says. Sonny frowns. Jimmy holds up a hand. "Alright, alright. That was a low blow, but it's been a few years, relax, will ya? I'm sorry about that, I liked her you know, she kept you... well she made you dress better. And yeah, we all know that he's dead, but that's not saying what the point is."

"I told her why I wanted to come to LA in the first place."

"And yet, you haven't told me—someone, who you said you were friends with—why you want to go."

Sonny crosses his arms. "I don't know if I want to tell you."

"If you want to go, you better damn well tell me, especially now that I said you can't go on your own, you're wanting the paper to flip the bill. That's just like you, saying you want to negotiate, but you aren't doing it right. Like a baseball team with the star pitcher and this second-tier team comes to them and is like, 'Let's trade,' and the team says 'No, we're good,' and so the second-tier says, 'Let's trade, and you pay us money,' and the first team says, "Yeah, sure, why not?'"

"It's not like that."

"It's exactly like that."

"You stole that from the internet."

"That's what the internet's for," Jimmy says. "Don't you know? I mean, how many of your pieces have been transmitted without your permission or mine? Why do you think I'm stressing about you not making a deadline or trying to manage an ulcer?"

"Paywalls are stupid," Sonny complains, falling into his assigned role in a conversation that both he and Jimmy have had for the last twenty years.

"They make us money," Jimmy says, parroting his line perfectly. "Just like selling ads, but now we're selling papers—"

"It's digital. We're not selling nothing."

"Anything," Jimmy corrects as any good editor would, but he ignores the rest of Sonny's comment and continues with his point. "Because I don't know if you know this, but we *are actually* in the business to make some *mon-ey*. I mean, you can't just feed the neighborhood and never charge for the service. Eventually, bills come due, and where I'm sitting, that's what I care about right now."

"You can still be stupid and make money. Look at who was just president."

Jimmy raises a graying eyebrow. "I think people would argue with you about whether he made money or not."

"They say he did it in office," Sonny adds, "so what's your point?"

"My point is, I started in crime, moved to local events—puff pieces and what not—then, moved on to local politics, and finally, national politics, then editor, and now I'm in charge of all that you see," he motions to the newsroom outside the doorway. "A dying empire but still mine."

"Well maybe if you stop running all the AP bullshit then people may actually buy the paper and *digital* copy."

Jimmy doesn't miss the contempt. "Well, the AP bullshit, as you say, also picks up your pieces and transmits them around the country, but I don't see you complaining when a dead basketball superstar's widow not only knows who you are but also agrees to give you an interview."

"It wasn't easy to arrange." Sonny drops into the one seat across the desk from Jimmy, a metal folding chair. "I wasn't going to tell you about the piece because I know how you don't like me writing about dead people."

"You're not a biographer."

"I'm not a biographer, but I figured, she's alive. She lost a husband and daughter, so why not make the piece about her? She's just as much of a sports person as he was, and she's probably more important. Plus, I've written about family members before."

"I know you have," Jimmy says, softer, signaling he has some idea where Sonny's going with this. "You've always had an ear for sympathy."

"Empathy."

Jimmy bristles. "I know what I meant," he snaps. "You know how to put *soul* in a piece. You're a dying breed, but the paper can't have you going out to LA to do something like that. That's why we have kids with computers and phones. We don't have to pay them as much as we pay you, and I don't have to put them on a plane."

"But they don't have rhythm," Sonny argues, leaning forward. "They don't have any *soul*, as you put it, no energy in their words."

"Since when has the paper ever cared about prose?" Jimmy sighs. "I know you do, but you write within certain established parameters, which allows you to do what you do. Again, you're good at it, but these kids write like they're trying to grow a garden, and I can't have that much copy; otherwise, we'd go bankrupt."

"Jim, I need to go out there, next week, just a couple of days," Sonny says, leveling with him.

Staring Sonny in the eyes, Jimmy considers it. "Just a couple of days?"

"Not long, but this is something I have to do."

"This Bryant piece, is that bullshit, or you really going to try to do something on his widow?"

"Not bullshit," Sonny says. "I had a contact at ESPN put me in touch with her. You remember Jennifer the sideline reporter?"

"The one who sent nudes to that quarterback?"

"No," Sonny states.

"Her name was Jennifer too, right? She was a sideline reporter, aren't all of them called Jennifer or Heather?"

Sonny shakes his head. "No."

"But the one who put you in contact with the widow is named that, so doesn't that sorta lend credence to my point?" Jimmy argues. "She's a sideline reporter, no? That's where they belong, by the way. At least, that's what my wife says. I frankly don't care, but she's got this thing about seeing them commentating."

"*What*?"

"My wife, she hates seeing women commentators," Jimmy exclaims. "Christ, you're getting old. Keep up lil' doggie. I mean for men's sports, manly sports, for like football—NFL. She hates it. Doesn't like listening to their voices or something. Maybe it's the tits on the display, but most of these broads used to play sports, and most of them, although not ugly, aren't exactly a thirty-year-old's wet dream. But still, she can't stand them. I mean I sit down to watch a game, and here she comes with the comments like the helicopter momma trying to shove the airplane down the baby's throat."

"So you're going to let me go?"

Jimmy closes his eyes and leans his head to the side to stretch his neck. "Are you going to tell me what this is actually about? I haven't seen you fight this hard for something since that story with the Olympic swimmer you got so hot and bothered about—didn't you win a Pulitzer for that—something about him being wrapped up with a cartel or something?"

"It's important, big."

"That's what you said then."

"But yes, I'll tell you what it's about; just it's a long story."

"We're in the newspaper business," Jimmy says. "Humor me; do it in five paragraphs or less."

"Alright," Sonny says. "It's my daughter; she's getting out of jail."

"Jail?"

"Like I said it's a long story, but I'd like to go out there for a couple of days, be there for her when she's released, and maybe... I don't know."

"You haven't gotten that far." Jimmy turns his head to look at the photograph next to his computer.

"No," Sonny says, "I haven't gotten that far, but it's a feeling, you know?"

"Ole Jiminy Cricket talking to you?"

"Not a conscience."

"You weren't there for her." Jimmy's meaning isn't accusatory or judgmental, but a plain statement of facts. Jimmy reaches down below the desk, and Sonny hears a drawer open. Jimmy comes up with a good bottle of bourbon. He reaches down again and returns with two small plastic cups; he sets them next to the bottle. "Emergencies and special occasions" is all Jimmy adds to explain. "Like two friends talking, not colleagues."

"Not after her mother died." Sonny looks down. "I sorta disappeared into my work."

Jimmy undoes the lid and begins to pour, saying, "As most of us do."

"She was old enough that she should have been fine."

"Obviously she wasn't." Jimmy sets the bottle down on the desk. "And obviously you weren't either."

Sonny nods.

Jimmy hands him a plastic cup. "So lay it on me, big Daddy, tell me what happened. Remember five paragraphs or less. I'd like to get home sometime tonight."

Sonny accepts the bourbon. "She drove a car for a friend. It was packed full of drugs. She was arrested, bonded out, and skipped town."

"I see." Jimmy studies the liquid in his plastic cup.

"A little while back, she got picked up in Texas, but now they're dismissing the original charges. Next week is the hearing, and the judge's indicated to her lawyer that she only had to wait because she skipped town, but he'll let her out next week."

"I like it," Jimmy says, nodding. "Not as much drama as I like or want. Where's the narrative here? Like what's the lesson or takeaway? Your lead sucked. Coming on strong like you were, asking for time off without saying what for, being secretive about it—that was annoying—making a big deal about it, and then bringing that sabbatical nonsense around, like that's going to make a bit of difference with me. However, I'll give you points for the stroke of genius of having an idea for a column ready to play, that was a good card, played well, you did well there. But all of that, just to ask me to let you have some time off to go see your daughter and be there when she gets out of jail?"

"Yeah."

"Drink." Jimmy tilts his cup toward Sonny. They take a hearty sip of the bourbon. "You know, you could have just opened with that, and I would have said yes, right?"

CHAPTER TWO:
MAURIZIO DIMAGGIO

CHRISTMAS: IT'S THE MOST WONDERFUL TIME OF the year. Yeah right, not for Maurizio "Maggie" DiMaggio. Not for someone like him, a workingman. Not when he has to kill someone.

But today is Christmas Eve, so here he stands, someplace that ain't his place. He's used to it because, for years, he has traveled across the country; there've been normal days, holidays, and every day in between, and except for a few exciting bits, he is doing things most people would consider boring such as sitting in cars, lounging in diners, working out in hotel rooms: basically, waiting. Sometimes, he runs in parks—he has run in all sorts of parks, all kinds everywhere 'cause staying fit is important—but not in the winter. He'll stick to the treadmill or elliptical, thank you very much. He hates the cold. And every now and then, he kills people, which is its own form of cardio.

That last one is far and few between, but it does happen.

Maggie works for Siriano, who has been in prison for the last couple of years serving a sentence equivalent to chicken shit, considering all the things Siriano's done. The man went down for embezzlement, accused of taking money from his own legitimate company. How does that work? Maggie's never been able to figure it out.

But that's why he's here. Branson Henry, Brandy to his friends.

This house sits in a neighborhood in Colorado Springs and is covered in fresh powder, with wood siding, broken and rotting. The place looks like it's been here a hundred years, at least that's how it looks. Christmas lights hang like limp strands of hair over the front door, wrung out and tired bangs. The colorful bulbs shine off the fresh snow, lighting the place up like it's ... well Christmas ... and give everything a Roy G. Biv reflection. It shines off the white siding, or what's left of it: Maggie's shoes; his face; the car in the driveway; and the front window, which looks full of warmth and love. And that's the pain here, seeing windows like that, golden squares of something Maggie's never had. Covered in cardboard and plastic sticker cut-outs of snowmen and gingerbread men, faux frost mixed with the real frost collecting on the outside of the window, and paper snowflakes, taped in the corners, stuck on the center of the glass, it looks like a home.

Here he is, standing outside, wearing his tan overcoat with simple clothes underneath: black turtleneck, black jeans, black shoes, shined to a shimmer, and black stalking cap secured to his head, with his hands shoved into the pockets of the overcoat, fighting the cold.

"Fucking Christmas," Maggie mutters to himself.

"Can I help you?" a young female voice asks from behind him.

Maggie turns around to see this kid standing there holding a skateboard. She surprises him. He didn't hear her coming up behind him. That could've been a problem. "Excuse me?" he says, cutting off the front syllable.

"You're on my front porch," the kid says. "I'd like to go inside. It's cold and the lights are on." She points to the Christmas lights over the doorway. "When the lights are on, I have to be home. Well, I have to be home before they come on. They come on at dusk, but see, I'm not. I'm late. So with you standing here..." She smiles, "... I guess, I'll just blame it on you for blocking the way. You're blocking the walkway, and I don't want to get snow all over my boots when I've been stomping my feet halfway down the block."

"Kid." Maggie puts it as a challenge, shaking his head. "That's your fault. Your choice. Not mine."

The kid, maybe twelve, is obviously a tomboy, with a hat on her head, gloves with the fingers cut out and wearing warm clothes, standing with her hip cocked to the side, showing attitude, showing spunk, skateboard under her arm.

Maggie starts to say, "Listen, kid—"

"—Mister, what are you?" she asks, dropping the edge of the skateboard onto her pink and polka dot rain boots.

"What do you mean?"

"You a salesman or something?"

Maggie rolls his shoulders, up and down once. "Something."

"What's that mean?" the girl asks, picking the skateboard up and tucking it under her arm again. "Are you or aren't you? Are you here to sing carols or something?"

"You here to start being smart?"

"You're the one standing in my way."

"Well, I'm here to see the man of the house," Maggie admits while dropping down to one knee. He notices the girl has Brandy's eyes, he can tell, ice blue, his attitude too. "He around?"

"Who around?" The girl laughs. "The man of the house? Who's that? He have a name, this man of the house? Who are you looking for?"

"Branson Henry," Maggie says. "But he might have changed it. I don't know what he's calling himself now. He your father?"

The girl half-closes an eye and studies Maggie's face while sticking her tongue out of the corner of her mouth thinking it over. Finally, she says, "He's not here."

"Where is he?"

"Hell if I know," she says. "It's Christmas time. He isn't here, that should be enough. Hasn't been for over two years."

"What?"

"You're thick-headed, aren't you?" the girl says. "I think that hat is boiling your brain or something."

"Ha, ha, very funny." Maggie stands because the crouching is killing his knees. He reaches out to place a hand on her shoulder. "Brandy here or not?"

But just as the girl's about to answer his question, the front door of the house opens, casting a curtain of warm orange light across the snow and the walkway, the unattainable glow of heart, soul, and comfort. The kid glances at the door, drawing Maggie's eyes with her. In the doorway, he sees a woman with a faded dye-job, blonde, standing in the doorway, brushing a strand of hair over her right ear, and then hugging herself tightly against the cold. As she crosses her arms over her off-white sweater, she braces against the doorframe. Addressing the girl, the woman says,

"Brandy," sharp and with a bit of concern. Maggie does not miss the concern, and her eyes tell Maggie that she recognizes him. She knows him for who he is and knows immediately what it means to see him standing here. She has a hand out toward her child, but she does her best to play it cool, staying calm. She yells sharply at the girl, "Get in the house."

The kid says, "I'm sorry I am late. Jennifer wouldn't—"

"Just get in the house," the woman snaps, cutting the kid off.

Brandy rolls her eyes, gives Maggie a look, and races off into the house, passing the woman on the steps, pausing briefly to apologize. The woman says something to her that Maggie can't hear.

Dropping his hand to his side, Maggie stands straight and squares to face the front door.

"What do you want?" The woman's hands grip the frame tightly.

"I met you once." Maggie shakes a finger at her, nodding, and taking three large steps forward. "It was a couple of years ago, you might not remember, but I met you."

"Stop." The woman thrusts her palm out toward him. "Don't come any closer. What do you want? Why are you here?"

Maggie stops at the foot of the steps and runs his hand over the stalking cap, adjusting it on his scalp. "You were... you were a dancer, right? I mean, you weren't blonde then, but Brandy said you danced. I think I saw you once, but that wasn't my thing. Brandy's thing though, obviously. I gave him a hard time about it, falling for a girl like that, well like you, but he said he loved you. Said you been dancing since you were ten. Said you wanted to follow after some woman, Vara—oh, what was her name?" he asks, snapping his fingers.

"Vera-Ellen," the woman supplies the answer. Maggie's not sure what's colder: her or the outside.

"She was in that movie—"

"White Christmas."

"Yeah," Maggie says, chuckling. "With Bing Crosby. Huh, Christmas, what a bitch."

"What are you doing here?" she barks.

"I don't remember your name," Maggie tells her. "I've been standing here, talking to your kid, cute kid by the way, talking to you, and I can't remember it. Driving me nuts."

"Oasis," she says.

"Like the band?"

"Or paradise in the desert."

"Where thirsty men go to get a drink," Maggie says. "I remember now. Brandy said that all the time. All the damn time. He loved you. I didn't know you all had a kid."

"She's a good kid," Oasis says. "I remember you. When we crossed paths, I'd already had her. Brandy didn't trust the people he worked with, I guess with good reason. Guys like you… when she was little, to keep her away from guys like you, she spent most of her time with my mother while I worked. You know the first night Brandy and I were together, he didn't pay for nothing. He took me out on a nice date, a real nice date; the only guy I knew at the time who actually cared what I thought about things instead of how I moved my body. But that first night we were together, I got pregnant. That's a bitch. But I wouldn't give nothing back. Brandy is my life, and all that's good." She pauses. "It's been a while since I saw you last. What do you want?"

"Brandy," Maggie says. "Branson, I'm looking for him."

"Why?"

"He here?"

Oasis lifts her chin, hesitant to answer, making Maggie wonder if she thinks he's here to kill her. "Why are you looking for him?"

"He's an accountant, right?" Maggie says. "Well, he needs to account for some things, settle some matters."

"He's not here," she tells him, matter of fact.

"Don't be offended if I don't take your word for it."

She pushes the door open more and retreats into the house. "Be my guest."

Maggie thanks her and ascends the stairs, peeling the stalking cap off his head. He steps across the threshold aware the woman could be reaching for a gun, or something hidden just behind the door. He pauses to wipe his feet on the mat. The house smells like a home.

"Something cooking in the oven?" he asks. "Smells like a roast if I'm not mistaken. I like roast. Like it with mashed potatoes. You making those? I love it with the roast, the roast being the base of the gravy. Brown gravy is the best gravy. Mashed potatoes, carrots, and peas. I love vegetables. Love them the most. I'm not much of a meat-eater, potatoes yes, meat no. Never have been."

Maggie scans the surroundings, glancing at any number of items that would constitute a weapon in his hands, but he finds nothing that would be effective against him in her hands, so no worries or concern.

Weaponless, Oasis nods and shuts the door behind Maggie. "He's not here," she says, protesting his intrusion once more.

Maggie gives her a fierce look, not with dead eyes although there's no life in his, but with eyes that could kill, filled with fury and venom.

She shrugs her shoulders and throws her arm out. "Take a look around if you don't believe me."

Maggie breaks the look and smiles with both his mouth and eyes. "No, that's alright."

"You're not going to look for him?"

"Oh, I'm going to look for him, just not here," Maggie says. "Cause he ain't here. If he were here, there'd be pictures and shit decorating the walls and that table over there. All of them showing him in them, or at least hint at him, but all I see are you and that kid. Nothing older than a year or two. And that kid wouldn't have reacted the way she did if her pops were really here."

The woman relaxes some, not all the way, but some. She walks a bit tense as she steps into the dining room, back straight like she's unsure if he's going to shoot her in the back of her head or follow. She beckons him farther into the house with a flick of the wrist.

As she makes for the kitchen, she says, "He gave her that skateboard as a Christmas present." Her voice fades as she retreats into the house, to safety. Maggie, gripping his stalking cap in both hands, follows in the wake of her voice. "Left it under the tree when he left, wrapped in this elf wrapping paper. You know that elf that goes on the shelf. It was paper with that on it. I like the Keebler elves, but I can't stand that creepy doll. He bought her one once back when we lived in Springfield, and I buried it in the backyard. She spent months begging us for a skateboard. I told them both that I didn't think a ten-year-old needed something like that. I guess I sounded like someone from that one Christmas movie, but instead of saying she'd shoot her eye out, I was telling them she'd break a leg or arm or something. A damn good way to break an arm. But Brandy, he just thought my reaction and protest of her getting one was the funniest, dumbest thing in the world. Called me 'Worst Case Scenario.' He left and left that as her present."

Stepping into the kitchen, which could have any number of weapons, Maggie sees Oasis, bent at the waist, ass pointed his direction, dancer perfect, tight and round, checking the oven. He says, "Kinda like a fuck you?"

"Yeah I guess," she says, closing the oven. "Kinda like that."

"I'm sorry," Maggie adds.

Oasis stands and talks over her shoulder. "Me too." She turns to face him. "But not really. It's better this way. You know, I don't remember your name. You think, with Brandy worried for years someone would come for him, that I'd remember the people from that life. I mean, I remember you, but I don't remember your name. Come to think of it, I guess it's fitting that it's you that's come for him. Brandy wouldn't see it coming. But he's not here. He left about two years—"

"—ago," Maggie says, "Yeah, the kid told me."

"I don't know your name, though. You know mine. I think it was a girl's name, like Brandy's, but I don't know. All that was so long ago."

"DiMaggio, Maurizio, but most just call me Maggie."

Oasis appears to think it over before turning around to check the stovetop. "Mashed potatoes are done," she says, lifting the lid of a silver pot and then placing it back on the pot. She does this well, this act, but he hears the fear in her voice, shaking in time with the slight tremor of her bottom lip, which seems to be radiating out and up from her shoulders. "Are you doing anything for Christmas? Dinner or anything? Any plans? Or..."

"I'm not," Maggie says.

"I'm cooking for tomorrow." She turns to face him again. She's pretty. Her hair is streaked with gray at the roots, but she's still the looker he remembers, the girl on Brandy's arm. "Cook the night before and then that way on Christmas morning, it's all about Brandy." She points to the ceiling, showing the girl's upstairs. "That way she can wake up and come down to the tree and open presents, be like a real freaking kid for once. I had to grow up quick. Her father had to grow up quick. I'm sure you're no different, but I don't want her growing up like that. I want her to have the childhood I didn't. Course, I'd have to get rid of all men from her life. I'm not going to do that. But I'm not going to have those types around either.

"My mother and stepfather will be over tomorrow," she tells him. "My sister and her piece of shit boyfriend and my cousins. I love my cousins. They're more like siblings. Love them more than my sister. You know, when we were in the program, that was the hardest part—not contacting family. Were you looking for us then?"

"Yes and no. The big guy wanted me to find Brandy and bring him to court, so to speak, kinda how I came to be. But it wasn't until Junior came around that I was hired, officially."

"I thought—"

"—not anymore; not since the big guy legitimized Junior, now Junior runs things."

"I had no idea."

"No reason you would."

"We left the program for a couple of reasons. My family being one. Brandy never trusted them, you know. He felt like they tricked him into doing everything, threatened to arrest me, take Brandy away from us—she was six at the time—I don't know, I think he talked to a lawyer who told him he had to cooperate or things wouldn't work out in his favor. But you know what I figured out after everything was said and done and he'd gone and plead to get his deal? Lawyers are only in it for the paycheck. Of course, this guy wanted to extend this out, get Brandy to cooperate with them and continue representing his client. Get more money that way. Brandy and I had a deal that if he went down, he'd cut the easiest deal, go down, and we'd see how long he got. I mean, he wasn't you. He's an accountant; how long would they give him? Those guys from Wall Street, they got nothing, not really. But he didn't follow the plan, and well, here we are."

"Everyone makes mistakes."

Maggie doesn't miss that she keeps a hand behind her back near the cutting board with carrot pieces piled up on one side. Would she stab him? He would if he were in her place. Could he pull his father's police special from his pocket before she clears the space between them? Maybe. Or he could just pull it now and send a message, but that's not how he works, not how he wants to work.

"What do you do for them now? To be looking for Brandy, you must work for..." Her voice fades, not wanting even to say names because saying names is why Maggie's here looking for Brandy. "... what'll you do when you find him?"

"I'm in the restoration business," Maggie says. "When you knew me, I drove. I was a gopher, but now, I'm somewhat in business for myself.

Sorta freelance, sorta not. Something goes wrong, a disaster, the types of things that cause certain people problems, gets other types' attention. You know, something like sending you to prison puts you in the news, drags what shouldn't be in the light out of the dark; then, you hire me to assess the damage and make repairs. Something like this, like with Brandy, that's my specialty. Track the person down. Do what I do. Hefty fee. Lots of work but pays well." He steps forward. "Do you know where he might have gone? Or what he's calling himself now?"

"Jefferson and I have no idea. If I had to find him, I'd look where he's been. Maybe back in Tulsa."

"Why there? Why not stay with you?"

She fixes her eyes on him the same way he glowered at her just moments ago. The look tells him a couple of things—mainly, trouble at the Oasis.

"Did he stay paranoid? Think someone was going to come after him?"

"Every ... damn ... day," she says. "But he likes it out there. That's where I'd look for him 'cause he always thought it was easy to hide in Oklahoma. Thought, if he stayed close, Siriano'd never think about looking for him in his own backyard."

"I've not been back there in a while. My work keeps me on the road."

"That's where I would start looking for him," she says and then pauses. "Do you want to stay for dinner? We were going to have some roast, dip into what I'm making for tomorrow. There's more than enough. I could..." But her voice dies in her throat. Her body shakes, but she plays calm well; it must be all those years of dancing in the soft light with lecherous fingers groping at her, acting like it wasn't a problem to get tips, keeping the pasted-on smile, which might as well be the grimace of a cheerleader.

Maggie looks around the kitchen. In the corner is a small table, with two placemats set out. Four chairs. Fridge to the side, artwork on it. A piece of paper with a large red A and a note saying, "Good job." Dirty dishes. Scuff marks on the cabinets. But still, her kitchen, her house.

Their house.

Maggie tells her, "I couldn't impose."

"It wouldn't be an imposition."

"You want him found?" Maggie asks, going back to why he's here. "Like really? Want him to come back? Say he's sorry or something?"

"Not really, Not now. Not after the last year of being on our own. The first year was rough, the shock of it. But now, let's just say I'd only want to see him again for sentimental reasons. I don't need him."

"Like if I found him, I'd let him know his wife says hello?"

"Something like that." She lets out a held breath.

And now the moment of truth, Maggie, still holding his stalking cap with one hand, slips his other hand into his coat, grips the butt of the pistol. Plays relaxed. The way he sees this, if she charges him, he's just going to poke the revolver forward and pull the trigger. Shoot through the coat. That way he's not going to get hung up trying to get it out of his pocket. Then, he'll have to do something about the kid but first things first.

Oasis asks, "Am I a problem? You said you were in the disaster business, and with what Brandy did, talking the way he did, well, that's a disaster from their point of view. Not his. Not mine. We got a chance to start over, a few times, but from theirs, that's a disaster. That's what you fix."

Just then the kid comes bounding around the corner, surprised to see him standing in the kitchen, blocking the fridge. She says, "First the sidewalk and now the fridge? Come on, man."

Maggie steps to the side to allow the kid to pass. She steps around him and opens the fridge door. She pulls out a carton of milk.

Oasis asks again, "Are we...?" She doesn't say the word problem, not with the kid in the room. She keeps her hand behind her back, pressed against the counter.

Maggie removes his hand from his pocket and uses both hands to reaffix the cap to his head, taking his time. He glances at her. "Not as long as Brandy isn't here. See no reason to go fixing things here. Wasn't paid for that; paid to find him. He's the water leak, not you." He lets the news sit for a moment. "I'll see my way out."

The kid says she was glad he took the hat off for a little bit, let his head have some air, otherwise she'd be worried about him, boil his brain like a frog or, worse, turn his head all red and scaly like a lobster. She told him to have a safe trip back to wherever he came from.

Oasis says nothing, but Maggie doesn't miss that just before leaving the kitchen, she slips the knife back onto the counter.

"Merry Christmas," he says as he closes the door behind him.

CHAPTER THREE: KELLY CHAMBERS

DEPUTY U.S. MARSHAL KELLY CHAMBERS RESTS HER back against the driver's side door of her issued vehicle, a white Chevy Impala, and tries to relax while contemplating death, probably by ambush, could be a sniper, maybe a lone gunman, all most likely mob ordered—JFK style. The vehicle is the new workhorse of the Marshals Service and the Crown Victoria's latest replacement, but her partner likes to complain, as he does now through the open window.

"Nothing compares to the utility of the old Ford. I miss that. Look at this. I feel like I'm sitting in some sorta Tupperware."

Kelly rolls her eyes in response not only to his near-constant bellyaching about the vehicle but also to the whole situation. Frustration wouldn't describe what she's feeling. This is a setup. It has to be. She keeps her eyes on the doors of the courthouse, watching people enter and leave, aware of her surroundings. The tall buildings make the muscles between her shoulders tense into tight, nearly unbearable, knots. Kelly says, "It shouldn't be like this."

"What, the car?" her partner asks from inside the vehicle. He pauses and continues, "I mean, I guess this is a nice car."

She looks without looking like she's looking, watching the world around her. She uncrosses her arms from over her light pink blouse, which complements her skin tone, shows just the right amount of cleavage and frames her mother's Saint Michael's medallion, a gift to her mother from her Uncle Frank. She clutches a half-burnt cigarette between her fingers, trailing more smoke than what's entered her lungs. Her nails match the blouse. It's a Wednesday afternoon, warm for February, and her navy pinstriped business suit does nothing to hide her feminine figure. It accentuates her slim frame almost to the point of absurdity and is a far cry from the pantsuits of her mother's generation, which is where her partner Patrick Ryan belongs. She is sans overcoat, enjoying the sun's warmth against her skin. Her jet-black hair is pulled up into a tight knot. Either the wind pecks at the raised hairs on the back of her neck or it's her frustration and anxiety. She hasn't decided yet.

"No, this—this circus." She slices the hand with the cigarette out to the activity around her that has nothing to do with the operations of the courthouse. She motions at the various news vehicles, the vans and cars sandwiching her vehicle parked on a dead-end street that terminates in a parking garage between Tulsa County courthouse and the Tulsa Library; at the station, logos pasted on the sides in fancy vinyl wraps; and at the reporters and producers claiming ground around the courthouse entrance like explorers planting flags, except it's tripods. They're setting up for live reports for the five o'clock news. All seemingly waiting for something to happen.

"It feels like a setup or something, like something's going to happen. I don't like it."

Pat Ryan, in his low, white-man, southern, gentlemanly voice, jokingly says, "You might be right. These people, whoever they are, don't they have somewhere to be? Somewhere more important? Surely, something somewhere is happening that deserves more attention than this judicial farce. I mean, I get it, there's only one case being heard today that matters, but that doesn't make it newsworthy. This man isn't newsworthy—far from it."

Pat's pretty much her opposite, and that's why they get along so well. He's a Pat Conroy novel come to life, dysfunctional childhood with an education beat into him through the Marine Corps. Pat did it the hard way, enlisting and then applying to the Citadel, where he graduated with honors, went back to the Corps, then transferred his Federal time over to the Marshals Service. He plans to retire in a year or two to write books about southern living while threatening Kelly that he'll really write cookbooks specifically aimed at those with Type-2 diabetes, which he affectionately calls his "Fat-Man disease," but Pat can't cook. His cookbook would be a curse upon society.

Pat's right. This isn't newsworthy, except it is

"Which is probably why the courthouse is dead."

"Well, yeah, *I get it*," Pat says. "What's happening inside there, in some courtroom on the fourth floor is that notorious—infamous would be a better moniker, I'm partial to the label 'crime boss'—Rosario Siriano (Russ if you want to be informal) stands before a judge to get his case dismissed. And he'll be a free man once again, maybe not a contributing member of society—I don't believe he ever was one of those."

Kelly watches a busty redheaded female reporter, better known for her weather reports, struggle with setting up her equipment solo while wearing a coat that belongs in *A Christmas Story*. "I can't believe the State charges are being dismissed."

"Overturned is the proper word," Pat corrects her. He has the charm and low drawl of someone born in the backwoods outside Charleston, filling each of his words with the grace and bull honky of an elder southern attorney, although Pat likes to say he's a statesman. "That's what you get with the McGirt ruling. It's like it never happened. Siriano's not a convict. Not for this. Not for nothing he's done here. The State had a procedure issue that voided the earlier conviction. Though, really it shouldn't have made a lick of difference. The man's as guilty as they come. And then, in the middle of the State's appeal, the grandest court in all the land comes up with McGirt and decides this wonderful state is to be the Wild West again, so today happens."

"You think we'll pick it up?" Kelly asks, meaning the Federal Government.

"Buddy over at the FBI, so take what I have to say with a pinch of salt, grain wouldn't do it—I don't know why you ever wanted to work for those blowhards—he says maybe," Pat responds. "Tells me, now mind you he is not on the case, he thinks that's what the Grand Jury's all about. He said he wouldn't be surprised if ole Siriano's going to play canary to something else he's got going on in exchange for the Feds laying off him for a while. You know the old game of 'which pan do you want to watch on the stove.' But then my buddy said something about murder and didn't explain who got murdered, so don't do that thing where you ask me who died or who committed such a *heinous* crime when you know we both don't know the answer."

She stays quiet.

Pat goes on. "My buddy said the State's appeal was going to be dismissed anyways, even if Siriano hadn't been Indian. Something to do with their primary witness, which might be why we are trying to get him to testify for something when they know there won't be any charges on this embezzlement shit. The witness failed to appear or something. My buddy thinks he's fled."

Kelly nods: she knows about it.

"I heard something about that," Kelly says. The State contacted the Marshals for assistance. The request landed on her desk just before the Supreme Court July decision. "I don't know what good it would do for us to find him. He left the program..." She lets her voice trail off thinking about the world post-McGirt and about how the Marshals Service is too busy chasing real criminals and picking up the massive case influx. Pat calls it an "overload" to spend time trying to find someone who doesn't want to be found.

Pat stays quiet.

"I guess I feel like the guy stuck his neck out once, so why's he have to do it again?"

To which Pat replies, "I bet he's been running for his life ever since. If he did appear in court, you and I, and he, know what's going to happen to him."

"Siriano would come after him," Kelly says, knowing Pat's right. "Make him disappear."

They both know the word on the street says Siriano's been looking for the witness, or at least, Siriano's son, Wilson Notaro, is looking for him. Wilson's taken over for Siriano, and Pat wonders out loud what's going to happen now that the old man's getting out.

Speaking with some lament, Pat says, "That boy was always so handsome. He could have been a movie star with those looks. But no, that was not to be. He had to follow his dear old dad into a life of crime and minor celebrity."

"Maybe he just likes the celebrity part."

"Wilson's always reminded me of Rocco DiSpirito when he was trim and fit, not the bloated mess he looks like now."

"Wilson or Rocco?"

Pat's tone is flat. "*Rocco*."

"Did you know he's in his fifties?" Kelly questions. "I didn't know that."

Last week, when she was watching one of those cooking shows, she looked him up. She found out that piece of trivia and logged it away to share with Pat in a moment just like this. She looks everything up. Her Uncle Frank taught her early on that knowledge is power except that she's full of useless knowledge. Some of which gets twisted around in her head. Pat makes fun of her for it.

Pat refrains from making fun of her now, assuming she is telling the truth about the chef's age. "I'm in my fifties," he says. "So what are you saying? Are you saying I'm bloated now that I'm in my fifties?"

Kelly plays it coy. "You know what I'm saying."

"You think I'm bloated," he utters, pretending to be hurt.

He is bloated. He knows it. It's why he got into Rocco in the first place, trying to lose weight and get down in size, and it's why he threatens Kelly with cookbooks.

"Whatever, it's more than looks. His looks are yummy. I wished I could just eat him up. But *what I'm saying* is Rocco could have been one of the greats, and he walked away in favor of celebrity, or so the gossip says. I was hoping Wilson would have done the same thing, but his family ties are strong even with a philandering daddy like Siriano."

Taking a drag from the cigarette, Kelly expresses, "I can't stand this. I can't stand men like him. True criminals, who think they run the world, not just the city, and he's the worst."

"That they are," Pat agrees. "And he is."

"I was there when the State did what the Feds couldn't—put Siriano behind bars. It was a sweet thing to see. And I loved how this little accountant..." Kelly remembers him as a small dark-haired man, with beady, bright blue eyes hidden behind thick black glasses, with a severe widow's peak and a well-trimmed black beard, named Brandon or something "... stood up to Siriano. Feds couldn't make a case. We can never make a case, not in any amount of time that matters, not on guys like Siriano, not anymore. Maybe in Uncle Frank's days," she pauses, "in your days—"

"Hey," Pat yells. "Be nice. First, you call me fat, and now you're calling me old. I don't know how I feel about that."

"You don't like it," Kelly tells him, glancing over her shoulder at him in the car. "What I remember most about this guy, the accountant, was his smile. The guy couldn't stop smiling."

She doesn't tell Pat that something seemed off about the guy's smile. There he was sitting on the witness stand, smiling bright like he couldn't think of anywhere else he'd rather be, but something seemed ... off. Maybe it was the smile of doing the right thing, but to Kelly, it was like the guy knew as soon as the party was over, he was gone.

"I kept track of the guy. I heard he skipped out on his wife and kid. Uncle Frank always referred to those people as 'Gone to Kansas. Dust in the wind.'"

Pat makes a guttural noise in agreement, somewhere between an *un-huh* to a clearing of phlegm from his throat, and adds, "And Siriano went to prison."

Except, he didn't because, like most men in positions of power, his type of influence buys favors, the appeal, and then, the United States Supreme Court ruled that this area of the country belongs to and has always belonged to the Muscogee Creek Nation, making it the largest reservation in the country.

Kelly, staring at Pat and mocking his southern voice, says, "And now, thanks to McGirt, and Siriano's fractional blood quantum, he's been given his providential freedom."

Pat waves a hand in front of his face, adding a dramatic flair, "And so today is a dark day, where the State is dismissing the case, right now, right in there," pointing toward the courthouse. "And the plan, or how we understand it, is as soon as Siriano exits this glorious house of Western justice, he will surrender to us, the Marshals Service, superb representatives of the Federal Government."

"Did you know he only wanted one Marshal?" she asks.

"Yes, except there's never just one Marshal—so he gets you and me. Low-key. No cameras. No hullabaloo. No problems. But we both know there are always problems." Pat pauses. "And cameras, obviously."

"You hear about the guy who set this up?" Kelly asks, knowing Patrick Ryan plays golf with the Assistant United States Attorney , Eli Buchanan—Bucky—every weekend. They're friends, good friends.

Pat says he has, with some defensiveness in his voice. He asks, "What have you heard?"

Really, he's asking if she's heard the rumors.

Like how the AUSA might have gotten some people killed.

"You know what, don't answer. I'll tell you how it is. Whatever you've heard, it's false. The DEA couldn't fly straight any more than I can."

"Did your FBI buddy tell you that over pillow talk?"

"Be nice," Pat says. "He's a friend. Bucky might be a lot of things, and I'll admit he feels he might be the reason why a couple of their people ended up dead last winter, but he's as ruthless as an opossum in a hen house. And my FBI friend is straight, if you must know; maybe, if you decided to take an interest in the finer aspects of the human condition you would enjoy a conversation or two across cushions of head comfort."

He means pillow talk, but Pat can't just say that.

Turning back to the courthouse, Kelly pats the folded warrant in her pocket, unable to ignore how uncomfortable this is, the idea of waiting outside the courthouse for Siriano to just come out and walk to them.

"I don't like this," she notes. "I feel standing here, we're like two pigeons waiting for a slingshot."

Pat laughs. "Now you sound like me ... and what's there to like? We get told what to do, and we do it. Simple, really."

"You know what I mean," she remarks, taking a drag and blowing the smoke out through her nose.

"I know a lot of things." Pat leans over the driver's seat to speak to her through the open window. "I know that if you stop smoking those things that you might run better. Just as I know if you stop smoking them, you'll live longer. I also know if you put that cigarette out, you could take a load off, relax, sit in this car instead of standing out there in the sun."

"There's a light breeze."

The breeze kisses her smooth skin.

"It's a cool one," Pat says, "which means, I'd be able to roll up this window. I'm getting cold." He mock shivers.

Kelly rolls her eyes. Pat can't see her do it, but it comes through in her voice. "No one says you can't do that anyways."

"Manners say that," Pat responds, voice raising so she can hear him clearly, "Manners and my morals. And if you're going to be cold, then I need to be cold. If I were warm and you were cold, well then there would be something very wrong with that picture. My mother would beat me. Not that my father didn't do enough of that, but she taught me how to treat women, and she'd think it were a shameful thing to let you stand out there all cold and lonesome."

"Pat, you don't have morals." Kelly ignores his pleas for her to sit in the car. She doesn't want to sit. If she's going to be in a gunfight, she'd rather be on her feet. With what they do, the chance of a gunfight always looms over them, but like most things looming over people, when expectations are seldom delivered, it breeds complacency. Pat is smug.

"I have a lot of morals."

"Name some."

"I'm a lover of those who play the piano, and I have dedicated my life to pursuing such men."

"And that's a moral, how?"

"It's a personal motivation."

Kelly laughs.

"I don't like this," she vocalizes again. Her thoughts turn to Bucky explaining how this would work and Marshal Kalka going along with it as if it was the most natural thing in the world. Kelly argued against it, but they threatened to bring her up on insubordination if she kept at it, so she stopped.

How it should be done, is through a Write Ad Test, that way Siriano would never be released. The Marshals would take possession of him from the State facility, and he'd be held in custody as a witness. But the freaking hard-left sheriff looking at cementing his legacy and pandering to his liberal base refused to work with the Feds and released Siriano as a giant middle finger to Marshal Kalka and the Federal Government as a whole.

"What's not to like about this?" Pat says. "It's an easy thing. We do what we do best. We wait. It's what we get paid for. I hate to break it to you kid, but we are babysitters, and babysitters wait."

"Don't babysitters get paid?" Kelly asks. "So wouldn't we just be getting paid to be here?"

A quick check in the side mirror, Kelly spots Pat shrugging. "Whatever it is, it's easy work; you should relax sometime and try it." His eyes search hers from the mirror.

"Easy," Kelly says. "Easy would be handcuffing him in the courtroom. That would be easy. That would be the right way to do this. Doing it this way, it ain't the right way. It feels wrong."

"Which is what you argued for," Pat says, "but that's not going to be. So why don't you try it my way and relax? There's no reason to get upset about it now. That's the past. It's over and done. You lost, kid. Now sit down, enjoy being paid to do nothing, or as near as nothing as I could find in the civilian world."

Kelly snorts. "Look, if I wanted to relax, I'd take a vacation. I don't like this, Pat. Something doesn't feel right. Don't you think it's weird that we're not in there waiting at least?"

Pat reminds her, "Bucky said he needed Siriano to appear before the Grand Jury as a willing participant. How would it look if he was forced into the room? Or had a dust-up with the local sheriff?"

"Like we're doing our jobs."

Pat makes a clicking noise with his tongue against the roof of his mouth, something he does often. A wet-sucking noise. It's annoying. "And where's the fun in that?"

"I don't like fun. At least not when I'm working. I like simplicity. Safety. You know what would be easy? Doing it in there, that'd be easy. We stand in the back. The judge makes his or her judgment, case dismissed, and we step forward and pull out the shiny bracelets. Order the son-of-a-bitch to turn around. And bam, we're done. That's easy."

"That would be easy," Pat agrees, whistling but hinting at an understood *but*.

"So why aren't we doing it?"

"Those things are overrated." Pat chuckles. "I don't think we should be out here either, *but* what use is it to fight the 'Powers That Be.' They're grand and mighty and sign my paycheck. So I concede to their undying and unyielding will."

"That may be so, but it feels like we're making concessions to a criminal."

He corrects her. "Accused criminal. Suspected. Alleged."

"Don't play word games with me, Pat; I'm not in the mood."

"I'm not playing word games; I'm telling you how it is. Those 'Grand Cosmic Powers' have deemed it so. You and I both know Siriano's as dirty as they come, the devil incarnate if it pleases you, but as far as the official record is concerned, he's a fine and upstanding citizen, a distinguished businessman, a captain of industry."

"So we're just supposed to forget he's the head of the mob?"

"Didn't you hear?" Pat says. "The mob doesn't exist. Not out here. Never has. J. Edgar just couldn't admit he let the other side of the coin manifest under his leadership, and we've dealt with it ever since. Two great corporations at odds with each other, one trying to turn a profit and the other trying to stop it, with us deputies left out in Indian Country holding our revolvers watching both sides: one that doesn't exist and one that wants nothing to do with the dirty work of actual police work. And no, Tulsa's never been a playground for them," he adds, nearly singing it. "They didn't come here in the eighties, and they haven't stayed while working out a pretty glittering symbiotic relationship with the cartels, who also just so happen to run this area of the country from this fine jewel of a little town. No, to them, it's Dallas and Kansas City that get the ink in print and the attention—except the Indians have gone and brought a whole lot of trouble to the way things are done. Upsettin' the apple cart and all that. It's Indian Territory again, 1864. Welcome to the untamed Wild West. I'd think your uncle's having a heyday. Isn't this right up the alley of a cattle cop?"

"This is bullshit."

"Exactly, but what are you going to do about it?" he questions, half-heartedly chastising her while reminding her of her place in the bureaucracy. "If you wanted to pretend to fight crime, you should've joined the blowhards."

"But they wouldn't take me."

"Exactly, and why do you think that is?"

Echoing her uncle's words, Kelly admits, "I'm hard-headed."

"You applied three times to the FBI," Pat says. "I figured you would have discovered that the first time you tried."

"I thought it might've had something to do with my upbringing or—"

"—Oklahoma isn't exactly the land of opportunity and higher education, but more than likely, it had to do with the fact that you didn't walk through life with a chip on your shoulder or a stick up your ass. They do."

"Uncle Frank would never have allowed it, anyways," Kelly says, "and besides, I only ever wanted to join the Marshals."

"That's because that's where your Uncle Frank made a name for himself."

"But they just weren't hiring at the time I was applying. So I applied to the FBI."

"Which might be the real reason why the blowhards never picked you."

"They ask me 'If you want to work for them, the Marshals, why don't you apply with them?' I just said, 'Hey, you asked, I'm being honest. They aren't hiring.' They said 'Well, we aren't either.'"

Pat laughs. "Sometimes you're too honest; you speak your mind too much, do what you shouldn't when you should and what you should when you shouldn't."

Checking her watch, noticing it is about time for the show to begin, she mutters, "That's what Uncle Frank says."

Pat chuckles in agreement. "That's because you have too much of him in you." He turns the key in the ignition, starting the engine.

Kelly wants to say that he's not really her uncle, but she keeps her eyes on the front windows, watches bodies shift and shuffle beyond the glass inside the building. Then, the front doors of the Tulsa County courthouse explode open and a flurry of movement spills out onto the pavement. A throng of reporters shouts questions at Siriano's lone attorney as he escorts Siriano toward the two Marshals. Behind them, the sheriff deputies pull the doors of the courthouse shut almost as if they're locking the world out or cutting off any avenue of retreat, eyeing the Marshals the whole time.

That's fine. They're probably happy to be rid of the sideshow traversing the space between the building and the dead-end street.

"Look alive." Kelly tosses her cigarette and stamps it out with her sensible shoes; she's not one prone to heels. From time to time, there are special occasions for them, but working isn't one. "The party's started."

Kelly hears the squeal of the passenger door opening. Pat groans loudly as he exits the vehicle, which shifts free of his weight. He hoists himself out of the car. Where a normal person would just get out, he makes a production out of it. Gray-headed and overweight like a linebacker put to pasture but not the slaughterhouse, as he puts it, he rounds the rear of the vehicle, pulling at his belt, black against his charcoal suit with his Marshals' star on his left side and gun on his right. He sniffs as he joins her on the driver's side of the vehicle.

"You ready for this?" Pat asks.

Kelly gives him some side-eye.

"You know the thing about waiting?" Pat asks, stepping forward but then pausing to allow the media figures to ask and get answers to their questions. "At some point, something's bound to happen and then it's sheer terror."

Kelly stays silent. Pat laughs.

"Come on, kid," Pat says in a soft patient voice. "Let's get this over with."

The two Marshals march toward the crowd. Siriano notices them and turns the corner of his mouth up in his patented sly smile. "Deputies," he says, voice smooth, before he is briefly eclipsed by a cameraman moving to get a better angle, mid-size camera over his shoulder, wireless, antenna sticking up like animal whiskers, and a large bright light illuminating both Siriano and his attorney, before flipping Kelly's way, camera lens capturing her brown eyes. "What can I do for you?"

Kelly lifts a hand to shield her face from both the camera lens and the bright light shimmering off her dark skin. She says, "You know why we are here." She pulls the warrant from her pocket and presents it to the attorney, who is already holding his hand out. The attorney, J. Gould, unfolds the warrant. His eyes bounce over the wording, skimming the page. He folds the warrant and stuffs it in his pocket.

Shouts ring out as the reporters turn their attention, cameras, and digital recorders on Kelly and Pat. Pat, being the southern diplomat he is, exercises that southern charm and tries to calm them and answer their questions without actually answering any questions. It's a gift and a curse. He does his best approximation of a politician, something he's almost too good at, holding a hand out and saying, "Come on now, come on, one at a time. With y'all shouting like this, I can't hear a thing." Continuing, he adds, "I'm an old man, come on, come on. Make some space so I can have a nice conversation with that man there," pointing Siriano's way, which only increases the barrage of questions from the reporters, which raise in intensity as each star reporter tries to get his or her questions answered, stepping over the others.

Siriano's attorney claps his manicured hands together to catch the reporters' attention and promises to give them the answers they seek, while stepping to the side, causing them to follow him like a school of fish. Now, performing his one-man show, the attorney says, "Why yes, my client is going to appear before a Grand Jury." He brings the reporters with him, leaving the Marshals and Siriano alone, "And yes those are two fine representatives of the Federal Government here to take my client into custody." He says, "No, I don't know what it's about, but the Feds seem to think Mr. Siriano needs to answer some questions," adding, "No, I don't believe my client is frightened of our friends in the US attorney's office. I imagine the Grand Jury will have their decision and will find Mr. Siriano didn't do the things the State seems to think he did. Otherwise, why'd the State Appeals court overturn his conviction," ending with, "and yes, I'm aware that the recent Supreme Court decision has allowed for Mr. Siriano's freedom, and yes, it's the Federal Government's prerogative if they wish to pursue egregious charges against my client even despite his overturned conviction in State court."

Whatever Indian blood Siriano claims to have hasn't overcome his Italian heritage. He'd be dark-headed if not for the graying temples. He lost weight in prison and gained some muscle, reverting to the man Kelly's examined in file photos: toned, lean, with just a slight belly, skin bronzed, well-groomed for his appearance in court, wearing a tan suit with a brown shirt, tan tie, matching shoes shined to blind, with a deep purple handkerchief square in his front coat pocket, and that stupid grin pasted across his face, which highlights his polished dentures. Reading his file revealed his real teeth were knocked out when he was in his thirties during a disagreement with a construction union.

"Turn around," Kelly demands, reaching behind her back to withdraw Uncle Frank's handcuffs from the handcuff holder secured to the backside of her belt. She holds the handcuffs up with a finger. They sway on the end of her finger. "Time to put these on."

Siriano rolls his shoulders forward. "Is that really necessary?"

"Can't ride in our car without them."

"Front or back?" Siriano asks, weight on his back foot.

"Turn around," Kelly orders.

"That's not what I meant," Siriano says, voice deflated. "I meant am I riding in the front or the back of the car."

Pat steps forward. "Front and we can put those in the front."

"Do we have to do it here in front of all these people?" Siriano asks, glancing toward the reporters. "I'm sure you understand how it must look for an innocent man to be bound the minute he steps out of the courthouse."

Kelly says, "Yes," as Pat says, "No."

Kelly stares daggers at Pat. "We need to get this over with."

"We can do it over at the car," Pat says, stepping over her and swaying his bulk forward. "But no problems, yeah?"

Siriano grins. "Certainly."

Kelly tells Siriano to "March."

Siriano motions Kelly forward. "Ladies first."

Kelly grabs his wrists and snaps the handcuffs over them.

Astonished, Siriano looks over to Pat. "Did I say something wrong?"

Pat shrugs and tells him, "Just walk to the car, will ya?" He motions to the waiting vehicle. "You offended *the lady* by treating her like a lady. She's a Marshal."

"Whatever." Siriano shrugs and takes one step forward, Pat to his left and Kelly behind him.

It's at this point that Kelly sees her career evaporate in front of her eyes.

The squeal of tires catches her and everyone else's attention. The tan panel van hops the curb, threading through the space between a reporter's sprinter van and the Marshals' Impala, the van scraping its underside against the concrete. The side door slides open as it nears, revealing five men in black ski masks carrying black rifles—AR-style. The van skids to a rough stop just on the other side of the concrete pillars and the five men file out of the side of the van, pointing their rifles at everything and everyone.

Of course, the cameras and reporters turn from Siriano's bewildered attorney toward the commotion, and they capture everything on camera as the lead gunman shouts, "Don't!" Motioning to Pat to keep his hands where he can see them. He buries the muzzle of his black rifle into the soft fat of Pat's double chin. Kelly moves to draw her weapon. Pat motions for her to hold off, hand down at his side, palm toward her. His eyes are wide. The lead gunman presses the rifle into Pat's neck, which causes him to twist his chin away from the barrel. The gunman orders Pat to stand down, shouting, "Don't move."

A second gunman steps forward, lowers his rifle, held in place with a sling, and pulls a black pillowcase from under his shirt, tucked into his waistband. He slips it over Siriano's head, pulling it tight at the neck, just under Siriano's chin, yanking on Siriano's wrists with his hand, forcing the crime boss to step forward. A third man, with his rifle switching between targets—the courthouse, the reporters, the Marshals, and the attorney—shoves Siriano forward with his left hand. The other two position themselves off to the side, guards, rifles scanning the area, making sure no one interferes.

The first gunman yells, "Don't," again before taking a step back, meaning don't draw your weapon. Don't follow him. Letting the rifle speak for him as he backpedals toward the van, unconcerned with any potential resistance.

Unable to process what's happening, Kelly shuts her eyes. When she opens them again, the last she sees of Siriano is his well-dressed form being half shoved and half hauled into the van.

Then, it's over.

The door of the van slams closed as it drops off the curb, and shoots out into traffic, running the red light, nearly hitting a crossing pedestrian.

The cameras swivel to her and Pat, and there is only a moment for Kelly to ponder her career stolen from her at gunpoint and for her to memorize the last three digits of the license plate before the tide of questions crashes against them.

CHAPTER FOUR: EMERSON ROWAN

EMERSON STROLLS INTO THE STARBUCKS AND maneuvers to the to-go shelf at the expo counter, with its freshly-made drinks waiting for their lovely new owners. This is Emerson's Tuesday and Thursday routine, at least for this location.

And at this location, in the heart of South Tulsa, hidden among the rolling hills and the migrating rush-hour traffic, confidence is the key, but not too much confidence. She doesn't want to overplay it and stand out or be remembered, which is why she is dressed the way she is. Something simple but accented with enough flourish to distract if need be, sort of like a tree frog in the rainforest, the bright colors warning off unwanted predators. With just a slight shift of body language, the frog can disappear into the undergrowth and blend in with the environment. It's a delicate balance, and she's good at it. Her whole life has taught her how to blend into the world around her, her personal undergrowth. Jail only accelerated and added to the knowledge in the way a trade school trains a mechanic.

Today, she chose a gray top with brown buttons, long sleeves, blue jeans, brown belt, and brown boots, with her hair tussled up behind her in a loose curly hold. Something unassuming and plain, but on her body, she rides too close to the edge of remembrance. The whole getup is otherwise known to her as the disguise of a suburban woman—a species more dangerous than something you'd coat an arrow with. But then again, Emerson's choice of men could offer a rebuttal.

At the counter, she bends at the waist to make sure the teenager behind the twisty tube burnt metal art deco designed espresso machine has a chance of ogling her modest cleavage, if he wants. However, this one doesn't look. He keeps his head locked down on his task, making the never-ending flood of drinks in ever-increasing varieties and combinations. He must be gay; usually, she gets some sort of eye undressing. This one goes on making drinks as if she doesn't exist, just another customer, which at this point, and if Emerson is honest with herself, she prefers. Men make her uncomfortable, and it's not like she entirely trusts them either. Her experiences with the other sex have left her empty.

Her green eyes scan the black sharpie scribbles on the side of the cups, studying the names and drink combinations as if she's looking for her drink, the one she ordered from the app or called in. She's searching for something that looks like something she would drink, and when she finds it, she takes it. Today, she feels like something straightforward, a latte with vanilla coconut milk, large, but it's not called large here, it's venti as if that makes it sexy. Emerson prefers to call things what they are.

It's not tall; it's small.

It's not shoplifting; it's taking advantage of shrinkage.

It's not stealing; it's reapportioning.

She's not a criminal; she's opportunistic.

Emerson plucks the drink from the shelf, glancing around to make sure no one is looking at her as she does it and making sure not to appear too guilty because that's as good a giveaway as any, especially on the cameras, and cameras are a big deal. They catch you. They remember you. They are like T-Rex; they will see you. If Emerson makes a sudden furtive movement, a twitch, she'll find her face plastered on some cyber-justice, neighborhood watch, wannabe social media warrior's weekly indictment of local criminal behavior. Or she'll find herself in handcuffs. If she plays it cool, she'll blend into the flow of daily life, especially in this place. Who knows when the barista, a barely paid 20-something, usually high or living a vaguely accepted millennial hipster life, made the drink? They make hundreds of drinks, and no one expects this one, or any of them, to remember the one drink that showed up missing among the flood of daily concoctions.

Perhaps, they never made the drink.

But it happens: grab the candy bar, the drink, the t-shirt, or whatever and shove it into a pocket only to glance around like a sly raccoon and garner the attention of watchful eyes. Here, doing this, it's low risk and well worth the return. All she has to do is act: use her body in all the ways the nuns of her parochial schools condemned. She'll apologize, saying something like, "Oh, I'm sorry I meant to take one of the other drinks" or "Oh, silly me" and hand the drink over to the proper owner with a schoolgirl giggle.

Stealing doesn't bother her, never has; it's her personal philosophy, a clean conscience and her mantra: "Screw the Man." The Man took two years of her life for a bullshit charge, which ended up dismissed, all because she had a shitty taste in roommates and boyfriends. So for her, "the juice is worth the squeeze," and God does she love Al Pacino and Robert DeNiro in *Heat*, especially the criminal mystique. She used to watch it daily while her father scratched out his column or chased some story, in other words, not around. She learned there is nothing she's not willing to walk away from in thirty seconds flat. In the age of online ordering and corporation superiority, Emerson can go days without spending money, not on food or drink, or clothes, or most of anything she needs. Her record is a month. If people are too lazy to actually drive through the drive-thru or walk inside to place an order, that's not her fault.

This time though, no one is looking her way. No one says anything or even gives her a second look. She lifts the drink from the shelf and takes a quick sip.

The sip is in case someone says something like "That's mine" or "What are you doing?" it's already too late and also to make sure the drink is still warm—or good. If it happens, she has a line for that too. She'll say something like, "Oh, I'm sorry, well, I've already drunk from it,"—turning to the confused mildly irritated barista—"Do you mind making them another? I drank from this one."

They never mind. It always works. And when it doesn't, she can always call dear old dad, who will bitch about her sticky fingers, but not really do anything of consequence because when she's not stealing, he's paying her bills as a way to make up for his parental absenteeism.

Today though, like most times, it's silent. No protests. No accusations. Nothing but a sweet sensation of accomplishment coursing through her veins. The thrill tickles her nerves.

Emerson smiles and turns to leave, twisting away from the counter and taking her premier drink, and it is at this point, over the lid of the newly liberated cup, that she notices two brilliant blue eyes, a man staring at her from a table far across the coffee shop, near the door. The eyes belong to a handsome man with mostly black hair. There are gray flecks speckled throughout his short cut. The hair goes with a distinguished-looking face, weathered but healthy, a man who takes fastidious care of his health and diet.

This man stares at her with an amused look, a lopsided grin due to the faint impression of a scar on the left side. For some reason, he seems familiar, as if she knows him from somewhere but she can't place it.

Her mind runs through options. An actor maybe, one in town to shoot a movie, here for a drink? No, that's not it. Maybe he's someone she went to school with, but Emerson doesn't remember anyone she went to school with or their names. She dropped out in the ninth grade. So that's not it either. Maybe he's someone she met in passing or during her visits to this Starbucks on a Tuesday or Thursday? Maybe she's brushed past him?

Her throat contracts as her heart flutters, half-coughing choking on the liquid in her mouth.

Did she steal his drink? Oh god, does he remember her for that?

Glancing at him again, she discounts this. He wouldn't look so amused if that were the case. This hiccup will bother her, but now she needs to leave. The longer she stays around, the greater the chance someone will shout at her or call the cops.

Emerson shuffles away from the counter as a woman approaches from behind, smacking her lips as she studies the orders on the rack. Her shape is reminiscent of a large squash, a gourd hanging from her father's study wall, with an elongated neck, framed in thick brown hair, tapering to a round full body, which lacks any definition or shape except for general plumpness. She is dressed in brightly colored eighties-style workout clothes that have probably never been used for exercise.

Emerson walks calmly toward the exit, careful not to run or make a sudden movement—T-Rex is watching—and toward Mr. Blue Eyes. She watches the woman from the corner of her eye, dimly aware of the female name scrawled across the side of the cup in her hand. Her thoughts should stay focused on the woman and leaving, but they flit back to the man, Mr. Blue Eyes, aware of how he sips his coffee, watching her watching him, intently, with humor dancing at the edges of his low-key, King of Cool, squint. Oh, how the crystal blue eyes perfectly highlight his tan olive skin.

Is he Italian? Mediterranean? Something. Maybe Native? There are a lot of those here. Not so much in California. Mexicans in both places, but he doesn't look Mexican. His face is too shapely, and he possesses the calm grace of a model, like an athlete. That's it, that's what he reminds her of, an athlete, like a David Beckham, no not Beckham, but the streamlined body of a soccer player. Like Cristiano Ronaldo, older of course, but lean and muscular, sitting in a way that displays his aloofness, serenity too, not smug and certainly not unattractive.

What type of man is he? What's he do? What is he drinking? Does he drink it black? Or is he more European, favoring teas? Espresso? Or maybe he's a frilly lawyer, wanting something picky?

He's not a soccer player. Those don't really exist out here. If she were back in LA, then maybe, but even then, the lines on his face hint at experience, aged, but not old—a wine that her eyes eagerly drink in as she approaches him.

He's a black coffee drinker, and it would be good coffee. The kind that he doesn't mess up with sugar or milk. His build says he doesn't consume unwanted calories. His clothes do the same thing; they are unadorned, high quality, and well made. Dark colors and earth shades complement his skin tone.

Emerson's had experience with guys like him and knows that whatever he does, he's an expert—he has that look.

The eyes stand out, crystal blue, with deepening shades radiating outwards from the irises. Even from across the room, they captivate her, and now, as she approaches him, she's drawn into them even more, like she's diving into a glacial lake. But he's a witness to her little crime, which is the gamble, or the hazard, of this particular jaunt. Someone is always bound to see something, and sometimes these goody two shoes say something, following the juvenile programmed credo of "see something say something."

How about "see something, shut the hell up?"

She's far from a goody two shoes, and she's had her fill of living by rules, living by a system, living by what others think of her, and being taken advantage of. She's not a sucker, not any longer. She grew up the hard way, and she paid for believing in others. Now, she's living life on her terms, and that means sticking it to the suckers who think tapping on a screen to order food is hard work.

Hard work is the guy behind the counter putting up with people who don't see a problem with paying six dollars for a drink when the guy behind the counter only makes a few dollars more an hour.

Almost on cue, from behind her, Emerson hears the woman at the counter say, "Where's my drink?"

"I'm sorry," a barista says, more questioning the outburst than apologetically answering her.

"My drink, it's not here," the woman goes on, throwing the beginnings of a tantrum, unaware of the scene she's making, "Did you not make it? I placed the order ten minutes ago. It should be here by now."

"Did you check the shelf?"

"Did I check the shelf? What do you think I've been doing here? Plucking my eyebrows? Of course, I checked the freaking shelf. Vanilla coconut latte. It's not hard. It shouldn't take but a few moments of your ever-precious, minimum-wage time to make, but it's not here. Why have an app where I can place an order any time I want and not have the drink ready? That seems silly."

"I'm sorry," the barista says, but this time it is an apology, and his voice disintegrates into subservience. "What was that drink? A vanilla coconut latte? I'll whip it up in just a moment."

"You better *whip* it up now," the woman sneers as Emerson stops listening to the exchange.

The man with the blue eyes, sitting with an arm draped over his crossed knee, shifts his gaze from Emerson to the woman at the counter, hardly acknowledging Emerson as she nears his table.

Emerson can't keep her eyes off him, studying him, undressing him the way she expected the barista to undress her. Just when she decides she's delighted in this romance long enough, he reaches out, snagging her arm like snatching a fly out of the air as she brushes past his table.

"Excuse me," he says, not looking her way, disinterested, fingers like ice. Grip firm, but not hard. Skin rough, but not broken.

Emerson turns toward him, blazing a how-dare-you-touch-me look, "Excuse me? Excuse you!"

Fighting the urge to swat at his hand. With someone like him, she knows better than to twist away. His grip is solid, but it doesn't hurt. He can't be a cop. They hurt. They grab, squeeze, pull, and twist, and he's doing none of those things. He's stopping her, yes, but not hurting her.

"I think you have that woman's drink." He tips his cup toward the scene unfolding behind her. The amused look still twinkles in his eyes. He's still not looking at her.

Emerson plays the confused woman, shaking her head side to side and blinking rapidly. Stunned. She can't have him catching the attention of the others at the expo counter because that's how bad things happen.

"What woman's drink?" Emerson asks, looking down at him.

"That lady over there." He tips his drink a second time. He lets go of her arm and puts his arm back on the knee, hand hanging free. "I think you picked hers up by mistake."

"No, this is my drink."

The blue eyes shift toward her, then down for a moment, and then back up, staring at her, staring through her, almost, intense, warm, but frightening, going from ice to fire and back again, fluctuating between the two.

"Without looking at the cup," he says, "what's the name on the side?"

"This is just some lame attempt to get my name," Emerson says.

"No, this is an attempt to prove you didn't just steal that cup."

"Why would I want to tell you my name?" Emerson asks, pulling her arm back, protecting her midsection, cradling the coffee cup under her chin, and playing coy, like he's trying to pick her up. "I don't have to tell you anything."

She's used this line before when someone like him has done something like this, but he seems different.

"You don't know what name is written there on the side, do you?" he asks with confidence in his voice. "You don't look like a Ruth."

"What do I look like?"

"Something worth looking at."

He delivers the line smoothly and with direct eye contact, and for a moment, Emerson's heart skips.

Emerson keeps her voice low. "No, I'm not playing this game where you hit on me, just so you can get my name. I don't use my real name when ordering drinks just like I keep pepper spray in my bag for guys that don't take a hint. When I say no, it means no. I don't want to give you my number. Just as I don't want to give you my name. Go flirt with someone else."

"Is that what I'm doing?" The man showing he's amused.

Emerson shifts her feet. "I don't know what you're doing. I know what I was doing before you stopped me—leaving."

"You were, but now you're not."

"You're really enjoying yourself right now, aren't you?"

"I wasn't, but now I am." The man motions to the table. "Have a seat."

"No."

"Sit down, and I won't get their attention. I'm sure they'd like to correct the mishap. Maybe make you your drink; what was it supposed to be? The same type of drink, a latte, or did you order something else?"

Emerson stays silent.

"Did you forget or just get confused?" he pauses. "Let me guess, an honest mistake, that's what this is. I bet that's what you say. 'I'm sorry. I must have picked this one up by mistake.' Don't you ever do that? And then do some stupid giggle, probably a cute one, but stupid."

"I don't have to tell you nothing." Emerson weighs, her options.

"You don't, that's true." Then offers his name like she's asked. "My name's Maggie."

"Maggie?"

"Maggie." Maggie motions to the table with his free hand again, inviting her to take a seat.

Even though she's free, her arm still feels the lingering sensation of his grip wrapped around her biceps.

"Sit."

"I don't want to sit."

"It's really not a request," Maggie says. "I could ask that woman over there if she would like to sit. Say: 'Ruth, funny story. I think this woman knows something about the mix-up.'"

Emerson locks her eyes on him. "You wouldn't?"

Maggie shakes his head. "She's not my type, but I'm sure we could find something we have in common."

"You do this often?" Emerson questions as she plops into the seat across from him. "Blackmail women into having a conversation with you?"

"Is that what I'm doing?"

"What do you want to call it?"

"A friendly conversation."

"Well then, Mr. Friendly, what do you want to talk about?"

"Why you feel the need to take something that doesn't belong to you." He smiles trying to disarm her. "Can't be a healthy living."

It works.

She doesn't like that it works. It shouldn't work. But it does.

She sets the latte on the table.

Now, she's disarmed.

"Oh, you think you're cute, don't you?"

"I don't really think about myself one way or the other."

"Oh, mysterious, let me get a napkin for the seat," Emerson says. "Is that how it works for you? You turn on the charm, squint those brilliant blue eyes, and make me all squishy in the knees?"

"Not on purpose." Maggie smiles. "But if that is what's happening—"

"No," she snaps.

But it is.

To which he follows with, "Because if it were, I'd have to tell you that I'm not really attracted to thieves. The liability would be outrageous."

Emerson crosses her arms. "I'm not a thief."

"Well then, what do you call yourself?"

"Rosina," she says. "Fine, there you go, you have my name, happy? And it's Rosie if I like you."

"Rosie," he says, turning the name over on his tongue. "Eh, I don't think so. It's not Rosie."

Emerson nods. "If I like you—"

"—Rosina," he concedes.

"And you're Maggie."

"I am."

"What sort of name is that?"

"One I chose for myself," he says. "Not my real name, but what I call myself."

"Great. I'm glad we got that cleared up. Now, what is it you want from me?"

"I want you to relax."

"Why?"

"Because the woman over there was staring daggers at your back as you were about to walk through that door, and I figured, one of two things was about to happen. Either she was going to capitulate and let you leave with your drink, which doesn't seem like her style, or she was going to make a scene. I'll let you decide which one she'd do."

Emerson takes a drink of the latte.

"So I figured, well, here is this cute woman that knows what she wants although she has to get really close to it to read it. Do you need glasses? Anyways, I figured I'd save everyone an embarrassing scene and act like you were with me."

"My knight in shining armor," Emerson says.

"I'm far from a knight," Maggie adds.

"I don't need your help."

"You don't?"

"No, I'm done with men."

"Are you?"

Emerson crosses her arms. "Are you going to just keep repeating things back to me? That's annoying."

"What is?"

"That," she says.

"What?"

"Stop it."

"What do you mean?"

"I'm going to get up and walk away."

"No, you are not," he says, confident in his statement.

"Oh, I'm not, so sure of yourself?"

"Yes," he says.

Emerson picks up the drink and sips, her lips caressing the plastic, using the quiet to study the man who thinks he's playing with her. It's the other way around. "You did it again."

He's a cop, has to be. He has that self-assured asshattery all cops have.

She asks, "You a cop?"

"If I were?"

"Didn't anyone ever tell you not to answer a question with a question?"

"Who would have told me?"

"God, you're unbelievable. I don't know. Your mom. Your teacher. How the hell should I know?"

"You seemed to have someone in mind when you asked is all." Maggie motions to her as he adjusts in the seat, uncrossing one leg and resting both arms on the table. Hand open, jutting toward her. "Did someone tell you that?"

"No," she says. "You know what, we're not doing this; we're not going to turn the conversation back on me. You're the one that's holding me here."

Maggie looks around. "No one is holding you here. I'm saving you. You can leave at any point. No one's stopping you."

"Saving me from what?"

"Possibly," he responds, "going to jail."

Emerson rolls her teeth over the backside of her upper lip. "I've been there before."

Maggie leaned in, interested now. "Have you?"

Emerson leans back, crosses her leg over her knee, comfortable, her act becoming real now. "I don't have to explain myself to you."

"You don't."

"What sort of name is Maggie?"

"What sort of name is Rosina?"

"My mother's name."

"Then, it's my father's name."

"We're going to keep doing this, aren't we?" she asks.

"Depends," he replies.

"On what?"

"If you'll answer questions truthfully."

"How do you know I haven't?"

Maggie is silent for a moment, eyes studying her again. "Let's say I know. I have a talent for these things. What's your real name?"

Emerson hesitates a second too long. "My real name is Rosina."

"No it isn't. Just as it isn't Ruth or Karen."

"Karen?"

"That's what she is, right, a Karen?" Maggie tilts his head toward the woman who's half leaned over the counter yelling in the barista's face. "I just can't believe it's Ruth."

"I don't know what her name is."

"She doesn't look like a Ruth, does she?" he asks. "Turn around. Look at her. Does she look like a Ruth to you?"

"I don't know who she is."

"You don't?" he questions. "It's on the cup."

"You don't stop, do you?"

"Nope," he says.

"So if you're not a cop, what are you? What do you want?"

"I watch things," he replies, not answering her question but answering her question.

"You watch things?"

"Like how last week, I watched you come in here, go to the counter like you were going to order something, and then, you made a big show about remembering you ordered something online as you plucked granola bars off the front display while the barista was looking the other way like you were picking pecans or something. Granola bars, really? If you're that hungry, let me take you to dinner."

"I don't..." she starts to protest but then stops.

"And then you went over to there, like you did today, and stole this poor person's drink."

"What was poor about it?"

"She was a mom," he says, deadpan, "with two crying kids. Carrying things. Strollers, everything. Whining. Used her last penny."

Emerson fails at suppressing a smile. "I did not."

"You did," he says, nodding. "And then you did it again today. Here I am, sitting right here, and here you come again. Straight over to the counter. Select what looks nice, and walk out. Except, this time I had to stop you."

"Why?"

"Didn't you hear me before?"

Emerson stays silent.

"I told you why. Weren't you listening?"

"What?" Emerson says. "You didn't tell me why you stopped me. I don't need your help to keep me from going to jail."

"But I told you." He leans in and his voice drops quieter.

Emerson says nothing.

He leans back in the chair, grinning. "I said I want to take you to dinner."

"When did you say that?"

"When I told you if you're hungry enough to take granola bars, you should let me take you to dinner."

"That's not what you said," Emerson retorts.

"There, that proves it; you were paying attention, so the answer's going to be yes, yeah?"

"Yes to what?"

"Dinner," he says. "Maybe I don't want to take you now. You're pretty slow on the uptake. That'll be an adjustment to the women hanging off me, beatin' my door down to take me to dinner. See, what's happening here, is an opportunity. Think of it like picking teams for kickball, but instead of teams, I'm offering you first dibs. Your choice what you do."

His smile says everything he just said was bullshit.

"You don't quit, do you?"

"Not usually, no."

Emerson thinks it over. "All right, Romeo, where would we go?"

Maggie shakes a finger in front of his face. "No, no, you don't get to do that. You have to give me an answer first. This isn't a 'I tell you tell' type deal. This is a you say 'yes,' and then, you find out when I take you. A leap of faith thing."

"I could tell you where to leap."

"You could." Maggie crosses his leg again, relaxed. "But then you'd be missing out, which means I'd be missing out."

"You know what; I wanted to talk to you," Emerson adds, turning the conversation back on him.

"You did?"

"Yeah, you think this aloof act's real cute, don't you? You think if you play Mr. Smooth, I'm going to fall all over you. I bet you're right; there's a whole stable of women out there just waiting for the wilted rose of your love, is that it? But that's not why I wanted to talk to you."

"It's not?"

"You look familiar."

"I look familiar?" he asks. "I told you, I was in here the other day? That solves it."

"No, that's not it."

"That's not why I look familiar."

"You're the big expert on what I'm thinking."

"A novice really."

"You do remind me of someone."

"Who's that?"

"I don't know." Emerson motions with two fingers. "That's the problem. Maybe if you helped me out here. Tell me what you do. Then, I'd figure it out."

"I do this and that," he says. "That help any?"

"That's old and means nothing."

He chuckles. He sips his drink. "I'm in restoration."

"Seriously?" she asks. "That's all you're going to say?" She drops her voice down, mocking him. "*I'm in restoration.*"

"You have a problem; I'm the guy you hire to take care of it."

"That doesn't sound like restoration."

"What's it sound like, then?" he asks. "And that's the definition of a restoration."

"Whatever. If you're not going to tell me, then I need to be going." Emerson stands but then she pauses. "Wait, what did you say your name was?"

"Maggie."

"No, not that name, your real name."

"I didn't give you my real name. You didn't give me your real name. I would like to know who I'm going to take out to dinner, but if you don't want to tell me, that's fine too. I've gone on some blind dates before. That's what I'll pretend this is."

Emerson sighs. "Fine, it's Emerson, happy? What's your real name?"

"Maurizio—"

"—DiMaggio?" She fishes the name from one of the few happy moments of her past.

Which surprises him almost as much as the joy it causes her.

"You know me?"

"God, I can't believe it's you."

His face collapses into suspicion.

Emerson leans back into the table. "Jesus, it's you. Really you! I can't believe it."

His lips pull into a hesitant grin. "So that's a yes then?"

"My father would love to meet you," Emerson says.

Maggie frowns. "I... I don't..."

Then, from behind Emerson, a deep voice booms, "Ma'am," breaking the mood, just when it starts getting interesting for her.

Emerson snorts and whips around. "What?"

The two cops, standing there, wear seriousness like it's part of their uniform.

CHAPTER FIVE:
PABLO JIMENEZ

PABLO STARES AT THE CAR AS IT CIRCLES THE ABANdoned drive-in parking lot, a Buick sedan, goldish-brown, day burnt and weathered two-toned, with the sun glinting off the hood's remaining paint. The approaching car kicks up a cloudy wake of grit and dirt that billows behind the tires. Once again, Gabino is driving too fast.

Pablo has talked to him about this. The Buick's close enough for him to make out the familiar dented driver's side door as it passes right to left across the half-circle parking lot. The exhaust is louder than it should be, altered after Omar gave the kid the car. The dirt flung up in the car's wake is a rusted reddish-brown, mixed with the decaying tan soil and the red clay Oklahoma's famous for, the red dirt Pablo hates. The cloud blots out the rotting white signposts or number racks, remnants of the ancient speaker system, white totems of some silver screen spectral graveyard—tombstones of another era.

Maybe that was the era of his youth, with lush fields, green and expansive. When Pablo's grandfather, arm around him, scoops up a handful of soil and promises all of this is to be his, fields extend into the horizon, dropping away at the edge of the world. That was before Pablo's forced march north—migration is the better word. Truer too. Another would-be refugee.

War came, a drug war, a senseless war, bloody, immortalized in successful fiction, factions fighting factions, circles within circles, chaos ignored or inflamed. A time when people like Pablo and his family, the mildly successful farmers, the little ones, suffered, caught in the churn of struggle where life became less about the future and all about the now. About survival.

About power.

Pablo's life has always been about power.

The power of choice. The power of life. The power of being oneself. The power of others. Rebellion. Honor. Duty. Service. Death.

His family sent him to distant relatives with the hope of a better life. In reality, their actions fostered his sense of abandonment and honed a distrust of those who say they love him. He was forced into a life of servitude, little better than an indentured servant to a man—dead now—named Alejandro Danois.

From the entrance of the garage, shielding his eyes from the sun with his hand, Pablo watches the vehicle with dread. He drops his hand in a crisp salute as he turns toward Omar who is in the office, turning his back on the vehicle, disgusted with Gabino's driving. "That kid needs to learn to drive."

From the office door, seated at the desk going over the books, Omar glances at him, his thick black glasses perched on his nose.

In Spanish, Pablo clarifies, "They're here."

Omar sets the ledgers down on the metal desk, pulls the reading glasses from his face, placing them next to the ledgers, inserts the half-chewed cigarillo into the corner of his mouth, and exits the office to look at the vehicle. The ledgers are for Alejandro's breakfast café that Pablo let Omar take over after Alejandro's death and the place where Omar worked as a line cook for years. The ledgers contain Alejandro's scribblings, which detail his accounts and daily produce totals. Omar, a lean and compact man, dressed in tan work pants and a blue denim shirt, wrinkled and in a way that it seems permanently covered in dirt, shuffles his weight in the doorway, left to right, something he does when he's nervous and has learned from a life on his feet in the kitchen.

"I still don't feel comfortable about this," Omar says in Spanish. He withdraws the chewed cigarillo from his mouth when he steps out of the garage and into the sunlight, still watching the approaching vehicle.

"Didn't that car use to be yours?" Pablo says from the shadows of the garage door, referring to the car Gabino is driving. Then, replying to Omar's comment, he continues, "We talked about this. Nothing can tie back to us. I don't need cops looking for us. It's already going to cause enough of a problem in the media." Pablo adds, "He's your brother. You'll need to do something about him, about that," meaning the loud music, the loud personality, and the free spirit hatched in the ignorance of youth.

"I will," Omar says, defending his little brother. "He's still finding his place in life ... with us."

Gabino is only eighteen and chafes under Pablo's rule. He was Alejandro's last acquisition, which is how the old man viewed all the members of his little neighborhood organization. A week before Alejandro's death, he hired the boy as a table busser because Omar kept bringing him to the café so that the troubled youth could finish his homework, much like Renaldo's mother used to do with Renaldo. Alejandro took to the kid and said, "If you're going to be here you might as well make some money."

Alejandro cared about keeping the kids off the streets and out of trouble, not that they didn't commit crimes for him, they did, but he ran a neighborhood improvement project and everything Alejandro did, everything he stood for and represented was for the neighborhood, for the betterment of his people. His people were anyone from Latin America imprisoned in a second-class American life.

Now, with the old man gone and Pablo's ascension to the top, Omar has taken Gabino under his wing to teach him the ways of their business, which is controlling all drugs and other racketeering-type crimes in East Tulsa. Alejandro carved out a nice little empire acting as a mediator between the Mexicans and everyone else. It was easy. He spoke the language of both sides fluently—money.

Pablo and Omar started at the bottom of Alejandro's world, and now they are the top two. Maybe Omar should have been the heir to Alejandro's throne, but Pablo seized the opportunity.

So when Pablo asked Omar about the kid, who's always around, Omar defended his actions by saying, "Life's short, keep family close." Pablo reluctantly accepted it because Omar accepted Pablo's lie, but involving family in this life is a dangerous proposition. Family makes things personal, makes things difficult, messy, and complicated. Family means dynasties.

Omar should be where Pablo is, and Pablo should be dead.

But he's not.

Omar knows. He has to know. Every time the little bald man stares at him, Pablo sees it in his eyes, in the tilt of the head, the examining look; he is searching for the truth, suspecting the truth, questioning the lie, seeing the truth, and peering into Pablo's mind and past the false claim.

Now Pablo asks, "Why doesn't he listen to me?"

"He listens to no one," Omar says. "Don't worry about the car. He was supposed to switch vehicles. If he's in my old car, then he's made the switch. I told him no less than three cars in three separate locations. Drive around for a day; keep the cars moving. If he's in that thing, then we're all good."

Pablo doubts it.

Omar licks his lips. "Vega called and said he dumped the van down by the river."

Raising an eyebrow, Pablo searches Omar's eyes to see if the man is making a Saturday Night Live reference or if he's serious. "The river?"

"Yes, where the old pedestrian bridge used to be," his tone serious. "I'll talk to Gabby." Omar flicks his eyes away. "You know, he looks up to you ... with what you've done, what you've made, salvaged from all this ... death."

"Someone had to do it," Pablo says. "It was necessary. With the old man gone, I..." He shuts his eyes. He doesn't want to discuss this right now or think about it. "Your brother may look up to me, but he only listens to you."

"Barely," Omar says. "But I'll talk to him if that's what you want. See if I can knock some sense into him."

"He should listen to me."

"He will come to his senses. All young men eventually do."

"If he doesn't listen, death will come for him."

Omar stares at Pablo, and Pablo watches the cook contemplate the veiled threat. Pablo may be uncomfortable with his newfound power and position, bestowed upon him, or taken, depending on who's talking, but that doesn't mean he's not a tough man or doesn't know how to make his point.

Accepting the situation as he accepted the lie, Omar licks his lips. "I'll talk to him."

Pablo retrieves a beer from the fridge in the corner of the garage's small workspace. "This is war, what we're doing today. They declared it, but we're better at it."

"This is different." Omar's eyes still sun-blinded flicker Pablo's way.

"Yes, it is," Pablo confirms. "So talk to him and tell him he can't fuck up. Neither can his friends. If they fuck up, they're dead. Either Siriano's men will get them or something else. I need you, so I need them."

"He'll listen."

Pablo sits in the chair under the hydraulic vehicle lift, a rusted piece of equipment languishing in the berth of the garage that makes up the northern boundary of the parking lot. He's unsure of Gabino's dedication to what Alejandro built. The kid wasn't around. He doesn't know. He has dedication, but not to Pablo—to his brother, big brother, Omar. Pablo slashes the beer bottle down, using the edge of the hard plastic chair to pop the cap. He takes a swig.

Omar continues to watch the approaching vehicle. The loud music overpowers the exhaust now, the thump of bass and reverb of vibrating speakers.

Between guzzles of beer, Pablo says, "This is a big step, what we're doing. A power move: expand or die. We can't be this neighborhood thing any longer."

He eyes Omar waiting to see how he's going to take it.

Alejandro was against a close relationship with their cousins down south, preferring to keep the violent nature of their way of life at arm's length, but now, it's Pablo's turn. If he's going to war, he's going to need reinforcements. It's better to obtain them before starting the war, which is why Pablo entrusted Vega, his new attack dog. Pablo needed someone he could trust, and his cousin seemed like a good choice.

Alejandro always loved Omar, and Pablo knows Omar loved the old man, which is perhaps why he can never be honest with Omar about what really happened that night, the night Pablo learned an unspeakable truth about himself: a truth he can't accept or admit. A man came in the night and killed Alejandro. Pablo did nothing to stop it from happening. He was there; the gunfire startled him. He let the perpetrator go, and he doesn't know why. He suspects it was out of self-preservation. After all, what was there to do? Die? That served no purpose. Deep down, inside his troubled heart, Pablo knows the truth—he's a coward.

And like all cowards, he lied. Lying's a skill Pablo was untrained in but quickly developed as his panicked mind listened to Renaldo Luna's rationale for letting him live. It wasn't hard; the offer was attractive, so he decided and he lied and he's a coward.

In Pablo's retelling of those events, he rushed out of the house ready to confront Renaldo, Alejandro's beloved protégé, who turned his back on the old man. The same Renaldo that Pablo failed to kill. In Pablo's version, Renaldo stands over the dead boss, pivots, and says, "Stop!" and Pablo stops mid-step. Eyes shifting from Renaldo to Alejandro, who is dead in the chair, bleeding into the pool where he would soak his feet after working in the restaurant.

This is where the story diverges from the truth.

In Pablo's story, which he later backed up with evidence that he added at the last minute, a flourish to sell the story, they exchanged gunfire, which brought the police to Alejandro's house. Pablo had already removed the family for safety reasons. In this version, there was a shootout, and Renaldo fled.

But that's not what happened. What happened was that Pablo shot into the house, shattering the sliding glass door. He quickly dismantled the gun and disposed of the pieces in a nearby storm drain, careful about how he touched the gun. Then, he fired into the fence with his own gun. Self-defense. It's not illegal to own a gun in a house, especially when using it after someone was murdered.

Assassinated is a better word, but the police, the white men, don't see it like that. They saw it as murder, homicide.

Also, Pablo leaves out the part where Renaldo, head still bandaged from where Pablo shot him, pleaded with him. "Think about it," Renaldo had said. "He's dead. It's over."

Pablo remained quiet, with fury burning within him, radiating out in embarrassment, eating him from the inside out. How could he fail Alejandro so badly? His mind processed the fact Alejandro was dead and there was nothing he could do. Pablo had one mission, one responsibility, and he failed.

Even now, Pablo, sipping his beer and staring at the suspicious Omar, can hear Renaldo's words, "It's yours. I'm done." He doesn't understand why Renaldo let him live. It would have been easy to shoot him and be done with it.

Pablo shot him, tried to kill him for Alejandro. Did Renaldo not care? Was he not as guilty as Alejandro?

But that's not what happened.

"He's dead," Renaldo had said, gun on him. "You don't need to die. You're the heir, yes? You don't want this. I don't want this. I'm done. I leave tonight. This was between him and me. I don't blame you for what you did. It was only business. This wasn't that. It was something else."

The words *this was something else* turning into a rationale in Pablo's mind. A lie. An opportunity. Freedom.

Renaldo made Pablo step back from the pool and back into the house, hands up, with the gun on him the whole time, until Pablo disappeared into the darkness of the old man's house.

That's when it struck him, this unbearable truth. He is a coward. He followed every command Renaldo gave him. He slid the door shut, locked it, and shackled himself to a lie forever, unable to admit his greatest failure to anyone.

Now from his seat of power, a lawn chair in an abandoned automotive garage, Pablo surveys the dusty, dried, dying earth of the parking lot, part of the abandoned drive-in that dissolves into the rickety horse farms and stables of the southern boundary. This is most of what Pablo inherited per Alejandro's will.

Pablo has taken to confiding in Omar as a way to keep a rapport between them and to try to find out what the man's thinking.

Pablo says, "Either this is a preemptive strike or retaliation. Either way, Renaldo started it when he shot Alejandro."

Omar stares at him and chews on the cigarillo, shaved head catching the sunlight in the way the hood of the car did. Since Omar either spends most of his time in Alejandro's restaurant or under a vehicle, he's usually covered in some kind of grease stains, and his skin's taken on a splotchy pallor.

Pablo shuts his eyes, fighting his mind, trying to prevent it from sliding back to the past, to that night. To the bark of the gun, the surprise. That night, Pablo knocked his bottle over, spilling beer all over Alejandro's kitchen table. He rushed outside to find Renaldo, Alejandro's favorite, with the gun in hand, standing over the old man's body. Renaldo pleaded with Pablo to stay quiet. To listen to him. To think. Pablo did what Renaldo wanted and went back into the house to the confused family of the man lying dead outside at the feet of someone who had been family, at the feet of Renaldo Luna, a man who had betrayed his roots for a white man, Siriano—for power, for ambition, for all the things Pablo isn't and has never wanted nor sought.

Pablo returns to the present and opens his eyes.

"Still," Omar says, "no one's heard from him since it happened. You were there." The tone of voice hints at something unstated, but Pablo ignores it, and Omar goes on, "You'd think if he made the hit, then *he'd* try to take advantage of it, *they* would try to take advantage of it, but nothing. Nothing happened. He just disappeared. Makes me think maybe it wasn't a hit; maybe it was something else."

"What else could it have been?" Pablo asks, knowing what else it could have been, personal. He tried to kill Renaldo for Alejandro and failed. Renaldo didn't.

Simple really.

Besides, his lie wasn't a big one, just a small one. He told the others he was pissing at the time. Who can fault the guy for peeing? He heard the gunshot and got outside just in time for a gunfight as the perpetrator runs away.

"Renaldo was Siriano's second-in-command after all," Pablo says. "It doesn't matter where he is now. He could have run to hide under the skirts of the eye-talian."

What he doesn't say is, "Who knows? Perhaps Siriano did order Alejandro's death. Maybe Renaldo did it for two reasons. Why not, serves him, and serves his white master."

But after today, it won't matter.

"Doesn't mean they didn't send him somewhere, these *eye-talians*, you can't trust them. You watch the movies, maybe they stashed him somewhere in Sicily, where he's living on some sandy beach watching the Mediterranean wash in and fade out. The old country," spitting the last words with a sneer and venomous contempt.

Omar doesn't sound convinced. "Renaldo was a lot of things," he argues. "He wasn't someone you just sat to the side. His ego wouldn't allow it. I think that's why he went to work for the white man. You knew him, and you knew how the old man was. Renaldo either needed to be in charge or go. That's what the old man wanted. That's how he was. Just as that's how Renaldo was. His ambition was too great. Alejandro loved him, but that didn't keep him from telling us to kill him."

"He tried to kill him," Pablo says, wanting to end the conversation. "We tried to kill him. We failed."

Omar doesn't say it. He knows better. But it's Pablo who failed. Renaldo twitched at the last moment; the bullet struck his skull, skimmed off the bone, and gave him a concussion.

"And he killed Alejandro." Omar licks his lips once and then smashes them together to keep himself from saying more.

Pablo notices the contempt, the questioning eyes. If he were in Omar's position, he'd probably feel the same way, but his position is infinitely more complicated. He doesn't want to be here. He doesn't want any of this.

That's the funny thing about lies, once told, either you have to stick to them or you don't. Pablo's stuck to his, and now, he and the rest of Alejandro's fractured organization have crossed a line that can't be uncrossed. He knows it just as much as Omar, but Omar can't seem to work it through his simple head that Alejandro is gone, and now, Siriano is going to pay for it, whether he had anything to do with Renaldo shooting him or not.

It's not about facts. It's about appearances.

And they've acted.

Publicly.

Omar adds, "All I'm saying is Renaldo wouldn't just disappear. That's not his style." He shrugs.

Pablo doesn't say anything. Omar better be careful with his next few words.

Omar continues, "Maybe Siriano didn't order the hit."

The man won't drop it.

"Does it matter at this point?" Pablo says.

Omar shifts his weight again, planting the chewed cigarillo between his clenched teeth. "I guess not, but this worries me. Once they stop, there isn't a way back. He'll know. I still think we should use ski masks or something. There's no reason to tip our hand to him."

"There's every reason." Pablo snaps his fingers together. "All you do is talk, fret." He's getting angry now. "Where was this advice, this morning, before we did what we're doing? Where was this counsel when Alejandro died? We failed. This is fighting back. They took our king; we take theirs."

Omar shrugs. "I'm just saying, if we do this, we start something we can't end."

"I intend to finish it," Pablo says. "We win."

"If we don't?" Omar raises an eyebrow.

Pablo starts to answer when the Buick comes to a screeching halt outside of the open garage doors, brakes squealing, ceramic hot from the drive, releasing a chemical smell as it cools. The driver, Gabino, looks across Omar's wife, Flavia, in the passenger seat. She's a pretty woman, but severely skinny and malnourished. Pablo's grandfather would call her field trash.

Pablo bends at the waist and places his elbows on the passenger window. Gabino turns the music down as Pablo asks, "How did it go?"

Gabino starts to say something, a half-strangled syllable.

"Better than expected," Flavia says before Gabino can speak. She's a defiant woman, strong, nothing like any of the women Pablo's used to or prefers. He prefers someone quiet, meek, who will listen, but Omar doesn't. Omar has allowed Flavia's independence to fester. She runs him. She runs the restaurant. And Pablo reads in the woman's face that she isn't happy that Omar is Pablo's second.

Pablo shifts his glance to Flavia, slowly. "Any problems?"

"None." Flavia refuses to look at him. She stares straight ahead, wringing her hands in her lap. Omar takes a half step forward.

Gabino asks, "Where do you want him?"

"Pull it inside, and we'll get him out." Pablo steps back from the car's window.

The semi-defunct automotive shop sits far back from any of the main roadways. Sometimes Pablo brings cars here to be "chopped," but today it will house Siriano. No one will hear anything or care.

Flavia glances at Omar. Gabino too. Pablo catches it. His orders should be carried out without question. Omar nods once, giving his approval.

Pablo will have to do something about it, but this isn't the time or the place. After today, he and all of his organization will need to play very carefully or risk losing everything. What they did was public, very public, already splashed across the news.

Omar and Pablo move out of the way to allow Gabino space to back the car into the garage part of the shop, under the hydraulic lift. Gabino backs in without any trouble, smoothly positioning the car between the rusted-red pylons of the lift. He's out of the driver's seat before the engine's off.

At the opening, silhouetted in the sunlight, Omar pulls the garage door down. The automotive shop has been cleared of anything that could be used as a weapon. The windows were painted black. The rollers on the door make a thundering sound. Omar throws a latch that was put in place to lock the door like the back of a truck.

With the beer still in his hand, Pablo moves to the trunk. He sips the beer and demands the keys. "Keys." He looks at Gabino, who's standing there, useless, thumbs jammed into his tight pockets.

Gabino blinks once.

"Keys," Pablo says again, holding his empty hand out.

Gabino jumps, removes his thumbs from the pockets, and turns to retrieve the keys from the ignition, but Flavia, exiting the passenger seat, tosses them at Gabino over the top of the vehicle before he can duck into the driver's seat. Gabino catches them and bounds over to Pablo to hand the keys over.

From near the door, Omar says, "Do you want a mask or anything?"

Pablo considered it. He thought a lot about it. He probably should hide his face, but the whole idea is to show Siriano who he is, make it very clear.

Pablo says, "No, let him see my face. Let him know what this is about."

Omar nods.

Flavia joins her husband, taking her place at his side. Omar wraps an arm around her waist. Pulls her close. She's wearing a simple denim outfit, button-down top, blue jeans, and tan work boots. The outfit works on her body but isn't elegant.

Pablo tells Gabino, "Go open up the other office, the one with the restroom."

The one Pablo's made into a makeshift cell.

With the kid gone, Pablo inserts the key into the trunk lock, turns the key, and pops the trunk. The trunk raises with ease. He helps it the rest of the way.

Inside is a battered man, dirty and crumpled. They took him yesterday. Pablo watched the news, watched it happen, watched how his men rolled up, rifles ready, and kidnapped him right off the courthouse steps. This man barely resembles the crisp, clean man from the news. His tan suit is dirty and scuffed; the shirt underneath is torn and sweat-stained. He's a shadow of the powerful figure that stepped out of the courthouse and into Pablo's grasp. But despite the man's appearance, his face shows proud defiance. He doesn't yell or complain, and from what Pablo understands from talking with Vega, he hasn't complained once. He only asked, "Where are you taking me?" and "Who are you?"

Both are reasonable questions.

The man looks up at him as Pablo holds the trunk open, arm resting on the lid.

The man's eyes are wild and white.

Pablo says, "Welcome."

The man's eyes turn from confused to focused as he runs through an internal Rolodex of names and faces until he finds Pablo's, as Pablo knew he would. The man was always good with faces. Always good with names. He made it a habit to be well-mannered and brought gifts every time he visited Alejandro. Often it was some shitty red wine, cheap, but Alejandro accepted the gifts graciously. And every time Alejandro received these gifts from this man in his sharp-tailored suits and expensive colognes, Pablo stood there as his bodyguard.

This man remembers. This man knows.

Nodding in acceptance, Siriano, still inside the trunk, pastes that annoying smirk across his face, checks his suit with a smooth brush of the hand, and asks, "Do you have any gum? My breath stinks."

CHAPTER SIX: FLAVIA SANCHEZ

FLAVIA FUMES AS SHE PACES BACK AND FORTH OUT-side the automotive shop in the noonday sun. She's trying to get her husband to see reason, hurriedly talking with her hands, flailing them at him in tight circles in front of her body every time she turns around to face him. He's blinded by his subservience, blinded by his love for Alejandro, so much so that he doesn't see what's happening around him, what's happening now. She sees it. How could she not? Doom, destruction, death, choose the word, that's what's coming if they aren't careful. She sees it.

Flavia says, "I don't trust him."

"It's not about trust, *mi reina*," Omar says, his voice soft and filled with love. He reaches for her, and she slaps his hand away.

"Don't touch me," she says, finger raised. "How can you think of anything else? Think of anything besides what's happening right now? Do you not see it? Are you blind?"

Flavia steps back, repelled by her emotions and actions because her words hurt him. She sees the hurt creep across his normally placid features.

In a strong voice, he says, "I am not blind."

She snorts, jaw clenched, teeth tight on a piece of gum, and struggles to calm her mind. The last few days have passed in a whirlwind and have chipped away at her silent resolve.

She can't be silent any longer.

Flavia reflects upon the situation. Maybe she's too hard on her husband. He looks like a battered puppy dog right now, with his beautiful brown eyes pleading with her to talk to him, hug him, hold him. Stuck between doing what's right and doing what he's been conditioned to do.

It's not his fault they are here; it's hers. Hers for not speaking up sooner. Hers for giving bad advice.

The dark-sleepless circles under Omar's eyes show how tired he is.

He says, "We've been up all night. Maybe, if we try talking tomorrow, calm down some, we can figure this out together."

They do everything together. That's how they have survived.

Looking just as tired as he does, her dark hair pulled back and tied with a piece of ribbon at her shoulders, Flavia hugs her arms against her chest. Her sleeves are rolled up, and her skin's cool from the air but kissed warm from the sun. "I don't think I would be any calmer tomorrow than I am now. I may be even more agitated the longer this goes on."

Omar, his brown shirt already sweat-stained, steps forward. "It will be okay."

Flavia feels the blood rushing to her cheeks, the throbbing veins in her neck and forehead, all signs her husband should see.

She squints. "It won't be. It won't be okay. That's what I want you to understand. Maybe if we talk tomorrow, you might understand. Sure, you might comprehend the situation Pablo's placed us in, but the problem is there may not be a tomorrow. The US government could kick down our door at any point, and Siriano's son is flooding the street with eyes and ears demanding to know what happened to his father. He's turning the full might of the Siriano criminal machine toward finding out who the five men in the van were."

"I know this."

"If you know it, do something about it," she says. "No one's looking for me. No one cares about me. I drove the van, no one counts me. I'm not being looked for—no one saw a woman. It's the five with the rifles that are plastered all over the television screens. It's that man in there that the world cares about. And when they find him, it won't matter who gets caught in the crossfire."

"*Mi vida*," Omar says, reaching for her again, hand outstretched, not even trying to touch her, but again, Flavia steps back.

He knows she's right. He has to know it.

"It's only a matter of time before someone says something," Flavia says, "and the Siriano organization knows *exactly* what happened and who made it happen. All it takes is one word. One weak mind. One misspoken outburst. Pablo trusts the men who carried this out, Gabino and his friends, but if someone with the Sirianos gets a hold of one of them..." She stops talking. Omar needs to see reason. He's the only person who can stop this ... this *insane plan* ... before it gets too far, before they commit too much to Pablo.

Omar can stop this insanity, but he must act.

Her husband is unwilling to do so, and Flavia isn't sure what's upsetting her more: her impotence because she's a woman; her opinion always discounted because of what's between her legs, or lack thereof; or her frustration with Omar for not understanding what she's saying.

What she's saying is she didn't like Pablo's idea to begin with, and now that she's spent time watching him with Siriano and been around his new dog, Vega, she's convinced this is wrong. He is wrong. He's a coward. She doesn't trust him. Never has.

"It's not about trust; it's about making a statement. We have to show Siriano we aren't afraid of him. Show that we will stand up for what's right. We have to show Pablo that we support him."

"Do you even hear yourself right now?" Flavia asks, pressing her lips together to keep from yelling at him.

Omar drops his outstretched hand and slips his fingers into his pockets, defensive. "I said the words. You didn't. Maybe you don't understand how this works. There are rules. In this world, there are rules. Pablo's living by those rules. It's not about trust."

"Not about trust?" Flavia shoves the rolled-up sleeves higher on her arms. "It's about nothing else. It's always about trust. That's the most important thing here. We can't do what we do without trust. That was Alejandro's currency: trust. He spent a lifetime building it. Trust with you. Trust with me. Trust in Pablo, but Pablo's spent no time building anything. He assumed power. And he assumes you and I are going to go along with him. That's not how this works. Those aren't the rules. That's not how my world works. I don't trust him, but you do, and I think you are wrong."

Omar frowns. It hurts her to talk to her husband this way. She loves him, but he must see the pain it causes her because she sees the pain she causes him. "We've talked about this."

Flavia crosses her arms over her denim outfit and cocks her hip to the side. She's wearing the same clothes she's worn for three days. Last night, however, she snuck off to the back of the automotive shop to take a shower. When she turned the water off, Vega was there, his dark sunken eyes watching, unblinking, but she won't tell Omar about it.

Vega was pissing into the toilet next to the shower, smoking a cigarette as he did it. He finished what he was doing, shook his endowment at her once, twice, and then put it away. Took the cigarette out of his mouth with two fingers and a flourish as she told him to get out. He didn't, not right away. Just as she didn't ask him why he was there. She knew, and he knew she knew. It was a game for him.

She said "leave," and he grinned, a half-smirk, one side of his mouth lifting like he had a stroke. Flavia figures it has something to do with the scar in the middle of his cheek, a star-burst puckered thing, just as he speaks out of one side of his mouth. He had stared at her naked wet body, his tongue caressing the threshold of his lips. Her hand searched for the towel that he had moved out of her reach. He didn't say anything.

He had moved the towel on purpose to make her ask for it, to provoke her rage and show his superiority, his maleness, his depravity. He had forced her to get out of the shower naked and show him all of what he wanted to see, giving in to his puny show of dominance.

With those two fingers, he placed the cigarette back in his mouth, rather dramatically, and kept the smile. Then, he zipped his pants.

She asked for the towel, projecting strength into her words while pretending that seeing him there wasn't upsetting. He handed her the towel, and she said "leave" again. He shrugged his shoulders once and left the room. Smoke trailed behind him, leaving a distasteful smell in the bathroom.

Flavia didn't bother shutting the bathroom door. The damage was done. He saw what he wanted to see, and he communicated what he wanted to say without saying anything. His eyes showed desire and dark bent of control. She quickly dried off and dressed. When she came out of the bathroom, dark splotches of water seeped through her shirt. Omar commented on the water, but she didn't tell him about Vega. She can handle him. Omar needs to handle everyone else. They don't keep secrets, but that doesn't mean telling everything right away either.

Flavia says, "Yes, we have talked about this, and I still think you are wrong."

"I can't go against him." Omar's expression sours, showing he is torn between the community he's devoted his life to and his wife's desire for him to seize power.

"He's going to get us killed," Flavia says. "He's a coward. I see it. How can you not?"

"He's not a coward." But Omar's tone and voice don't line up with the words.

Flavia points to the automotive shop door. "What shows that he's not a coward? Why is he alive and Alejandro dead? I know why. Do you know why?"

Omar closes his eyes. "I know why."

"Then, you know we can't trust him."

"It's not that easy," Omar adds. "That's not how this works."

"You should be in charge."

"It's not... I can't," he argues.

Flavia knows what he means. It's not easy for someone like him to buck the system, to go against everything he's known.

God, he has to see the light. He has to see how wrong this is.

"What's hard about it?" she questions.

"He is in charge," Omar says, which is the truest thing he's said, but it's only true because Omar's allowed him to be in charge.

"And look how well that's going." Flavia gives her back to her husband. She can't look at him right now. She hates when he gets like this. Alejandro loved Omar, but he respected Flavia. He respected her opinion. He listened to her counsel—if only Pablo would have gotten it right, but he failed to kill Renaldo.

Alejandro didn't respect Omar, not the same way. Omar says *yes sir*. Omar does what he's told. Omar is the type of guy to hold the line. Flavia isn't; she does what needs doing.

"We kidnapped him. We are at war, and we can't afford to be at war."

"We're sending a message," Omar says, parroting Pablo. "We're showing them we can stand up for ourselves."

"I don't believe it was a power move. The old man was in prison. He had no idea what Renaldo was doing. I think it was personal. I think, and I know you don't want to hear this, I think Alejandro let emotion override his good sense, and he picked a fight he couldn't win."

"That... that wasn't him."

"That's exactly what happened. I know it. I just wish my husband would see it too."

"What do you want me to see?" Omar flips the conversation around. "Who had Alejandro's ear?"

"No," she screams. "You will not make this about me. It's about that man." She points to the door again. "It's about both of those men; it is not about me."

"You want me to go against who I am?" Omar questions. "Go against you?"

"I want you to be who you are," Flavia argues. "Who I know you to be!"

"I am who I am. I'm your husband."

Flavia shuts her eyes. Tears are there now. She hates it. "You are more."

"Alejandro listened to you," Omar says, as if he's reminding her of something she's forgotten.

"No," she whispers, refusing to turn her thoughts toward those memories.

"You want to criticize Pablo and what he's doing, but have you thought about what we did?" Omar asks.

"You did what you were supposed to do," Flavia says. "I did what I was supposed to do."

"Provide counsel."

"And I did that," she declares. "It's not my fault Pablo couldn't carry out the order."

"But what if it wasn't personal, what if Alejandro ordering Pablo to kill Renaldo was the act of war Siriano's been waiting for?"

"What if it wasn't?" she asks. "What if it's all personal? I know what you are trying to say, that we shouldn't have encouraged Alejandro to get his... to kill Renaldo. But if Pablo would have carried it out, did it right, then it wouldn't be a problem now."

"It's not like he didn't do what he was supposed to do," Omar says. "I was there. He shot Renaldo in the head. I saw him do it."

"He should have shot him more.".

"Maybe God spared him."

"God doesn't work like that," Flavia says. "Now Pablo's in there talking to Siriano."

Omar nods as he corrects her, "Watching him, but yes I understand what you mean."

"What if Siriano convinces him that he didn't try to kill Alejandro?"

"What do you mean?"

"What if Pablo finds out it was us?"

"He won't find out."

"But what if he does?"

"How would he find out?"

"Siriano's smart. He's ruthless. You don't get to where he is without being the baddest man in town. Alejandro wasn't like that. He cared. Siriano cares about nothing but Siriano. What if he convinces Pablo to release him. What if he convinces Pablo he had nothing to do with Alejandro's death, and Pablo finds out it was us who convinced Alejandro he had to kill Renaldo."

"But we didn't kill Renaldo."

"That's the problem, had Pablo done so, we wouldn't be in this situation."

"Pablo trusts us."

"Pablo's keeping his enemies close," Flavia says. "That's what giving us the diner is all about. He doesn't care about the restaurant or who should run it, he cares about himself, and he cares about power, and he cares about people not seeing him for being a coward."

"A coward wouldn't look Siriano in the eye to show him who took him."

Flavia steps forward. "Okay, well then, how did Pablo know?"

"Know what?"

"How did he know Siriano was going to be released? Have you asked him?"

"I've... no." Omar shakes his head.

"How did he know?" Flavia says. "I think he's talking to someone."

"He wouldn't."

"But what if he is? What if he likes power? What if he never thought he'd be here but now that he's here he wants to hold on to it?"

"He wouldn't."

"Why did he send for Vega?" Flavia says. "Vega is the boogie man. He's the man you call for when you need the dirty work done. Why did he send for him?"

"Because this is a war, and we need men."

"We have men, and look where that's gotten us."

"Don't be like this," Omar comments.

Flavia marches toward him, her words in rhythm with her steps. "Be like what? Speak the truth. We have your brother. We have his friends. We have all the people that have been with us since the beginning. We don't need Pablo. Who cares if Alejandro saw him for the role you should have? Pablo should be dead. If he didn't die saving Alejandro, then he should die for not saving Alejandro."

Now, Omar steps back. "That's a cold way of looking at it."

"That's the only way of looking at it. How is he still alive? Why?"

Omar's shoulders slump. "I have to go along with him because that's what Alejandro would have wanted. Alejandro had the succession plan in place. It's not like Pablo assumed power out of a vacuum. Alejandro dictated it would be him. He dictated we would get the restaurant. Pablo isn't trying to placate us. He's trying to carry out the old man's wishes."

"By kidnapping another old man?"

"By making a power move to show disrespect won't go unanswered."

"So it doesn't matter to you?"

"Doesn't matter that Renaldo killed Alejandro? Of course, it does. But this is our world now. We have to live with how it is, not how we want it to be."

Flavia's eyes narrow, surveying who her husband has become. "You should be in charge."

Omar is quiet for a moment, staring past her as his mind goes someplace else.

He looks at her and surprises her. "Okay," but then he adds, "but that's not how it is."

He reaches out for her again, and this time she accepts his affection, hugging him, burying her head into his shoulder. Flavia adds sweetness to her voice. "I want us to be safe. I don't feel safe."

"I know," Omar says. "I'm working on it."

"What are they doing in there?" she says. "Pablo isn't talking to him, and he won't shut up, but he doesn't sound afraid."

Flavia looks up into her husband's eyes and sees he doesn't know. Pablo only shares so much with Omar. He hasn't shared his grand plan.

Before Omar can answer, the maroon door of the automotive shop, with the streaked peeling paint and the cracked window at its center, swings open and bangs against the wall. Vega appears, stepping into the light.

"Jesus," he exclaims, holding up a hand to shield his eyes with his rumpled, once off-white now sweat-stained straw cowboy hat. "It's bright out here. What are you two doing?"

Flinching against her husband because of the sound of the door banging against the wall and slamming shut, Flavia doesn't answer. She firmly embeds herself against Omar.

Omar replies, "Nothing."

"Doesn't look like nothin'," Vega says. He sets the hat on his head. "Looks like you two were doing somethin'. Lookin' like you're up to somethin'." He makes wispy chirping noises while flapping his hands out, arms tight to his side, mimicking wings. "People whisperin' like little birdies all over this place." His alligator cowboy boots crunch the gravel. He stops and straightens his spine, hands at his love handles, pushing. He strikes a cowboy pose, looping his thumbs in his overly large belt with the turquoise stone at its center. "Why don't you tell me what that was."

Not a question.

Omar glances down at Flavia. "We were talking."

"What you talkin' about?" Vega's not letting it go, getting at it again, talking out of one side of his mouth nearly chewing his dark brown lip off as he speaks. He digs a crumpled pack of Turkish Golds from his back pocket and shimmies his left hand into his front pocket to reach for a lighter. He pulls the lighter out, and while lighting the cigarette, he says, "Course, you don't have to say what you were talkin' about. I guess whatever you have to say has to stay between you, husband and wife." He snorts at the concept, huffing smoke from his nose and mouth. "Never been married myself. Never saw the use of it, tyin' yourself to one woman, like ropin' yourself to one pole, never to see what the rest of the world has to offer." He adds, for Flavia's benefit, "I've been all over, so I know what I like."

Omar doesn't say anything. He doesn't move.

Vega studies them a bit more, body relaxed, hip cocked to the side like a bull rider, the bulge of his gun in the small of his back, another one in his left boot. He withdraws the cigarette from his mouth, holds it down at his side, looking at them, smoke floats away from the tip.

He notices Flavia looking at him and winks at her.

Omar asks, "Where are you going?"

"I got a thing." Vega drops the lighter back into the pocket. He inhales through his nostrils and exhales and places the cigarette back in his mouth.

"What thing?"

"A thing," he grunts. More smoke in the air: it hangs around his head like a dark haze.

Unperturbed, Omar repeats, "What thing?"

Vega tilts his head up, eyes on Omar. A hard look. "You ask a lot of questions." He shakes his head. "Not a good habit."

"I ask what needs to be asked," Omar says.

Vega considers the words for a moment. "Do you?"

Omar nods.

"Alright," Vega says. "Tell the big man I'll be back later, but if he needs somethin', I got my phone."

"Where are you going?" Omar asks, not giving up.

"Man, you sure like to latch on. I bet you're good at some things. But judging from the way she's gripping you tight, I bet you got some bark." He barks like a dog. "Ruff. Let's just hope it's not all growl with no muscle." Then, he adds for Omar's benefit, "I bet she latches on too."

Flavia feels Omar tense, muscles flexing under her fingertips, anger feeding his nerves. Her nails bite into him to keep him still. She whispers for him to breathe.

"I don't answer to you," Vega says. "So I don't have to tell you nothin'. You got a problem with that, go ask the big man."

"He still inside?"

Vega, nodding, says, "'Cept he's outside the room now. He wouldn't stop talkin', and the big guy wasn't sayin' nothing back, so he decided it would be better for everyone if he left him alone for a while, which is why I'm goin' to do my thing. That alright with you?"

Vega removes the cigarette. Cranks his neck to the side, cracks a couple of joints.

Omar nods.

Vega reinserts the cigarette. "Alright."

CHAPTER SEVEN: SONNY ROWAN

SONNY PULLS UP TO THE SHOP AND, THROUGH the front windows, sees his number-one critic cough, hand to mouth, announcing his arrival to everyone else at the table. The guy in the golf outfit: plaid shirt, plaid shorts, both different colors and patterns clashing with each other. For some reason, on his bloated overly tanned body, held together with plastics and titanium, it works. The donut shop is where Sonny has his morning meeting with the time warriors and their incredulous opinions. The meeting takes place after Sonny has already put in an hour of work at the office, arriving at 5 a.m.—Sonny's usually up before four and out the door by half-past that. He works hard until three in the afternoon, but after six in the morning, he cuts out for a bit to grab some coffee and to meet with what he calls his sources. He really means his source of community wisdom. These men keep him grounded and do, from time to time, provide some great ideas for his column. They are sports lovers who love to talk about past glories and encounters.

He spots Carlos coughing a second time as Sonny parks his truck in front of the shop, the bright lights from inside painfully luminous against the still predawn morning. Carlos does a third cough as Sonny opens the door and enters; the chime above the door dings.

Sonny used to eat donuts, but his health issues dampened his appetite. So once a week, on Fridays specifically, he allows himself an apple fritter with a healthy heaping of criticism from Carlos, the second-youngest of the group who is currently enjoying his administrative leave. He shot a guy, but he didn't know if he killed the guy or the girl who put some more bullets in him. Either way, Carlos hasn't taken it personally, choosing instead to enjoy some earned time off—how he puts it.

"Look who's finally decided to show up." The golfer and critic exaggeratedly checks his watch, leaning back in the chair, donut in his other hand. "About time."

Sonny, not wanting to give Carlos the pleasure of getting under his skin this early in the day, ignores him and goes to the counter to place his order. He has to wait in line behind a dad, probably some type of construction worker based on the heavy boots and work clothes, who's trying to wrangle two kids, no more than four and five, both with blonde hair, who can't seem to go the same direction or decide on what they want. One of the kids places his grimy fingers on the glass display case, leaving fingerprints like a series of greasy smudges, pointing to which donut he wants. The other one runs back and forth from dad to the side door, yelling the entire time with gleeful abandon, making the construction father, and everyone else, visibly nervous. The father grabs the running child and ushers him to the case. He holds him in place at the shoulders while trying to tell the thin brunette behind the counter that he'd like two jalapeño sausage rolls and a large coffee before asking the boys what they want. They tell the dad through hand motions, and he relays the info to the woman, saying, "It's for here."

Sonny wonders if the brunette is thin because she knows how these things are made, even if he knows why she's thin. Just as he knows her name is Rachel. She helps the construction father, with nun-like patience, waiting for him to dig a card out of his wallet while grabbing at each kid's shoulder and steering them back to the shelter of his legs. The kids are both eagerly digging into their donuts.

"I'll take care of it." Sonny leans around the father to get Rachel's attention.

The father half turns to look at Sonny over his shoulder.

Mid ringing his purchase up, Rachel asks, "You sure?"

"Yeah." Sonny steps to the side to give the father an exit lane. "I know how it is. Just put everything on my tab."

The father mutters a thank you, lifts his tray from the counter, and moves to a table. The boys follow in his wake, staring up at Sonny over the quickly disappearing curves of donut, mouths half-open, chewing. Fingers wet.

Sonny steps to the counter.

"It's Friday," Rachel says. "Does that mean you're going to eat something?"

She's worked the counter for four years, helping her family business. Her father reconciled with her after coming to terms with her other profession. Her father used to be a football star, college, not professional. Sonny did a piece on him a while back, got to know him pretty well, Rachel too. She also went in his piece because Sonny doesn't hold back. Stripper daughter of a down-and-out football star, busted knee, prostate cancer, and small business owner; the story wrote itself. Sonny leaves nothing out. It's one of his writing rules, forgoing the emotions and feelings of the people he writes about, a personality flaw or so he's told, so he can elicit those things in the readers. Readers are the only ones that matter, and people seem to forget a reporter exposed all their painful truths when someone like Sonny renders their life in the written word as beautifully as a Renaissance painter. His column has no set word limit, to the chagrin of his editor.

Rachel's father didn't mind, said Sonny's always welcome.

Sonny nods to Rachel and points to the stack of paper cups behind her next to the coffee pot. "I'll take a large coffee too."

"Large," she says, "must have had a rough morning."

Usually, he drinks a small or medium when he's sitting at the table with everyone else, favoring the cheaper option and refills, but not today. She accents her statement with a smile; she's cute and she knows it, but she's got that "rough mystique" that women who are up before dawn have. Sonny's spent a career getting to know people like her; he loves people like her. These are his people, those who live on a different time schedule than the rest of the world, which is partly why he can't sleep past four. Rachel may be a stripper, but this is her job and the more important one. Besides, she says she makes more money here than working at the club.

Sonny explains. "Got an early phone call."

"Musta been early to wake you up," she says. "I know what time you get to work."

"It was." Sonny chooses not to explain. "I'll take the coffee, as much as you've got and one of those apple things."

She raises an eyebrow. "It's a fritter, and you know that. You know what it's called."

Doing their weekly bit, he falls into his expected dialogue.

"I like *apple thing*; it's more descriptive," Sonny tells her. "I love the crispy edges. I can't get that anywhere else. That's why I come here ... and I get to see you."

"Whatever." Rachel taps the cash register keys with a long-nailed finger. "Anything else?"

Carlos clears his throat. Sonny sees Carlos's reflection in the counter's glass, distorted through the greasy smudges the kid left behind.

"And whatever else Carlos wants." Sonny fights the urge to glance over his shoulder. He watches Rachel's eyes instead, tracks them as she looks over to Carlos.

"Hey." Carlos turns his attention to the other three old men sitting at the table with him. Sonny knows what he's doing; he's been doing it for the last three weeks. "Don't forget about my friends over here."

"What, you want me to buy breakfast for everyone here?" Sonny asks, finally giving in and turning toward Carlos.

"I'm not the one paying for everyone. You are," Carlos says. "And yes, that sounds nice. It's like a round for everyone, except, you know, we're here, not the bar."

Spencer, skinny as a rail, a marathon runner, who flirts with training for triathlons he's never going to complete, speaks up in his nasal voice that reminds Sonny of Steve Buscemi from *The Big Lebowski*—looks kind of like the guy too. "Nothing for me, thanks though."

Spencer ran the Sahara one time. Sonny did a story on him; they talked about his issues with being adopted, coming to terms with having dual families. After the Sahara run, his biological brother reached out. It was a good family piece. Spencer still runs in several dozen marathons a year, makes a nice retirement career out of it. He finished first in his age bracket at some pretty big races last year.

"What's wrong with you?" Carlos questions him, slapping the table. "He's offering something free, the big shot, Mr. Newspaper man, the man with the golden column, coming down to us mere mortals. He's offering something free. You don't turn down something free."

Rob—the most unhealthy of the group, maybe the oldest, but it's hard to tell with his hunched body, oxygen tank, and thin white hair all over his body, the biggest patch of it growing on his chin like a billy goat—says, "If the big shot doesn't want to, he doesn't have to, Carlos. Don't pressure him like that."

Carlos looks at Rob, eyes wide. "What is this? A rebellion?"

David—a Mitt Romney-looking guy, straight-laced, blessed with dark hair, even though he's far into his seventies, with good looks, a regular Mr. Rogers type, considering his penchant for sweaters and his last name's the same—says, "No, it's telling him he doesn't have to be so nice to us."

"But he loves us," Carlos says. "He doesn't know that guy." The construction father turns his head toward Carlos, who mutters, "No offense."

Sonny pays, and Rachel steps away from the register to fulfill his order.

The door chimes as Bing, the last of the group—real name Birmingham Gentry—opens the door and steps in, cane click-clacking against the tile floor. Everyone stops talking and looks up. "I miss anything yet?" he asks, studying each man's face.

"Carlos was going to tell us about the man he shot," Spencer says, having fun at Carlos's expense. Spencer pops a donut hole into his mouth.

"I was not." Carlos steals one of Spencer's donut holes.

"You have to now," Spencer laughs. "Those aren't free."

"No, that one was paying for everyone, have him tell you a story," Carlos says.

Sonny says, "I think you were."

Carlos, not liking the table turned against him, retorts, "Don't you have a story to go chase or something?"

"That's why I'm here," Sonny responds. "I come to you all, you tell me who I should talk to next, and then, I go bug them until they give me an interview."

"How's that work?" David asks. "You just call them or something?"

Sonny nods. "Or e-mail."

"They answer their e-mails?" Carlos asks, delighting in the turn of conversation; the focus is off him.

"Not always," Sonny says. "That's why I have to call them."

Spencer asks Bing, "Your son coming in today?"

Bing groans and answers, "Nope, he's minding the office." He takes his seat at the table. "Can one of you get me some coffee?"

On cue, Rachel drops a small cup of coffee down in front of Bing before he's gotten settled. "Here you go, Luv."

Bing cants his head to get a look at her, smiles large, and says thank you.

David comments, "Sonny, you look tired."

Bing's feeble old hand picks up the coffee. He sips it while still holding on to his cane like he's about to get back up, elbow bent toward the ceiling. "You do look rough."

"I didn't sleep much," Sonny admits. He rubs his eyes.

"Why not?" Carlos questions, voice hinting at something more.

Stopping the rub, Sonny says, "Not like that." He cuts Carlos off before he can start razzing him for sleeping with someone.

Rob speaks up this time. "What?"

"Yes, what's it like." Spencer eyes Rob, telling him to stay quiet.

"I got a phone call," Sonny tells them.

"Not your kid again, is it?" Bing inquires.

David adds, "She in trouble again?"

Sonny nods. "Jail," he says. "She called to tell me she got picked up for shoplifting."

"What'd she steal?" Spencer asks.

"Coffee." Sonny hardly believes the words. "Seems this cop has stopped her a couple of times. Couldn't just write her like they've done in the past, so he arrested her."

"Are you going to bail her out?" Carlos asks. "I mean it's a misdemeanor, not a big deal, considering what trouble she's been in before."

Sonny shakes his head. "I don't know. I've done that a few times lately, and it's getting old." He doesn't say expensive, but it's that too.

"What she needs is a good outlet," Bing says. "Or an influence." Bing believes in humanity, Sonny's undecided, and Carlos has given up.

"She needs a swift kick in the butt," Carlos expresses. "Why do you keep bailing her out? She keeps screwing up. You went out to California, brought her here, and got her back on her feet. Why do you let her lead you around by the nose like this?"

"Because he's a father," David states. "That's what fathers do."

Sonny watches the construction father finish the last of his sausage roll and wipe his mouth with the napkin he drops on the tray. He throws the trash away and hustles the kids out the front door.

Sonny addresses the table. "I guess, I feel like I owe her." He looks at Carlos. "I don't know if you'd understand. You don't have kids."

Carlos stays quiet, which is unusual for him, which means Sonny struck a chord.

"I'm not trying to say something by that," Sonny tells him. "Just, I wasn't around much when she was young, and when I was, I was working."

"On your column?" Rob asks, jumping into the conversation. "You should write about that gangster getting kidnapped. Did you see that?"

Spencer rolls his eyes. "Yes, for his column, but that's not what he's talking about." Spencer shifts his attention back to Sonny. "Although, I will say that'd be a good column."

"Where's the sports angle?" Sonny asks. "The column deals with former athletes. Not crime."

"The angle is it's interesting," Carlos says. "The guy was supposed to go to the Grand Jury, but then, these guys with rifles roll up and kidnap him right off the front steps of the courthouse. That's theater. If I'd have been there," Carlos mimics drawing a pistol from his hip, finger gun pointed, "I'd have shot those men, right then, right there."

Spencer says, "No you wouldn't have."

"He's all talk," David agrees.

"I've shot someone," is all Carlos says before growing quiet.

"That's not how you act in that type of situation," Bing declares with an authoritative voice.

He's the most experienced shooter at the table. He used to be a Deputy United States Marshal before retiring and opening Bing's Bail Bonds. His boy followed in his father's footsteps and retired from the Marshals Service. He's now working at the place with his dad, whose health hasn't been good lately. It's how Sonny got to talk to that Olympic swimmer a few years back. His boy got the swimmer out of some hot water down south, the Mexico way.

Bing explains, "When men with guns put guns in your face, it's better to listen and follow directions. Those men weren't there to hurt no one. They were there to take the gangster. My feelings on this matter are, good riddance, let them have him."

"Siriano's a big deal," Carlos says. "Guy like him, getting out of prison due to McGirt, should have gotten some people's attention, but you know how it is, if it doesn't affect them it doesn't matter... that is, until it affects them."

"Native pride," Rob interrupts. Rob's fractionally native; he just won't say what tribe.

"Quiet down," Spencer tells him. "Go back to gumming your donut."

Bing shakes his finger. "He'll screw up... that is when he turns up... and the government will get another crack at him. They always do."

"Your kid call you last night to tell you she was in jail?" David asks, bringing the conversation back around. "Wake you up?"

"Yeah," Sonny says, "she called when they got to the county jail."

"She sit in some city jail for a few hours?" Carlos asks.

"Yup, but once she was transferred, she got through to me. I guess I slept through the first half dozen calls or so. She said she didn't get to call for the longest time, but I'm thinking it's because she threw a fit about being arrested. She doesn't like authority."

"Who does?" Carlos questions.

"Speaking of columns," Spencer changes subjects, "you think of something for this month?"

"I don't like having to wait so long between them," Bing expresses. "I liked the one every two weeks. This once a month thing's getting old. I like reading what you write."

Sonny shakes his head. "I'm not really sure what I'm going to write about. I'm kinda in a slump."

Carlos says, "I read that piece you wrote on Kobe Bryant's widow and how you wrote about going out west to get your kid to bring her back here. A sorta father's journey, talking about how she lost Kobe and a daughter and how you're a father trying to regain yours. It was a nice piece."

Sonny takes his first drink of coffee awed by Carlos's surprisingly sweet words. "Thank you."

"But that was two months ago," Bing says, staying on him about it. "You should write something and get it out there. Aren't you worried about them firing you?"

Sonny defends himself. "I do other things at the paper. Some copy editing and other smaller pieces."

"But they're not what they once were," Carlos says. He juts a finger out at Sonny. "Face it. You're a has-been."

Bing makes a brooding sound, smacking his lips at the end. "You know, I know the lady that was outside that courthouse. You could talk to her."

"But where's the sports angle?" Sonny asks again.

"Why's there have to be a sports angle?" Bing asks. "You are in a slump, everyone goes through them. I did. That's why I retired. I think you are about due for that, either that or wait until the rug's pulled out from under you and you find yourself without a job."

"Paper business is dying," David adds.

"You could talk to that girl, see what she has to say," Bing says. "She's a nice girl. Her Uncle Frank, he used to work with me."

"Uncle Frank?" Spencer asks.

"Yup, she grew up next to him," Bing says. "Frank was my partner for years, younger than me. He looked after her and her mother when she was young. I can make a phone call. Get you an interview. See here I go, I'm giving you some good stuff. Imagine how she feels, losing someone like that, so publicly. She can't speak for herself, but you could speak for her. You got the column that looks at the way the world is, not how we want it to be or how we're told it is: what's true and what's not."

"You did that piece on that girl's father." Carlos points over to Rachel, "and you see how well that turned out. You get a discount, which is why you always pay for people."

"I think you should do it," Carlos continues. "I know if I was that girl and was embarrassed like that, I'd want to tell my side of the story." Giving his cop opinion, which for once sounds reasonable to Sonny.

"Besides," Bing says, "you can't always look for an angle. Sometimes, things just are, and if you're patient with them, treat them nicely, what you're looking for will show up anyways. The girl was an athlete when she was younger, nothing special, but a mighty fine soccer player. You've not done one of those in a while. Do something on her. Talk about a career when career aspirations don't work out."

Sonny thinks it over. "I guess so. I'll have to pitch the idea to my editor."

Rob jolts awake in his seat. "Not Frankfort, Frank?"

Bing looks over at Rob as he recovers from the sudden, startled exclamation.

Bing says, "Yes, that same Frank."

"Who's that?" David asks.

"Frankfort Corbin," Bing clarifies. "He's one of those cattle cops now. He was a damn good partner. Did ten more years after I left. I can proudly say I taught that man everything he knows, and I will say, he probably was sweet on that girl's mother. She may call him uncle, but he's not blood to her. Although, if things were different back then, I believe she'd call him daddy now."

Everyone looks to Carlos to make a joke, but Carlos, shaking his head as he speaks, says, "No, I'm not touching that one. He T-d it up too well. There's no fun in it."

Sonny's phone rings. It's the jail; he knows from the caller ID. He excuses himself and turns to answer as Rob asks what's happening, and Spencer tries to recount the conversation to him, loudly, which makes it hard to hear the automated voice. "This is an inmate at the David L. Moss Criminal Justice facility..." Sonny clicks the number one on his touch screen to skip past it.

The line's quiet for a moment. Sonny can hear the bustle of the detention pod in the background.

"Hey," Emerson utters.

"Hey." Sonny plugs his other ear with a finger to focus on the phone call and not the men at the table, who seem to talk louder the more Sonny tries to focus.

"You going to come get me?" Emerson asks, different than the demanding tone she had this morning.

"I was thinking about it," Sonny responds.

"I'd appreciate it if you did."

Sonny tells her, "I can't keep doing this."

"I know," Emerson says. "I've been thinking a lot about it, and I know."

"This is the fourth time in two months," Sonny says.

"Dad," Emerson pleads.

"I am running out of money," Sonny says, breezing past her statement. "I... what?"

"I met someone," Emerson adds, excitement in her voice. "You're not going to believe who."

"You met someone in jail?"

"No," she says. "Look, if you come get me, fine. If you don't, that's fine too, I guess. I deserve it. I mean it's not a big deal, but I might as well accept that I put myself here."

Sonny's glad to hear her admission, but now he's interested. "Who'd you meet?"

"I met DiMaggio. He's in town."

"Who?"

"Remember, we watched that Driller's game," she says. "Remember the pitcher? Maurizio DiMaggio?"

He sure does and with the memory—one of the few good ones between him and her—comes the whiff of a story. "What do you mean, you met him?"

CHAPTER EIGHT:
MAURIZIO DIMAGGIO

WILSON NOTARO TAPS HIS PHONE AGAINST THE table; tap, flip, tap, flip, tap, fingers working the little silver flip phone around in tight circles, studying Maggie's face as Maggie enters the apartment. Kevin Alexander, Wilson's gopher, opened the door and showed Maggie into the one-bedroom apartment, 700 square feet, not much, but enough for business meetings: black sofa in the center, table and chairs behind it, furnished kitchen to the right of the door, where Kevin now stands, vodka bottle and a few glasses on the counter near his hands, which rest flat on the counter. The table is a card table with a couple of brown folding chairs around it. The radio's on in the background, something current, between rock and pop, purring at the undercurrent of tension heavy in the room.

Through the doorway into the back bedroom to Wilson's left, Maggie catches a feminine glint of red hair and smooth pale skin, Iris King, Wilson's woman. She pulls a deep blue dress up her elegant nude body, heavenly and luminescent in the pale light of the back room, mid-thigh, rising to midriff before the parade is out of sight. She reminds Maggie of a movie star, something like a redheaded version of Natalie Portman, body soft and pink, ample and slight at the same time, but Iris is older than Portman; she's seen more.

And standing off to the left, at the balcony door, Maggie notices the slouching form of someone he doesn't know. The initial impression is male, probably Mexican, stout, not short, dark hair, shoulders heavy, looking like a gemstone cowboy fond of turquoise and all things shiny. The man clutches the folded brim of a straw cowboy hat, which was once one color and is now something else. He's smoking a cigarette, blowing the smoke out the balcony door, his eyes on the parking lot bathed in the afternoon sun.

A cigar sits in the ashtray, the only item on the card table.

Maggie stops just inside the doorway, reading the room. He's dressed in blue jeans and a yellow button-up, wears a thin black leather jacket, semi-automatic shoved in his waistband, his father's .38 in the jacket pocket. He allows the door to shut behind him as Kevin starts to pour vodka into a glass; the door lock clicks.

"Welcome," Wilson says, pausing the phone mid-flip. "It's about time you got here. I've been waiting, for what?"

From the kitchen to Maggie's right, Kevin says, "An hour," mid-pour.

"An hour," Wilson says, talking with the phone still in his hand. He wears a black shirt, black tie, and black slacks. A sports coat hangs over the back of the couch. "An hour I've been waiting, waiting for you." Wilson sets the phone down and picks up the cigar in the ashtray. He places it between his lips, inhales, the cherry glowing red-orange. He sits the cigar back down on the table as he releases smoke, blowing it down at his feet. "I don't know about you, but I got places to be. People to see. All that..." He holds the comment for a moment and then smiles. "I'm just fucking with you. I got tickets to... what was it?" Wilson glances over his shoulder

From the backroom, the female voice replies, "Madame Butterfly."

Now, back to Maggie. "Madame Butterfly," he repeats. "Whatever the fuck that is." He holds up a finger to shush Maggie so that he doesn't say anything about Madame Butterfly, not that Maggie knows what the fuck that is. "Don't say nothing. I know what you are going to say. You're going to say you're still looking for him, give you more time. Well, I think I've given you time."

"You have," is all Maggie says after a pause. He knows how this works. Be quiet. Speak when spoken to.

That's how Wilson's daddy introduced Maggie back in the day. Outside another door in another time. Right before stepping into this life, Russell said, "You don't talk, got it? Not unless someone talks to you, but even then, you wait a beat like you're wondering if it's a rhetorical question or something. After waiting, you can say something. But what you don't do is say something that pisses someone off. You piss someone off, the wrong person, I can't protect you. I can win with you, but not if you piss someone off, so that means you don't talk, got it?"

Maggie got it.

"Well, you're home now." Wilson nods a few times. "You're home, and now that you're here, I got some things to say to you."

Wilson's up, nearly knocking the folding chair over, and moving across the small living room toward Maggie, hands outstretched, presenting himself for an embrace, the phone and cigar left behind on the table. He walks toward Maggie with his arms open the entire length of the living room, ten steps maybe. That's a long walk for a greeting.

Maggie prepares himself for the close contact, watching the surreal performance unfold in front of him—this isn't the impatient youth from Maggie's college days. This isn't the Wilson he remembers. The Wilson he remembers wanted nothing to do with Maggie, resented him because Siriano never legitimized Wilson and showered Maggie with attention.

Maggie forces his shoulders to relax as the two men collide in an embrace. Wilson wraps his arms around Maggie, enfolding him. Uncomfortable. Unexpected. They weren't close, but things change. Time can transform a passing acquaintance into a battle-worn companion.

Maggie mutters, "Nice to see you too," as Wilson squeezes him tight. Maggie's unsure if this is normal, Wilson's way of doing things, or if this is because of what's happening now with his daddy, the kidnapping.

"How you doing?" Wilson asks, immobilizing Maggie.

Maggie's a strong man, but Wilson's on another level, muscles hard under his shirt, which doesn't do much to hide them, tight like a vacuum-sealed steak, smooth and sleek. It complements the man's good looks.

Wilson says, "How does it feel to be here? Been a while."

Maggie prepared for the encounter, but he isn't ready for this. Coming here had to happen since Wilson took over. His work takes him all over; he doesn't care for Tulsa, not since he was a kid, not since his father's death—murder—but the city's part of him. Facing his past is part of the deal, especially when Wilson hired him through an intermediary to find Branson. Before that, Maggie hadn't dealt much with the Sirianos, not since being traded, his way of looking at it, to Jackie C.

Maggie kept in touch with friends who are with the Sirianos, the same friends who told Maggie about Iris and Renaldo and Wilson, warning Maggie to be careful. Working for Wilson, not his daddy, always meant he'd end up here, standing in front of him. It doesn't mean he likes it any, but he and Wilson came up together; they were something like brothers once ... though, Russell took to Maggie more, teaching him how to swing a bat a little differently than he was used to. Taught him to go for the legs, the hips; take a man at the hips, you take him down. Destroy his center of gravity, and he won't get back up. As far as Maggie's concerned, Russell's still in charge; it doesn't matter if it was Renaldo before or Wilson now. He answers to the man in charge, that was Russell's and Jackie C.'s rule.

Thinking about Wilson's daddy, Maggie asks, "How are you doing?" emphasizing on how Wilson's feeling, not the organization. "I saw the news."

Wilson breaks the embrace, arms and hands sliding down Maggie's shirt, shoulders to elbows, fingers and thumbs pinching, gripping tightly, constricting his movement and locking him in place. Wilson's arms extend straight, and he leans back, looking at Maggie. Examining him, Wilson starts at the waist up until he is looking Maggie in the eye.

"I'm worried sick."

Wilson's face doesn't match his words. "I saw the news." Maggie is careful to not say more. He doesn't want to step out of turn; Russell's lessons are still fresh in his mind, even after all these years. Wilson's in charge now.

Wilson nods again. He enunciates his words in a staccato fashion for effect. "I bet you're asking yourself what happened. Like how did this happen?"

"I am."

"Those are questions I'm asking myself," Wilson says. "I want to know too. But that's the thing, I don't know how this could have happened. It's not like we were out there advertising it, saying, dear ole dad is going to get out of jail on this day. But it wasn't exactly a state secret or anything. Someone knew something. Knew someone. I want to know who. I want to know how."

Wilson dips his head to the side, nearly touching his ear to his shoulder. He inspects Maggie again, searching him, maybe trying to see what's changed. They've changed. They're both different men. Older. Wiser. Different. Then, satisfied, Wilson pats Maggie's right elbow once and releases Maggie's arms. He holds up a finger. "One way this happened," he says, "only one way. Someone said something, and I want to know who. Kevin wants to know. Hell, everyone wants to know who. That's what the news keeps asking when they say *daring kidnapping in broad daylight*, how could this happen? Course they don't mean how could someone like my dad be kidnapped. They don't care about him. He's a sideshow to them, a novelty. No, they're asking for all the people not in the game, the people who sleep secure in their beds at night, unsuspecting and weak. *How could something like this happen?* Shocking. What they're really asking is who did it?" Wilson lifts his chin. "But that's not why you are here."

"It's not." Maggie relaxes some.

"You're here because you're looking for Brandy. That's what I hired you to do."

"You did," Maggie agrees.

Wilson steps to the kitchen counter. Kevin hands him a glass of vodka. With his back to Maggie, Wilson drinks the vodka in one gulp. Slams the glass down on the counter.

Then, Wilson questions, "What have you found out?"

"Wife," Maggie starts, "maybe ex-wife now. I don't know. She said he's not been around for a while."

"They all say that," Wilson says.

"They do," Maggie says. "I made sure she was telling the truth."

Wilson turns around, eyebrow raised. "What'd you do?"

Maggie stays still. "I made sure."

Wilson smiles and goes back to what he was doing. "Of course, you did. And she said what, he's not around? Hasn't been around for a while? Go figure. Someone like him running out on his family. That's what he did to us. What made her think she was any different? That he'd do anything different? He ran out on her like he ran out on my father."

"Except he didn't put her in prison," Maggie says.

Wilson agrees. "No, he didn't do that. Except he sorta did, right? I mean, he made her go in the program, took her all over the place. Took her away from everyone she knows. Everything she knows. That's sorta the same thing. Everyone has their prison—like everyone has their crosses."

Maggie doesn't say anything.

Kevin pours another glass of vodka. He picks it up and moves from the kitchen to the sofa where he sits, mumbling something negative as he passes Maggie.

Maggie lets it go.

Wilson glances at Kevin then back at Maggie. "So, what'd she say, he's here?"

Maggie nods. "Said he thought he could hide where no one would think to look for him."

From the couch, Kevin says, "You included."

Maggie says, "I'm here now."

"Yes, yes." Wilson's face contorts as he works through what Maggie might've been doing in the last few months.

Kevin doesn't let it go. "Took your sweet time about it, coming here."

Maggie better not let this go on. These things have a way of escalating, getting out of control. "I wanted to make sure she was right," he says. He doesn't look away from Wilson. Maggie watches his face, watches the mood shifts, the changing expressions, from interest to frustration, to mild confusion mixed with irritation. "Made sure she was telling the truth; followed up on some other leads."

Wilson hums to himself.

Maggie steps forward, taking the gun out of his waistband. They're in a dance now, not one of feet and twirling bodies but rather egos, circling each other like sharks. He sets the gun on the counter. He takes off his jacket, throws it over the gun. He turns and leans against the counter now. "They checked out."

"The leads?" Kevin asks, obvious to Maggie he's out of turn.

Maggie says, "I wanted to make sure he was here before coming here. Didn't want to waste a trip."

"Jackie C. said you were the guy," Wilson says, hand on the counter, drumming his fingers on the Formica. "On his deathbed, cancer, there he is, lying in bed, sick as a motherfucking dog, pale as a ghost. Anyways, I'm legitimized after removing an obstacle."

Maggie knows he means Renaldo.

"We don't have to get into what or who right now. I'm visiting Jackie C. asking him how I can get to Brandy, what's the best way, who do I send, that type of stuff. My old man liked him." Wilson points a finger at Maggie, grinning. "Jackie C. says I should send you. Surprised me. I didn't know you did that type of thing. Said my pops had you do some jobs back in the day. Said you handled yourself alright." Wilson frowns. "I didn't know you did that."

"I drove, mainly."

Wilson bobs his head up and down. "I knew you did that. That's how you and Brandy got to be buddies, right? Good thing he didn't involve you in his mess. I always thought you were all about baseball. I mean, I know you did some collections and stuff, heavy work, but you did the heavy major stuff too?"

"Jackie C. was after baseball."

"Right, well Jackie C. likes you. Said you handled yourself well. Said you expanded, tried to make a go of it outside the umbrella of the Siriano name. Something my pops allowed, apparently. Follow in Jackie C.'s footsteps, called you a restoration man, like he used to call himself."

"I do," Maggie says. "The restoration business..." Maggie's words trail off when he sees the face Wilson makes.

Wilson asks, "Why's that?"

"I wanted to see what the world held. If I stayed here, working for your dad only, I wouldn't have. Your dad understood. He set me up with a good deal."

"You don't like it here." Wilson guesses correctly. "You don't like this town, why? Because your father was killed here?"

"Among other things," Maggie says.

Baseball too. Siriano. Finally, Brandy doing what he did. Although, Jackie C. was already tutoring Maggie when that happened.

Something black crosses Wilson's features at Maggie's non-answer. "Whatever," he says. "So Brandy's here, somewhere, in Tulsa?"

"Looks that way," Maggie responds. "Checked with some banking contacts—the wife gave me a name he might be using—I might've got a lead, but we'll see."

"Good, good." Wilson walks back toward the table. Toward the cigar. He scoops it up and tries to take a puff, but the cigar has gone out. He frowns and talks to Iris, "You about done in there?"

Iris appears in the doorway, hands at her throat, fastening some sort of pearl necklace. The pearls fall in the valley, hanging there before constricting her slender neck, creamy skin. "Almost," she says. Her eyes flick across to Maggie, undressing him up and down like the girl did in the coffee shop. "Who's this?"

Wilson looks from her to him. "This is an old friend of mine."

Maggie and Wilson haven't ever been friends, but Maggie lets it go. It's better to have time-honed friends than go through life without them.

"More like brothers, not close brothers or anything," Wilson says, staring at Maggie again, getting to be unnerving for Maggie. "My father connects us, took to Maggie when he was young. Didn't he, Maurizio?"

"He did," Maggie tells Iris.

"He worked for my father, well from time to time. Now, he's working for me, helping me find a guy, sort of a freelance thing right."

"Is that right?" she responds with a smile on her lips. Her eyes still on him. Lingering, teeth caressing her lower lip.

Kevin breaks the moment. "He still works for us." Like he has to remind her to keep her hands off him or something. "Wilson's in charge now."

Wilson falls into the same tone. "He's just visiting. We're almost done. I promise."

"You sure?" she says. She doesn't look at Wilson. "I don't want to be late." She disappears back into the room.

"She doesn't want to be late," Wilson repeats. "If it weren't for her, we'd be there by now. She's the only reason why we are still here after waiting for you for an hour. I wouldn't have waited for you. We would've rescheduled or something. Speaking of, where were you?"

Maggie says, "Getting reacquainted with being home. Things change."

"What's changed?" Kevin asks from the sofa. He sips on the vodka.

Maggie ignores him. "I come home, from time to time, but I don't come here. Sometimes, I stay for a day, maybe more, but this work's brought me here for the longest. Tracking leads on Brandy, hitting the pavement. I'm late because you called this meeting at the last minute. I had to move some things around," he lies. "I'm sorry for being late. It won't happen again."

Wilson dips his head to his chest. "You know what." He looks up. "Don't worry about it. You're here now, and you're making progress on that Brandy thing, so that's all I can ask for, right? You're going to let me know when you've done it, right? That's one of Jackie C.'s rules, there's none of this questioning your methods or anything. Jackie C. said he would handle situations as they needed to be handled, bragged that's how he did it out east. What I want to know is, how do I know when it's done?"

"When I say it's done," Maggie says.

"Meaning you send a picture or something?"

"Meaning, it's done when I tell you it's done."

Wilson studies him for a moment. "Alright, alright. You play it like that; that's fine. Jackie C. said you might be like that. He said don't expect quick results. Said Brandy's been on the run for years; it's not an easy job. Is there anything you need from me? Money or something?"

Maggie considers the question: is it genuine?

"You paid me enough upfront to cover those types of costs." Thinking about how the trip to Colorado, to the wife, cost him time and money, but he decides it isn't worth telling Wilson. Maybe a point for later.

"Right," Wilson says. "Well, I'm glad you are here. Jackie C. said some other things about you. He said you are the best he ever trained. Is that right?"

Maggie agrees with a nod.

"Good, because I want you on this thing with my father. I want you to figure out how it happened, why it happened, and who did it."

Maggie stays silent.

"Can you handle that and find Brandy?"

"I can."

"You sure?" Wilson says.

"Anything else?"

"You find the problem and fix it. You're asking me if I want you to fix it? I do."

"What do you want done?"

"I'll leave that up to you. My pops said that Jackie C. always did what needed done without any direction from the top. For two reasons, one it's so no one knows anything that gets them sent up the river. He meant prison, but the guy couldn't just say that. He'd have to be all dramatic about it. The other thing is that it's better to stay out of your way, which I've tried to do, especially on the Brandy thing. I don't like it taking so long. But if Jackie C. vouches for you, then you're doing what you need to do. He's not an easy man to win over." Wilson waits for a moment and then adds. "Neither is my father."

"Your father trusted me."

"So I trust you."

"I'll see what I can find out."

Wilson likes that. He smiles and holds a lighter to the end of the cigar. "You do that. You do that."

With a slight flick of his head, Maggie asks, "Who's this guy?"

"What guy?" Wilson asks, between breaths, bringing the cigar to life. "Kevin? You know Kevin."

"No," Maggie says. "That guy." Meaning the guy in the door.

"That's Vega," Wilson says. "You know this used to be Renaldo Luna's apartment? That's what accounts for all this furniture." Like it's a joke, meaning there's not much of anything here.

"After what happened to him, I had to hire a bodyguard. Vega..." Wilson drops the lighter in his pocket.

Vega turns from the balcony and squints at Maggie.

"Vega meet Maurizio DiMaggio, but he don't like that name. He didn't like people calling him Maury in school, so he started goin' by Maggie."

"Maggie," Vega says.

"Maggie." Wilson does introductions. "Meet Vega Bolivar."

Maggie acknowledges Vega. "Nice to meet you."

Vega nods.

Wilson tells Maggie, "Vega's my bodyguard, for now. He's on loan from our friends down south. With Renaldo gone, things have been... let's say, tense. They liked Renaldo, go figure. They're the only ones that did—"

"Why the girl's name?" Vega, having been content to stand at the door and smoking his cigarette, asks now that he's been introduced.

Maggie gives the man his attention. "Excuse me?"

"The name. Why Maggie? Why not your real name, Maurizio?" Vega asks, rolling the cigarette over, smoke trailing his words like sparks from a streamer.

"Your real name Vega?" Maggie questions.

Vega smiles, which shows his clean teeth, which tells Maggie some things. One, everything Vega's doing right now is an act. The slouching. The costume. The cigarette. All of it. Like the homeless guy on the edge of the highway holding a sign only to strip off the garb and climb into a BMW. Two, he isn't someone Maggie wants to tussle with. If he had Wilson's ear, he'd warn the man. Vega isn't someone you trust. He's not Renaldo. He's not Maggie. Russell wouldn't trust someone like him. Vega's a pit bull, but not a trained one. He doesn't have a master. And if he does, it isn't Wilson.

Maggie bets Vega's master is money, and he doesn't concern himself too much with where it comes from.

Wilson steps forward. "Think about it, will ya? If you think you can work on finding my father while you're working this Brandy thing, I'd

appreciate it. Something like this, it isn't in the rules, not Jackie's rules. I figured, my father being who he is to you, you'd be willing to help me out, help get him back."

Maggie considers everything Wilson's said, then nods once, agreeing to do what he can. But as far as breaking Jackie C.'s rules, he'll have to think on that one. Wilson's leaning hard on Maggie's relationship with his father, and that's the Wilson Maggie remembers—the manipulative little shit.

CHAPTER NINE: KELLY CHAMBERS

UNCLE FRANK SITS IN THE BOOTH ACROSS FROM Kelly, drinking coffee, even though it's 8 p.m. on a Friday. The steak house is packed. The hustle and bustle of dozens of conversations, glasses clinking, plates clanking, and silverware scratching against ceramic fill the place with a unique atmosphere, a popular warmth, a high-end family feel. They're in their booth in the corner of the restaurant in the one spot where they can have their backs to the walls and still be able to see the door, except Uncle Frank's not looking at the door. He's staring at her, saying nothing as he sips the coffee from a little cream-colored mug, droplets of the brackish liquid hanging from the edges of his graying mustache. "How do you feel?"

"You should really switch to decaf," Kelly says, plopping a carrot into her mouth. While perusing the menu and enjoying hors d'oeuvres, they've chit-chatted for the last ten minutes; while putting off talking about work, they've caught up on the minor stuff in her life like her ex-boyfriend, the news, and a book she read. He used to do what she does. He likes to talk to her about what's going on. She likes to get his advice. But not tonight. Not after this week.

"I don't like decaf." He examines the mug for a moment and takes a drink. More coffee on the mustache. "I like this."

Frank's wearing his typical attire, a tan hunting vest with all the pockets, over a gray shirt, buttoned to the neck with a bolo tie, tight blue jeans, and cowboy boots. She can't see them right now, but he's always wearing cowboy boots. Just as he's pretty much always wearing this combination of clothes, the only thing changing is the color of the shirt and clean blue jeans every two days. His cowboy hat rests, properly, in the seat next to him, a white felt Stetson.

"Decaf's better for you," she tells him. "How do you not stay up all night, drinking that?"

"I don't drink." Frank offering his classic non-answer. "So I drink this."

Kelly doesn't see what one has to do with the other. As far as she can remember, she's never seen Frank touch alcohol, except for two times, and neither of them could be confused with a relapse, more joyous celebrations. He's never fully explained why he doesn't drink, although he's pointed it out numerous times, so many times she's lost count. She kept count for a whole year, two thousand nine hundred and thirty-three mentions, which seemed excessive until she realized her mother would tease him about it over a glass of wine at their dining room table during their dinner and after-dinner conversations.

"Decaf would be better for you, better for your body."

"I don't recall asking you for your opinion on my body. I do recall askin' you how you're feeling." Frank speaks in his slow cadence and low baritone, taking another sip between sentences as if he's trying to make a statement without actually saying more than necessary. But that's Uncle Frank. "Decaf isn't decaf. Can't remove all the caffeine. Always some leftover. Why would I pay more for something when it's less, and not a very good job of it at that?"

Kelly wears her dark blue business suit with the medallion around her neck. She spent the day in meetings, doing what Lucille Ball was famous for, explaining. But she's, tired of explaining, and doesn't want to talk about it. "You know what I'm trying to say; you should take better care of yourself."

"Well then, say it," Frank says. "Don't just try."

Uncle Frank's all she has left. Her mother died last year. Frank paid for the funeral, and he helped Kelly move into her mother's place, which is next door to his. There's a gate in the middle of the fence, with a wooden arch, something Frank made way back when Kelly was a kid. The gate's open and has been for years.

Frank lifts a finger and points to the table next to them, without looking in that direction. "See that table over there."

Kelly side-eyes the table and leans in so the neighbors can't hear whatever Frank's going to say. "What of it?"

But Frank, being Uncle Frank, doesn't change the volume of his voice or lean into her. "Both those people are drinking soda pop," he says. The couple glances their way. "You think they're drinking decaf soda pop? I don't. I know the man isn't. He's drinking prune juice." He means Dr. Pepper. "I heard him order. And the woman, she's drinking sweet tea, which might as well be soda pop with all the sugar."

The woman snatches up her drink, almost instinctually, and sips from the straw.

Kelly says, "You shouldn't listen in on other people's conversations." She leans back in the booth, lifting her napkin-roll off the table, unrolling it, and placing the silverware on the table. She adjusts the napkin over her lap.

"Like I shouldn't involve myself in other people's health issues?" he asks.

Kelly smiles brightly while refolding the white napkin into a tight triangle, which she places on her left thigh. She pats it.

Frank licks his lips, cleaning off the coffee still drenching his mustache.

Kelly dips her chin down. "You could use the napkin."

"I could," is all Frank says, sucking in on the longer hairs of his mustache.

"I can't take you anywhere."

"No, I don't think you can." He changes the conversation back to what he was saying. "I'm drinking water and coffee, black." He holds up the mug of coffee for effect, one hand wrapped around the small half circle handle, raising the mug to bring it even with her face. "You can say it's not good for my health, and I might go along with you on that, listen to you even. My doctor probably would too. I stopped drinking about the time you all came around, right before I met your momma. What I'm going to tell you, what I loved most about drinking, was pairing food with drink. Whiskey, beer, wine, you name it. That was the joy. Researched a lot of different ways to eat food, went to Greece once, Italy twice."

She knows; she went with him on a few of his later global trips, and her mother loved showing people the pictures of her wearing the grass skirt in Hawaii and drinking a fruity tropical drink on a Jamaican beach. Kelly remembers when Frank and her mother returned from Moscow and how her mother talked about the people there staring at her, how unnerving it was, until someone explained to her they'd not seen a black person except on TV, which didn't help with the unnerving nature of the stares, but it gave her some context. Her mother always wanted to understand other people, something Frank and her shared. Frank was with her the whole way, by her side until the end.

"Now, we've had this conversation before. I believe we had it last month, in this very spot." He points at the table, jamming his index finger into the table. "Right here, and I told you then what I'm going to tell you now. I drink coffee because it goes good with a steak. I don't eat much red meat these days, you know, looking out for my health, but I sure do spend a lot of time looking after the fine providential providers of this here meat. I don't want to look at them all the time and not enjoy the one day a month when I get to partake in their succulent flesh, their offerings if you will. That'd be disrespectful to the animal, to what I do. The people who count on me. Now, I get it; you're not tracking with me, and that's alright, I'm good with that."

"So what you're saying," Kelly retorts, throwing his attitude back at him, "is that you don't care what I think?"

"I'm not just saying it," he expresses, sipping the coffee. "But I asked you how you're feeling. I did not come here to offer you a treatise on why I drink coffee—and to answer your unasked question—I'm going to work tonight, a stakeout, some rustlers down south of here, see if we can catch them in the act, but I didn't want to cancel on you, especially with what happened this week. I want to be awake for the drive. Hence the coffee."

"I sense an *and* coming."

"*And* I like to pair the black coffee with the red meat," he says. "Whiskey and red wine go with red meat too, but I don't touch that stuff no more." His face softens. "And if you're worried about my health, rest assured, with the way Ibrahim makes his coffee, there's not a lot of caffeine to worry about."

"I still worry about you." Kelly plucks another carrot from the relish tray, picks through the celery and pickles, sorting them into nice little separate areas, and bites off the tip of the carrot. She doesn't like pickles, and the celery is a non-factor. She forgoes the hummus, which Uncle Frank loves. He comments that it goes well with the black coffee too.

He dips a piece of celery into the hummus, a big glob resting on the tip of the celery, and threads it through the mustache, chewing while talking.

"And I care about you, which is why I'm here, asking you, when I could have canceled for official reasons"—there are no other reasons—"how you're feeling."

"Like shit," Kelly admits. "I don't like how it's being played in the media."

"Don't get me started on them," Frank says.

"What do you have to complain about, they love you."

"They may do the occasional piece on cattle cops, but that don't mean they love me. I just happen to be the epitome of what they think a cop who goes after cowboys should look like."

"I never understood that."

"What?"

"'Cowboys,' how movies and stuff depicted them. That was sort of an insult. The word. Cowpunchers and all that. People didn't want them in town. Sort of the riffraff of the West. But when you see a western sheriff displayed on the screen, he's called a cowboy."

"Except the cowboys weren't cops," Frank finishes. "Yeah, I know. Marshal maybe, city marshals. US marshals too."

Kelly reflects upon it. "I agree, you are the epitome of what someone who does what you do should look like."

Frank thinks on those words while he eats another piece of celery with hummus, ignoring the pickles. He sips his coffee, washing everything down. "So are you."

He means it; she blushes. "I'm not what people think of when they think of a marshal."

Frank speaks an uncomfortable truth. "They will now."

"You've seen the video?"

Frank nods. "Watched it a few times. Not discounting what you or your partner did, I think if I were in the same spot, I would have acted the same way."

"Tell that to my boss," Kelly says. "Tell that to the media."

"No one cares what they think," Frank says. "And I'm sure your boss understands."

"He does, just not happy about what happened."

"Who would be?"

"Not to mention Kalka has the AUSA breathing down his neck."

"Well, it was his rodeo that got busted up; of course, he's not happy about it."

Kelly is silent for a moment, thinking over what happened. She notices the twinkle in Frank's eye. "You have thoughts on this?"

"I don't know if you want to hear them," Frank says. "That's why I'm holding onto them."

"If I said I did," she says, "would you tell me?" "Maybe, maybe not. Haven't figured out which yet."

Kelly frowns because he's making her ask. It's something they do; something she doesn't like. "Tell me."

"You sure you want to hear? You might not like what I have to say, might make you uncomfortable."

"Tell me," she says again.

"Alright," Frank says. He sips his coffee and places the mug back on the table. "First things first." He leans to the side and withdraws a folded piece of paper from somewhere and slides it across the table. "I want you to call this man and talk to him." Eyes motioning to the paper.

Kelly accepts the paper, unfolds it, and reads the name and number. "What is this? Why?"

"To help you with your media side of this problem," Frank says. "My friend, you remember Bing? Well, this guy's a friend of Bing's. They eat donuts or something together. I've met him a few times myself. Been to their morning spot, had coffee, broke bread so to say, with him, and I liked what I saw. He's honest, and I like reading his columns. You know who he is right?"

"I've read his columns," Kelly says. From time to time she's checked them out.

"He's willing to talk to you about what happened," Frank says. "Which is serendipitous because it has to do with my other points on this matter."

"Which are what?"

"We're still on my first point," Frank says. "We don't want to get ahead of ourselves here."

"So call him tomorrow?"

"Call him when you're ready to talk. I'm sure you could call him tonight."

"I don't know," she says. "I don't know if I can talk to him. I might get in trouble. Kalka might have a problem with it."

"Of course, he's going to have a problem with it, but screw him," Frank says. "Sooner or later, Kalka, if he's not already doing it, is going to throw you to the hounds. Now, you're seeing some of it because of what happened in front of all the news cameras and with who it was, which I'll come to in a moment."

"Taking your sweet time."

"Best advice comes after patience."

Kelly takes a deep breath. "I feel this is going to come back on me. Pat doesn't. Pat thinks he did the right thing, not engaging them in front of the courthouse. With all those people. He thinks we'll be fine."

Frank echoes his earlier comment. "I think you did the right thing. If I failed in conveying that from the start, hear me now as I say it. You kept those people safe by keeping your head about you."

"I appreciate that."

The validation feels good. Uncle Frank's taught her everything she knows about law enforcement with his old cronies filling in any gaps in her knowledge. His opinion matters.

"That's what I watched for when I watched the video," Frank says. "I watched to see what you were going to do. Your hand did what it should, down to your holster, the butt of your weapon. You can't teach that."

"That's what I was taught," she interjects.

Frank fixes his statement. "Of course, you can teach the reaction, but when the moment comes, you can't teach what people are going to do. You never know. People surprise you. Hotshots aren't so hot when the guns clear leather. Some freeze. Some flee. Some fight. You were willing to fight. That's not something taught; that's just who you are,"—pointing the last piece of celery at her as he says it—"so you should feel proud that was your initial reaction. Then, I saw something more. I saw you think about the situation, who was around, what was happening, and I believe you made the right call. You were smart about it. You can't teach that either."

"Pat urged me not to engage with a motion of his hand."

"He made the right call too," Frank says. "I imagine, having a rifle shoved in my face would be pretty frightening. I don't know if I would have had the sense to hold myself together the way he did."

"You've been in situations like that."

Frank's eyes dissolve into a vacant look as his mind goes back to some of the situations he's been in. He doesn't talk about them, never has, not about the times he's killed someone, but Kelly knows he has, both in the Marshals Service and as a cattle cop for the State. Finally, voice cracking slightly at the beginning, he says, "I have, but you know what I mean."

Kelly pokes at him again. "No, I don't."

He comes back to the present, eyes regaining focus. "Kalka will throw you to the hounds."

"Just a matter of time."

"If it matters any, Bing feels that way too. Call this Sonny fella and see what he has to say. I'd rather get in trouble for something I did than for something I didn't do, and they're aiming to get you in trouble for something you didn't do. Not engaging in a firefight in front of the courthouse is admirable, but they're going to make it sound like some sort of dereliction of duty."

"Okay," she says. "What else do you have rattling around under that hat of yours."

"I'm not wearing the hat right now," he says.

"So lay it all out there, old man."

Frank smiles and asks, "You going to try to find Siriano?"

"Don't know if that'd make the situation worse or not."

"It'd make the situation both," he says. "Worse, because the smart move is to stay away from this thing, far away, but better because if you brought him in, well, that'd sure inspire some little girl somewhere, seeing what a real marshal looks like."

She blushes again, warmth flooding her cheeks. "You're going to make me want to have a cigarette."

"You shouldn't smoke," Frank says. "But I've told you that since you were twenty years old."

"I still remember you catching me when I snuck out of mom's to smoke, telling her I was taking the trash out."

"I saw you from the window, came out, asked you what you were doing. You nearly swallowed the thing to prevent me from seeing."

"Mom wasn't happy."

"She didn't ever like being lied to."

"I thought about hunting Siriano, but Pat thinks we should lay low."

"Pat's like butter left on the table too long; he's melting and just waiting for a time he's not needed."

"So you think I should go after him?"

Frank shakes his head. "No...I do not. I think that would make some problems for you, but I'm also not telling you that you shouldn't go after him. Sometimes the right thing is the wrong thing, and the wrong thing seems like the right thing."

He would do this from time to time when she was growing up, not wanting to influence her decision. He lay it out there, telling her what she should do by telling her not to do the very thing he's talking about. It's very confusing, but that's how Uncle Frank communicates.

"And your other thoughts?" she asks.

"Do you wonder why what happened happened?"

"What do you mean?"

"You're thinking about who did it, and all that, and I'm sure, knowing you the way I do, you have a lead to go on. You wouldn't be you if that weren't the case, and I'd be disappointed in you, but since I'm not, quite the opposite, have you asked the question of how or why what happened happened?"

"You mean, why did five armed men and a female driver kidnap Siriano?"

"Ah, you caught on to the driver." Frank sips the last of the coffee and sits the mug on the end of the table. "I wondered how long it would be until people started talking about her. People should talk about her. My experience in life, someone like her, with guys like this, willing to engage in activities like that, she's pretty important. You find her, you find them."

"I noticed her. Female driver. Face covered up."

The waiter brings their steaks, dropping a handful of plates on the table, the steak drowned in the liquid smoke the place is known for, pooling off the steak and soaking the underside of the foil-wrapped baked potato.

"But that's not what I mean," he says, unrolling his silverware. "What I meant was: did you ever ask how someone, people like them, knew Siriano was going to be there that day?"

Kelly hasn't.

"I thought about it, the first question I asked, how did that happen?" Frank says. "I know you didn't tell anyone, and Pat's not going to tell anyone; he's still a Marshal. Wouldn't have come from a Marshal, then, who?"

"You know who."

"I have an idea." Frank holds the knife in one hand, fork in the other. "Call it an old man's hunch."

Kelly cuts into her steak to check that it's done. "You going to share this hunch with me?"

Frank is silent until she looks up at him. "I don't know if you want to hear it. It's pretty far out there."

"You know who?" It's phrased as a question, but it's more a statement.

Kelly slices off a piece of meat and sticks it in her mouth. It nearly melts.

Frank, still holding his unused silverware, continues, "I think it was your AUSA, which is why I want you to call that reporter and talk to him. I think you do that as a way to protect yourself."

"Why do I need to protect myself?"

"Because you're now trapped in a game that you didn't know you were playing."

"What game?" she asks, cutting another piece of meat off her six-ounce sirloin.

"The game of Monsters and Men," Frank says. "Every so often, people get wrapped up in things they had no intention of being a part of, get involved in something they didn't know was going on, or with people who want something. That's you, my sweet girl. You're in a game, their game, and you don't know the rules, but don't worry, you know an old man who knows some other old men, and we're willing to get you caught up so that you're not left holding the pieces at the end, wondering what happened."

Kelly swallows the piece of meat. "What are you talking about?"

"I'm talking about the thing that makes police work interesting. It's never about what's happening on the surface; it's what's happening behind the scenes that's interesting. You know we used to, in the rustlin' business, arrest someone for minor possession as a way to get them to flip on their dealers. We don't care about the minor stuff; we want the major pushers, but now the State's changed all that, and we can't do that no more, which means we've had to adjust our tactics and come up with new ways. Which means new rules."

"I'm still not following."

"That's okay. You'll catch up eventually. I raised you, so I have faith," Frank says. "What I'm saying is, there's always more going on. We arrest the minor guy for minor possession because we're working on building a net, trap, whatever, for the guy supplying the drugs, who's also stealing our cattle. It's never just as simple as a minor possession, something those bleedin' hearts don't consider or want to consider. You're caught in a similar game. Someone's playing a bigger game out there in the world, and with Siriano's kidnapping, things just got shaken a whole lot up."

"Okay?"

"To answer your question." Frank draws the suspense out as long as he can. "I think it was your AUSA. I think he didn't like how things went a few months back, and this was his way to get his interpretation of *justice*."

"That's crazy."

Frank grins and starts cutting into his steak. "Ever hear the saying about a fox?"

"Don't let them in the hen house."

"Which is why my associates, some roosters at the DEA office in Tulsa, want nothin' to do with your AUSA, and so the final question you have to ask yourself is, 'why is that?'"

CHAPTER TEN: EMERSON ROWAN

HER FATHER'S TRUCK RATTLES SOMETHING AWFUL, nearly vibrating the teeth out of her head. The sun's breaking the horizon outside the window, flooding the valleys between the buildings downtown, casting cool blue shadows on the empty streets. Kaleo is on the radio, playing one of their slower songs, a current favorite band. Music's always been how she and her father communicated, and she's sure he's letting the CD play through the truck's speakers as a way of setting the mood so that she feels comfortable enough to talk to him. This is one of his tricks. He did this when she was a kid, on those few precious weekends. He'd play the music, and she'd break down telling him about her life because that's what little girls do when they're with their daddy, except it feels like she's never been a little girl, and this is just him manipulating her like he does all those other poor saps he tricks into revealing their deepest darkest secrets. "You didn't have to wait so long to come get me," she says, lashing out at him, not meaning to and not upset about it either.

After emerging from under an old bridge, driving the truck with careful precision, he lets the chorus of the song roll over him. "I didn't have to come get you at all."

Fair point, but Emerson's not going to admit it. Instead, she says, "I called you yesterday."

To which he says, "And I came and got you today."

Even though the glass feels good against her forehead, she pulls her head from the window and faces him. "What were you doing?"

Without turning his head more than a fraction, he glances at her. "I was working." Hands tight on the broken-down steering wheel, with its chipped and ripped plastic, showing just how dilapidated this truck is.

Emerson throws her hands up and lets them slap loudly against her thighs as they come down. The blows sting. "Well, there we go. Nothing ever changes."

"Hey, I have to be able to pay for you," he says, tone sharp but still amiable. "Pay your bonds. Get you out of jail, this being the... what is it? The fourth time?"

She shakes her head. "You don't have to look out for me."

"And you don't have to call me to come get you, but here we are."

"It's not like I want to be here," Emerson didn't think she would be here. "Coming home wasn't supposed to be like this."

They were going to reconnect or try to connect in a way they'd never been able to. It was a new start for her, getting her away from a city that did nothing for her, but for whatever reason, Emerson couldn't get into it, and her father was not willing to bridge the gap.

Her father hasn't changed. He's still just as driven as he was when she was a kid—when her mother left him, when she died, when Emerson left for what she thought would be good. He's not changed at all. In all this time, he's still the same man. He's eternal, the man with the golden column. She didn't even know what that meant when she was a kid. Now she knows that it means he's good at what he does, in the top of his bracket. Yet he's never left Tulsa, so what's that really say about him? It says that he's comfortable, and he's been so comfortable doing what he's doing that he's decided to not mess up a good thing and do it until the day he dies or until they bar him from the newsroom, whichever comes first.

But for her, the golden column just meant he was never home, not for her, not for her mother, not for nothing. He worked all the time. So much so that Emerson doesn't know who he is, not the real him, and certainly not the version of him her mother complained about, and he doesn't know who she is any more than she knows him.

And now it seems that neither one of them is willing to try to figure the other out, which means they just sit here, in silence, in his shitty ass truck, as he drives her out of downtown and away from the county jail.

The truck smells like lilacs, nauseating, but it does cover up her smell. Being in jail has a certain smell, and she doesn't like using the facilities there any more than necessary. It's not that she's worried about the bullshit shown on TV; she just doesn't like it. She won't even shit in a public restroom if she can help it. Right now, she could use a shower or maybe even go in all the way and soak in the tub, take a bubble bath, and shave her legs, spending an hour or two, pruning up real nice.

Of course, that's assuming he's driving her back to the house. He could be, or he could be taking her someplace else, like out of town, to the airport, or somewhere, tell her to get out of the truck.

So maybe, Emerson will just tell him to pull over, and she'll get out, give up on ever having a relationship with him and cut him loose. Do it to him before he can do it to her. That's what she does to everyone. Push them away, shove really. She learned it from him.

While stopped at the light before getting on the highway, he turns in the seat some, his expression gentle and throws his arm over the back of her seat. "Did you really meet him?"

Briefly, an unfamiliar feeling of positivity arises within her, filling her chest with a buzzing, soaring joy. Emerson wants to tell him she did. She wants to say he's everything she ever dreamed of him being. Tell him how cool he was, handsome, and how, before the cops hauled her off, he gave her his number. He told her to call him when she got out, like shoplifting, getting arrested, and being locked up didn't mean anything to him. With his history, Emerson knows he's been on both sides of the law. Talk about how calm he was. How cool. But the anger and resentment are too entrenched within her. The bitterness poisons her thoughts as well as her words.

"Why, so you can do a story on him? Do something for your *golden column*?"

Her father opens his mouth to say something, to make some pitiful response, but then he snaps it shut. Eyes moistening.

That's exactly why he was asking.

He isn't interested in her or what she has to say. He never has been. He's not interested in what happened because they are a father and daughter who share a connection—a game, made special because of what happened at the game, and she just met the man who made all that happened—but little else. He just wants something he can use, something he can write about.

He's not changed in all this time. He's still the cold-hearted bastard she grew up with, except that she didn't grow up with him, she grew up around him. He was a visiting presence. Like Santa Claus or the tooth fairy, she wasn't even sure she really had a father. She had this mythical figure, who would come at odd times, shower her with love and affection and gifts, before disappearing back to wherever he faded off to.

A few minutes pass in silence, he clears his throat, surprising her. "Yes, I'd love to do a story on him."

"You're unbelievable. You don't change," she says. "You're the same guy you were when I was younger. You don't care about me. You never have. You care about sports. Care about the story." Emerson bounces her index and middle fingers up and down on both hands, using finger quotation marks, making a show of it. "You let it control your life. It's pathetic."

Her father's speechless as he digests her comments.

Then, he says, "That's not why I want to do a story on him."

"Oh yeah," she says. "What are you going to say in this story? Talk about the game he threw? How great it was? Talk about taking your little girl there? Skipping school? Eating hot dogs?"

"Among other things," her father says. "Have you ever read my column, not what I did when you were younger, but the one I do now, this *Where are you now column*?"

"You mean, did I read the disingenuous piece of shit you wrote about coming out to LA to get me, and linking it to an interview you did with Kobe Bryant's widow, which is pretty fucking morbid, just so you had some excuse to fly out to LA like I'm not enough?"

"I didn't..." He starts to say and then stops, sounding like he was going to try to defend himself.

"What?" She tries to force him into a confrontation. "What didn't you do? Huh, are you going to finish that sentence?"

It's easier to drive others away when they get angry first. But he doesn't get angry. Instead, he smiles tenderly, mouth closed, lips pressed tight together.

"Yes, that piece, that is what I meant." Seemingly unoffended with her assessment of it and his actions.

"I read it."

What she doesn't say is she liked it. It made her cry. It filled her with hope. Made her believe maybe... just maybe... they can salvage their relationship, but then, she remembered who they were, him and her, and that hope quickly faded, evaporated might be a better word.

"I'd like to do a follow-up piece to that one."

"Talk about how full of shit you are?"

He thinks it over. "I've thought a lot about it, about you and me, about us. I thought about the past, your mother. And I feel like I have something more I can say. Something meaningful."

"Why?" she asks, shrugging her shoulders. "To win some award or something?"

He glances at her again, taking his eyes off the roadway. "No,"—jerking his head—"I want to repair this relationship."

"What relationship?" Though, she knows what he means.

"That's it," he says. "There isn't one."

"Well, *this* is new," she says. "What are you doing, trying honesty for a change? Figured out you can't hide behind words for the rest of your life? They won't take care of you when you get sick and decrepit? Won't carry on your bullshit? Call you for your opinion? Keep you warm?"

Her father nods, a quick taut bob. "I thought about your phone call all day yesterday."

He pauses as if he's waiting for her to interrupt him again.

Emerson crosses her arms over her chest.

"Thought about a lot of things," he goes on. "You learn some things as you go through life, some say grow up, but I'm not growing up to anything, I'm growing older, so maybe, it's wisdom. Maybe, it's the benefit of seeing mistakes from far away, unattached, and all that, but what I thought most about was you taking responsibility for your actions, and how if I keep coming to save you, I'm not helping you."

"You got all that out of me telling you not to come get me?"

He nods without looking her way. "Except you weren't telling me not to come get you. It was the opposite. I'm sure of it. You wanted me to come get you."

"Oh *yeah*?" she utters.

He says, "yeah," and then, adds, "I thought when I went out to LA, I'd come get you, save you, and maybe we'd repair ... whatever this is between us," he motions with his hand, "but after yesterday, I just got to thinking, I don't think I can repair it. Not if I keep saving you."

"No one asked you to save me," Emerson says. "No one asked you to come to LA to get me."

"No one did. I chose to. You needed help. I helped. My choice."

"Did you ever wonder why I never came home while I was on the run?"

"You didn't think this was a home."

Which shocks her into silence because it's the truth.

"You really mean it, don't you?"

"What? That I would like a relationship with my daughter? Find out who she is, not whatever it is we've been pretending for the last few months? Yes, I do."

"I don't know what to say."

"I don't know either. I've thought a lot about that too. I figured, when I don't know what to write, I turn on music, turn off my brain, look away from the keyboard and just let what comes out come out, which is why I shared with you what I shared. I don't want to go through life without knowing you, but I can't keep saving you either. That's not working."

"I'm sorry." She is surprised at her admission and how some of her fire's faded from within. "I don't know why I steal. I mean, I think I know why, but it's a bullshit excuse. I don't know why I keep doing it, even after being caught."

"You want to give it to the man. I know you. You were like that when you were younger."

"Something like that."

"You want to say you don't need anyone to get through life. But you do. We all do. I think I get it. It's sorta why I write."

Emerson stares at him. "I've never talked to you about your writing."

"I've never wanted to force it on you." Her father turns the wheel. "I could've forced it, but then, you would have resented me for that. I thought... I don't know what I thought. I just didn't want you to hate that... you could hate me, but not the writing."

"You are *really* passionate about it."

"Your mother didn't understand," he admits. "And I've come to terms with that. It was hard, but I am at peace with it."

"She didn't hate you."

"Yes, she did," he replies. "But I know what you mean. I pushed her away. I hid in my work. From her. From you. From life."

"You're not the only one."

He adjusts the mirror.

Emerson asks, "What were you working on?"

"That kidnapping," he says. "The thing in the paper. I was in the process of getting a bondsman to get you out last night, but then, I got a call from someone related to that thing, so I had to talk with her, figure out when we wanted to meet and do some background research. I figured you could wait, considering my recent revelations."

That doesn't make her angry. Progress? She questions, "The crime guy getting kidnapped?"

She thinks she saw the headline on the front page of the paper when she walked in to steal that coffee. The newspapers were right there, off to the side of the expo counter.

"Yes."

"Who called you that's related to that?"

"The lady marshal," he says. "She had just slapped handcuffs on the guy when he was taken."

"How did she get your number?"

Her father grins. "I have my ways. I'm really good at what I do."

He better be for all that he's committed to his profession.

"What did she say?"

"We just did the meet and greet type stuff... this is who I am, this is my idea about what I want to write."

"What'd she say to that?"

"She said she'd sit down with me," he says. "It's a bit outside of my wheelhouse, but I'm doing a favor for a friend, or a group of friends, I'm not sure which."

"Why did she let them take him?"

"Why did she let the guy get kidnapped right out of her hands?"

"Yeah that," Emerson says. "She tell you what happened?"

"She told me it was the right move, knew there were a bunch of people around. Didn't want anyone getting hurt."

"So not because she's a coward?"

"I didn't get that impression."

"But that's the impression she wants to clear up?"

"That's the impression in the news, right now."

"She wants you to speak for her."

"Could be," he says. "Maybe. We'll see. I still have to meet with her and then pitch it to my editor, you remember Jimmy?"

"He's still alive?"

"He's alive," her father laughs. "Anyways, the marshal and I didn't get too far into it. I don't like to do those sorts of things on the phone."

"You want them to trust you."

"I want them to be comfortable, but yes," he says. "Trust comes with it. If they don't trust me, then I can't write their stories. I don't write about the surface of the ocean; it's an ocean. There are only so many ways someone can say the surf was choppy, you know. What I write about is what's going on in all those places you don't see, everything under the surface. That's what I find interesting. More about the 'why,' then the 'how,' or the 'who.'"

"Have you always been like that?"

"Have I always been interested in the 'why?' Honestly, no, there was a time I was young and dumb and stupid, made major mistakes, things I wish I could take back, make right at least. I cared about money and my name in the byline." He looks at her. "But I've learned. I changed. My style at least. I feel like I'm a better writer. Better reporter."

Emerson pulls her feet up, hugging her knees, drawing them tight against her chest just under her chin, which she rests on her knees, thinking about how her father just leaned in for her to punch him square in the face, and thinking that she didn't do that even though she's dreamed about it for years. She was thinking about how brave he was to change and how hard that must have been for him.

So she'll do the same, share with him, begrudgingly if she's honest with herself, but why not try? If she wants this, which she imagines she does, otherwise she'd have taken off long ago. She might as well put herself out there, at least as far as he did.

Her mind returns to Maggie. She says, "He was really cool."

"Who was?"

"DiMaggio," she says. "Look, if you're going to trust me, then I'm going to have to trust you. You're right. We can't keep on going the way we're going. It's not good for either one of us. Look at where our lives are. Either we change it, or I get off this ride and fade away, maybe go back to Texas where that bondsman found me working the diner."

Her father is silent.

Then, he asks, "What made him cool?"

"His confidence," she blurts out without thinking about the answer. "He was so calm, so sure of himself."

"Has he gotten fat or—"

She laughs, giggling some, which she didn't think would ever happen especially with how she was feeling when she got in the car. "That happens, doesn't it? They get fat, bloated, disgusting. No, he was trim, looked better today—well, the other day—than he did when he was playing."

"Did you get to talk to him about that game?"

She shakes her head, chin still on her knees. "No, the cops showed up before we could get to it. I did say you would love to meet him."

"That's a shame," he says. "I'd love to tell him how special that day was."

She's not sure what made the day special. Was it because it was one of the few good memories they shared? A father and daughter playing hooky from school, going to the ballpark on a perfect day, watching the local farm team play, got a chance to see some big players at the time who came to the little town and hit the ball, or the fireworks at the end of the night? Or was it what Maggie did, the accomplishment, the feat?

"I'm sure that day was special for him too."

Then, it hits her why her father related, and relates, his columns and subjects.

"Oh," she says, like air escaping from a hatch.

"You get it, don't you?" he says.

Emerson digs her chin into her knee. "No, but I'm starting to."

"I've never seen anyone play like him." Her father breezes past her revelation. "That was a hell of a day. For us, for him. He threw a no-hitter and hit the cycle. That's rare. I hadn't seen it before or since. Haven't even heard of anyone getting close. It's something that would never happen in the Majors. College, the minors, maybe. But not the Majors, not now with the DH. The only type of batter I've ever heard of doing that—seen film, of course, because I wasn't alive when he played—was Babe Ruth. A hell of a thing for a hell of a day."

"It was a good day," she adds, "wasn't it?"

"It was." Her father agrees and guides the truck through a turn in the suburb neighborhood. Close to the house now. "I've never forgotten it." He pauses as he pulls the truck into the driveway and parks. "I've never forgotten any of our days together."

CHAPTER ELEVEN: PABLO JIMENEZ

THE OLD MAN WON'T SHUT UP; THREE DAYS NOW— nearly—he's gone on and on and on, talking and talking, asking questions like, "Who are you?" and "What do you want?"

Then, trying to guess what's going on. "Are you going to kill me?"

Answering his own question. "No, you're not going to kill me; if you were going to do that, you would have done it."

Yelling at Pablo. "You ain't got the balls to kill someone like me!"

Challenging him. "Whip them out, show me you got some fucking balls, I don't believe it. You got balls? Show them. Do it. Fucker, fucking kill me and get this over with."

Then, moving on to just talking nonsense.

He talked for six straight hours this morning like he's filibustering a piece of legislation. He started just after Pablo entered the little room. Never getting tired of talking. Going on about ancient Rome, apparently a favorite topic of his, but considering his mafia roots, not totally unexpected. The whole time, pacing back and forth in front of the cot, mainly because he's chained to it. The chain is wrapped around his left ankle, just under where the pants break, connected to the horizontal bar of the bed. He wears his pants like an older man, letting the bottom hem break just above the ankle. He talks with his hands, bouncing them in time with each of his six steps to either side of the cot until he hits the wall, about twenty steps total.

Then, after the six hours, he just sat on the edge of the cot, looked defeated or winded, Pablo wasn't sure which, shoulders heaving as he stared down at the floor, maybe at the chain, and then, he stared at Pablo. A cold hard look, the same look he gave him in the trunk of Omar's car. The same lopsided grin.

And he went right back to it, talking about lions of the Serengeti and how in Rome they used to feed people to the lions, how it wasn't like in the movies where there's this big crowd of people, no one nearly as pretty as Russell Crowe up on the screen. Saying the actor's name with affection like he's kin to him or something, probably for having the same name. Going on and on about how it wasn't in the Colosseum; it was these nowhere places, where punishments were handed out, but yeah, it did happen in the Colosseum too, he read about it. He read it wasn't just Christians, more like just let the beasts feed on anyone deemed unpopular.

Now, Siriano continues, "Throw those sorry fuckers in with all sorts of wild and ferocious beasts, cats and pigs—they say boars, but let's be real, they're fucking pigs like that fat fuck from the *Lion King*, but with tusks out to here—make you fight for your life like you're going to fucking punch your way out of those freaking jaws, like those sorry fucks who punch sharks. *Pow, right in the kisser*. Like that fucking works with something with teeth. Not just Christians either, although I'm sure some self-agonizing Catholics want you to believe they were special, those cult of Jesus types. Ignatius—my fucking confirmation name. Fed him to the lions. Paintings and shit depicting it. I thought that was a way to go: in a crowd full of people, for their entertainment—big fucking beast, pacing back and forth in front of you large, powerful, regal—persecuted but wanting to live the right life, be a martyr. Course, that was before I grew the fuck up. Who wants to die by being fucking mauled to death?"

Pablo sits mute throughout the entire tirade. He thought about blindfolding Siriano, maybe even gagging him to get him to shut up, but it seemed pointless after the scene in the trunk. He figures he should just let the old man wear himself out.

"You ever fucking see a caged lion?" Alluding to the idea he was the lion, hunching his shoulders and lunging at him like he's a Saturday afternoon bully and Pablo's intimidated. If Pablo squints, then yeah, the hair running up the back of his neck, the pelt across the guy's shoulders, could look like a mane. "TV has you believe you have to use a fucking whip with them. You got whips for me? I don't know about that. The whips sound kinky. If you had the whips, I'd bust your balls over it, call you names. Some S and M type shit right there."

Pablo doesn't answer.

But that doesn't keep the old man from going on, ceaseless. "I know you," he continues. "I know you. You're that fucking pipsqueak who used to hide behind Alejandro's shirttails."

Pablo says nothing. He stays in his seat by the door and sips his second coffee.

It is better this way.

It started as a power play. A way to mess with the guy. Then, it turned into Pablo didn't know what to say. He planned this elaborate speech, a monologue about Alejandro, Renaldo, all that, about how Siriano's son's fucking nothing and is screaming at people like an impotent child, about how his son's the reason he's here.

But when Pablo opened his mouth to say something to the old man, his mind reverted right back to Siriano in the trunk and how his plan was fucked from the moment Siriano recognized him, not because he recognized him but because he wasn't afraid. He wasn't scared. The look on his face showed it was a game for him, and so far, even chained to a shitty bed, he was winning, and Pablo hasn't worked out how to challenge the move. Like Siriano, in that one look, knows who Pablo is, not his name but the truth of his being.

Watching the old man do his theater bit, Pablo keeps turning over that moment in the garage—Siriano in the trunk. How the question about the chewing gum surprised him so much that he didn't know how to act, so he hit the man, one sweeping backhand across his face. Like hitting stone. Siriano turned his face with the blow, deflecting most of it, but then, as his hand cleared flesh, Siriano went right back to staring at him and asked, "So you got gum or what?" Like it wasn't a big deal. Not him in the trunk. Not him getting slapped. The guy seemed amused, even did that lopsided grin.

So Pablo hit him again, punched him this time, which drove the air out of him. He didn't say anything the whole time Vega and Omar helped Pablo haul him out. Not speaking didn't equate cooperation. He was dead weight. First doing the potato sack act for Pablo when Pablo reached in and grabbed the man's armpits, which were wet and sweaty. The guy didn't budge, just went limp, his shoulder pulling with Pablo's strain, like tugging on a noodle or a wet and sweaty rope, body not going anywhere.

And then, when Vega came over, the guy smiled even wider, looking from Pablo to Vega and at Omar then back to Vega like there was some sort of inside joke. Challenging them. Playing the little kid that didn't want to go to bed. Daring them to get him out.

They got him out, but it wasn't easy.

Now, Siriano buttons his slacks after pissing in the bucket in the corner of the room by the wall, dressed down to his white tank top, dirty with sweat. "All you do is stare, what the fuck are you staring at?" He grabs his crotch, bunching the fabric, and shakes his junk. "You like what you see, you fucking fairy?"

Trying to goad Pablo into talking. Sensibility and questions didn't get a reaction, so now the crime boss decides to move on to trying to elicit an emotion. Anger being his current emotion of choice.

Pablo chooses to remain quiet just as before. He's never been one for anger. And he's not worked out what to say to the old man.

How does he convince Siriano that kidnapping him prevented a war?

That's what Pablo couldn't tell Omar. Even though he told Omar it was their way to go to war, it's not. Pablo did it to shore up his position within the carcass of Alejandro's operation and to show the city, at least the people that matter, that he had balls to strike back. Pablo did it to have this one-on-one conversation with Siriano, to tell the man that he's not here to hurt him—it plays well for the public—and he's in charge of Alejandro's operation. To make him listen.

"Not going to talk, huh?" Siriano lowers himself down onto the cot, slowly like an old man, groaning with the strain.

All this time, in this room, it seems to be taking a toll on him. He looks like an old man, the saggy tits and wiry white hair dusting his body all over except for the salt and pepper mess on top, which Pablo figures is a die job, a refusal to accept reality. Siriano pulls his pants up past his belly button when he's feeling insecure. He is a strong man gone soft but on his way back, as though getting out of prison changed him, made him healthier, but he'd really let himself go there for a while.

"How long I been here?" Siriano asks. "Couple of hours? Days? How many? I've lost track. All this time, you've sat there, right there by the door, saying nothing, crossing your legs like you got to tinkle or something the whole time, little Miss Muffet on your fucking tuffet. What's wrong with you? You don't talk? You one of them..." he snaps his fingers, "whatchamafuckingcallit.... A mute, that's it, gotta be. Is that why you're the one in here with me? Cuz you don't fucking talk?"

Pablo just shifts his weight in the chair and stares back at him.

"Do you know who I am?" Siriano asks. "I feel like if you're doing this, then you must know, but I've worked with some dumb fucking people in my life, and sometimes they do some dumb shit. Stupid fucks all of them. Once knew a guy, he broke into a car, and a woman comes out of the cupcake shop, sees this guy in her car and how he acts like it's the most natural thing in the world and doesn't hurry his stealing any. But this woman, she's got some balls. She goes back inside the cupcake shop, gets some friends. They come out as this stupid fuck's getting into his very unique shitty-but-okay muscle car, engine growling like a broken air conditioner swallowed a cat, and the pussycat's angry as fuck about it. And they fucking throw cupcakes all over his car. Guy drives away, car covered in frosting. Needless to say, the cops knew him on sight. He didn't get very far.

"I tell you this as an example of the stupid fucks I've worked with." Siriano touches his chest with the splayed fingers of his left hand. Then, he motions out to Pablo. "But what I don't get is, you don't strike me as a stupid fuck. You don't wear a mask, so that tells me you're not worried about me seeing your face. You're not going to kill me, so I think it's this, you don't wear a mask because you *want* me to see your face. There's a reason behind it. I just haven't worked out what it is yet. But hey," he touches his chest again, "what do I fucking care? You got me out of a quagmire. I don't have to testify in front of the Grand Jury about shit I did and don't want to talk about or shit I didn't do and don't have a clue about. So I'll give it to you, you seem smart. Noticed you got rid of that fresh off the boat bowl cut you were sporting just a few months back. How long you been over here?" Saying it like he's truly interested in who Pablo is.

Pablo says nothing.

"Still not talking, huh?" Siriano keeps going. "Okay, okay, but just so you know, I know you." He shrugs and points. "I remember you. I know who you are ... or were with the *Jefe*. Whispered in the man's ear when we were meeting like you're his conscience or something, so I know you talk. I liked Alejandro. The man knew how to speak the language of money. He fucking talked. Made good eggs too. But what I liked most about him was he didn't let emotions get in the way. Never. He was always about what was best for the whole. Not me, I'm a greedy fuck. So let me ask you, who fared better? Me the greedy fuck? Or your boss the emotionless one?" He tries to elicit a different sort of emotion.

Pablo considers the question but says nothing.

And Siriano doesn't supply the answer. Instead, he transitions to history and tries to suss out information. "Let me ask you, where you from? Mexico? Is that where that big ugly fuck is from too—the one I've not seen before? The bald guy. I know he's from here. He and Alejandro been together a long time. I liked the bald guy, reminds me of Ben Kingsley, except the spicy jalapeño version—like when the guy played Gandhi. Me, my people are from two places." He holds up two fingers. "Well, more than two, but my name, my identity comes from two places that aren't here. Italy—Napoli, home of the pizza pie, crust so thin, you got to fold the pizza and you don't feel like nothing's there on the bottom but some dough to keep the whole thing from sticking to the oven. And Sicily, obviously."

He pauses for effect.

Then, Siriano says, "I try to live up to my ancestors. They don't mix until they come to the giant mixing bowl that is this fucking country. So now, I have two patronages I have to fucking lug around like bulky luggage, but I like them both.

"You know where the Roman people come from, right?" Siriano asks. "Couple legends, let you sort out which you want to believe, but the fuckers ran from Troy and ended up there, in *das boot*, had some kids—lost them in the woods or maybe the parents died; who cares, you choose—who were then raised by motherfucking wolves. Hard mothers, if you ask me, flee a burning besieged city, find a place, fight the wild, thrive. Now, I don't believe the wolf bullshit. I think fleeing an ancient city like Troy could be true. *Head West, young man*. I'll get on board with that, but then, it's not hard to understand why Americans did what we did, when Romans did what they did, expand. We are a fucking Republic after all. It's in our DNA, which is USA.

"That's what they did, the Romans, founded a city, raided their neighbors, folded their culture into theirs, and proceeded to conquer the mother fucking world, taking everything they wanted. Reminds you of someone, don't it? America, Manifest Destiny. All that you see is yours, from sea to shining fucking sea. Not hard to understand how that might upset the status quo. Ever play *Risk*? People don't like those who overreach. I run things with that in mind. I don't want to rock the boat too much, but I'll sure as fuck drill a hole in the bottom and let the other guy's boat sink. I think you need to think about that and about what you're doing before you do it."

Pablo says nothing.

"I've thought about it, thought a lot about it," Siriano adds. "Not just what the fuck you're doing but also about why the wolf legend is so popular, but then, I'm not a smart guy. I just like the metaphor. I think it's like what Byzantine Emperor Justin I said about Rome, which means he's talking about himself, he's not much different from me. I grew out of the ashes of something already existing and made it my own thing. We think alike, but what he said was, 'It is only to be expected that they should have the hearts of wolves. *They're fucking bloodthirsty, and insatiable in their greed, lust, and power and riches without limits*.' That's not exactly what he said, but what he's saying is—they're fucking wolves.

"But I'm not Justin I," Siriano continues. "I'm a Caesar though. I bring peace, but you, you're Augustus; that's what you are." He pauses to see if Pablo will respond or argue. He doesn't. "You know who that is, right? Being from Meh-hee-co, I don't know if you do or not. I don't know what they teach you. I don't know what you've picked up living over here, but he was this guy, some kind a small-town gangster who arose to become Julius Caesar's adopted son—now how can I not enjoy the metaphor here. I'm a Caesar—the Ambassador has bequeathed me all that you see, his son was killed, and no not by me—but not like you, not like this guy, he's a nobody. Some say he was Caesar's nephew, I don't know, but he was ruthless, a cold-hearted bastard by some accounts. To quote, 'rise to become the first emperor of Rome,' by using the murder of his *guy* as a springboard into gathering power around him. Never let a good tragedy go to waste, right? Then, he did some things with some people, like murder and fight a civil war, all against and with people he thought were friends, or they thought they were friends. Know what else he did. He kidnapped rivals, murdered them—now, who does *that* remind you of?"

Finally, Pablo, who at first was merely half-listening like he's done the last few days, clues into what Siriano's getting at. "Me," he says.

Siriano stares straight at him. "He speaks, for the first fucking time. He speaks. Thank the gods, or whoever the fuck you believe in. Feel better? I feel better. Feel like we just fought twelve rounds here. Spent all night figuring you out."

"You think you have me figured out?"

"I do," Siriano says. "I do. I wouldn't say it if it wasn't true. It's not like you were fathered by Mars, the god of war. You're a person, and I like people, like seeing how they think. That's interesting to me. But what I don't know, what I'm still trying to figure out, is just what sort of Augustus you are?"

"I don't know what you mean," Pablo says.

"Are you the somber fellow, gloomy as a fucking storm cloud? Are you the party goer, playing everyone with your charm, slimy and elusive like a fucking snake? Are you the lion, who won battles? The man who outmaneuvered all his enemies. Or are you someone else?"

Pablo stays quiet, but he leans forward, revealing he's interested. A small concession.

"Well, I think I have you pegged, but I wanted to give you an opportunity to speak for yourself," Siriano says. "So now that I got you all chatty Cathy and all, why am I here?"

Pablo leans back and crosses a leg. "To talk."

"Well, swell fucking job doing that." Siriano points at him. "I'm so *overwhelmed* with all the fucking talking you've been doing."

To which Pablo asks, "Does that mean you're thirsty yet?"

Siriano's lopsided grin breaks into a full toothy smile. "There's the bowl cut I know. Got some bite in you. I heard you did."

"What else did you hear?"

"From prison," Siriano says, "that you're in charge of Alejandro's shop."

Pablo nods. "I am."

"So if you aren't going to kill me, why am I here?" Siriano asks. "You looking to renegotiate or something?"

"Something like that," Pablo says. "I just don't know how to say it to you."

"Well shit boy." Siriano stands and continues to dress, putting his shirt back on, buttoning the buttons in silence, tucking the shirt in, slowly, pants flapped open, Siriano shoving the ends in as he pulsates on the balls of his feet. He slips the sport coat over his shoulders. Once he's dressed, he's dirty, but composed, he sits down on the bed. "I found when you don't know what to say, just start talking, it will help knock it loose." He holds out both hands at his side. "So just consider me listening."

"Did you order Alejandro's death?"

"No." The answer is the truth.

"Did you sanction Alejandro's death?"

"No," Siriano says, same as before.

"Did you want Alejandro dead?"

"Honestly?" Siriano displays a smug look. "I did, but I didn't, you know. I mean, it does me no good to rearrange the board without options out there, but at the same time, the old man was awfully stubborn about business."

"But you didn't want him dead because of it?"

"I wasn't going to kill him if that's what you mean."

"Yes or no."

"No, *Jesus*, don't you understand a thing I'm saying?"

"Not really," Pablo says. "Did you know what Renaldo was doing?"

"In what regard?" Siriano asks, but his features break showing he's unsure of himself, not as confident. "You mean with Alejandro? I don't know why he reignited that relationship. I told him to leave the old man alone. I scooped that boy out of this life and made him into something, but the catch was that he had to leave that life behind. I guess it made room for you, no?"

"My parents sent me here after Renaldo left Alejandro, but he was a relative."

Siriano nods, hands on his knees, the imposing crime figure returned. "So you're in charge of all this, all that was his?"

"Yes, I am."

"And you think Renaldo killed your boss? Is that what you're getting at?"

"I know he did."

"But Wilson said something different, so I know Alejandro died, but I don't know how he died. If you say—"

"I don't care what your bastard said," Pablo says. "I was there. Renaldo killed him."

Siriano leans back, placing both hands behind him to support his weight. "Now, why would Renaldo kill Alejandro?"

"Alejandro tried to kill Renaldo. Renaldo came around asking for help. Alejandro was offended by the entitlement. Renaldo thought he could come back here, say he was sorry, ask for resources, and all would be forgiven."

"Obviously, it wasn't," Siriano says.

"He ordered me to kill Renaldo," Pablo says. "I shot Renaldo in the head."

"But he survived?"

"*Somehow* and he blamed Alejandro. Took his revenge. I was there."

Siriano whistles. "Well, then Mr. No Emotion felt emotion, and it killed him. That's ironic, no? I like it. The guy who always tried to be the most controlled one in the room lost his cool and then lost his head." Siriano laughs. "That's fucking rich."

"So now I'm in charge."

"And it gets better," Siriano says. "You in fucking charge. I love it. So what, this is your way at getting back at me, except I did not know any of this."

"No," Pablo says. "I don't want a war."

"You don't want a war," the old man repeats. "Well, what do you think this is going to do?"

"Ensure you listen to what I have to say."

"What are you saying?"

"I'll cut you loose if you promise not to come back on us."

Siriano twists his face thinking about it. He rocks in his seat. "I think I can do that. That's why you did all this? Kidnapped me so we could have a chat?"

"There was more I wanted to say, but yeah, that about covers it. I figured I'd lay it out there, let you think about it, come back tomorrow and get your answer."

Siriano nods. "You know what Augustus's problem was?"

Pablo doesn't.

"Your face says no," Siriano says, "so let me leave you with something to think about, tit for tat. Augustus, he had a hard time with his friends. See, his friends were Julius's friends, and with Julius dead, they thought they'd be the ones in charge. Think about that. Think about the people around Alejandro who thought they'd be in charge."

Pablo stands, hand on the door. "I take it you'll think about it?"

"I'll think about it, but I'll tell you, I'm leaning toward 'yeah, sure, okay, why the fuck not?' But, remember this when I said I've worked with some dumb fucking people. The guy I told you about, he didn't think nothing about the cupcakes, but at the end of the day, the cupcakes were the reason he was caught—you need to think about the cupcakes."

CHAPTER TWELVE: FLAVIA SANCHEZ

THE GUNMEN COME FOR HER ON MONDAY AFTERnoon—two of them, meth heads—skinny white wraiths barely dressed. Flavia's would-be assassin wears a white stretched-out t-shirt and ripped blue jeans with flip-flops. He walks with a staggering swagger, somewhere between heavily intoxicated and whiteboy smooth. Gabino's would-be assassin is dressed in a green basketball jersey with holey blue jeans—he's the healthier looking of the two. Flavia's window is open, which is why she hears one of them sneeze as they approach. It causes her to check the mirror where she spots them. As they near Omar's old Buick, they split in two directions, and Flavia watches them in the mirror. She watches to see where they go, see what they're doing. She watches the one in the white t-shirt hang back rubbing at his nose and scratching at his forearms and face, picking bright red sores.

She doesn't like Gabino's driving, and after he showed up the other day at the automotive shop, she told Gabino that from now on she's driving. So she drove today, and today is the first time they've left the automotive shop. They left to get Gabino a snow cone to show their appreciation for him hanging out at the shop overnight and keeping an eye on Pablo. Gabino loves snow cones.

The other, Mr. Green Jersey, crosses the parking lot and rounds the car. When he passes the passenger window, he keeps his head locked straight and pointed forward as if it's in some invisible neck brace. A gun handle sticks out of the back of his waistband as he makes his way toward the snow cone shack. Gabino is inside. The man yanks open the door, steps inside, and disappears. The windows are too dark for Flavia to see inside. The door swings shut.

Flavia gathers her purse and slips her hand inside, her fingers searching for the reassuring cold metal of Omar's gun. The pads of her fingertips brush the rough plastic of the Glock's handle. Flavia slowly removes the nine-millimeter from the folds of the purse while keeping her eyes on the pale man in the white t-shirt. She crosses her arm over her body and lodges the muzzle of the gun against the driver's door. She positions the purse over her hand and arm to hide the gun.

The gunman glances at her in the mirror, his eyes locking with hers, staring now. He starts his lumbering amble towards her, scratching at himself. He tugs at his waistband to keep his pants from falling off his hollow body. The confrontation is unavoidable.

Flavia glances down at her phone in the center console cup holder. She could make a call. Does she have time? Could she warn Omar? Warn Gabino? Should she even try? She doesn't think of calling the police. That's never been an option. Alejandro was clear about that. Anyone who lived under his rule called him, not the authorities. He was the authority.

Flavia curses under her breath. She knew this would happen. Her husband told her not to worry, and she told him this would happen, told him there is no way they could keep a lid on this thing for long. The Siriano organization was bound to find out who did the kidnapping. She told him using Gabino's friends provided manpower but was a liability. They are young and dumb, and Flavia was never convinced they could keep their mouths closed especially if someone got a hold of them and forced them open.

What she didn't tell her husband was that she worried about Vega. She was worried about how he was there at the kidnapping, the main one with his finger on the trigger, ready to shoot; about how she doesn't trust him; and about how something is wrong. He's wrong. But she doesn't think Siriano will get to him, will make him talk. Vega is a lot of things, but he's not a talker. He'll keep his mouth shut. She worries about him for other reasons. Where do his loyalties lie? Where did he come from? Where did Pablo find him?

Flavia recognizes the man in the mirror for what he is. A killer. He's here to kill her. That's what his eyes say. Focused but blank. Soulless. A hired gun. Green Jersey is in charge, which tells her two things. One, they think Gabino is more important. And two, they underestimate her.

Flavia's eyes veer from the phone to the snow cone shack, thinking Gabino's love for snow cones may be the death of him and her. Again, she briefly considers calling him, to warn him, but she knows it won't do any good. It won't help. This will be over long before she can punch a number into the phone. If the gunmen are here, it means Siriano's bastard got a hold of someone, one of Gabino's friends, and frankly, she's surprised it took them this long. She expected some sort of reprisal sooner. She just didn't anticipate someone would be coming for her.

When her eyes return to the mirror, the man hasn't deviated from his course. He's at the rear of the Buick. He touches the lid of the trunk as he passes, walking up to the driver's side, strolling alongside the car like she's seen a dozen cops do on traffic stops. It makes her wonder if he's watched those videos too. Has he studied them like she suggested Gabino do so that he knows how to walk up the side of the car, protect himself, where to stand? Is that why he's doing it this way?

Flavia turns to her left. She'll face him. He won't surprise her. She bites down hard on her cheek to control her fear. Then, abruptly, he's in the window, appearing there as if he just blinked into existence, bringing the sudden smell of body odor and stale cigarette smoke.

Now that he's closer, Flavia can see the meth damage. His face is a red mess, pockmarked. His head's shaved smooth, and she spots the SS lightning bolts on the side of his neck, near the break between skull, neck and chin. She sees the green clover on his collar bone and the cursive writing trailing from the edge of his right eyebrow. She watches the sweat roll down the side of his head in big beads. His teeth pull on his lower lip, nibbling on the pink skin, drawing blood. He's high and his mind is racing a mile a minute. He can't speak, can't think of what to say, because he's thinking of hundreds of things to say as the bugs crawl under his skin. He's used to this, so he reverts to a tried-and-true tactic, a drug-fueled muscle memory.

"Do you have any money?" he asks, spitting the words while his eyes search the inside of the vehicle, studying her, scanning her from ponytail to button-up blouse, to blue jeans.

Does he see the gun? Does he know? Is he going to try to kill her? Or does she have it wrong?

She could be wrong.

Flavia forces herself to stay calm. Stay cool. Breathe. She furrows her brows. "Excuse me?"

"Yeah." He scratches at his shoulder. His fingernails are bitten to the quick and covered in black dirt. "Money, you know money. *Dinero*. I'm hungry. I wondered, I thought... Want to help me out? Surely, you got money if you're sitting here."

"I don't have any money."

He surprises her. "What about a kiss?" He smiles now, his thin skin stretched back at the edges making his face more skull-like than before.

The smile shows that he thinks he's clever. His drug-infused mind turns toward sex as it probably always does. That has been her experience with meth heads.

"Can I get one of those? I wouldn't mind kissing you. You're a pretty girl. A pretty girl. Smooth skin. Skinny. I like that. I like your hair." He tries to reach into the car with his dirty hand, swiping at her hair.

Flavia leans to the side to prevent him from touching her.

"That hair, I bet you like to have it pulled. *Ye-ha!*"

He reaches for her again, fingers whiffing through her hair, the black strands running across his fingertips. Flavia shakes her head and ducks out from under his hand, pulling hard away from him, without dislodging her gun, or revealing its position.

She reminds herself to stay calm, stay with it.

"No, you can't have a kiss," she barks.

Her blood's gushing, pounding in her ears, at her temples, behind her eyes, which are locked on his hands as her finger tightens on the trigger of the nine. Her thigh quivers, bouncing in place as every muscle fiber tenses within her, telling her to run.

"Come on, let's party," he says. "I got a room at this motel down the street. You and me. I'll go all night long... all day long. I bet you quit before I do. Let's see, dare you, triple dog dare you to suck my cock."

"I don't want to have sex with you," she insists. "I'm married."

"That's what I thought." The man scratches at himself with one hand while the other disappears behind his back. She watches the muscles of his shoulder bulge and strain as he reaches for something.

Her breath catches in her throat.

This is the moment.

This is it.

Then, she sees it. He starts to bring the revolver around the right side of his body, lazily like he's unsure of himself, thinking if he moves slowly she won't see him. She sees it all. And she's ready for him. He doesn't present the revolver yet. The slow movements mean hesitancy, and a quick read of his face says he has to be sure. This has to be the right person. He hides the revolver down at his side, behind his thigh, as he asks, "Flavia Sanchez, right?" Before moving to present the revolver.

Flavia doesn't answer with words or a nod, and she doesn't wait for him to fully raise his hand or the gun, she fires through her driver's side door, not once, but three times, the first two hit him, boring into his stomach. She doesn't know where the third goes. Maybe that one missed him. Maybe the door caught it or deflected it.

Her eyes blink rapidly, reasoning through the events. Her mind screams at her to leave.

The meth head doubles over as if she punched him in the nuts, and he lets out a high-pitched squeal. There's blood on the pavement, the shells are ejected, and she's tearing the gun from the door and planting it over the lip of the window, firing once unexpectedly in the process, which makes her flinch and jump in the seat. That bullet strikes the brick wall of a shop and drills into the pavement somewhere in the distance.

With his body bent at the waist, spasming, the man tries to straighten. She's on him now, settling the muzzle right on him, pivoting off the window lip, and firing until the gun clicks dry. The gun scratches the already ruined finish of the Buick. Flavia doesn't count the shots, and she can't be sure how many times she struck him, but he drops his revolver. It clanks against the pavement. He topples to the ground, legs underneath him, one at an awkward angle, hands groping at his body, at the white shirt blooming red, drenched in one spot. He groans loudly. His gurgled noises reveal he hadn't expected her to strike first.

Life's taught Flavia to bite, to be decisive and act. So that's what she does. She shoves the empty semi-automatic back into her purse and throws the purse into the passenger seat. Her heart thumps against her chest wall. Her eyes shift from the meth head to the purse to the door of the snow cone place in one surreal movement, seamless and disconnected with time and space, the edges a faded blue blur. She flicks her wrist to turn the keys in the ignition and slams on the horn, laying on it with her left hand as the car comes to life. Belts under the hood squealing, slipping, squealing, and the engine growls in response to her command.

Just as the engine turns over, two shots ring out from inside the snow cone shack and punch through the front window. The shack's door flies open, straining at its hinges. The upper portion of the glass door breaks as Gabino scrambles out of the snow cone shop, ducking, body low, taking large lunging strides with his barely tied tennis shoes. Something Omar's teased Gabino would be the death of him.

Gabino scrambles for the passenger side of the vehicle and loses a shoe in the process. He makes it to the passenger door, tugging at the handle with an outstretched hand before realizing he lost a shoe. Squatted with his white sock pointed toward the door, he pivots to retrieve the shoe, but the second gunman, with blood flowing from his nose and down his shirt, appears in the door of the snow cone shack, gun in hand. Flavia doesn't wait to see what type of gun he has; all she sees is the black barrel. He fires twice. Gabino drops to the rough pavement, his hands and feet out wide as if he's doing a wide stance pushup. The shots miss. Flavia throws the car in reverse to get out of the parking spot. The gunman's head jerks her way. He realizes that she's not dead and that his cohort has failed. Her foot lets off the brake. The car lurches backward. Spinning her hand over the wheel, she cuts hard, pulling the vehicle's nose to her right and away from Gabino, who's up now, clambering back to his feet, his gold chain dangling from his neck and swaying with his actions, hands touching the ground like a linebacker at the line of scrimmage, as he crawls back toward the car.

The gunman in the green jersey steps out of the snow cone shack, gun still raised. He looks at his groaning cohort withering on the ground near where Flavia had been parked. His eyes flicker back to Flavia, and the gun drops some. He aims for her. She sees the muzzle flash but hears nothing. Two bullets impact the door behind her. Her foot alternates from the gas to the brake as she shifts from reverse to drive, and she shifts back, foot hammering the gas.

Open-mouthed and breathing hard, Gabino knows better than to try to enter the vehicle through a door. Instead, he hurtles himself onto the Buick's hood; his hands grab ahold of the windshield wipers; he tries to secure himself to the hood like a tick attaching to skin as Flavia punches the gas. One of the windshield wipers breaks off in Gabino's hand. He stares at it in disbelief and tosses it to the side, nearly sliding off the hood in the process. He digs the tips of his fingers down on the slight overhang of the hood near the windshield. He holds on tight and stares at Flavia through the windshield, his face a mask of terror.

She focuses on driving. Determined, tongue pressed against the side of her mouth, with the burnt smell of rubber in her nostrils as the tires spin on the concrete. She presses hard on the accelerator and directs the vehicle away from the snow cone shack and out of the parking lot. The vehicle bounces over a parking median and down a curb. The Buick charges out of the parking lot and onto the main road.

The gunman grows smaller in Flavia's rearview.

Gabino struggles to hang on, but he manages until she's approximately half a mile away. She comes to a rough screeching halt and reaches for the passenger door at the same time. Popping it and pushing it open. Gabino scampers off the hood, half sliding, half scooting, and hits the ground. He dives into the passenger side as Flavia hammers the gas again and makes for a getaway. The door nearly shuts on Gabino's stockinged foot as she leaves black marks on the pavement.

CHAPTER THIRTEEN: SONNY ROWAN

THE GIRL WALKS IN AND TAKES A GLANCE AROUND the room, surveying her surroundings like an expert, so smoothly in fact, if Sonny didn't know better, she'd be just another woman stepping into the darkness of this bar, pausing to peel off her sunglasses, sunlight outside behind her, turned onto full afternoon blast. But Sonny knows better, and he knows this is her way of buying time to look around, helping her be aware. Like all the cops he's met, she's hyper-vigilant. Her eyes land on him, and she struts over to his spot at the bar, straddling up to the bar next to him, taking her place on the stool.

The first thing Sonny says: "I heard you smoked, so I thought this place would work, maybe buy you a cigar, maybe some whiskey, figured you might need to be comfortable to talk to me," getting right to it, which is the best way with these cop types.

The woman—not a girl, she's too woman to be a girl, even if she's short and petite—doesn't speak right away, choosing instead to give him a once over. Her eyes glance down at the whiskey sitting in front of him. It's fine. It gives Sonny a moment to take a mental snapshot of her.

She's wearing something similar to what she wore in the videos of the kidnapping, but the videos didn't do her beauty any justice. She's a black girl, dark skin, the type of skin just now making it onto TV, and the world's better for it. She's beautiful because she doesn't play into her beauty. Her skin is smooth and creamy in texture, especially on the cheeks, which are rounded orbs, shiny in the light, in a way that makes them look like a master's sculpture—God's handiwork. Her dark hair's pulled back in something functional, and her expression is neutral, if not bordering on disinterested.

Sonny didn't know how to dress, so he chose something simple: a bowling type shirt, black with a broad white stripe down the front and blue jeans.

The woman is silent.

"I took the liberty of ordering you a drink." Sonny motions to the bartender, who picks up a glass, fills it with whiskey, and slides it across. "Whiskey straight up… you're not working, are you?"

The woman shakes her head once.

"Good," Sonny says. "I didn't think so, considering it's Saturday and you're a fed, but you never know."

The woman is silent.

"You're not much of a talker, are you?" Sonny asks, trying to get something out of her.

The woman picks up the whiskey, lifts it to her nose, takes a quick sniff with her perky button-nose, and sips it.

"I don't know what you like," Sonny says, "so I figured you could start with what I'm having, and if you don't like it, then I'll get you something else, but I don't want you feeling like you have to be here."

"I don't," she says.

Two words, not much but enough to show some cracks in the dam.

"Alright, alright," Sonny says. "This isn't easy for me either, full disclosure. This ain't my thing." He takes a sip of whiskey. "So if it feels like I'm just getting to it, I am, in a way, but that's because I didn't peg you for someone who beats around the bush, not with someone like Bing talking about you the way he does."

"I like Bing," she says.

Three words, improvement.

"I have a whole bit I like to do," Sonny goes on, "bullshit I say to get people comfortable with me, get them started, get them talking."

"I do too," she says.

Still three words, but hey, they're talking now, a genuine back and forth. It's a full-blown conversation. Progress.

"Right," Sonny says. "I figured you did. Most of your types do… cops that is. Jesus, I'm screwing this up. This isn't my thing."

"It's not?"

"No," he stammers. "I'm more comfortable with sports figures. That's my thing. Always been my thing. Sure, I help out here and there, do the odd political piece, background on major stories, go talk to the widow whose husband died in that car crash—"

"Or plane crash."

Sonny shuts his eyes for a moment, pinches the bridge of his nose with his forefinger and thumb, then opens his eyes. "Or *that*… you've read my stuff?"

"Some of it," she says.

He resists asking her if she liked it, if it's any good.

"I liked some of it," she offers. "That piece with the swimmer, that was good."

"I liked that one too."

"But didn't that ESPN reporter do something on him, on that?"

"Oh yeah, she did," Sonny says, "but see, you have to look at mine as sort of a follow-up, see what's happening in his life since that moment. I mean, it was big deal. And she used to screw the guy, so how objective is she going to be?"

"You've never … screwed anyone…?" She lets the question fade for effect, but there's something in her voice like she's interested, and if he said yes, she'd be even more interested, and he can't blame her because he's interested too.

God, look at her, who wouldn't be?

Sonny laughs and shakes his head. "I'm not answering that question. Even if it is a no, I don't feel like I need to answer that question."

"Cause that's not how this works?" she says, finishing where he was going with it but not sure if he could say those words to someone like her.

"No," he says. "I'm here to ask you questions, not the other way around."

"You haven't asked any."

She's right; he hasn't. "Okay, well how about this: what do you like to be called?"

"What do you mean?" she asks. "Like in bed or something? Don't you think that's a little forward of you?"

She's playing with him, smiling.

"Not like that," Sonny laughs, leaning into the humor. "What name should I use for the piece?"

"Use my name," she says. "What name would you like to use? "Her lips stretch wider, showing she's enjoying this now, comfortable with him. She bites her lower lip, "I could suggest a few; make it easier for you."

"I will use your name," Sonny quickly says. "What I want to know is what you want to be called. What name do you want me to use?"

"Kelly," she says. "What's it matter? You're the one writing the story. Call me whatever you like. Ms. Chambers. Marshal Chambers, whatever you want."

"I like Kelly. It's a good name. A strong name, especially with the last name. Say everything together, Deputy US Marshal Kelly Chambers, makes me think of power."

"That's the idea, isn't it?"

"Some people like to be called different things. I want to make sure I call you what you want to be called. It makes the piece more *personable*. If I'm referring to you as just Chambers, well then, it puts too much distance from our readers. Makes it sound like any other fluff piece. We want them to learn about you, not some automaton bureaucrat."

"Oxymoron."

Sonny holds up his hands. "Woah, you're right. My bad."

"But I get what you're trying to say," she adds. "What name are you going to use for Siriano?"

"Probably Russell."

"Not Rosario?"

"That's his legal name, but you and I both know, as well as anyone who's lived in this city and not buried their head in the sand that it's Russell. He doesn't like Rosario. Like at his last trial, he interrupted the official reading of the record—"

"You were there?" she asks, seemingly surprised.

He throws out the next bit for points. "So were you." He pauses to see if he gets a reaction; she takes a drink, eyes on him. "I saw you. You sat in the corner."

"Why were you there if this isn't your thing?"

"Filling in for the guy that was supposed to be there. He was sick, got asked to go and see what I could see, hear what I hear—my specialty if you ask me."

"So you're good?" Kelly says. "If you remember me, then you are good."

"I'm paid to be the best," Sonny says, "but I'll take good. What I was saying, Siriano cleared his throat and said, 'It's Russell… Russ if you want somethin' shorter.' Stopped the Assistant District Attorney cold. The judge had him repeat it, asking him, 'What was that?' and then admonishing him for speaking out of turn. Dressed him down in front of the jury."

"Which didn't make sense to me," she says, "asking him to repeat what he said and, then, admonishing him. It's like when I have a guy at gunpoint and I yell freeze, and then, I tell him to turn around. Like which is it? Do I want him to stand still or turn around?"

"Anyways, the name thing, I want to call you what you like to be called. If you're unavailable for comment, i.e. I'm unable to ask you this question, like with Siriano, since he's kidnapped, then I rely on the official record, interviews, court documents, that type of thing."

"So when he stands up and says I'm Russell or Russ that makes your job easier."

"It does. There's none of the guessing I sometimes have to do. Take this guy my daughter ran into the other day, for example."

"You have a kid?"

Sonny nods. "She's not a kid anymore. She's an adult. Not much younger than you are."

"You know how old I am?"

"Mid-thirties," Sonny holds up a hand as if to say hold on. "I'm not going to tell you the exact age, but it's going to be printed. Bing told me. You want to confirm?"

"My age?" she asks and shakes her head. "Nope, not at all."

Sonny didn't think so. "This guy, he was a pitcher for a local team back in the day. My kiddo and I, we played hooky and went to the game. Well, she skipped school. I was able to do a write-up about it for work."

"Like take your daughter to work day," she says. She digs cigarettes from her suit coat pocket, a pack, knocking one loose, and Sonny supplies the flame, the bar's butane torch used for the cigars.

Holding the flame to the tip of her cigarette, the blue-orange jet whirring in intensity, Sonny smiles. "This guy, he makes it special. Does something I've never seen before, or since. He hits the cycle and throws a no-hitter."

"What's a cycle?"

"You hit a single, a double, and a triple—this guy hit a home run in the eighth just for the hell of it," Sonny says. "I don't have to explain what any of that is, do I? And I assume you know what a no-hitter is? It's sorta in the name."

"What's a home run?" she asks, playing with him again.

"I'll take that as a no." Sonny pauses to take a drink, urging her to do the same. He toasts to new friendships, and they drink before going back to what he was saying. "But what I'm gettin' at is that this guy does that, and I want to write a piece about him. I did. I wrote a great little piece, but only after it's published, do I find out he likes to be called what they call him on the field."

"What do you mean?"

"His name's DiMaggio, but he goes by Maggie; that's what his teammates call him. I didn't use Maggie in the piece. I thought that might be too informal, and the editor thought so too. This is one of those few times I was wrong. I find out later he likes to be called Maggie."

"This bothers you?"

"It does. I want to be right."

"But you weren't wrong."

Sonny's wrist is against the bar, and he motions with his hand. "But I could've done better, been closer to the truth."

"I know what you mean," she says. "It's like that with us in an investigation. We know what happened, but it's like a zero-curve. You can only get so close to the truth; you can always do better."

"Just like that."

"What's the pitcher's real name?"

"Maurizio DiMaggio."

"Jesus, no wonder he goes by Maggie, that's a mouthful," Kelly says. "So your daughter ran into him the other day?"

"She did. She saw him..." Sonny's voice trails off. How's he explain this to a cop? Less is more, he guesses. "... saw him while she was getting coffee."

"And let me guess." Kelly takes a turn at reading him, gauging his personality. "You want to see if he was: A. offended at being called DiMaggio throughout the piece; B. what he's doing now; and C. if he even remembers the piece you did ... or the game?"

"That's the idea," Sonny says. "I'd love to sit down and talk to him about that game."

"Do you think he'd remember it? I mean, it was a while ago if your kid's the same age as me and she was in school then."

"I think he would remember, yes."

"I suppose a lot of those types are like that, then. They like to talk about the glory days. A lot of Uncle Frank's friends are like that, telling cop stories around the fire while drinking a beer."

"They are, they remember games, sometimes better than most people who watched them, sometimes not, but what they remember and don't remember varies from time to time. I imagine it's the same with witnesses. Has been for all the ones I've interviewed. They remember weird things, get big things wrong. Not always but sometimes."

"Like taking red for blue and vice versa," she says. "I know what you mean."

"To be honest."

"I thought you were...Say, how old are you?"

"What?"

"You know my age."

Sonny tries to deflect. "I've been at this awhile, but I had her young if it means anything."

"So in your sixties... fifties... forties?" Kelly stair-steps her answer, pausing between each decade to see if he says anything.

"Fifty," he says.

"And she's what?"

"Thirty-something."

"You don't remember?"

"I forget those types of things."

"How's she take that?"

"We don't have that type of relationship."

"Well, what type do you have?" Kelly asks before realizing she's teased him a statement too far. "I guess, you're like those guys you talk to. You remember certain things but not some of the details."

Sonny shrugs. "You could say that," he says. "I was young when I met her mom, like still in high school. By the time she was a toddler, I was chasing stories, worked my way up, more or less."

Kelly inhales on the cigarette. Releases some smoke. "This feels like a date."

"Excuse me?"

"I feel like this is a blind date," she says. "Like we were set up. Bing, through Uncle Frank, set me up with you to talk to you about something extremely personal. To me, that's what a blind date is."

He hadn't thought about it like that. "You could say that I guess."

She finishes her drink in one gulp staring at him and then looks away.

Both of them fall silent, stealing glances at each other while letting the mood of the place, the laid-back easy feel, wash over them. The bartender refreshes their drinks for another eighteen bucks of Sonny's money.

She finishes the second drink and sits it on the bar, eyes flickering towards his drink, a challenge, playful. So Sonny finishes his with a snap of his wrist, throwing the alcohol into the back of his throat.

She orders the third round, telling the bartender to let her pick it up this time.

Sonny's wallet is thankful.

Watching the bartender do his thing, filling their recently empty glasses in front of them to save on dishwashing, she says, "That guy you were talking about, Maggie or whatever, are you going to do a story on him like you're doing on me?"

She ashes the cigarette into the ashtray lying between them. The bartender walks away.

"I want to," Sonny responds, thankful for the turn in the conversation. "I have to find him first."

"Why him?"

"Other than the fact he did—"

"Yeah, other than that, what makes him so interesting?"

"His father used to be a cop," Sonny says. "I learned a lot about him for that piece."

"Used to be?"

"Killed in the line of duty," Sonny tells her. "Happened when Maggie was a kid, eighteen or something."

"You don't remember like you don't remember your kid's birthday?" busting his balls about it, but Sonny can take it.

He smiles. "Yeah, something like that. His father tried to stop a robbery. Maggie was playing at a tournament down the road."

"That sucks," she comments.

"You have a father?"

The coldness returns to Kelly's face stealing the lightness from her voice. "I have Uncle Frank," telling Sonny more in those few words than anything she could have said.

Course, he can't use any of it. It'll be supposition, not fact, but the way she says it, it's a fact.

Then, the coldness fades from Kelly's face. "What do you think about what happened?"

"What I think doesn't matter."

"It must if you're here talking to me."

"I think you didn't get a fair shake in this whole deal."

"Meaning you've already formed an opinion before doing any work on this piece. Is that how you normally do things?"

"No," Sonny says. "I usually wait and see how things shake out. Write what falls out. Falls on the page, so to say. But that's the going trend in news right now, write with a narrative take."

"You don't like that?"

"I like to see where the story takes me," he says. "Sure, I'll start with an idea of what might've happened, a hypothesis, but as the research and work go on, I find myself open to letting the narrative come out of the facts instead of putting the facts in the narrative."

"I see, so like what I do?" she says.

"Yes, like what you do."

"None of that bullshit tells me what you think happened."

Sonny raises an eyebrow and tells her plainly, "I think you did the right thing."

"So you don't think I'm a coward?"

"Do you think you're a coward?" he asks, reading into her question.

"I don't know. That's how they're playing it everywhere else."

"If I thought that, do you think I would have wanted to know what to call you? Take time to make sure I get your name right?"

"You aren't a coward, are you?" she asks. "You just do things differently."

Sonny shakes his head. "I don't think you are a coward. I think you did the right thing."

"In calling you?"

Is she flirting with him, or is he just reading into it?

Sonny transitions from a shake to a nod. "Yeah, in calling me," he says. "Are you flirting with me?"

"Are you opposed to it?" she flirts, coming on a little stronger. She smiles broader than she has the entire time she's been sitting here.

Sonny reaches over, and Kelly lets him; his fingers caress the end of the cigarette near her lips, almost so that the backs of his fingers are touching her lips. He plucks the cigarette from her mouth, places it in his, and inhales.

Sonny shakes his head . "No, I don't mind."

"Good, because if I'm going to trust you." Kelly pauses to take the cigarette back from him; she inhales. "Then I might as well get something out of this in return."

"So will you talk to me about what happened?"

"Like this is a blind date?"

"If you want to think about it like that then sure."

"Answer the question," Kelly demands, circling back to her earlier question. Sonny sees where this is going. "Have you ever screwed—your word—anyone you've interviewed?"

Sonny thinks about the time the tennis star came to the interview, wearing that tight, skimpy tennis skirt, except there weren't any bottoms, and how when she crossed her legs, she looked him dead in the eye and said, *I'm a huge fan*, which meant, the interview ran a few hours longer than he'd expected.

"Yes," he says, straight-faced.

"Good," she says. "Then you won't have any problems with what happens after we're done."

CHAPTER FOURTEEN: MAURIZIO DIMAGGIO

MAGGIE ARRIVES AT THE DIVE BAR TO MEET WILSON Sunday night. He didn't intend to see the man so soon after meeting with him. That's not how things are done. Those aren't the rules. But Wilson sent Kevin to tell Maggie that he needed to scoot on over to Harjo's, a bar Maggie's somewhat familiar with, a generational staple, to have a chat with the big man. Kevin said Wilson's there waiting for him and wants to talk.

Kevin didn't say what Wilson wanted to talk about, but Maggie's pretty sure it has to be about his father. Wilson knows better than to bug him over the Brandy thing. Maggie will find him. That's a guarantee. It's done when it's done.

In fact, Maggie just obtained an apartment number from an old source for someone who resembles Brandy and is using the last name the wife gave him. The first name isn't Brandy or Branson; it's Bradford, and the similarities are too blatant to ignore. It's Brandy's old neighborhood. His mom lives around the corner. It's like Maggie's come full circle looking for the man. He's hiding in the neighborhood where Maggie started his search, which took him all over the nation. To think Brandy was there even then burns like hot coals in Maggie's stomach.

Maggie pushes those thoughts to the side for now. For Wilson to want to see him so soon after their last meeting means something's happened or changed with his father's status, and he wants to update Maggie. He asked for Maggie's help because Maggie's good at this sort of thing. It's what someone in restoration lives for. Fix the problem. This isn't a conversation you can have over the phone. Phones are dangerous. Too easy to record. And if the federal government wanted Siriano Senior to appear before a Grand Jury like the papers say, Wilson shouldn't talk on the phone either. Maggie wouldn't. Everything he does is face-to-face. It makes a reluctant world move slower when all it wants to do is spin off the carousel. If Maggie were under that type of pressure, he'd just leave town. Get away for a while, let things cool down, but then again, Maggie's father's dead, not kidnapped. So the situation's different.

Maggie enters the bar and looks around. The place is what one would expect to see where everyone knows everyone's name, and the lights rarely shine brightly in the dimly lit room. Neon signs decorate one wall, and a shuffleboard set up is on the other. Rose tinted glass everywhere, wooden paneling, and some pool tables. Maggie finds Wilson seated at the u-shaped bar in the middle of the room, his eyes on the pool tables. A billiard break, a sharp crack rises over the loud music and the roar of voices; the place is fairly crowded. Maggie knows a little about its history, how the place acts as neutral ground for the Tulsa criminal element. It's in a suburb, on the city's far edge, which is probably why Wilson's here and not at Kevin's bar or another establishment owned by the Sirianos. Same reason as the phones.

Maggie marches over to the bar and takes the empty stool next to Wilson, who is slumped forward, head hanging over a tall glass of what smells and looks like cheap whiskey. He's still wearing his black suit, collar undone, shirt wrinkly: a mess. This is the man Maggie expected to find back at the apartment, worried and frazzled about his missing father; it's not the man he encountered.

With his hands on his forehead, Wilson shifts and glances over at Maggie from under heavy brows. "You came."

Maggie settles onto the stool. "You asked me to."

"I didn't think you would."

"You sent Kevin."

What he doesn't say is that when Maggie returned to his little one-bedroom apartment, Kevin was inside, sitting at his table, waiting, trying his best to appear menacing. Maggie's heard the stories about Wilson's gopher, about how the Fred Durst wannabe likes to break into people's homes and shit on people's floors. Since he's been back in town, Maggie's heard other things too, rumors, like how Kevin somehow fucked over both an old friend and his ex-boyfriend, and how it had something to do with Wilson's bid for the throne.

"I still didn't think you would," Wilson says.

"Why's that?"

Wilson stares at him for a moment. Desperation flickers across his features. A plea for help. Suspicion. Something. Then, Wilson says, "We just had a meeting that's all. You don't make it a habit of meeting more than a handful of times, at least that's always been Jackie C.'s policy. And you made it pretty clear I'd know that the job was done when you tell me it's done. Sending Kevin around was a long shot, but I had to try."

Wilson doesn't come out and say it's about his father, but his words communicate the message. This meeting's about his father.

Doesn't say he's desperate either but same difference.

Maggie says, "What do you want to talk about?"

"You ever meet Jobe?" Wilson motions toward the bartender.

Maggie looks at the native man with dark graying hair cut almost into a mohawk working behind the bar. "No."

"Jobe owns this place." Wilson's finger circles the rim of his whiskey glass. "Used to be his grandmother's. It's important you know that. Know this is about family. Of course, you knew that didn't you?" Wilson points a finger at Maggie, the tip glistens. "He always liked you better. I hated it, but I guess I understood it. I… I represented his past. You… well you represented something different. He liked that."

Maggie says nothing.

"My father brought me here," Wilson says, "for my first drink, the first time, and a few times after. I was young. Younger than I should have been being in a place like this. Not old enough to drink by a long shot. Closer to enlistment age, but even then, I don't know if I could have lied and convinced the recruiter to let me in."

Maggie searches his mind, recalling what he knows about Siriano and his relationship with his son. Wilson has several sisters. Maggie dated one once; none of them are related to Siriano. Wilson's mother and Siriano had a thing when she was a dancer and cocktail girl at one of his clubs, and Siriano quietly supported the mother of four because she bore him a son when Siriano's legitimate wife, who divorced him when he went to prison, couldn't.

Wilson grips the glass in front of him as if it tried to slink away. He lifts it to his mouth and sips the whiskey. "He came back into my life when I was a teenager," he says. "I was a shithead, angry at the world. A dumb fuck. Fat too, but that didn't last long. That's the first thing he said to me when he came back around. I'd just gotten into it with my mother and my oldest sister Sara. I had told my mother to fuck off and stormed out of the house. He happened to stop by after I'd stepped out the back door to try to cool off. You could say I was feeling my oats, but I don't know what the fuck that means, but know what it means, you know?"

Maggie does, but he remains quiet. Better to let the boss speak.

"There I am, fucking seething, and here he comes out the back door, this fucking guy, wearing this charcoal-colored suit but wearing it in this real relaxed way. Like he just stepped off the set of *Miami Vice* or something. White shirt underneath. Loafers but no socks. Rolled up sleeves. He sits down on the back porch. Takes his time about it, flicking the jacket back, swiping at the wooden steps as if his hand could sweep away all the dirt. Not wanting to risk ruining his shit. Sat down, stared at me, rubbing those hands together like people with arthritis do. Like when you're washing your fucking hands. Get all the dirt off. Motions me over with a twist of his hand. He wore so much gold I didn't know what were and what weren't fingers. Fucking blinded me with all that gold. He's since stopped wearing all that shit. Course, seeing him for the first time, something like that, a guy like him, I didn't move right away. I didn't know what to fucking do. I wasn't angry anymore. I'd forgotten it. He motions again. Says, 'Hey, Dumb Fuck, when I tell you to come here, you fucking come here.' Said it just like that. Sounded just like that."

"Did you go over to him?"

Wilson nods. "Yeah, I did," he says. "I sat next to him and stared at the fucking ground. I didn't know what to say. What do you say to a guy like him? I didn't know who he was. He didn't look like a cop, but with the fight we had, my mom and I, I thought maybe my mom called the cops. I thought, maybe this guy's some detective she knows from working the clubs. Some guy that is sweet on her. I had no idea who he was. Still don't, if you get what I mean. Then, he turns to me and says, 'You and your mom fightin'?' I told him no, and he rears back and slaps me across the face, a backhanded thing. All that fucking gold hurt. Cut my cheek open right here." Wilson points to his left cheek. Even in the low lighting of Harjo's, Maggie sees the faint outline of a faded scar. "He was quiet after that for some time, staring at the yard. I let the blood weep down my cheek. Then he says, 'Good, you're not a pussy. I like that.'"

"What did he want?" Maggie asks, remembering the first time he met Siriano, a chance encounter. Maggie mopping the tile floor at the pharmacy, Siriano snapping his fingers, demanding kid Maggie jump behind the counter, put in his lotto ticket numbers. Maggie didn't work the counter, and yet that didn't stop history from happening.

Wilson sips the whiskey, his eyes staring off into space. He cocks his head to the side and continues with his story. "He asked, 'You know who I am?' To which I said, 'How the fuck would I know something like that?' He told me he was my father. I asked him how he knew that, and he told me to shut the fuck up and listen. He said my mother works at his club, which I kinda figured with all that gold. Had to be someone rich. Cops don't have gold like that."

"What's the point of all this?" Maggie asks. "Why are you telling me all this."

"Thought you wanted to hear about him and me."

"That's the past. It's done."

"Sometimes you have to understand the past to know why what's happening is happening," Wilson says. "All of this could have been avoided had he come to me sooner, had he said, 'You know, Dumb Fuck, you're a shit head of a son, but I need you on the outside. I need you to run things.' He shouldn't have ever let Renaldo rise as far as he did. That guy..." Wilson shakes his head. "I just need you to understand why it's all happening because I need to understand it."

"And what's happening? You getting drunk, drinking... what are you drinking? Well, whiskey?"

"I just wanted you to know how he came to be in my life," Wilson says. "He appeared. Sorta like he appeared in your life. It's funny; a guy like him, once he is in my life, in your life, it was like he never *wasn't* in my life. Invested in me. Taught me. Loved me if he knows how to love. I think he knows affection but not love. I don't think that man's ever loved. My mother, she loved. He covets. Takes. Possesses. Uses. He has fondness for possessions, things, but not love. But when you haven't had a father, well, that's love. I went from barely having clothes to wear, having to adapt t-shirts and shit my sisters had and passed down to me, to not wanting for nothing. In fact, although my mother was uneasy about it all, he sorta adopted all of us. My sisters looked at him like an estranged uncle come back into our lives."

"They didn't have their own father?"

"Who the fuck cares about him," Wilson says, bitter, "he was never really a part of their lives. He was the reason for their being after pumping my mom with his fucking seed; he left after the twins came along. Sara was..." Wilson's eyes dart to the side, pausing to think of her age. "She was two ... three, I don't remember. Twins come along and he bails because he can't handle it. Who does that? I mean, I get it if the guy dies, or there's a divorce, but who the fuck just runs out in the middle of the night on a single mom with three kids. But my mom, she was a strong woman. She raised me as best she could, which wasn't all that great. She was only like twenty years older than me, so she's out there trying to live the life of a young woman, but she has four kids. Can you imagine? Imagine what life's like working the club? Dancing every night, taking care of kids all day? I can't. She's a strong woman, and when Russ started coming around, she breathed a sigh of relief, not because she entertained any hopes he would come into her life and shower her with love, but ... she wasn't alone, you know?"

Maggie nods. "Why did you send Kevin around?"

Whatever vulnerability was displayed on Wilson's face, the openness etched into his features, evaporates. "I need your help."

"With what?"

"I don't need you to find my father," Wilson says. "Not anymore, so you can stop looking."

"I've barely started," Maggie says. "Still trying to find Brandy. That's the job you hired me for."

"Don't be such a hard ass," Wilson says. "I got a phone call a couple hours ago. Seems all this may be over soon. As long as no one screws it up."

"What kind of phone call?"

"The call was from them, whoever it is that took my father."

"How do you know that?"

Wilson looks at him again; the same look as before crosses his face. "They said some things only my father would have said."

Maggie pushes him harder. "Like what?"

"Like invoking my father's contingency plan, using the code we came up with, telling me to come here," Wilson says. "My father always said if something happened to him, being in the life he was in, he planned for shit like this, or if something ever happened to me, he would call this phone number." Wilson points to the phone behind the bar.

Jobe motions to the phone. "Been the same number since the place opened."

Wilson continues, "Jobe's grandmother was always fond of my father. Guess he invested in this place."

"She told me I couldn't refuse a Siriano." Jobe adds, "You need anything else?"

"Get my ... friend a whiskey," Wilson states.

Jobe does while Wilson explains, "The phone call was supposed to let me know it's him. This business, you can't trust people, not like you want to and not like you should. Think about all those made men back East. Think about how when the government really started cracking down on them. They couldn't help themselves, jumped at the opportunity to turn state or fed witness. Climbed over the others like crabs in a fucking pot, all pulling each other down, but all trying to crawl the fuck out."

Maggie sips the whiskey. "When he calls this number, then what?"

The phone across the way rings, a shrill sound, catching Wilson's attention. He doesn't say anything. Jobe answers the phone, says a few words, and places the receiver back on the base.

Wilson's mind turns to something else, distracted.

Maggie asks again, trying to figure out how he could help him, "He calls this phone and then what?"

Wilson finishes his whiskey and sets the glass on the table. "They said, 'Know the place where your father told you to take a call?' and I told them I did. They said go there and wait for a call. I asked why, and they told me, it's so I know it's legit."

Maggie tries something different. "So you're waiting for a phone call?"

"I'm waiting for them, yeah..." Wilson's voice drifts away as if something's wrong.

Maggie picks up on it. It explains Wilson's inability to answer any of Maggie's questions. "What's the problem?"

Wilson is quiet. After a moment, he says, "I hit them back."

"Hit them how?"

"Vega found out who they were," Wilson announces. "I should have told you, but like you said, you're looking for Brandy. I figured I'd let you be my control or some shit, verify the information, an independent source."

"You could have said something."

"Would have screwed up the experiment."

"Why tell me now?"

"Vega's guys screwed up."

"Tell me what happened," Maggie says.

Wilson's appearance makes sense now. He gets a phone call from the kidnappers, which can only mean one thing, they want to work out a deal, and then, his new bodyguard did something to screw it up.

"Vega hired some low-level hitters," Wilson says. "Guys not associated with me, per se. You see the news footage of my pops being taken?"

"I did," Maggie says. He watched several times. Noticed the female driver and wondered why the news didn't talk about her. It was her long dark hair. He noticed something else, a bracelet on the lead gunman's wrist, but he doesn't mention it to Wilson.

"Vega found out who those guys were," Wilson says. "Said he heard about one of them bragging about it, so he started asking around. They were all like nineteen years old or something. Stupid kids. Couldn't keep their mouths shut."

Not all of them, but Maggie doesn't say this.

"These kids run some fucked up street gang, so Vega paid a few of them a visit."

"How many did you get?"

"Three," Wilson says. "Two escaped. There was a shootout."

Maggie fills in the rest. "So now you're worried. The kidnappers want to open a dialogue, and you just shot a bunch of them."

Wilson slaps his chest. "I didn't shoot no one."

"But that doesn't change the fact that you hit them back," Maggie says. "So who were they?"

"Who do you think?" Wilson says. "Alejandro's old crew, or what's left of it."

That makes sense to Maggie, but there are other things that don't. "What'd they tell you on the phone?"

"Said they took my father in response to Renaldo's cowboy antics."

"That you had nothing to do with?" Maggie offers.

Wilson pauses before answering. "Sirianos didn't, that's for sure. We had a good working relationship with Alejandro. Why would we want him dead?"

"Father getting out of prison," Maggie says. "Shake things up. Take control of the city again under one power. Been awhile. Mexicans running most of the drugs. Everyone else just sells for them. I could see your father having a problem with it."

"You think my father would take on the cartels?"

"He's safer here than in Mexico," Maggie says. "And I think he would. I think him getting out worried some people. Sure did the federal government."

Wilson waves his hand. "My father likes money."

"Meaning what?"

"That's not going to happen."

"You sure?"

Wilson rolls his top lip under his teeth. "I'm sure." Then, he says, "So now you know the predicament."

Maggie summarizes the conversation. "You hit them, and you want your father back, but you worry that striking back may have jeopardized your father's release."

Wilson nods. "Vega says not to worry about it. Says they shouldn't play these games if they don't want to get hurt."

"Says they should have expected this?" Maggie asks.

Wilson crinkles his brows. "Yes, he said that."

"I'll say this once. I couldn't tell you in the other setting. You shouldn't trust Vega."

"Why?" Wilson adds. "He came highly recommended."

"I'm not going to argue with you. Jackie C. taught me a lot of things. One of them was reading people, and the other was reading situations. I'm reading him and the situation. Don't trust him."

Wilson snaps his fingers for Jobe to bring him another whiskey. Jobe fulfills the order.

After taking a sip, Wilson asks, "Are you jealous?"

"Jealous? What would I have to be jealous of?"

"Me taking over, my father not needing you."

"You think I wanted to be your father's son?"

"You wanted to be someone's son."

Wilson's trying to upset him. He's losing it so why shouldn't everyone else.

"I'll find Brandy," Maggie says. "When that's done, I'm done with you."

Wilson smiles a wicked smile. "I hurt your feelings. Are you going to cry? Cry about your dead daddy?"

Maggie grips the under edge of the bar. "When this is over, don't call me. Lose my number."

"You want out?" Wilson says.

Maggie is quiet.

"Fine, do this one thing, and I'll never fuck with you again. No skin off my back. That's for sure. Whatever these fuckers want, I'm sure they're going to want a meeting. I want you there. My father would expect me to bring you in on this. He's always liked you."

"Which you've resented."

Wilson glares at him. "He's always liked you, and he'd expect me to bring you in to help out. Do that and find Brandy, and you and I are done. I won't call you. I won't use you for nothing."

"I'll think about it."

Wilson's about to say something, but then, the phone rings.

CHAPTER FIFTEEN: KELLY CHAMBERS

KELLY WATCHES THE MAN SLIP BEHIND THE BUICK, a run-down, dilapidated piece of shit, with bullet holes in the driver's side door, cracking the front windshield, and lining the hood. He's a Hispanic man, wearing a navy-blue track suit with white stripes down the shoulders and arms, looping back under the arms and extending down his sides from armpit to waist, possibly Adidas, with a white wife beater underneath, the zipper halfway up his chest. The wife beater looks as white and bold as Superman's S. The man's body and height are average. His thick black glasses and a bald head that glistens in the sun complete the well-off mechanic look.

Kelly watches him from the front seat of her white Impala parked away from the main part of the Walmart parking lot, which is heavy with traffic, both vehicle and foot. It's midday, and the sun's warmed the interior of her car. Kelly's windows are halfway down, which is letting in a pleasant breeze flowing through the cabin. A half-eaten sandwich rests on the crest of her dashboard, wedged against the windshield glass baking the outside of the sandwich, spreading germs, not that she's going to eat it anyway. It's all part of the illusion. She isn't the only law here. Several others sit in various positions, all watching the Buick and the bald man getting into it.

The radio in a cup holder of her center console buzzes as Pat says, "Look alive."

Kelly flicks her eyes from the Buick to the radio and back again, wondering why the man came back for the car.

"Why not leave it?" she asks to herself. "Why come retrieve it?"

"What was that?" Uncle Frank says from the passenger seat. He is leaned back in the seat, cup of coffee in his hand resting comfortably on the bend of one knee. He has his cowboy hat pulled down low over his eyes. He was sleeping, or at least, Kelly thought he was sleeping. He hasn't moved for more than an hour. She knows because periodically she would look over for the fluctuations in his mustache to tell the difference between him awake and not moving to him asleep and not moving. The differences are slight and require a keen eye.

Kelly glances at the unmoving mustache. "The car," she questions, "why come back for it?"

"I suspect there's a reason." Uncle Frank's face is hidden under the rim of his cowboy hat, the whiskers bouncing with his pronouncement.

Kelly rolls her eyes and turns back to the man in the Buick, fiddling around somewhere inside. "I know there's a reason."

Uncle Frank smacks his lips. "My guess is he's tied to it."

She glares at him even though the hat hides his features, keeping her eyes from meeting his. Otherwise, he'd see the annoyance. Not that her tone doesn't do the job. "Of course, he's tied to it."

The mustache says, "Well some people, not all but some, have a hard time letting things go. You sure do. You're stubborn, been so most of your life. Like your mother, a mule. Course, your mother would have been a wonderful mare, which makes you the result of a half-assed relationship with an ass."

Her boss, Marshal Kalka had a problem with Kelly's attitude too, yelling at her about how she can't let things go, especially when she's been told to let it go. Ordered. Getting onto her in his office this morning about her looking into the missing person case—he meant Siriano—and she's not sure why the hell he couldn't say the damn gangster's name. Chastising her for talking to the media. Throwing a copy of the morning paper, with a tease of Sonny's story across the vertical fold in black and white, down on the desk like he was trying to swat out her insolence. He said things like, "What the fuck were you thinking?" and "Don't you know they have a job to do? They'll fuck you over in a moment's notice."

Kelly wanted to tell him that was the best part, the fucking her over. It lasted longer than a moment, longer than Kalka can yell at her, and she's partial to the reporter now, unsure how she wants to proceed with him. He's sweet. He likes to talk. They've planned to meet again.

She didn't say any of that. She knows better than to push it in a moment like that. This is war, and that meeting was only a skirmish. One where Kelly smirked and let Kalka rant and rave. She had already planned a full-scale frontal assault for after the meeting, one Kalka knew nothing about, which is going to cause a bit of a stir, possibly result in some disciplinary action, not that she hasn't earned some kind of action already.

Kalka said it himself, telling her he should write her up. Get her drummed out of the marshals or at least sent to some shit posting like the longitude of You Done and the latitude of Fucked Up. He accused her of running to the media, of seeking glory. He said he can't trust her, not now, not ever. But he put it as a question, saying he doesn't know if he ever will be able to trust her, finishing it with, "How do I know you won't try to become a TV star?"

To which she replied, "The moment I was caught on camera, I became a TV star, or at least an interesting current affairs piece." She added that talking to the reporter, she's not talking about anything to do with the Marshals Service, not when she's talking about her feelings and personal history. No one said she can't talk about herself, the private citizen. They only said she can't talk about herself as a marshal. When she said it, she knew that wasn't the right thing to say, and she might not be in the right on this one, but it felt good to stand up for herself, to tell him she wasn't at fault here and to tell him she's a person, she has feelings, and she intends to find the sons of bitches who took Siriano. She told him that he can either suspend her for talking to Sonny—she said reporter then—about her past in sports and talking about a moment immortalized in celluloid or he can allow her to do her job and find the asshole who embarrassed the damn United States Marshals Service.

Kalka stared at his desk for a moment and said, "It's all digital now. No one uses celluloid for local news."

Two weeks ago, Kelly wouldn't have said any of that, but something's changed, more than having a rifle shoved into her face. Something wonderful, scary, almost as scary as having a rifle shoved in her face. Something which made her face herself, do some deep reflection, think about the person she really wanted to be, or wants to be. She now sees her future isn't written, which is something Uncle Frank's fond of saying, and he likes to chase it with, "It's never too late."

So now she says, "Yeah, well, they have a hard time letting go when it's registered to them and tied to a crime... well, two crimes."

With two fingers, Uncle Frank pushes up the rim of his cowboy hat, revealing his eyes. One eyebrow raising, it matches the mustache. "Yours and theirs."

"It's a miracle we found it," Kelly says.

"No miracle," Uncle Frank says, "just good police work, but then again, it's like that nerdy British fella who wrote them science books said a while back about technology and magic."

"What's that?"

"Hard to tell the difference."

Kelly turns in the seat, lodging her elbow against the top curve of the steering wheel, hand against her cheek. "Do they sell books on that shit, or do you just pick the bullshit through trial and error?"

Uncle Frank sits the coffee cup on the dashboard. He removes his hat and plops it on his knee. He runs both hands over his face and through his wispy hair. After a moment, he says, "Wisdom comes with age."

"Is that in the book too?"

Uncle Frank doesn't answer her question. "How'd we get here?"

"A friend of Pat called, a friend that works in the Tulsa Police Department's Homicide unit. Detective Color. He told us they found it."

"Found what?"

Kelly motions to the windshield. "That Buick."

"Alright, but that doesn't tell us how we got here, now does it miss prissy pants."

"I did some digging on my own."

"What did Kalka think of that? Didn't you say you met with him today?"

"I didn't tell him we were doing this."

"Don't you think he should know?"

"I think he told us, Pat and me, to work with Tulsa and arrest some bad guys while our case is pending review. So that's what I'm doing. I found out this Buick was our Buick, and it was involved in a shooting yesterday. Some meth head got shot. Died."

After leaving the reporter's house, the night was still young, so Kelly drove straight to the office and spent all Sunday working, still wearing the clothes she's wearing now. She had a hunch. The Marshals Service and the FBI had found the husk of the van, found where it had been dumped, burnt, and crushed. And like a dead body missing feet and hands and a head, the thieves had stripped it of all identifiable numbers and parts. They won't have gotten them all, but they got the easy ones. It will take time to disassemble the van after processing to get to the numbers imprinted on pieces not easy to get at. The Marshals Service had hit a standstill. They will eventually work through the issue; the Federal Government never rests. From the burnt-out husk, the kidnappers got into another vehicle, which had been identified. The service and the FBI believe they changed vehicles two to three times more. The first vehicle had been found, but no usable evidence was collected to help in identifying the suspects.

Kelly decided to work in the opposite direction. She found a likely candidate for the van—actually she found ten. Tulsa, on average, has had over 4,000 vehicle thefts, and the number's rising. White vans are popular. The fourth one she found and followed up on was buried in a stack of reports and felt like the right one. She pulled the report and called the officer who took it. He was awake and working. It was the middle of the night, Sunday into Monday—so there's one for small miracles. She asked if they conducted a canvas of surrounding businesses, and he said no.

So, long before the sun broke the horizon and before her meeting with Kalka, she did the canvas. At a 24-hour gas station down the road, she found what she was looking for, footage of a van traveling down the road in the middle of the night—the van had been stolen the day before the kidnapping—followed by a gold/tan Buick sedan. The two vehicles stopped at the station. One person got out and put gas in both vehicles. She got lucky. The person paid in cash; he entered the store, a teenage to early twenties Hispanic male. She called Pat and told him about it, waking him up early on a Monday morning, which he didn't appreciate.

"What are you doing?" he said.

"Working," she told him.

"That's what I mean, you aren't supposed to be working... what time is it?"

"Well, I had a hunch. One I felt good about."

"You talked to your uncle, didn't you?"

"I may have."

Pat laughed. "And got laid," he said. "You always have a certain uplift to your voice when that happens, and you do better work. Who was it?"

"Pat—"

"Just wondering, so I'll know to stay away from him, but I need to know so I won't go hitting on him."

"Pat," she said again.

"Pat what?"

"I'm calling because I have a lead." She paused to allow him time to process.

He was silent. "Well, spit it out."

"It's not much of one, but I have a car and a picture."

"That's better than what we have. The FBI, still shocked you ever wanted to work for them, can't find their way out of a paper bag without filling out ten forms and getting approval from a pogo stick in Washington. You give it over to them yet?"

"Not yet," she said. "I wanted to run it by you first."

"What for?"

"You still know that guy at TPD?"

Pat murmured into the phone. "I know several. What are you thinking?"

"I'll send you what I have. You send it to whoever over there you trust, and we see if it means anything."

"You just want to lose your job, don't you?"

"Just do it, will ya?" she urged but with a questioning tone.

"That it?"

"I promise I won't leave the office to get involved, but don't you feel like we have to fix this?"

"No."

"Pat!"

"Alright, yes, I feel, for pride purposes," he chuckles, "that, yes, I need to fix this. I don't like being embarrassed like that. It's a matter of personal honor."

She sent him the photographs. Within ten minutes, he called her back and said, "How dead set are you on not leaving the office to get involved?"

"It's me."

"That's what I'm afraid of," he said.

NOW KELLY SAYS to Uncle Frank, "And that's how we ended up here. Detective Color called Pat, said not only was that car a suspect vehicle in a shooting, the picture of the guy who paid for gas matched the description and surveillance photo of a possible person of interest. And guess what? The driver of that Buick was female. So, if Kalka asks, I'm not looking for the kidnappers, I'm helping Tulsa find their shooting suspect, which is what Pat and I do for the marshals anyways, violent fugitive task force."

Uncle Frank smiles. "If I had a grasshopper in my hand." He unfurls his left hand, palm up, fingers straight, thumb nearly at a right angle. "You could not only take it from me but eat it."

"Seriously, is there a book? Did I miss this on-the-job training? A class? Or is this just some country white boy shit?"

Uncle Frank withdraws his hand. "How'd things go with the reporter?"

Kelly's features freeze. She faces away from him, smashing her lips together to keep him from seeing the quiver in her throat. "Good."

"Good, good?" Probing her for answers. "Or *good*?" He raises an eyebrow again as he says it, with a grin forming under the bushy mustache.

"Is there a difference?"

"Good, good, is good."

"And *good*?"

"Is when you show up to a stakeout still wearing the clothes from two days before."

Kelly shakes her head. She's not talking about this with him for several reasons. Her love life is one of them. "I'm working a hunch."

"I used to get those, but that's when things with your mother were *good*—"

Kelly holds up her hand, nearly shoving it in his face to get him to stop talking. "I don't need to hear it." She knows what he was saying, the hidden meaning under his words, because she knows him, and she knew her mother too.

Frank smirks. "All I'm saying is you're good at what you do, and I think you've learned all there is to learn from me."

"Not everything."

"Well, no, not everything. That wouldn't be possible; otherwise, how am I going to write my sequel to my runaway bullshit bestseller White Boy Wisdoms?"

"So there is a book?" Kelly says.

Uncle Frank just stares at her.

"The hunch panned out."

"You know," he gives her a look, "I used to be a detective. I'm a skilled and trained investigator, and obviously, if we're sitting here staring at some jerkoff trying to start a car that has no battery, then your hunch worked out."

"Pat thought it'd make a great trap."

Several TPD detectives swarm the car, wearing bullet proof vests, some in windbreakers, some in sports coats, all holding guns and shouting. The driver's hands are trying to stick through the roof.

Uncle Frank says, "Pat's *good* at what he does."

"No, stop," Kelly says. "Stop saying '*good*.' You're not allowed to use that word anymore."

"You going to see him again?"

"Who?"

"Who?" Frank repeats with his eyes on the scene unfolding in the parking lot. The car doors are thrown open and arms are reaching in and yanking the bald man out, forcing him to the ground. "What are you an owl? The reporter, that's who. Why are you asking who? You know what, never mind, I know why. You like him. So you are going to see him again, which is why it was *good*."

"You're doing that just to mess with me aren't you?"

"I mean, isn't that my job as a stand-in father? If I didn't do it, well, you could bring me up on charges of dereliction of duty. Your mother would have something to say about it, I'm sure."

"You're not as cute as you think you are, old man, and if you're not careful, I'm going to have you placed in a home. Find one with a memory care unit with locked doors, the kind with a keypad on it. Trick you into going to see one of your *peers* and then leave you there, telling the staff you're a patient... I figure they'd keep you for a couple of days before they figured it out. If I broke your legs and then wheeled you in there in a wheelchair, I think it goes from days to weeks."

That shuts Uncle Frank up for some time.

Then, he remarks, "Tell me again how'd you figure this out from a hunch when I told you not to get involved."

"I was involved whether I wanted to be or not. My handcuffs were around the man's wrists, and it was my face the rifles were shoved into,"

Kelly says. "And we both know you mean the opposite of what you say because you can't talk like a normal person. You spend too much time out in those fields, breathing all that methane, makes you high or something."

His words come out honest and sincere. "I don't smell the cow shit anymore."

"That's what I'm saying," Kelly expresses. "You wouldn't stay out of it. You'd get right in the middle of it."

"Would I?"

Kelly turns in the seat. "Why do you think you are here? What possible reason could you have for being here?"

Uncle Frank's mustache trembles and shudders as his cheeks split into a wide closed mouth grin. "Pat asked me."

CHAPTER SIXTEEN: EMERSON ROWAN

WHEN EMERSON FINALLY WORKS UP THE COURAGE to call Maggie, his voice tells her he didn't expect to ever hear from her again. Maggie giving Emerson his number was a lark. He sounds tired, but it is late, and he explains he just left a meeting with a client. She tells him she didn't notice the time; says she was out of jail; and asks him if his offer for dinner was still open.

After a pause, he says, "It is, but I can't do dinner anytime soon. I'm working." His words insinuate work keeps him busy in the evenings, which might be why he sounds tired.

That's a bummer. She really wanted to get to know him better.

Then, just as she is about to hang up the phone, he asks her about lunch, with an uplift in his voice. He asks if that would be alright, "Say in the morning, an early lunch?"

"Sure. Where at?"

He asks her to meet him at the place they met, laughing hard when he says it.

The next day, in the late morning, Emerson sits across from him at the same table they had their first conversation. "I never thought you would agree to see me again."

Maggie wears the same type of clothes he wore on their first meeting and sits relaxed in the chair the same way he was when she was arrested. He looks up from his coffee cup. "Why's that?"

"I was arrested. Not exactly the best way to start a relationship."

"There are worse ways."

Emerson snorts when she laughs and nods. "Yeah, I suppose so," she says, thinking of her ex-boyfriend, the same one who set her up, which resulted in her getting arrested and spending two years in jail awaiting prosecution. "Still, it's not a great way to get the ball rolling."

Maggie shrugs like he doesn't care. "I've been arrested."

Emerson raises an eyebrow. "What for?"

Maggie doesn't answer. He just sips his coffee, dark blue eyes watching her.

Emerson tugs at the fringe of the beige vest she wears open over a black t-shirt. The t-shirt is tight on her body, so much so the contours of her bra struggle against the fabric and hint at the color underneath, and that's totally on purpose.

There's something about him, in his look, in his eyes, something about how he makes her feel, something about his presence too. It makes her uncomfortable but a good uncomfortable. The flavor of uncomfortable she read about when she read all those Harlequin Romances and similar books in jail, like how those books talked about love, both the carnal and the emotional kind. It's like her insides have coiled into a tight spring, and she's ready to happily pounce on him in any moment with the right word—happily being the keyword for her. Just like those springs in a box leaping out saying *surprise* with their bright colors and sudden appearance. Now, wouldn't that leave an impression with the folks who work behind the counter of this coffee shop? First, she steals from them; then, she's arrested in front of them; and then, she returns to perform a pornographic act on one of their tables.

Emerson places her coffee cup on the table. "You think they had a hard time seeing me again?" meaning the people working at the coffee shop.

His eyes flick to the coffee bar and back to her. "No, you paid this time."

She shakes her head. "No," dragging the word out, "*you* paid this time."

Despite his best efforts, Maggie allows a slow grin to form on his lips.

Emerson traces the outer rim of the coffee cup, removing any traces of coffee that splashed out of the lid. The expelled liquid is cool against her fingertips, in contrast to the contents inside. She moves her finger in a slow sensual manner—also on purpose—and places the fingertip into her mouth, licking the liquid off with a quick twist of her tongue.

"What type of man are you?"

Maggie, quiet for a long moment, clearly studies her. He is trying to read her and what she wants. Not that she isn't advertising exactly what she wants. It should be obvious to him or anyone else watching, but then again, she's had experience with men, and they don't exactly clue into womanly wants and desires. Not like her girlfriend did, but women know women. Men usually require a more straightforward approach. If she sat on his face, then maybe he'd understand.

Emerson licks her lips. "Like who are you? Not who you want to be, but who you are."

"That's a strange question."

"This is a first date, right? Well then, that's the type of question you should expect on a first date. Answer the question. What type of man are you?"

After a hesitant breath, he asks, "What type of man do you want me to be?"

He's elusive. It should be a red flag, and with anyone else, it would be, but with him, it only entices her more.

Maggie rests his coffee cup on the table. He crosses a leg over his knee and, with both hands, clasps his kneecap. "Let me put it to you this way," he says, "because I see the way you look at me..."

Emerson's eyes meet his like she's a fly who's found itself inside the maw of a Venus flytrap. The blue orbs don't let her go.

"I saw the way you reacted when I said my name—you knew me, were surprised—made me feel like you know me. So let me ask you this, who am I to you?"

Emerson blushes. "I did jump at your name, didn't I? I brushed you off too, when you asked me about it the other day, I said something about my dad and then didn't really have much of a chance to explain..."

What would he think about what he means to her? To her relationship with her father?

When she stops talking, he probes for an explanation. "I am someone to you, right? You know me from somewhere, but it goes beyond just knowing me, knowing who I am. There's an experience there. A moment."

"Honestly?"

Maggie grins wider. "Does anyone ever want honesty, like a hundred-percent-tell me the truth-honesty?"

Emerson shakes her head. "I don't believe they do, but what I'm asking is do you want to know? There's a difference between everyone else and you."

"That's what I'm saying." He laughs. "There is a difference between everyone else and me. The way you look at me—"

"You're a hero," The words spill from her mouth before he can finish.

Maggie chuckles. "I'm not a hero."

"To me, you are ... to my father. You were a hero."

"I was one?"

"You are one."

Maggie shakes his head while leaning forward and snatching his coffee cup off the table to take a sip. "I'm the opposite of a hero. I work in restoration. That's not a glamorous job or anything to aspire to. Kids don't go around telling parents how they want to pick up after people and fix their shit."

"That's not what makes you a hero. You asked me what you were to me. I'm telling you. You're a hero."

"Why?"

She thinks about it. Then, she thinks about her father. "You're tied to an event—"

"—an event or an emotion?"

"Both." Emerson struggles to find the words between his interruptions and her raging emotions: lust, embarrassment, shame, and joy. "Damn, it shouldn't be this hard to explain to you what you mean to me ... and my father, but then again, if I tell you the story, it'll make me sound like a crazy person. Except, I'm not a crazy person."

"You're not?" he asks, playing with her.

Twisting her nose, Emerson sticks out her tongue, playful. "If anything, you're the crazy person for injecting yourself into my life. You could have let me just walk out of here, but you didn't."

"I did not."

"You grabbed my arm. Held me up. You are the one who initiated the conversation."

"And that makes me a crazy person?"

"No," she says. "Well, yes, but no."

Maggie waves his hand in front of his face. "Is it because of baseball?" Guessing at what she's talking about. "Can't think of any other reason for someone—you—to know my name."

"Yes," she says. "My father... god, you're going to think this is crazy."

"Your father's a fan?"

Emerson nods, impersonating a bobblehead. He's going to think she is crazy with all the nodding and the smiling. Neck and chin bouncing up and down. Think she's unstable. "He's more than that."

"You know where that word comes from, right?" he asks.

Emerson tells him she doesn't.

"Fanatic," he says. "Means crazy. Meaning there must be some sort of emotion tied to whatever it is you're talking about."

"There is," she says. "You're tied to both. The event and the emotions of the event."

Maggie cocks his head to the side.

"You remember when you played ball for the Drillers, what like ten-fifteen years ago, and you hit the cycle and threw a no-hitter?"

"I do," Maggie says. "Jesus, you remember that?"

"I was there with my father. He worked for the newspaper, still does. I've watched a lot of baseball growing up. Watched that game with him, right before everything went to shit. Well, everything had gone to shit, but it was a good moment before a whole lot of bad."

"How could I ever live up to that?" Maggie says. "I'm just a guy."

"That's what I'm saying," Emerson says. "The moment, your moment, took on this meaning ... for us. So yeah, you did something pretty freaking cool and memorable, but then, there's this whole other layer to it that has nothing to do with you but *everything* to do with you. So I guess, if what you're asking is how you live up to this version of you I built in my head or the teenage-version built in my head—you can't."

He is silent again.

"I guess you could, but that doesn't happen most of the time, does it? Our heroes don't live up to our expectations. Don't meet them, right? That's what they say. Don't meet your heroes because they'll let you down."

"But I'm not a hero, so you don't have to worry about that."

"No." She pauses. "You're different though. Different than you were that day. I can still remember it. Your eyes are the same. I remember those from the promotional flyers and posters. You know, those things they hand out at the gate. Well, when you're with the media like my father is, he gets all that shit. He calls it swag. I used to eat it up. I was a bit of a tomboy, but then there came a point where I wanted to grow up, and he kept wanting to be a kid and watch the game."

"People change."

"They do, but still, you're different. Your eyes are the same but different."

Those blue eyes swallow her attention and scrutinize her for a moment. "Different how?"

"Well, you're older."

"That was years ago. It happens."

"No. I mean, yes. You are older, but now there's a different type of energy with you. You're more relaxed."

"Aging is one of those things."

Emerson bites her lip. "I remember hearing stories about you. Remember hearing about how much of a hothead you were and how you worked harder than anyone else on the team. My teenage self thought it was pretty freaking hot."

"Just your teenage self?" he asks, but before she can think too much about the blatant pass at her, he says, "It's what cost me my job. The passion. Being passionate means sometimes tempers flare. Mine did. It is what it is."

"What happened?"

"You don't know? Your pops didn't tell you about it? Report on it." His words come out almost cutting, hinting at something deeper under the surface. Maybe the media did him dirty. She'll have to remember to ask her father about it.

"When you're a kid, you try to avoid hearing bad things about the people you like," Emerson says. "Why do you think my pops couldn't ever tell me how terrible all my boyfriends were? He did. I just didn't listen."

Maggie rocks in his seat in agreement. "Well, during the pre-game warm-up, I got into it with the pitching coach, who wasn't coaching. It pissed me off. I thought he was the reason why I wasn't getting called up to the Majors. I had dreams of being in LA, playing with the Dodgers for real, not stuck in my hometown bagging groceries when I could do what I could do."

"You felt held back."

"I felt held back."

"I know exactly how that feels."

That's why she left and didn't want to come back.

"We got into it. It wasn't pretty."

"What happened?"

Maggie leans back from the table as if he's pushing the memory away. "I lost my temper, and there was a bat involved."

"You hit him with a bat?"

Maggie's eyes say "yes." He sits the coffee down on the table and talks with his hands. "Luckily, it wasn't too bad. Several of my teammates tackled me before we got too out of control."

"They fire you?"

Nodding, he shrugs again. "What can you do? It was better than getting the cops called on me," he says. "Yeah, they fired me on the spot. Didn't even let me collect my gear. Escorted me out of the gates. A guy I was friends with on the team stayed with me while my other friend collected all my shit from my locker. Then, when I was leaving, they just looked at me, shook their head, and said nothing before disappearing into the gates with all the early arriving fans. Some friends. That was it. When you're out, you're out. In their eyes, I was nothing. Nothing but a washed-up baseball bum who couldn't handle his temper."

"The home office didn't have anything to say about it?"

Maggie hesitates. "It wasn't the first time my passion flared into a physical outburst. I broke a couple bats one time hitting the ground—I was a stupid kid."

"But you aren't that anymore?"

"No, I'm not that anymore," he says. "I'd like to think I've focused on myself, calmed down some. Jackie sure helped me with that, gave me an outlet. Pointed me in the right direction, so to say."

"Jackie?"

"Guy, I knew." Maggie dismisses her with a half-wave of his hand. "He's dead now."

"How'd you meet him?"

Maggie pushes air out through his nose sighing heavily. "Jackie C., he and I hooked up while I was working for Russ."

"Russ?"

"Russell Siriano." Maggie keeps his head down, but eyes up and on her.

"You worked for Russell Siriano?" Emerson can't believe it. "The guy that just got kidnapped?"

Maggie nods. "He took me in after I got fired. I had nothing. I've known him since my pops died. For some reason, he was always interested in me, in my career. I don't get it. He and I met one time when I was working at a pharmacy. From then on, he was always around, coming to find me in bars and coming into the store to buy groceries. When he heard I batted myself out of the game, he hired me as a driver."

Emerson is flabbergasted. Her words are slow and pointed. "You work for Russell Siriano?"

Maggie tilts his head forward and flicks his wrist. "Worked. I don't work anymore, not really, but every now and then, he calls me and offers me some work."

Emerson raises a questioning eyebrow.

"Not that type of work," Maggie says quickly, but something in his voice, and especially in his physical demeanor, the shape of his body, the hard terseness of his muscles, says what she's thinking is exactly the type of work Siriano reaches out to him for. "From Russ, I went to Jackie C. who was a better influence. But, he's dead now. He taught me everything I know about the ... *restoration* business. Taught me the rules. Taught me how to be good at what I do. Taught me to control my temper, not let it get the best of me."

"How'd he do that?"

"He beat me with a baseball bat when I got out of control."

"Seriously?"

Maggie chuckles. "No, he helped me work through my emotions. Got me to talk about them. Face them. Realize some of the passion I felt for things was anger at losing my dad. See, my father died when I was eighteen. His dream was to watch me play in the Majors. He never got to see it. Never got to know if I chose to be a hitter or a pitcher."

"No wonder you threw that game that way," she says. "Was it the anniversary, or something, his birthday?"

Maggie's cheeks glow red, bashful. "You going to tell your father about all this?" His way of turning the conversation around. He doesn't like talking about himself, and Emerson guesses this is the most he's shared with anyone in a long time.

The look he's giving her now, she can't look away. She has never seen anyone look at her this way. She doesn't know how it makes her feel. It makes her feel something. That's for sure. She just doesn't know what. Doesn't know how to respond to it. It's uncomfortable but exciting.

Emerson touches her hair, sweeping it back over her ear, a nervous gesture. "I've thought about it," she says and pauses. "Would you be willing to talk to him? I think he'd like that."

She's surprised she's wanting to do anything nice for her father, but his words the other day while in the truck struck a chord with her. Maybe their relationship is done, they missed their moment at reconciliation, but that doesn't mean they can't have another moment, one with a common thread—that thread being Maggie.

"I bet he would."

"Funny," Emerson says. "My father's working on a story having to do with the Siriano kidnapping... how'd you meet him?"

"Siriano?" Maggie says. "I told you. I was working at a pharmacy. This was about a year—maybe less, I don't remember—after my father died. My father got shot trying to stop a robbery. He should have minded his own business, but he didn't. He wasn't perfect, and there were some things that came out about him after his death, but all in all, he was a good guy. He tried to do the best by me, invested a lot of time in me. My career. My baseball. Barely ever missed a game. And when he wasn't there, he was there, you know.

"Siriano—this guy's larger than life, old school mob guy from out East, dressed the part, acted the part. So much so when you think about it. He fits every stereotype there is about these guys. Wise guys. But then, you sit down with him, and he's this different person, says he always wanted to be a cowboy. He's got feelings. Wants. Aspirations. And he ain't dumb. The guy's a businessman at heart and loves making money. So yeah, from time to time, he takes exception with how limiting the rules are or how a competitor's treating him, and he does something about it. Does this make him a criminal? What makes him different from the oil barons or Bezos? You think these guys, from the '20s to now act any different? Think the Clintons aren't tied to the Dixie Mafia and don't have people disappear? Think it's something less than a Republican fever dream?

"These fucks, these types, they do what they want because they can afford it. Siriano's no different. One thing he did and still does is play the lotto. Why the fuck he does, I don't know. He likes to say it's for the kids, but you and I both know Oklahoma's lotto system has never gone to the kids like Brad Henry promised it would. That was a ruse, hook, line and sinker, and so Siriano thinks he has to *invest in the future*—his words.

"I worked at the pharmacy, mopping and stocking, and stuff like that. Siriano came in every week. Played the same numbers. Came in at the same time, wearing nearly the same suit, with a toothpick in the corner of his mouth, and hair all done up, slicked back, shiny. Looked like a proper Providence mobster. One day, he comes in, and the woman who works the counter is in the shitter. I don't know why. Broke up with her boyfriend, shitting her pants, I don't know. So he says, 'hey kid, I don't have all day.' Course, I point at myself, and he nods and says, 'yeah you, you dumb fuck. You think you can help me out?'

"I could. It's not hard to punch a couple of buttons, but I know who this is, and I know what he's capable of—who he really is. So I set the mop to the side and slinked up to the counter. Took me like twenty minutes to get the nerves right so that I could steady my finger to get the numbers punched in right. He plays everything. But the big one, the jackpot, he plays those same numbers every week and I, the dumb kid, don't know any better, punch in an eleven instead of a ten. Minor deal, but he fucking plays ten not eleven in that spot. He's in such a hurry he doesn't catch it right away, but then he's walking out the door, looking at the card and he says, 'Hey, you fucked up.' I offer to fix it, but then he looks at me funny like this is some crossroads moment for him. He's got to choose what's going to happen, his face all concerned. 'Nah,' he says, 'if you fix it, then surely I'm going to win with what I have, and I'll be kicking myself. So let's see what happens.'"

"What happened?" Emerson asks.

"He fucking won," Maggie says. "Couldn't believe it. The next week, he comes in, and points me out to the manager, and tells the guy that I'm his lucky kid. The kid that won him five hundred bucks. That kid will be putting his numbers in from now on because I had the lucky touch. Called me Midas for a while until he learned my name's as Italian as his, and then he started calling me Maurizio. Refused to call me Maggie. He said, 'Maurizio's your fucking name. Why don't you go by it? Your father gave it to you. If it's good enough for him, then it's good enough for me.'"

"Why don't you go by it?"

"Too hard to explain to everyone," Maggie says. "Try explaining to them how to fucking spell it—people who don't really care, teachers, coaches, bosses, whoever the fuck comes along, how to spell the whole thing. Easier to just say Maggie and move on. They can still fuck it up, but then, it's not that big of a deal. Makes them pay attention too. It's like some chick being called Michael."

"That's my middle name," Emerson says.

"No it's not." Maggie leans in toward the table.

CHAPTER SEVENTEEN: PABLO JIMENEZ

JUST AS HE PICKS UP THE PHONE ABOUT TO MAKE the call to set up the final details for the exchange with Siriano's bastard, Flavia bursts into the room, a raging thunderstorm of emotion, thrusting the door against its hinges until it collides against the wall with a solid thump. She's crying—dark eyes, red cheeks, hair a muss. "What the fuck are you doing?" she yells as she enters the room, her voice accusing him of something, but Pablo doesn't know what. "What the fuck is going on? What are you doing?"

Pablo looks up from the phone. Scrunches his eyebrows together.

The door crashing against the wall, and her yelling cause Siriano, who's over on the cot still chained up, to look at her too. He must see the same frantic look in her eyes that Pablo sees, all that hurt, anger, a swirling mess of emotions.

Pablo stands there with the receiver in hand. He's never seen her look like this. Usually, she's calm and restrained. She normally looks angry, but he has always chalked that up to the fact she could never hide her contempt for him. She never acts like this. This open. This raw. Pablo used to tease Omar about Flavia, asking him what she's like in bed, is she better than a fish; she looks like she would be a fish, cold and unapproachable. Omar would smile and say she was like a hurricane, calm at the center, but when the winds of emotion began to blow, she'd become an unstoppable force.

Remembering Omar's words, Pablo sets the phone down and tries to feel out the situation without upsetting her any further. "What are *you* doing?" he asks. "What's going on?"

In the back of his head, deep down, he's anticipated this coming storm. Vega had predicted this. Predicted she would act like this. That she would be the problem. Siriano hinted at it too, telling him to keep an eye on the people closest to him.

Flavia, dressed in a solid gray t-shirt and blue jeans, wearing sandals, crosses the room without saying anything more. She launches herself at him, arms and hands lashing out, trying to scratch Pablo's eyes out. He snatches her wrists out of the air and shoves her backward as Vega pushes against the closing door. He trails into the room behind her like he had been trying to stop her.

Behind him, Gabino, dressed in the same clothes he's worn for the last three days, comes into the room. His face asks what's going on, but he's wise enough to keep his mouth shut.

It's Vega who captivates Pablo's attention. At first glance, he thinks Vega's face says *sorry boss* as he tries to grab Flavia's arm, who is now rearing back to slap Pablo, but then, Pablo sees something different, almost lecherous in the man's look, desire for Flavia for sure, and he gets it. She's a desirable woman. Who wouldn't want her? Pablo wouldn't, she'd be like a fish with him, but if what Omar says is true, Vega might have some fun with her. He's seen the same lecherous look on the man's face these last couple of days. He wants her.

Pablo can use that.

Rushing to prevent the blow, Vega hunches forward and grabs Flavia around the waist, lifting her and dragging her back. She kicks wildly as he hauls her away from Pablo and Siriano.

Pablo raises a questioning eyebrow. Working with Alejandro for as long as he did, he's learned the most important rule of business: know when to keep quiet.

Flavia screams something guttural and digs her nails into Vega's forearms. He drops her. "Don't you fucking touch me," she spews in Spanish, slapping his hand away in a flutter of movement as Vega reaches for her again. "Leave me the fuck alone."

Vega barks something back at her in Spanish. Flavia yells at him more, and Gabino yells at him about not touching his sister-in-law. Vega ignores the kid and reaches to restrain Flavia. She slaps him away and lands a blow solidly across his face.

Vega absorbs the blow, chin reflexively turning with the slap. His way of showing the blow didn't hurt. A look descends upon his features, and in a flash, Vega backhands her. If Pablo had blinked, he would have missed it. His ears didn't though. If Flavia's slap was a crack, his was a whack. The lashing blow smashes across the left side of her face and sends her wheeling backward, stumbling to the floor at Pablo's feet.

It's the kid's turn to get involved, protect his family. Gabino rushes Vega, but Vega's ready for him and whirls around. He delivers a sharp elbow to the back of the kid's head.

The kid crashes to the floor.

Pablo steps to the side. "Stop!" he commands. "Alright, that's enough! Stop! What's going on?"

Flavia's on the floor at Vega's feet. "I hate you," she hisses, rubbing her palm down her face. "I hate you all."

Vega steps toward her.

Flavia scuttles back.

Vega smiles, showing off his dental-care deficient teeth. He inches forward until he's straddling one of Flavia's legs. She continues to crab-crawl backward trying to put some space between her and the hulking figure. She's stunned into silence now, scared. She bumps against the wall near the door.

Pablo holds up a hand, trying to stay Vega's anger. "What's going on?"

Vega remains silent. His eyes glower at Flavia and then flicker to Pablo.

"What's happening?" Pablo asks, trying a different tone this time.

"They arrested him," Flavia says from the floor. "They arrested Omar."

Gabino groans and rolls over to his side, hand on the back of his head, rubbing out the spot.

Pablo takes a moment to scan the room, the faces. Siriano sits amused. Flavia fumes. Vega seems pleased, and Gabino's confused. "Who arrested him?"

With her back against the wall, Flavia has nowhere to go. "The police," she answers. "They have him."

Pablo's mind reels with the revelation. "When?" He searches their faces for answers. He needs answers. "Where?"

Vega is the first to speak. "He went to get the punta's car," he says, half-turning to motion to the kid down on the floor.

"The car?" Pablo says. "I don't understand. What car?"

Gabino says, "My car."

Vega says, "The kid's... Omar went to pick it up."

"What, why?" Pablo asks. "Where's the car?"

The kid stays quiet.

Flavia chest heaves. "We dumped it after getting shot at. We didn't want to drive something filled with bullet holes around, so we dumped it in a Walmart parking lot. But we didn't think..." Her voice fades to nothing.

"It was stupid going back for it."

"It wasn't stupid," Flavia argues. "We couldn't leave it there. It ties back to us. To this. To all of this fucking mess."

Vega looks up into Pablo's eyes. Pablo reads the man's intentions and tries to shake him off. He knows what's coming.

Vega says, "Look, my friend, didn't I tell you she could be a problem, upset the plan—what little of it there is—she's always been a problem."

"My friend," Flavia spits. "That's rich. Who are you? We don't need you. No one asked for you to be here. No one needs you. Who invited you?" She levels her gaze at Pablo. "That shit?"

Her contempt's out in the open for all to see.

"Flavia," Pablo starts to say, but the cutting look she shoots him silences him.

Vega cracks his neck side to side and chuckles. "Tell her." His eyes back on Pablo. "Tell her the truth. Tell her what's going on."

Something in the man's tone hints at a deeper knowledge. Like he's trying to say something or make Pablo choose.

Flavia doesn't hide behind innuendo; she openly accuses him. "You're weak," she says. "You're nothing. You fucking coward. You did this because you have a small dick. Look at you, you've been in this room for days, talking to him, letting that white man twist your mind. They killed Alejandro, Pablo. Doesn't that mean anything to you?"

It does, but Pablo says, "No, they didn't."

"And then, they came after me." She touches her chest. "Me. They tried to kill me. Tried to kill Gabino." Her hand out towards the kid. "Killed all his friends. We've lost so much. And you want to do what? Let him go? Is that your grand fucking plan? There's been blood. You need to send a message."

The bed creaks as Siriano leans his weight forward. "What did you expect to happen?" he questions.

"Stay out of this," Pablo says.

Siriano shakes him off and continues to address Flavia. "That you could just kidnap me and there wouldn't be any repercussions?" He searches each person's face as the heads swivel his way and silence descends upon the room.

Pablo sighs.

Siriano lifts his hands and motions from side to side as he talks. "You hit us, so we hit you back. What did you think would happen? That we would leave you alone? This is business. This is how the game's played. If you don't like it, get out. If you can't get out, shut up."

Pablo cuts in, his hands outstretched. "Flavia, you need to calm down. Need to see the bigger picture. I'm trying to fix this. We have a plan. This is almost over."

"Fix what?" Flavia asks, resting on her elbows now, motioning toward him with her hand. "Sucking that dickhead's cock? Is that what you are doing? You got yours, so fuck everyone else?

Pablo snorts and shakes his head. "No..." She needs to understand. "We've made a deal."

Flavia squeezes her eyes closed and turns her head away from Pablo, toward the downed Gabino. "So you're just going to let him go? Fuck what we've done. Fuck who we've lost."

"We weren't going to kill him," Pablo says. "That was never the plan, you know this. Our cousins down south don't want the Sirianos gone. They want stability. We just wanted to show them we weren't to be fucked with. They didn't kill Alejandro. Renaldo did that."

"Did it on his own," Siriano adds. Pablo glances at the old man. He looks as smug as ever. He's enjoying this.

Vega steps forward and grabs Flavia's ankle. "I was right," he announces. "Whatever power you've gained, she's never going to let you have it."

She kicks at him with her other foot, losing a shoe in the process. It flies off and bangs against the wall. Vega seems unaffected and bats her blows away.

"Stop," Pablo tells the man. "This isn't the time for this."

Flavia yells and cusses, but her efforts are pointless. Vega yanks hard on her ankle, reeling her toward him, her back sliding across the linoleum floor. There's a soft screech like sneakers on a basketball court.

"Didn't you say she's always whispering in Omar's ear, offering counter opinions, poisoning her husband's mind to your ideas?" Vega patiently lists her crimes. "That's why you wanted me here, right? That's why you contacted my employers. You weren't sure who you could trust. Said it was Flavia who argued against you, against retaliation toward Siriano. Said she lobbied to get Omar elected to assume Alejandro's metaphorical throne."

Everything Vega says is true, and it's what keeps Pablo from acting. He stands there, near the phone.

"I said those things," he responds.

"Then consider this is what you hired me to do."

Pablo watches Flavia struggle. He doesn't move to help her. He doesn't say anything.

And then it hits Pablo. This wasn't just his plan, the kidnapping, it was a suggestion from Vega. He said, why don't you show them who's boss, show them you aren't to be fucked with. And the more Pablo thought about it, the more he liked the idea. "But how?" he had asked. "How would we even attempt such a thing?" Vega said he had heard rumors about Siriano, about how he was going to be released and he claimed he could find out when.

Vega's no different from Flavia.

It's games within games.

Vega has his own agenda just as Flavia has hers.

Vega twists Flavia's foot in his hands, flipping her over. He continues backing toward the door. He reaches behind him to open the door. He's going to take her somewhere.

"She craves power, amigo." Vega moves hand over hand from her ankle up her leg, toward her knee, yanking roughly each time to keep her off balance and to show his strength. Her gray shirt rides up and rolls over as it slides up her upper half, exposing her hips, smooth stomach, and the underside of her bra. "She craves your power. I'll show her what real power is."

"Let go of me." Flavia reaches for something to halt his progress. Her fingers latch around a chair leg. "Let go."

Flavia tries to kick at him again, but Vega doesn't let go. He laughs, unafraid of showing how much he's enjoying this.

Gabino scrambles to his feet. "Let go of her!" His voice breaks as he yells it. He takes a fighting stance, hands up, feet shoulder width apart. He shuffles forward toward Vega and Flavia.

Vega pauses, stares at the kid for a split second with semi-curious eyes. Then, there's a flash of silver, something metal, coming from under Vega's shirt, from the small of his back, and there's a loudness in the room, a thundering roar of three shots fired nearly simultaneously, a .45 handgun, and then ringing.

It leaves Pablo blinking, trying to understand what just happened. Flavia stops struggling. She goes limp. Like Pablo, she tries to process what just happened.

Gabino stops mid-step. He looks down, breathes heavy, eyes moist, looks from Flavia to Pablo, and then down at his chest where three blooms of blood appear on his shirt. He lumbers forward a few steps as if he's suddenly dizzy or the room's spinning. Pablo watches Gabino's left-hand grope at his shirt, at the wounds, and the kid topples to the side. He doesn't attempt to break his fall. His face hits first, then the rest of him.

Siriano holds up his hands. "Woah, hold up."

"Jesus," Pablo says. "What'd you do that for?"

With the gun still outstretched toward Gabino, Vega licks his lips. "He was a problem," he answers, emotion absent from his voice. "It's better this way."

Pablo says, "What do you mean better this way? Omar's going to fucking go berserk."

"He can't," Vega says with a twinkle in his eyes, meaning Omar's in jail.

Flavia comes back to life. "You did it," she yells, struggling once more, kicking, and trying to crawl away.

Unconcerned, Vega drops her foot and calmly shoves the gun back in his waistband.

Flavia drags herself toward Gabino, her arm stretching for his. "You fucking did it," she cries over her shoulder, despair filling the void where anger had been. "You called the cops. You told them where the car was. You did it."

"So what if I did," Vega says.

"What do you mean?" Pablo asks.

Vega cocks his head to the side. "What do you mean what do I mean?" He drops his shirt tail and extends his arms out to the side. "Don't get your panties in a bunch. With the kid gone, and those other fucking kids gone, there's just me and her—no one else is tied to the kidnapping. Did you think about that?"

Pablo hadn't.

"If I make her go away, then there's just me... well technically there's me and you. And you're not going to say nothing. You're going to finish our little renegotiation. And then I'm going home, back down south, maybe find myself a beach to hole up on for a while."

"There's Omar," Flavia yells.

"He's in jail," Vega says. "You think he's going to tell the cops what he knows?"

Flavia stares daggers at him.

"He's not going to say nothing because I got you. And that's how it's going to stay. See, I suspect he'll be calling us as soon as he can, and you're going to answer and you're going to tell him that you're with your ole *Tio* Vega. Let him know who's really in charge."

Pablo opens his mouth to say something but then decides against it.

Siriano claps his hands together. "Family, you got to fucking love it."

Pablo turns his head toward the man.

"This is fucking entertainment is what it is," Siriano says. "Here, I thought I was destined for the fucking witness box, but then you stupid fucks come along, change the plans, and for a day or so, I thought, hey maybe they're going to kill me, but then would that be such a bad thing? I could finally get some fucking peace." He chuckles. "But as time went on, and you started talking to me, I realized, this is a fucking vacation. I'm out of prison. What's being locked up for a few more days? I'm out of prison and free of the fucking Grand Jury, so what do I have to worry about. Now this, I get some melodramatic family inner-workings—I love it. You were paying attention. Saw what I said about them cupcakes?"

Pablo says, "Yeah, I saw."

"What's he talking about?" Vega asks.

"Nothing," Pablo says.

Suddenly, the kid gasps for breath, and Flavia squeals as she pulls the kid's arm toward her, saying, "I'm here, Gabby. I'm here."

But just as quickly as before and as calmly, Vega, standing over the kid now—Pablo didn't see him move—withdraws the gun from the small of his back and shoots the kid in the back of the head. "He won't be coming back from that."

"You fucking monster!" Flavia shouts.

Vega squats down next to her, his knees bending at sharp angles, and lodges the gun against the back of her head, tapping her skull with the barrel in time with his words as he says, "Shut up or I'm going to..." then Vega's voice turns into a whisper, his lips millimeters from Flavia's ear, telling her something only she can hear.

Pablo doesn't hear the rest of the threat, but he sees her eyes, how wide they grow, how fearful she becomes, and knows whatever Vega promises her got under her skin.

When Vega's done, he forces the barrel against the back of her head once more and stands. Flavia doesn't move, only whimpers and squeezes Gabino's lifeless hand.

Siriano, still on the bed, motions to Pablo and the phone. "You going to make that call or what?"

Pablo reaches behind him and picks up the phone. He dials the number.

CHAPTER EIGHTEEN:
FLAVIA SANCHEZ

VEGA DRAGS FLAVIA TOWARD THE GARAGE, WITH her hair bunched tightly in his fingers. He walks ahead of her at arm's length, yanking and tugging to keep her moving, upright and off-kilter, preventing her from having a moment to collect herself. She cries; the tears sear her cheeks, which smolder red with anger and grief over Gabino's death. Omar will be devastated, just as she is. She never thought her own would turn on her, but then again, Vega isn't one of her own. He's one of Pablo's, and Pablo is a coward who will do anything to stay in power, even sell his soul to his "cousins" down south, who want nothing but blood and mayhem—Vega's kin—no friends of hers or Alejandro's.

In the long two-toned hallway, seafoam green over dusty gray, Vega tells her things: give up hope, quiet down, and quit crying. He tells her to get over it; the boy's dead; he tells her to shut up. He takes large loping strides and wrenches her forward, roughly, which nearly causes her to lose her balance. She falls twice. Vega keeps a firm grip on her hair so that her upper body stays up. His momentum never slows despite her inability to keep up and stay on her feet. He half drags her body down the hallway with her hands wrapped around his wrists until she can get her feet under her again and get back up and moving.

At the end of the hallway, they reach a metal door with a square window in the top part. Vega throws the door open. "Would you stop somethin'?" He looks over his shoulder. "This will be easier if you just cooperate."

Flavia digs her fingernails into his hands, trying to pry his hand off her head, as she clamps her heels to the floor. She manages to break his skin, but Vega doesn't seem to mind. He looks at his hand like it's a foreign object but still he doesn't let go.

She cries in a small voice. "You killed Gabby." She's determined to go no farther.

"What's wrong with you?" Vega lets her hair loose, with a shake of the hand. He turns in the doorway and sucks on the small beads of blood that bubble on the backside of his hand. "Course, I did, which is somethin' you're going to have to come to terms with." He studies her, amused at her distress. "Cryin' about it won't bring the kid back."

Vega punches her in the stomach, driving the oxygen from her body. The blow doubles her over. It's probably to get back at her for causing him pain, coming back at her tenfold. His speed surprises her, and the blow steals her voice. She struggles to breathe as his fist lingers against her midsection, wrapped in the thin fabric of her shirt. Reflexively, her body fights to take a breath. Her lungs quiver. The first intake of air sounds like the high-pitched whine of someone inhaling through a snorkel before collapsing into a wheezing coughing fit. She recovers and through choppy respiration, determination returns to her. She straightens up, eyes defiant. She blasts air through her nostrils.

He puffs up. "You're goin' to have to learn to love me."

"No," she says through clenched teeth.

"This isn't like before, not like it has been for you. When a man tells you to do somethin'—you do it."

In a savage strike, Vega backhands her hard across the bottom half of her chin. The blow wheels her body over into the wall. She bounces off, stunned.

"Struggle, struggle, struggle, all you do is struggle," he says. "Bitch, complain, question. Like every woman in this country. All of you, little birds, peckin' and tweetin' and chirpin'." He claps his hands together in front of her face and makes bird sounds. "Talkin' to each other, whisperin' in men's ears, distracting them, confusing them, fillin' their heads with delusion, not doing what you should be doing, which is minding the nest. I don't want you in business. You don't need to be in business. You need to be in the kitchen. Alejandro gave you a kitchen. You should be there. Women like you should be quiet. Do what they are told. That's the problem with your husband, which was why it was so easy to set him up. He listens to you. Should have left the car alone, but he didn't." Vega shrugs. "His mistake."

Vega told the cops where the car was. Vega is playing his own game.

She's sure of it. It's the only way any of this makes sense. "All of Gabino's friends, the snow cone shack, Omar with the car, it's all you. You talked Pablo into hitting the Sirianos and kidnapping the old man. Pablo wouldn't have had the balls to do it on his own."

Vega just grins. "Pablo did warn me you were smart."

Flavia told Omar. Omar should have listened. But now, she may never see her husband again.

"I'm not dead." Flavia works it out in her mind. "You want something from me, want me for something, but I can't imagine what that is."

He already made his intentions known in the shower, but then again, if he only wanted sex, every man wants sex, he would have taken it then, or shown he wants it now, or any time in the in-between. But he didn't. If he wanted sex, he wouldn't be acting like this. No, something else is happening. Vega's playing a game, one Flavia's very much a part of. And who are these other women he's talking about that are in business? No one in Alejandro's organization is like Flavia. She was at the top. Alejandro trusted her. Trusted Omar. And trusted Pablo, which was his mistake. The coward may not have killed him, but that doesn't mean he didn't benefit from his death. Who else does? Who else benefits from Alejandro's death? Renaldo certainly would, but he's nowhere to be found. Flavia doesn't know what happened to him and neither does anyone else. Siriano would benefit from Alejandro's death because it allows his empire to expand. Consume the neighbor and grow stronger. Siriano seems logical, but Vega's people wouldn't work with him. They wouldn't be able to communicate. So, what's going on here?

With all those thoughts flying through her mind, Flavia tries to stand upright to ask him and get it out in the open, but Vega grabs a chunk of hair again. He smashes her head into the wall, hard, denting the seafoam green drywall. Pieces of the wall come loose, and Flavia sinks to her knees as her body loses rigidity. She pees herself.

"With your hubby gone," Vega says, "I'll take good care of you."

On the floor, her hands snap to her skull and she squeezes her eyes together, fighting off the blistering headache. After a moment, the wave of pain subsides, and her fingers shake the strands of hair, loosening the drywall fragments in a cloud of fine dust.

"You done?" he asks, looking down at her. He motions at the wall. "Someone's goin' to have to fix the wall, and it's not goin' to be me. But I can make the hole larger if you're not done."

That last blow steals the fight from her. When she doesn't respond beyond whimpering and cowering, descending into a distraught mess, he makes like he's going to hit her again.

She squeals in terror, flinching. "Don't!"

Vega lets loose a deep belly laugh. "Good." His soulless eyes flick up to the pickup truck parked in one of the automotive bays. The truck is a maroon rusted piece of junk, twenty years old and dented to hell. It's Vega's work truck. "Get in the truck. We have an appointment. Don't want to be late."

"What sort of appointment?" she manages to say in the right submissive tone, with the pain from the last blow fading from behind her eyelids. Some of her internal strength returns. She flips the dark hair out of her face.

Vega jams his fists into his hips like John Wayne, still looking down at her, and snorts. He shakes his head. "Just get in the truck."

"What if I don't?" she asks, using the wall to steady herself. The head blow made her dizzy, so she uses the wall as a brace as she climbs back to her feet.

Vega withdraws the .45 handgun, a 1911, from his waistband and waves it in her face.

Standing with her shoulder touching the wall, Flavia tips her chin up. "Do it."

Vega lunges forward. His free hand seizes the back of her neck, putting his fingers through her hair, while he drives the barrel of the .45 into her forehead. The cold steel and ferocious speed surprise her.

"That's what you want, isn't it?"

Flavia stares at him, eyes narrowed.

She doesn't answer and neither of them moves, but the pressure increases and so does her resolve.

After a moment, when it's clear she isn't frightened of him, Vega, eyes blazing, releases her, throwing her head away from him. "Driver's side, you drive." He tucks the .45 back into his waistband.

Flavia shuffles forward. She gets in the truck. Once seated behind the wheel, she asks, "Where are we going?"

"I'll tell you as we get there." Vega pulls a zip tie from his back pocket. He zip-ties Flavia's left hand to the wheel. "In case you get any ideas. Believe it or not, I still need you. I can't have you goin' anywhere."

Shoving hard, he slams the driver's side door shut and gets in the truck on the passenger side. He withdraws the gun from his waistband and sets it on the bench seat between them almost like a challenge, tempting her to reach for it. His eyes say "I dare you." Then he pulls his door closed.

"When you pull out, take a left." He hands her the keys he digs out of his pants pocket.

Flavia slips the keys into the ignition, turning the engine over and bringing the truck to life. She puts it in gear and pulls out of the garage, saying, "Gabino was just a kid. He didn't deserve that."

"He was in the game." Vega reaches for the cigarette pack wedged between the glass and dashboard in front of him. He pulls a cigarette from the pack and tosses the pack on the dashboard. He points the tip of the cigarette at her. "No kids are in the game."

"You're crazy."

"Maybe so," he says, lighting the cigarette. "Turn right up here."

—

FLAVIA FINDS HERSELF in a living room in a part of town she doesn't belong. The word suburbs come to her mind, but this house, on the outside at least, isn't that nice. It's nice, but not what she would expect the widow of a cop to own. The living room color scheme is gold and white, with some cream. Pearled drawstrings dangle from the light fixture hanging from the vaulted ceiling, which looms over white furniture.

Flavia isn't dumb. The word living room isn't the right word for this cold sterile place. Sitting room? Theater stage?

Vega sits next to her. His hand shifts from her thigh to waving in the air as he talks about what's happened at the garage. He's smoking a cigarette; it's probably his fifth since they left the garage. Across from Flavia sits a redhead. She said her name was Iris King.

She's wearing a black kimono and smokes a cigarette from a black cigarette holder, very 1920s. She's pale and beautiful. Her hair and red lips contrast brightly with her emerald eyes and luminous skin.

The woman's eyes, watchful like a predator, notice Flavia eyeing the cigarette holder.

"Would you like a cigarette?" the woman asks. She tosses the cigarette pack in her lap onto the gold coffee table.

"I'm fine," Flavia says.

The room is silent as the woman considers her for a moment.

Vega yawns loudly, making a show of it, stretching his arms back, chin up, mouth wide. He touches his fist to his mouth before placing the arm on the couch behind Flavia.

Flavia asks, "Why am I here?"

The woman crosses one arm over her midsection, cupping her delicate perky breasts, and cradles the elbow of the hand holding the cigarette holder, which hovers just off the edge of her lips. "I need your help," Iris says. She turns to Vega. "Did you not explain to her what's happening?"

Vega shakes his head and withdraws the cigarette from his mouth with two fingers, mimicking the woman. He blows the smoke away from them both. "We didn't get much of a chance."

Iris hums to herself. Then, she asks Flavia, "Do you know who I am?"

Flavia doesn't answer.

Vega says, "She can be like that—stubborn."

The woman glances from him to her and then smiles. Her smile is as real as her offer of hospitality or claiming this room was built for comfort.

"This won't work if you don't feel comfortable talking to me," Iris says, matter-of-factly. "I need you to talk. If you don't answer my questions, I'll leave you to Vega and whatever he wants to do."

"He works for you?" Flavia says.

Iris laughs. "No, he doesn't work for me."

"Then who are you?"

"That's what I was asking you," Iris says. "Do you know who I am? Judging from your answer, I don't think you do. That's good."

"Is it?"

"You know Renaldo, yes?"

Flavia nods.

"I knew Renaldo," Iris says. Her eyes show delight then sadness at the memory.

She leans back in the seat and crosses one leg over the other. She's nude under the kimono, and Flavia examines the woman's sculpted calf hanging over the other knee.

"How did you know Renaldo?" Flavia asks.

"Renaldo was my lover," Iris says, bluntly, "but I've had many lovers. He was not the love of my life."

Flavia asks, "Who was the love of your life?"

The woman doesn't answer the question, but something in her face breaks for a moment, and Flavia realizes she touches a nerve. Iris recovers and announces, "I killed Renaldo."

"What?"

"I didn't pull the trigger of course." Iris pauses between sentences to smoke the cigarette. "But I facilitated things that led to his undoing. It was quite simple, actually, poor Renaldo. He loved me. He wanted to leave with me. Did you know this? I think when Alejandro tried to kill him, it killed a part of him. Suddenly, the beautiful strong man I had come to enjoy was replaced with someone I barely recognized—fevered."

The woman pauses to see if Flavia is going to say anything, but Flavia doesn't know what to say so she remains quiet.

"Still, Renaldo managed to enact his revenge." Iris chuckles to herself. "Which has worked nicely for my plans."

Iris leans forward and plucks her cigarette butt from the holder and stubs it out in the large rose gold glass ashtray. She withdraws another cigarette from the pack, and before lighting it, she once again offers one to Flavia, who declines. With it set in the holder, she falls back into the folds of the couch.

"Have you ever reached for something, only to discover you could have more?"

"I don't understand," Flavia says.

"Of course, you don't," Iris says. "That's why you are here. I require your help." She pauses to look at Vega who rolls his eyes, huffing. "Vega and I are at odds about this. He thinks we can do this without you. I, however, doubt it. But, if we did this together, then I believe we could both benefit nicely."

"Do what? What are we doing? What are you talking about?"

Iris licks her lips and considers her words. "I think I will ask you the question," she says as if she's having a conversation with herself. "I thought maybe I would just tell you what I need done and either you agree to do it or you don't, but I like you. I think I need to explain things a bit more. Vega here could be a factor in your decision process, but then I'm afraid it would get messy, and I can't have that."

"Listen, lady, whatever you want, just get to it," Flavia says.

Iris smiles and smokes the cigarette, puffing, and puffing, staring at Flavia the whole time. She looks at Vega. "I like that."

"I don't."

"Of course not," Iris says. Then, back to Flavia, she continues, "I asked you, have you ever reached for something only to discover you could have more?"

"I heard you the first time. I don't know what you mean."

Iris nods. "Let me put it to you this way: what do you want most in life?"

"My husband," Flavia says.

"Lofty goal," Iris says. "I was hoping for a bit more though. Sometimes wanting what you cannot have, your husband, isn't enough, and it's never going to happen."

There it is again, the crack. Flavia sees it and logs it away in her mind for later.

"To answer your question," Flavia says. "I wanted Alejandro's organization."

"What if you could have it?"

"I can't. I'm a woman," Flavia says. "What do *you* want?"

Iris moves her head side to side ever so slightly as she says, "More than you could ever know."

"What I want doesn't matter. Pablo is in charge."

"Not for long," Vega quips.

Flavia turns toward him. "What?"

Iris clears her throat. "I need your help. In exchange for helping, I'll give you what you want."

Flavia doesn't understand, but she doesn't ask. Instead, she just asks, "Why?"

"I need you to coordinate with Vega's people."

Flavia glances at Vega again and then at Iris. "His people?" The idea of it all dawns on her.

"You speak a similar language and are comfortable doing business together."

"What language is that? *Spanish*?"

"No," Iris says, chuckling. "Money. You have worked together for years. I don't want to step in now. I want to renegotiate the deal, during what you could consider a hostile takeover. And what better way to do that than bring senior executives with me?"

"You want to recruit me?"

Iris bites her lip in a soft smile. "I am recruiting you."

Flavia understands or at least thinks she does. Whatever is going on, whatever power or control Pablo thinks he has, he doesn't. Vega manipulated the situation with Iris pulling his strings, but Flavia doesn't know for what purpose.

She leans forward and selects a cigarette from Iris's pack, pausing just for a moment to silently ask for permission, which Iris gives with a head tilt.

Bent over, Flavia retrieves the lighter from the table and lights the cigarette, considering how she is going to play this. If she says no, she's Vega's to do with as he pleases, but if she says yes, then she's beholden to this woman and whatever goal she has in mind. Flavia would be a fool to agree to this arrangement without asking for something more in return because Iris is giving her what Iris needs: someone she can trust to take control of Alejandro's organization and act as the bridge between Vega's people and whatever Iris wants.

Somehow, Siriano is at the heart of this, but she doesn't see how or why. There's more going on, but she doesn't have the answers. The only thing she knows, the easy answer, is she's not fond of Pablo, but she is fond of staying alive, and with Iris's proposition, everything could be set right. This deal costs this woman nothing.

Flavia needs Iris to feel a cost; she needs Iris to concede in some manner.

Flavia leans back in the seat. "If I say yes, I do this with my husband. You get him out of jail, and he and I remain untouched in whatever game you're playing."

Iris studies Flavia and nods. "I think Vega can make that happen."

CHAPTER NINETEEN: SONNY ROWAN

"**I GUESS MY DAUGHTER SET THIS UP AS SOME SORTA** way for you and me to talk," Sonny says, leaning back in the seat, some faux wicker job, armrest in the middle with a cup holder. He battles nervousness creeping in at the edges, knocking it to the side, and exudes polite indifference. "And I guess this is for the beer." He circles the cup holder with his fingers. "Yeah, sure drink whatever you want, diet Coke, Dr. Pepper, water, whatever, but come on, when you're smacking a little ball around as hard as you want, you and I both know that's for the beer. Doesn't matter if there's a bottle or a plastic cup."

The nervousness makes him talk too much.

They are at one of those hipster-multi-tier driving ranges, the type that doesn't know if it wants to be an arcade or something more serious where people come to "train." Emerson likes it; she says it reminds her of her childhood. Sonny doesn't think so; they're too upscale to pass for putt-putt, and not serious enough to attract top-level pros, like the country club.

Two more faux wicker pieces bookend Sonny, with a matching trio across from him. A wedge-shaped counter in the middle separates this lane from the ten or so others all with the same shape and function. A few more levels, all looking the same, above, and below, with a glass-lined wall, show off the gaming floors or hallways decorated in generic sporting memorabilia.

Sonny watches the server, a nerdy-looking guy with long hair who looks far too old to be working as a server, sit down their drinks, fluttering about, holding a tray with skill. Maggie seems interested in him.

Sonny crosses a leg over the other, getting comfortable, and lobs an arm up on the seat back to watch Maggie pick up a club, examine it with a keen eye and slip it back.

Sonny says, "Don't like that one?"

"Dented." Maggie drops the driver back into the wicker umbrella basket. He rifles through the other house drivers stuffed in the basket. Like he's rifling through a series of CDs in a discount bin. His face shows he isn't happy with the house selection.

"Reminds me of selecting pool cues; you have to find the right one," Sonny says. "It's not about how good it looks or how bad; it's about what feels good, speaks to you. That's why I brought my own." He points two fingers at the golf bag leaned against one of the wicker two-seaters. "Feel free to try out my driver. It's the only thing I've spent any real money on."

Maggie moves from the AstroTurf pad to Sonny's golf bag. He leans forward and examines Sonny's clubs without touching them.

Sonny decides to go for it. "Let me ask you, where'd you go after they tossed you out?"

Maggie looks over his shoulder with his hand hovering over Sonny's clubs. "You talking about when I got tossed out of the minors?" Maggie selects the driver and lifts it out of the bag to examine it in the natural light, twisting it slightly to rotate the silver shaft in his hands. He runs his fingers over the rounded edge of the head, feeling for imperfections, admiring the craftsmanship.

"I've never really cared about golf. I just wanted something that worked and worked well. I told the guy at the store, give me something good, don't care what it costs and that's what he gave me."

"It's alright." Maggie drops the club to the ground, holding it like he should, like he knows his way around the game, and lines up with it like he's about to take his shot.

"I wouldn't know the difference anyways. You could tell me it's the most expensive thing out there, and I'd believe you. I don't really run in the circles where golf clubs become something I invest in, but I do like hitting balls. Helps clear my head."

Maggie hesitates before speaking. "Almost like running," he says. "Does the same for my head."

"I getcha, I getcha," Sonny says, nodding. "My boss loves it. Golf that is, it's why I have all them clubs—I don't think he does much running. I sure don't."

Maggie cuts a sideways glance at him, looking up from the pretend ball down between his feet and inches from the driver's head.

Sonny shifts his weight in the wicker seat, crossing one foot over the other. "Look… sorry if we're just jumping into it, but this is a meeting I've wanted for a long time."

Sonny pauses to see if the man will protest, but all Maggie does is wait to see what Sonny has to say.

"Don't worry about it," Maggie says, "the jumping to it. I prefer people speak plainly. I've had far too many people in my life that speak in some sort of half-assed code … but I don't know what you want me to say. You might have to help me along."

Sonny sips his beer and reads Maggie as a guy that's going to be difficult, but then he did have the reputation for not being easy to work with when he played ball. Too hot-headed. Too stubborn. Just like every other natural-born athlete destined to be something, and if that weren't proof enough, he did hit the coach with a bat and all.

"What happened to you? Where'd you go?" Sonny says. "Emerson said you started working for Siriano after leaving the game. I can see you're not going to volunteer information like that. So I figured I'm going to just jump out, right in front, and ask you what I want to know, tell you what I know to see what you're going to speak to."

Maggie shrugs. "I did work for Siriano." He admits to it like it is nothing. Like Siriano isn't a mob-connected guy running Tulsa like it's his own little kingdom. "Now, it's a gig thing, you know. They call, say they need some help with something, and I help."

Sonny picks his teeth with his finger. "They call you to help with this kidnapping thing?" Getting to it. His ankle rests on his knee, relaxed, showing off his skinny chicken legs, boney and pale as chicken skin.

Maggie nods, and all he offers is, "They called," before stepping back onto the AstroTurf. He bends down to retrieve a salmon-colored ball from the bucket. Holding the ball between two fingers, he places it on the tee, steps back, and admires the setup.

"And?"

"And nothing," Maggie says, moving into position. He grips Sonny's driver in his hands the way it should be, moving the driver back and forth softly working up to the shot. "They called, said they needed help, and then nothing."

"What'd they say?"

The driver's pendulum act pauses. "What do you care?"

"Let's just say I'm curious."

Rearing back like he used to bat, Maggie hits the ball with a brutal swing of the club. "Not that you're working on a story or something about the kidnapping?"

He pauses to put his hand over his brow to watch his ball soar into the distance.

Sonny follows the ball along until it drops below the raised deck. Judging by the arc, the angle, and the distance, it was a good hit. Better than anything he can do.

"Emerson said you wrote something about it." Maggie looks back at him. "Said it was in the paper over the weekend."

"I did write something." Sonny's insides tingle with thoughts of Kelly like he's a kid again. Puppy love. His night with her, thinking about how she came on to him and how he didn't dislike it. "It was in Sunday's edition. My editor has been on me about doing something else to get outside my comfort zone. But this, this is something different. This is a piece about you."

"For that column, the 'Where Are You Now' bullshit?"

Sonny shakes his head. "I don't know what the story is here, but my instincts tell me there's something, something big, like when you've caught the tiger by the tail but don't know what to do with it," Sonny pauses. "I guess you could say it's kinda like my relationship with my daughter."

Maggie turns from the driving range, letting the club slip through his grip. "Emerson made me think that's what you were wanting to do. Do a piece about me. Said that's all you have talked about for years, about how you always wanted to talk to me, but you never knew where I went and didn't know how to get ahold of me." Maggie walks toward him, the club in his left hand. "I think you're the only two people that remember I played ball ... outside my circle that is."

"She wasn't wrong."

Maggie slips the driver into the bag and leans against the counter. He picks up his glass of water. "What happened to you two?"

Sonny studies the man's face for a moment. "Emerson warned me about you," he says. "Told me about how you can switch things around on me with just a word in the conversation, but I didn't take it seriously. I should've. You've got chops—always been one to watch out for. I should've listened to her, but I guess that's our problem, we don't communicate well."

The cup hangs just off Maggie's lips. "So?"

Sonny tries to flip the conversation back around. "So what do you mean?"

But Maggie doesn't bite. "I mean, it's clear to me she's got some affection for you, but there's this block. She wants to like you, but she doesn't. She hates you, actually. And yet, when she realized who I was, you popped into her head." Maggie takes a drink. "'My father would love to meet you' type of shit. She wanted this for you. People that hate people don't do things like that. Don't want things for the people they hate."

Sonny sucks on his bottom lip, waiting to see if Maggie's going to ask a question. He doesn't so Sonny says. "I wasn't perfect."

"Wasn't or ain't?"

"Is there a difference?"

Maggie shrugs. "One's happening and the other is a thing of the past."

Sonny chuckles. "So are you working for Siriano or not?"

Maggie smiles and nods his head a few times. "Yeah, I work for him."

"Then I am not perfect," Sonny admits, waving a hand in front of his face. "I was a shit father."

"Feels good admitting things, don't it?"

"No." Sonny shakes his head. "It doesn't, but it is what it is."

Maggie freezes for a moment looking Sonny over in the chair, the muscles of his face relaxing. "Why is this moment... this thing with me," he touches his chest, "why's that special?"

Sonny tilts his head to the side. "She told you about that?"

The man rolls one shoulder forward, toward Sonny, while puckering his lips. "You said you were just going to jump in, so consider this me jumping in... what's the deal?"

"You know, I've not given it that much thought," Sonny says, which is true. "I don't know if I could put it into words. It's just one of those things—one of those moments between father and daughter that becomes immortalized in memory. Surely, you have something like that with your father."

Maggie diverts his eyes, looking down. "My father..." Maggie starts, but his voice trails off as he thinks of what he wants to say. Clearly, from his face, the guy doesn't like talking about his emotions.

Sonny stops him. "Don't bullshit me, the story. The column doesn't work if you don't speak the truth."

Maggie stares at him, saying nothing.

"Otherwise, we're just wasting our time," Sonny says. "I covered your father's murder as one of my first assignments. So don't stand here and lie to me about how you feel about him dying. If it's terrible, then tell me it's terrible. If you're happy the son of a bitch is dead, then tell me you're happy. I'm not going to judge you. I'll ask you why you feel that way, but I'm not here to judge ... and if you want to know a little truth, neither are my readers. Things I thought were the nastiest things someone could say end up filling readers' minds with compassion and empathy ... and you want to know why? It's because it was true."

With his head cocked to the side, reading him, Maggie shifts in his stance. "You think people don't judge?" He loosens up some, legs a bit wider, hip cocked to the side, relaxed, but gaining some edge too.

Sonny considers the question. "Alright, fair enough, there's plenty of people out there who judge, but most of them only want the truth. I think it's why people like sports. It's true; it's happening in the moment. Probably why they get so upset when they find out something's rigged or the outcome was predetermined."

"People don't want the truth," Maggie says. "People lie. They go around making up these little lies about things, about themselves, telling people fibs, stories they want to hear to make themselves feel better. Like when the wife asks about how the shirt makes her look. She don't want to hear the truth. She wants reassurance. Nothing wrong with that, but as long as everyone plays along, then it's fine, but the minute someone stops playing, then everyone cries foul."

"Or throws a flag?" Sonny suggests.

Maggie pauses. "Yeah."

Sonny agrees. "White lies are a thing for a reason, but I'm telling you, readers want the truth."

"No one wants the truth." Maggie's relaxed stance stiffens. "You think your readers—anyone—cares about my truths?"

He pauses and looks back toward the driving range. Several balls fly off the top tiers into the distance.

"No one wants to know that my father got murdered trying to stop a robbery, not because he felt some civic duty to intervene because he was a cop, but because the gas station owner paid him an envelope of cash every month, whether my father wanted—or asked for it—or not. The guy would tell him things like, 'buy Maggie some new shoes,' and shit like that. The guy knew what he was doing. He was older, been around. He knew the score, and my father knew it too.

"You think they want to know he's in there on that day getting a cup of coffee because I fucking woke up late for a tournament, and he didn't get his cup like he normally does? Know about how he drops me off at the ballfields, after talking about if I'm going to hit for a career or pitch? He wanted me to hit. He said play the fucking outfield. Be like Willie Mays. But I wanted to be the guy. The star. I wanted to be someone."

Sonny can relate. He wanted to be someone once. It cost him everything. He lost his wife to cancer and, then, lost his daughter because he couldn't pull his head from his typewriter.

Maggie goes on. "I wanted to hold the game in my hand, figuratively and literally ... my fucking ego. So you think they care if he goes into the store, gets his coffee, goes to the bathroom ... all according to the police report mind you, which is based upon the surveillance footage which I never got to fucking watch. You'd think that'd be something they'd let family look at, the fucking death of their loved one. Not this blank memory of him driving off, and then in the middle of the fucking championship game these two dicks coming over, wearing cheap suits, both looking like they haven't slept in six days, coming over to you and saying your pops was murdered. Like what the fuck... he's in there because he went to get coffee. He's in there because it's my fault. He didn't have to step in ... but because that guy financed my baseball equipment ... he does. He steps in and he gets blown away for it. You think your readers want to know that? Know some guy, an adult they said, was in there, and he was not seen until the last moment? My father had no idea he was there."

Maggie's eyes well up with tears, which makes Sonny hesitate before asking his next question.

So Maggie says, "Or how about the fact that it's unsolved? According to them, he was dirty, so who the fuck cares?"

"Do you feel like it's your fault?" That wasn't Sonny's next question. He's memorized a whole list of them, but when an interview starts flowing, you don't step on your dick by not asking the next logical question.

"Is that the truth you want? The truth your readers want?"

"I think so."

Maggie clenches his fists, his whole posture tense and compressed. "Your readers are a bunch of fucking animals," he snaps. "If that's all they want, consuming entertainment so easily but forgetting this is someone's life."

"You didn't answer the question," Sonny says, pushing. The man's all edge now, sharp, and lethal. The hotheaded young man with the anger issues arising out of the past to invade the present. "Do you feel like it's your fault?"

"Fuck you," Maggie says. "What do you want me to say? You want me to say, 'Yeah, I fucking feel like it's my fault. I got my father killed.' I've carried that around with me for years. No matter how often people tell me not to worry about it. No matter how many times I hear, there's nothing you could have done. You weren't there. It was out of your control. It's not your fault, but yeah, it's my fault. I could have gotten up like I should've. I could've asked him to stay at the game, or I could have said we could be late. There's a lot of things I could have said but didn't..." Maggie collapses into silence.

"Tell me about Siriano," Sonny says. "Where'd he come in?"

Maggie's chin tilts down to his chest like he's about to strike. "You want to know about Siriano? Know about our relationship? Know about it for your story?"

Sonny nods. "It would explain why you work for him now."

"I love that man," Maggie says. "He's like a father for me. He took me under his wing. Made me into the man I am today. Told me I couldn't act like I did. And if I did, I needed to funnel it into worthwhile pursuits. I hate his fucking son. I think he's a shit. But I love that man. He's not perfect, far from it, and he didn't get me into nothing I wasn't trying to get into myself." Maggie points a finger at Sonny.

"All your fucking readers, every one of them," he says, "they all see this guy that reminds them of Al Capone because that's what you think of when you think of mob guys, but he's like a Tony Soprano. He ain't out there making life difficult just to make life difficult; he's out there trying to run a business, and yeah, that business isn't the most legal of pursuits, but it's life and it's money and there's a certain level of heavy-handedness that exists in the world your readers know and don't want to know nothing about. No one does. No one likes the violence, just like they don't like the guys who pick up their trash. They don't want to know about them."

Sonny starts to say something, but Maggie claps his fingers together to keep him quiet. Looks like he's making a chopping motion with a hand puppet.

"I mean look at you," he says, starting his indictment of Sonny. Sonny's heard it before from guys. It's all part of the process—listen. "You write about people who made millions of dollars, not because you particularly care about them—I've read your columns; it's good shit—but because that's what your readers want. If it were up to you, you would be writing about the trash guys because you like the little guy. You like writing about guys like me, and in a way, you try to do that even when you're writing about them big guys. You like the wives and the family members who help those guys be who they are. You like telling the stories about the people who help them get where they are and the life struggles associated with them, like the man who served coffee at the Olympics. You fill in his life just as much as you fill in the *supposed* important people. You like the high school athletes and the down-and-outs. You like me, but you shouldn't. You shouldn't write about me. You don't want to know about me."

"I do," Sonny says.

"You don't," Maggie says. "What do I matter? I'm a nobody. A down-and-out who's out there in the world getting by doing things no one's proud of. I don't like myself. I don't think I'm successful because if I was successful, I'd be sitting with you in the mansion I earned with all the major league money. But that's not reality. The reality is, I'm a man who helps men like Siriano when they ask me to because I love him. I help his shithead son when he asks me to because of my relationship with his father. I don't want this life, but it's my life."

"You don't want this life?"

"Who would? I haven't really been home in years. Yeah, sure, I come through here every so often, and I spend time in town, but that's not home. Nothing feels like a home. Nothing has since my pops got popped in that gas station. Home evaporated. It was murdered that day."

"Why don't you leave?"

"Where would I go?"

"Someplace else," Sonny says. "Far away from here."

Maggie is quiet. "You only want to talk to me because I did something special on a day you were with your daughter, and that's what made it special; not me."

"No," Sonny says. "I've been interested in you since your father got killed. I thought you were going to be something."

"Yeah, well me too."

"It's not too late."

"What do you mean?" I can't get into the Majors now; I'm too old."

"That's not what I mean. There's more to life than a career or what we do."

Maggie doesn't speak.

"That was my mistake," Sonny says. "You don't have to make the same one. You could have a family."

"What are you saying?"

Sonny shrugs. He doesn't know what he's saying. "Look, this sounds silly, but I've been thinking a lot about things. My kid, she likes you. I think... I think you standing here says you like her and maybe that's not enough for a future together, but then again, maybe it is. Maybe if you decide you don't want to be in whatever life you're in now, you leave, and if you leave, take her with you."

Maggie shows some interest. "What about you all? Aren't you supposed to be working on your relationship?"

"Perhaps words aren't the way we communicate," Sonny says. "Maybe it's actions. Maybe that was the problem. I spent my life communicating with words, not knowing that actions were the thing that spoke to my daughter. And right now, what we are doing, it isn't working. But maybe, it's not too late for either of you. You're still young, relatively, maybe you two hit it off, or maybe you don't, but if you left this town together, then she wouldn't get arrested anymore, and you'd have a chance at having a life—a real life. Maybe even someone who loves you, a family."

Maggie faces away from Sonny. "What are you saying?"

"Take it from me, kid. Family's hard to hold on to, easy to lose. If you don't believe me, then look at your life and the people in it."

CHAPTER TWENTY: MAURIZIO DIMAGGIO

MAGGIE CHOOSES TO KEEP THE LIGHTS OFF, which means that when Brandy comes through the front door, he'll switch the light on, surprise him, and do what needs to be done. Sitting here now, in the dark, Maggie thinks about what the reporter asked of him.

Take his kid away. Start a family.

Like, what the hell?

Those things aren't him. They've never been him. Why would this guy even ask him to do that? But would it be so bad? Leave this life. Leave the city. Find someone he could have fun with, talk to... look at... and settle down some, have a life. A family. Maybe try his hand at being a dad.

Then, he chastises himself and tells himself, woah slow down. Don't get too ahead of yourself. The girl is a thief, and that brings attention, and the last thing he needs in his life is attention.

Besides, all he knows how to do is pitch baseballs and work in the *restoration* business. What would he do if he left the business altogether? What would he tell Siriano? If Jackie C. were alive, what would Maggie tell him? I'm sorry. I'm out. Thanks for teaching me your life's work, but see ya.

For the most part, Maggie has stayed out of trouble. He knows baseball, still follows it some, and he could probably find some high school hurting for a pitching coach and talk his way in. Maybe he could be a custodian or something while he works on figuring out what he wants to do with his life.

And beyond all that, what would the reporter's kid think? Would she even go with him? Something tells him yeah, she would. Something about Emerson, the way she looks at him. But she gets a choice too, right? He couldn't just kidnap her and leave town. He could tell her, "I'm leaving. Your pops wants me to take you with me. Wanna come with?"

What would she say?

More importantly, what does he want her to say?

Maggie's so distracted thinking all this over that he doesn't hear the key slip into the lock or the turn of the knob. Then Brandy's standing there, long hair and all. Maggie studies him, judging how the man's going to react.

"Shit," Brandy says, not surprised at finding Maggie in his apartment but sounding disappointed for not placing Maggie's face at the driving range. "It was you."

Maggie recognized Brandy instantly. It was the eyes. They had been friends once, but that was a while ago. Things change, especially appearances, or at least Brandy's appearance. But not the eyes. Maggie noticed the eyes when Brandy dropped off the drinks while Maggie was talking to the reporter. Afterward, Maggie followed Brandy home and waited until Brandy left again, probably an errand. Maggie entered the building and asked the adjoining apartment neighbor an old lady in a cardigan, if his *buddy* still worked at the driving range, which she said yes, he does and told Maggie that Brandy would be back soon. Said he ran to the store to buy her some groceries and said Maggie could wait for Brandy in her apartment. She made Maggie coffee while he waited. Then, she told him she had a key to the apartment if he wanted to wait inside for his friend. Maggie thanked her for the key, drank his coffee, and politely left.

Maggie wears what he wore at the driving range, but with tight black leather gloves. His gun, hand loose on the handle, rests on his knee. He waves it twice to get Brandy's attention. "Don't make a scene. Shut the door."

Brandy does as he is told. "You want me to lock it?" he asks, with his hand on the deadbolt.

"If it makes you more comfortable," Maggie says, gun lazily pointed at Brandy.

Brandy throws the deadbolt. "Oasis called, said you had come around."

"So she did know how to get in contact with you." Maggie works it out in his mind. "I thought she might. She warn you?"

"Sorta." Brandy steps away from the door. Fingers held wide, showing his clear hands. He looks around the room. "Mind if I sit?"

Maggie shakes his head. With his free hand, he clicks on the floor lamp hovering over him, illuminating the place.

The apartment is sparse, sad really. One lone couch/futon set. Black cushions which look like they belong on outdoor furniture. The recliner Maggie's in isn't too bad, but it's second-hand, and the leather, or fake leather, is worn off in spots. A TV, Brandy's only real investment, hangs on the wall next to the front door.

The rest of the place isn't much better; it tells a sad story. The kitchen isn't any different than the living room, a generic wooden table, cheap, with four chairs. Something you assemble and made from MDF, which means dented corners and stripped low-budget screws. Appliances bought from Walmart or Target. The bedroom has a mattress on a frame, but a cardboard box acts as the nightstand. A quick walk-through the rest of the one-bedroom apartment told Maggie any furniture in there is second-hand, probably purchased at garage sales. Brandy used to go on and on about how he could find the best deals at garage sales, saying he got more bang for his buck. And when an accountant, a guy good with numbers, tells him that's where he should shop, Maggie listens.

"What's the deal with the shitty job?"

"I needed spending money," Brandy says but neglects to say any more. Maggie gets it. "I thought that was you. You haven't changed all that much; you look older, rougher, lost some weight, but it's you, even after all this time."

"You don't look like yourself. What's with the hair?"

Brandy doesn't explain the hair. "Mind if I make a drink?" he asks before moving. He knows better than to move without permission. He points a finger at the dented wet bar with obvious water damage, near the front door. It doesn't match anything else in the room. It's next to an old record player with records stacked under and next to it in milk crates stuffed full. "You want something? Whiskey, scotch, whatever?"

"I'm good," Maggie says.

Brandy doesn't offer to put music on, which is good. Maggie doesn't need the distraction, and Brandy probably doesn't want to get popped to a soundtrack. Maggie does briefly consider what would play underneath the scene. Would the needle drop be something dramatic or something ironic?

Brandy moves to the wet bar. Glasses clink as he talks. "Oasis and I, we talked about what would happen if you came around." He pulls a glass from the cabinet and sets it down on the mirrored surface. He picks up a crystal decanter, uncorks it, sniffs the liquid, and sets it down in favor of another one, which he doesn't inspect, merely uncorks and pours. "I said I couldn't stay there; I'd put them in trouble." He glances over his shoulder and goes back to pouring his drink. "I couldn't be sure who would come around looking for me, but I knew someone would, eventually. You see, all of them stories about the witness protection program, no way someone can just cut all ties with everyone in their life and go start a new life. Oasis couldn't do that. I couldn't. I knew that."

With a drink in his hand, Brandy walks from the wet bar to the sofa.

Maggie says, "So you left."

"Left the program." Brandy sips the drink as he takes his seat. "Yeah, I left, and then I left Oasis."

"She told me."

"She tell you about the skateboard?"

Maggie nods.

"I hated doing it, but it was the best thing." Brandy sips the drink again. "I figured I'd let them at least have a chance at a normal life. I know how Jackie C. was, and the odds were that Siriano would send someone from Jackie's stable to come find me. Whoever they sent wouldn't bother the girls if I weren't there." He pauses. "Didn't figure it would be you, but then again, I never thought I'd go to the cops."

"I still have trouble with that myself," Maggie admits. "I never expected someone like you would do that."

"I had a change of heart." Brandy shrugs. "I found out some things, saw how people were treated, how Oasis was treated." He tips the glass toward Maggie. "How you were treated. It wasn't right. Someone had to do something. Besides I had a kid I had to look out for."

"How'd Oasis take you leaving?"

"Not well," Brandy says. "I bet she's still mad. I'm sure she wasn't acting when you were there. She was pissed and has been pissed. Pissed at the situation. I knew she'd be furious at me for leaving. I waited a while before I called. I don't know where I was, Iowa or someplace. A truck stop. Grew a beard for a while, worked on growing my hair. Couldn't part with the glasses though. I just can't do contacts. Anyways, I called her and told her what I had been thinking."

"What'd she say?"

"It was a mistake but good riddance," Brandy says. He falls back into the seat. "She's family-oriented, believe it or not. I think removing myself from the picture allowed her to get back in touch with her family—her mom specifically. It's good for her. Good for the kid too." Brandy furrows his eyebrows, and the light glistens off the tears welling in the corners. "What's the kid like? Is she getting tall?"

Maggie's gun hand relaxes. "She's got spunk."

"Yeah," Brandy says, liking the sound of that. "Good, good. She's a good kid. I miss her. I think that's the hardest part. Missing them both. Missing her grow up. I think all this will be over soon enough, but I don't know."

"Why'd you do it?" Maggie asks.

"Leave?" Brandy doesn't understand the question.

"Go to the cops," Maggie says.

Brandy shakes his head and sips the drink. "You don't know what it's like to have someone like Siriano come into your life the way he came into mine. When he hired me, I thought I was going to be a controller for some locally owned company, corporation thing. I didn't know who he was. I didn't know what he stood for. I was a kid, no different than you were at the time. I wanted to put my accounting skills to the test, make something of myself. I thought this guy had a couple of businesses, cash mostly, needed someone to come in and straighten things up. How was I supposed to know anything different?

"Well, that wasn't what it was, but then I enjoyed the life too much at that point and wanted to enjoy it some more. Did I know it was wrong? Did I know I didn't like it? Did I know it was not healthy? Yeah, I did, but I wanted to enjoy the high life."

Brandy sips his drink and offers to get one for Maggie again. Maggie declines with a jerk of his head.

"You know, being an accountant isn't as glamorous as you would think. It's not like the sororities in school were beating down my door or the frat guys were letting me go to their parties. I was a nobody. The attention felt good. Besides, if I hadn't enjoyed it as much as I have, I would never have met you."

"What's meeting me have to do with anything?"

"We were friends. It meant something to me."

"Obviously, not enough to keep your mouth shut."

"Hey," Brandy says, "who's the one here with a kid, something to lose? You want me to have done what, just wait until Siriano decided I wasn't useful anymore? You know what he does with those guys. Retirement isn't exactly a thing. In fact, look at the old man? He was in prison, my fault, sure, but now he's been kidnapped. There's no guarantee in life. I thought I'd make something better. Enjoy my family. Have a life."

"How's that working out for you?" Maggie asks.

"Better than it's working for you," Brandy says. "You visiting Oasis was a test. I figured someone would come to her, and I'm happy it was you because I have something to tell you. Then you can do whatever you want."

"Like she knew what to say to me?"

"I told her if it was you, she was to help you, tell you where I was," Brandy says. "I figured the kid hired you to find me and kill me. It's what you do, right?"

"Something like that."

"That's what you told Oasis; it makes sense," he says, sipping his drink. "When you did something, you did it to the fullest. You play baseball, you were the best, course I didn't know you then. You drove for the old man, you fucking drove for the old man. Not a fender bender, not a scrap, car polished and detailed every week. You took pride in your work. Then when Jackie C. started coming around, taking you with him wherever you all went. I knew you'd be the best for him too."

"What do you have to tell me?" Maggie leans forward, elbows on his knees. "Flattery isn't going to keep what's about to happen from happening."

Brandy finishes the drink in one gulp, the liquid like mercury, disappearing between his lips. He sits the glass between his legs. "Nothing's going to keep what's about to happen from happening, but you should know something before you do what you've come here to do."

"What's that?"

"The truth," Brandy says.

Maggie smiles. "Seems to be a popular subject."

Brandy cocks his head to the side. "It's about your father," he says. "You ever find out what happened to him? The truth? Who did it? Anyone ever tell you?"

"No one knows who did it."

"Siriano told me. He was drunk."

Maggie jerks his head to the side. "Told you? What do you mean?"

"Look, I thought they'd send you around. You're the best, right? And when I found out the truth, I couldn't just come tell you. You had this issue with anger and outbursts. I didn't want to be the messenger who got killed, and I'm glad I didn't because then it would be someone else from Siriano's organization sitting here and not you. You tell me about how your father died. How many people were involved?"

"Where's this going?"

"Humor a dying man," Brandy continues. "Can I get another drink?"

Maggie says sure. Brandy extracts himself from the couch and moves to the wet bar. He starts to pour his second drink. Maggie adds after a sigh, "There were two people, a kid, teenager or something, and an adult. The cops said my father didn't see the adult. That's the guy that shot him."

Brandy sets the decanter back on the bar and turns. He leans against the bar. He sips the drink. "But they don't know who it was. The cops."

Maggie shakes his head. "No, they don't know who it was. No one does. No one else was there. The video doesn't show who it was, not that I ever got to see it."

Brandy holds the glass out toward Maggie. "Siriano was there." He kills the drink in one toss.

"What are you saying?" But Maggie knows what Brandy's saying.

Brand lets silence act as his punctuation. "The man you love, the one who picked you up when you got tossed out of the minors, the guy still paying your bills and pulling your strings—you know what I'm saying."

"You're saying he killed my father?" Maggie drops the gun to the side of his thigh, muzzle off Brandy.

"The kid, the teenager, who do you think that was if the adult was Siriano?"

Maggie repeats his question, still not fully understanding. "You're saying Siriano killed my father?"

"I'm not saying it," Brandy says. "I know it, 'cause he said it."

"How?" Maggie can't swallow right now, throat dry, brain running a thousand miles an hour, sucking up every bit of juice needed, every drop of lubricant to run the calculations and spit out the solution, except his brain doesn't have to work that hard, telling him something he already knows. It makes sense. Explains a whole hell of a lot.

Brandy shakes his head and steps from the wet bar. "You were such the good boy, the good employee, driving the car, taking hitman lessons, but when that screen went up, separating you from the cabin of the car, you couldn't hear a thing. Siriano used to cuss at you, mock you, make fun, and you couldn't hear a thing. You never let on you could hear, and if you could've heard, then you would know what I'm talking about."

"I couldn't hear a thing."

"I know, that's what I'm saying," Brandy says. "He told me one day, said it was his biggest regret. He didn't know it was your father. He knew the old man who ran that station wouldn't pay protection money to Siriano and threatened to get the cops involved. The man said there was one cop he paid protection money to simply because he wanted to and not because he had to. The old man was threatened into doing it."

Maggie doesn't know what to say.

Brandy smacks his lips and sits down on the couch. "I thought you should know before you do what you're going to do. I know what you are thinking right now, and yeah, I could be making this up, but you know it makes sense, explains why the old man was so fond of you. Maybe he does have a heart after all." Brandy chuckles to himself. "But I don't care anymore. I've held that in a long time. I knew what I was doing. I chose my family over this life." He holds up both hands. "I should have told you when I found out, but I didn't, and I'm sorry. It was a card I held onto to play later, and now I'm playing it. It's up to you what you want to do with it, but know this, Oasis... Brandy... they get to have a life. I gave that to them. Siriano took that from you. So now you get to make a choice. Do what you were hired to do or don't, but you should choose knowing all the facts."

What Brandy is really saying is Maggie could make the girl just like him, take her father from her like Siriano took his father from him. Is that true?

"Why tell me now?"

"I thought you should have all the facts," Brandy says. "If you don't believe me, ask the old man. Have him tell you who the kid was."

Maggie knows who the kid was. There's only one possibility.

Maggie's phone rings. He tries to ignore it.

"You should answer it," Brandy says.

The phone rings.

"I don't want to interrupt our conversation."

The phone rings.

Brandy sets the glass down and takes up the decanter. "It could be important. Answer it. It's fine. I won't go anywhere."

The phone rings.

Brandy holds up his hands, half-heartedly, takes a sip from the decanter. "I promise, I won't move."

The phone rings.

Maggie raises the gun to his knee and keeps it and his eyes on Brandy as he answers the call. It's Wilson.

"Yeah," Maggie says.

"The trade happens tonight," Wilson says. "I need you there."

"The trade?"

"For the old man," Wilson says. "I need you there."

Maggie looks at Brandy and, for a moment, considers telling Wilson he found him.

"And in case you were thinking about not helping out," Wilson says, "since you've been kind of distracted through this whole thing, well, that girl you've been spending time with the last few days, she might be thankful to see you show up at the meet."

And he ends the call.

The girl he's been spending time with. Emerson? How did Wilson know about her?

Brandy, looking at Maggie, asks, "So what are you going to do?"

Maggie lowers the gun. He reaches up and pulls the cord, switching off the light. He stands.

In the dark, he crosses the room, walks to the wet bar while tucking the gun into his waistband, and makes a drink, ripping the decanter from Brandy's hand. He finishes the drink off, silently, in one swig.

The entire time, Brandy says nothing and doesn't move. Maggie's not even sure the guy's breathing.

Maggie doesn't look at him. "Your wife says hello. You should call her. Go home."

And with that, Maggie sets the neighbor's key on the wet bar and shows himself out, leaving Brandy in the dark, not moving.

CHAPTER TWENTY-ONE: KELLY CHAMBERS

KELLY ENTERS THE SMALL INTERROGATION ROOM and sits across from Omar Sanchez. Omar looks up at her from the table and picks up his black frame glasses. He's sat quietly for the last hour. He had nothing he wanted to say to the police when they asked about the shooting his car was involved in other than, "I sold that car to my little brother." But when detectives asked who his little brother was, Omar shook his head, smiling slyly, and remained mute. When the detectives gave up, Kelly decided to give it a go.

The walls are covered in egg crate foam, a sickly pale brown caramel. The room smells stale, not sterile, like old cigarettes where the smoke's seeped into the paint. The table is a bent and beat-up piece of square composite—maybe pine or oak. The chairs are dilapidated computer chairs, mismatched, one a faded maroon turned pink. Omar's chair is a classic plastic school chair, metal rods for legs.

Kelly studies the man, the sun-drenched skin and calloused fingers. She sees signs of cuts, scrapes, and burns, all probably from working in the kitchen at the diner Alejandro used to run.

He's relaxed and seemingly unworried about being in police custody. He crosses his arms over his front now wearing his black glasses. He leans back in the chair, legs straight, ankles crossed. He stares back at her.

She scoots the computer chair back from the table. It threatens to tilt over backward. A wheel shifts under her, turning, and she fears the black plastic will crack, not from her abuse but from age.

She crosses one knee over the other and glances at her watch.

Omar says nothing and stays as he was. The glasses magnify his eyes some: big brown orbs. Kind eyes. It's not like what she's seen with some criminals, but then Uncle Frank would tell her that means nothing. He would say he's sat across from murderers, and they were the nicest, most interesting men in the world, but that wouldn't keep them from sinking an ice pick in some poor sucker's neck.

After a few more seconds of silence, she checks her phone. Sonny sent her a message asking her to meet him for dinner. She picks up the phone and returns the text asking where. Nails tapping on the screen in a quick staccato. Sonny responds after a few seconds as if he was waiting for her message. He suggests Waffle House, saying it's one of his favorite places. Kelly taps out a response, aware of her fingernails clacking against the touch-sensitive screen in the otherwise silent room. When she's done, she tosses the phone onto the table and withdraws her hands into her lap.

"So tell me," she says, starting mid-thought, "what was the thinking in kidnapping Siriano?"

Omar doesn't move except for a slight head tilt and eyebrow twitch, the left one. He does a fair job at hiding his surprise, more so than most, but those kind brown eyes don't hide it well enough. She sees it. Uncle Frank's taught her well, and she doesn't miss the interest.

Kelly points her chin at the camera hanging in the corner of the room and throws her head back toward the door. "Don't worry," she says. "I asked them to turn off the equipment."

Omar's eyes drift around the room, starting with the visible false camera in the corner to Kelly's left, down to Kelly, and then across the rest of the tight space.

"I want my lawyer," he says.

"This isn't that type of conversation."

He tilts his head to the side. "What type of conversation is it, then?"

"Just a conversation."

"Not an interrogation?"

"Nor an interview, just a conversation."

"I see," Omar says.

"But I want you to be honest with me."

"Do you think I would lie to you?"

"Do you think I would like you to?" She picks up her phone, unlocks it, and hands it to him. "I'm not recording, but if you want to double-check ... or make a phone call to your attorney, here you go. I don't want you thinking negatively of me."

Omar accepts the phone but places it face down on the table. "I don't think anything about you one way or another," he says, which in and of itself isn't much of a start, but it's better than nothing. It shows he's willing to talk but only about subjects he wants to speak on and with the right question.

"That's good," Kelly says. "A lot of guys, they come in here—maybe not here," she holds her hands out to her side, "but in rooms like this, interview rooms—and they either lie to us or bluster with anger and vigor to try to throw us off. Course, that's a sign of guilt if you know what I mean. Then there are guys like you—"

"Innocent?"

"You're not innocent," she says. "No more than I'm not black. But there are guys like you who still play by rules. You're not going to sit here and lie to me, and you aren't going to be disrespectful either. That type of behavior is usually a sign of guilt too."

"What about innocent men?"

"I don't know about these detectives." Kelly motions to the door behind her with her thumb. "But I don't get innocent men in this room. I am thorough enough that if you are sitting here, there's a reason."

"So why then is the equipment off?"

Kelly shrugs. "Because I'm not supposed to be here."

"Then, neither am I."

"How do you figure?"

"I stood mute. I answered the few questions I have any information I was willing to provide, and then, I was silent. You are supposed to quit asking after I go silent."

Kelly shakes her head and holds up a finger. "What's interesting is you only provided answers to questions you were willing to answer, which mean you were not telling us what you know."

From the slight shift in his face, a nod down, Kelly can see Omar concedes the point. "So why are you not supposed to be here?"

"Have you seen the news?"

"In general? Ever? Or do you have a specific date and time in mind?"

Kelly doesn't let his passive-aggressive attitude upset her. "I'll take that you have seen the news recently, so you know Russell Siriano was kidnapped outside the courthouse."

It wasn't a question, but Omar acknowledges it. "I heard."

Kelly leans forward. "He was taken from me with my handcuffs on him."

Omar studies her as she studied him when she entered the room. "Sounds like you are more upset about the missing handcuffs than his abduction."

"They came from my uncle."

"They were his handcuffs?"

Kelly nods. "And he has a theory. Well, he has a lot of theories. Likes to hear himself think. My mother used to entertain him, but I…I just listen. Sometimes his theories make sense. Most times not." She pauses to see if Omar stays with her. He does. "His theory is that crime, boiled down to its bare essence is nothing more than family squabbles."

Omar uncrosses his ankles and sets his feet under his knees, straightens his back some. He adjusts his black frame glasses, resettling them in place. "How do you explain white-collar theft, like embezzlement from corporations? How do those fit in?"

Kelly suppresses a smile because she had said something similar to Frank. She gives Omar the list of questions she gave Uncle Frank when he spouted that homespun wisdom, rolling her hand over and over as she speaks. "What's the motivation? The nagging wife? The poor childhood? The greed of never having anything?"

"You think that is related to the family?"

Kelly shrugs. "Honestly, I don't know. I'm sure you have an uncle that people don't listen to. I just make the mistake of listening to mine. He has that country wisdom born from spending too much time outside under the sun. I think the hat's boiled his brain."

"What type of hat?"

"Stetson, with a smart turn to it."

"What's that mean, a smart turn?" Omar's body opens up some, his shoulders widening as his face shows some expression. "I read, read a lot, read westerns because I like to think about another time, another place. I don't think the world's changed too much. We just ride in cars, not on horses. And most likely, I'd still work in a kitchen. I like cooking. I like food." He pinches his belly fat. "Flavia, my wife, she's always telling me to be careful how much I taste, saying I'll end up eating too much. And when you watch those networks devoted to food, not that I spend much time watching TV. Alejandro liked to turn the little TV hanging in the corner near the door to those networks because they were family-friendly, you see all those chefs with bellies bigger than mine. Anyways, in those westerns, they always mention how this guy, the hero or the villain, all wear their hats with a smart turn of the brim. I don't know what that means."

Kelly's never thought about it before. The term came from her mother. She'd always say that about Frank when she gushed about him to her sisters on the phone.

"You know what," Kelly smiles, "I'm not sure. I guess I've never really thought about it."

Omar shrugs, his face saying "Oh, well."

"I'm also not sure about his theory, but I've given it some thought. I mean a large number of crimes are family issues. Boyfriends. Girlfriends. Husbands. Wives. Kids. Maybe not on the federal level but local. Yeah, a lot of it is family at its core. How many serial killers had fucked up childhoods or how many sexual abusers were abused themselves. Family drives motivation."

"Nature vs nurture, huh?"

"Which is why I know you were involved with Siriano's kidnapping."

"You do?"

"I do," she says. "It makes sense when you sit down and put the pieces together."

"It does?"

"Start with the kidnapping itself. Look at the motivation. That got me for a while until I started asking around, unofficially. But you saw the news. I had to do something; I couldn't just accept the embarrassment of having that happen live on TV."

"What's the motivation?"

"Power." Kelly offers the only answer that makes sense to her.

Omar thinks the answer over. "For who?"

"That's the question, isn't it? Who benefits if Siriano isn't around?" Kelly scoots the chair back and stands up. She stretches her back, placing her hands on her hips. "You do. You benefit, or should I say Alejandro's neighborhood gang benefits."

Omar sighs. "I just don't see how."

But he has those glasses. He should see.

"Start backward." Kelly paces the length of the table, not trying to appear intimidating but inviting, relaxed. "Isn't that life: our past events influence our future events? Nature vs nurture as you said." Weighing the two with her hands. "Start at the beginning. According to my friend in the DEA who has some knowledge of Siriano—I mean he did lose a partner while trying to put charges on the guy—Siriano uses Alejandro to maintain relations with the cartels pushing in from the south. Hence, how the missing—and I assume is the dead—Renaldo Luna ended up changing positions from Alejandro's crew to Siriano's."

Omar seems unmoved with her standing over him.

"Except Renaldo screwed up. He set a deal with a couple of DEA agents, one of those guys ended up getting shot and killed, and now Renaldo's missing. But he only went missing after Alejandro ends up dead. So what happened? Siriano take out Alejandro? Or did Renaldo act on his own?"

Kelly doesn't expect him to answer her questions. He may not know. Omar may not be who she thinks he is. Maybe he really just works in the kitchen. Judging by his hands and forearms, real evidence, not conjecture, he's a cook.

Omar shrugs.

"So who is in charge now? Pablo? You?"

Omar chuckles. "It is not me."

That statement rings true. "I didn't think it was, or you wouldn't be trying to pick up a car full of bullet holes."

Omar smiles. "My brother called. Asked me to pick up the car."

Now they are getting somewhere. "Why?"

"He was afraid. Someone tried to kill him."

"Why?" she asks.

Omar smiles broader and adjusts in the seat, a dead-eyed smile, betraying the truth of the statement. "You know why."

Kelly spins the computer chair around, the back facing him, and squats on the seat. She folds her arms on the curved chair back. "I don't, but I'm trying to understand."

Her tone pleads for him to help her understand. That's the purpose of the conversation and not the interrogation. Kelly thinks he understands. His features show he understands.

"Say your theory is correct," he continues, leaning forward, throwing his arms on the table. "Who by your account should be in charge?"

"I'm not a kingmaker."

The desire for a cigarette crosses her taste buds. She licks her lips and flares her nostrils.

"Neither am I," Omar says. "So why would I kidnap Siriano?"

"To get back at him for killing your boss," Kelly says.

"And then what?"

"That's the question, isn't it? Are you going to kill him or ransom him back? Is this a power move, like a rape, a violation?"

"But you are not talking about me," Omar says. "So who of Alejandro's would need to prove himself?"

"Pablo. You're talking about Pablo, the bodyguard. That's what he was, right?"

Omar opens his hands wide, palms up toward the low ceiling. "Bodyguards don't make it a habit of letting those they protect die."

"But he's in charge?"

"If you say."

Kelly fills in the gaps. "Pablo goes to the Mexicans and invites them to back his play. He doesn't want you or your wife, my DEA friend said you both run the restaurant, taking over. So he brings in muscle he can control. The guy with the AR15. The one with the eyes. The others were kids, some stupid street gang or youngsters on the bottom. Alejandro was notorious for recruiting the smartest and brightest. I bet you he did the same with your brother."

"I tried so much to keep him out of trouble," Omar says. His eyes take him someplace else. "When Gabino was a boy, he got a new BB gun. He bought it from a friend. It was black and expensive, something, if a police officer saw it pointed at him, would get Gabby shot. Gabby wanted to go show a friend of his who lived around the block. I told him it wasn't a good idea. Mom, our mother, liked to have dinner at the same time every night. I told him if he'll wait until later, I'll take him, but we have to eat first. Our responsibility is to be home when expected. I go inside to go to the bathroom, leave him outside. When I come back out, he's gone. I don't know where he went. I go in for dinner. My mother beats me because I don't know where Gabby went. She yells and screams and cries that her boy's lost, thinking some man grabbed him off the street. She picks up the phone to call the police, handing it to me to speak to them because she only speaks Spanish and the police don't. But I think about it, and I say, he wouldn't let a man grab him because he had the BB gun. He'd shoot the man in the eye, and then I know where Gabby went. His friend's. I walk over there. He sees me. I tell him our mother's crying and worried and about to call the police. It makes him cry."

Omar pauses.

Kelly chooses to stay silent.

Omar adds, "He's a good boy, but he isn't right for this life."

"The restaurant business?"

Omar just stares at her.

"Good boys cry when they upset their mother." Kelly summarizes her thoughts. "Pablo kidnaps Siriano but doesn't kill him, to grab power. Siriano's son loses it, knows something we don't, since we just got on to you, and sends someone around to take off those involved. Your brother is one of them. Your wife another."

Omar raises an eyebrow.

"But you weren't there. So why are you sitting here now?"

"Why am I sitting here now?"

"That's the question. My uncle was with me in the car when you were arrested. He asked me how TPD got on you. I asked the detective, and you know what he said?"

Omar shakes his head, but he knows. He's figured it out. Her DEA friend told her Omar is smart. Omar was Alejandro's second in command. His true confidant. He has the restraint Alejandro needed. And now that Alejandro's dead, he has the restaurant.

"My TPD friend said they got a tip," she says. "A tip."

Omar snorts. "You think I was betrayed."

"No," she says, "I know it."

Omar is silent.

Kelly adds, "I can't prove it. Just as I can't prove my theory or my uncle's theory about crime. Who would call the police on you? Your brother? Your wife. No, I don't think so. Pablo is more likely, but if he kidnapped Siriano, he doesn't want us getting on to him.

"No, my bet is you're all being played. Pablo, you, Siriano's side. If you look at it this way, you have to ask yourself: how did they find your brother when they shot up the car? The answer, someone is playing both sides."

"If that is correct, what's it mean to you?"

"Nothing," she says and means it. "I started off hurt, confused, angry, embarrassed, but then, as I worked through it, talked with my uncle and others, did the work that has you here talking to me, I realized the kidnapping was out of my hands. We only live one life. I don't want to waste mine worrying about something I never had control over. So, what I'm going to do is leave you here and go meet a friend for dinner, and then I'm going to move on. I got my answers, or at least, some of them."

Omar motions to the room with both hands. "And what of me?"

"You? You'll get out of here, go back to whatever is going on. You can do whatever you want with my theory. We never had this conversation, and I don't care."

Kelly stands to leave.

Omar looks down at the table.

When her hand is on the door handle, Omar says, "If what you say is true, then my wife is in danger. Great danger."

Kelly pauses. She fights the urge to turn around to face him. She drops her chin to her chest, breathing heavily, waiting, and stares at a discolored knot in the wood grain of the door. She knows what's coming.

It won't be for her, she's not here, not officially, but it doesn't mean it doesn't fill her with vindication.

Omar says, "I know where Siriano is."

CHAPTER TWENTY-TWO: EMERSON ROWAN

EMERSON COMES OUT OF HER ROOM AT NOON. SHE crosses the hallway dressed in workout clothes, a pink tank top over gray shorts, both sweated through and disgusting with dark wet stains that make the clothing stick to her body. Emerson didn't sleep until noon. She got up at eight, started her day with an hour and a half of yoga and stretching, and ate a light breakfast, which consisted of a piece of toast, a small strawberry-based protein shake, and a cup of coffee. Her father made the pot and left it for her. After breakfast, she went back to her room to finish her workout. Today was a heavy cardio HIIT day.

Every morning she does *something* and follows somewhat the same routine.

She used to run, loved to run and could run forever, but running in the city had its disadvantages, and she'd rather do the minimum for maximum results than waste time running for hours on end. Lately, she has taken to doing one of those thirty minutes to an hour or more body-weight workout routines that used to be sold on CDs. Nowadays, she can sign up for a yearly subscription and choose to do any body improvement plan the company offers on her Smart TV from the comfort of her room. She doesn't like the ones that require any real weight-lifting. She finds her thighs get bigger than she likes when she's lifting weights. Her pants don't fit right, and she doesn't want to look like a man. All the instructors on these programs, the women and the men, but especially the women, are good-looking with well-toned muscles. Emerson doubts they got their looks doing their own programs. Consumerism magic.

It doesn't matter. Emerson's been successful enough with the routines she does do, and she enjoys getting her heart rate up, especially on the heavy cardio days. She feels the programs keep her body toned well enough to suit her purposes or any man she happens to be with.

When she had her date with Maggie, he mentioned he liked to run. She told him he could chase her if he liked. She said she's been told she has a nice ass; if he chased her, he'd get to look at it. He didn't say anything, just smiled.

Those blue eyes of his, that smile, it melts her every time.

Emerson got into streaming bodyweight workout programs while living in LA, trying to stay healthy while staying LA-worthy, not just to look sexy, but also so she didn't look ugly. The women out there, Jesus, Emerson never met more self-centered and vain women in all her life. Her life before LA was the Midwest, or was it the south? There's a bit of a debate. All of the women she knew were servers pretending to be actresses, who either had personal trainers or tortured their bodies to look like they did, throwing up, doing cocaine, not eating, and/or working out a hundred hours a day. It was all done to get the *right look*, but to Emerson, they never looked right. She couldn't understand why they all tried to be something they weren't. Isn't the most important thing about acting being comfortable on stage? How can you pretend to be someone else if you don't even know yourself and aren't comfortable in your own skin?

Halfway across the hallway, Emerson pulls the tank top off, over her head, revealing her nude torso and tussling her hair. She isn't concerned about her father seeing her half-naked, he's gone for the day, off meeting Maggie.

God, if he walked in on her nude, that'd be embarrassing.

It happened once when she came to visit years ago. She went out, got skunk drunk, passed out in the hallway walking from the bathroom to her room, bare ass up in the air, face down in the carpet. She didn't remember driving home, and she didn't remember him finding her, but he asked her about the broken towel rack and toilet paper holder in the bathroom the next morning. And when she didn't know what he was talking about, he showed her and explained how he found her.

Her father's meeting with Maggie is around now. She knows because she set it up. Somewhere deep inside she liked that. Liked making her father happy, giving him a special gift, something no one else could give him. It felt good. They may not get along and may not have mended their relationship like they thought her coming back would, but that doesn't mean they haven't made some strides in the right direction. Looking at it that way today, that's the point. At least, it's something.

Not to mention that she liked that Maggie was doing it for her, not because he had to but because he wanted to. He seemed excited about it. A lot more so than when she called him the first time.

She likes him, and the guy's special.

She twists the silver knob for the shower to get the water going and shoves the shorts off her hips. She steps out of the shorts, kicking them to the side, making a pile with her soiled clothes, and she notices her father didn't flush the toilet after he used it last.

"Gross." She taps the lever.

She sticks her hand under the shower water to feel when it's heated. It's an older house, and it takes the water heater a moment to catch up. The water changes temperature with the strain of the flushing toilet. Once the temperature levels out, Emerson jumps into the shower, rinsing off the workout and the night. Afterward, she spends extra time blow-drying her hair, hoping she can entice Maggie into meeting again, this afternoon or tonight. She'll ask him how the meeting with her father went. Emerson knows her father well enough; she's sure he's going to upset Maggie with all his questions—Maggie doesn't seem the type that likes being asked things about himself. But at the same time, her father's going to be on his best behavior because he's getting his meeting with Maurizio DiMaggio, which he's pined over for years. Maybe she'll feel those lips on hers. Stare into those blue eyes. Show him her gratitude for doing something nice for her when he didn't have to.

She comes out of the bathroom with a towel wrapped around her body, rubbing in the last bit of lotion on her arms and shoulders. She's in the hallway with the living room coming into view, with the big couch that could fit a whole family, and Emerson sees him. A figure sitting there wearing clothes that look too big for his frame, something a rock and roll group from the late 90s would find fashionable, flat bill Chicago Bulls hat, black on red, with a matching sweatshirt and basketball shorts that hang down toward his calves, a toothpick in the corner of his mouth.

He's lounged out on the couch as if he was waiting for her. When he sees her, he shakes and shuffles to attention, taking up the gun laying on the cushion next to him and smiles. He says, "Hello." Amused, not threatening.

Emerson freezes on the threshold, trying to feel out the situation. Aware of the towel shoved under her armpits. Who is this guy? What's he doing here?

The best play is to act nonchalant about him and the scene, like when she's caught shoplifting. Her left hand keeps rubbing the lotion into her right shoulder. "Hello," she says, smiling.

Emerson considers dropping the towel to take away his surprise advantage. He could be here to rape her, but she doesn't get that vibe. She's been with those sorts of men. It hasn't gone well for them. Not to mention, she spent two years in jail for something she did, but not something she should have been locked up for. She's had more instances like this than she's proud to admit, coming back to her cell to find a woman there looking to get something going with her. The first couple of times didn't go well, usually ending with a black eye, full-on nude catfight. But then, she figured it out; if there's one truth about jail life, it is life repeats itself, and there's always someone new.

The stranger tries to put her at ease. "I'm a friend of DiMaggio."

Her first thought is, if that was true he'd call him Maggie. He made that pretty clear from the beginning. Emerson knows how to talk to these people—meaning people who break into other people's houses and point guns. She knows how to play the game.

"*Really*?" Emerson adds a surprised and questioning uplift to the word.

"He said he'd like you to join us this evening." The stranger removes the toothpick and points it at her. "Asked me to come by and pick you up."

Emerson says, "And let yourself in."

The man starts to stand. "What was that?"

Emerson waves both hands in front of her body, moving at the elbows. "Nothing," she says. "And what are we doing this evening?"

The man stands with the gun at his side, showing he's smarter than he looks. He knows he doesn't need to use the gun to motivate her, and besides, she feels like she's done a pretty good job of not letting on that her legs are quivering or that her chest has tightened into a condensed ball that prevents her from taking a full breath.

The guy doesn't answer her question. He shoves the toothpick back in the corner of his mouth.

Every time she speaks, the evenness of her voice surprises her. "I simply ask so I know how to dress."

"No," he says.

"No?" she repeats. "No, I can't get dressed, or no you're not going to tell me what we are doing?"

"No, you can't get dressed," the man confirms.

"You're going to make me go out in a towel?"

"I don't care how you go out, but I'm not to let you out of my sight until we get to where we're going."

"And where is that?"

He tongues the toothpick moving it from one corner of his mouth to the other. "Not telling."

He thinks he's cute, clever, like he's in control here.

Emerson lets the towel drop to the floor. Full-frontal, but he doesn't react the way Emerson thought he would. Most men, when they see her, they smile. Faces beaming to show they like what they see. They show some desire. But this guy, there's nothing there, like in those movies where the hero kicks the eunuch or robot or whatever the bad guy is in the nuts, except, he feels nothing because there is nothing there, and the bad guy looks down at the hero, smiles, and then continues to pummel the hero. It's like that. No surprise. If she's reading his expression right, it's almost one of disgust. Definitely lack of interest.

Explains the toothpick fetish.

Eyes squinting, the guy tongues the toothpick back to the original corner of his mouth.

"Should I go put something on or just go out like this?" She motions to her body, highlighting her curves like a gameshow girl. "I think I'll draw some attention walking around out there dressed like this."

The man's disgusted, or uninterested, face gives way to him mulling things over. He simply says, "Okay, get dressed."

Emerson turns her back to him, faces the hallway, places one hand on the small of her back, and with the other, rolls a come-hither finger towards him. "If you're not supposed to let me out of your sight, you better follow me to my room."

The man debates internally if that's a good idea and steps forward.

Emerson saunters down the hallway, swaying her hips side to side. A read of his face says he doesn't know how to handle her. That's just where she wants him.

In the room, the man won't let her open a drawer or closet. Every time she tries, he says, "Nah-uh." Shakes a finger in front of his face. After a quick look around the room, she starts to dress, throwing on the only two pieces of clothing that are not in a drawer or closet, a white t-shirt that doesn't leave much to the imagination and a pair of jeans. No underwear. The guy won't even let her put on a pair of socks because they're in a drawer. When she asks about shoes, he motions to sandals near the dresser with the muzzle of the revolver.

Emerson pulls the jeans up and buttons them, staring at the guy. "Look," she says, "I'm assuming there's a reason for all this, and I'm assuming you're going to tell me what it is, at some point, but if you think this tough guy act's going to scare..." she was going to say "me" but he interjects.

"Let's go," he says. "I'm taking you with me and I don't want to be late. You can do this the easy way or the hard way."

Slipping her toes in the sandals, Emerson smiles. "You must not know me very well..."

The car skids around the corner, the stranger staring intently through the Toyota Corolla's windshield, ignoring Emerson, and acting like he's got somewhere he needs to be in a hurry.

Emerson is in the passenger seat, hand on the handle above her head, trying to hold herself in place. "How good of a friend are you?"

The driver, who introduced himself as Kevin, glances her way without taking his eyes off the road for more than a second. "Excuse me?"

"Well, I was just thinking about the scene at the house," she says. "You sitting there with the revolver—that's a revolver, right? I always get them confused."

Kevin places a hand on the revolver shoved under his right thigh. "It's a revolver."

"What's the other kind?"

Kevin doesn't look at her when he answers. "Semi-automatic."

"What's the difference between that and automatic?"

"One goes boom every time you pull the trigger, the other goes boom many times with one trigger pull. What'd you mean about being whose friend?"

"I was thinking about what you said when you saw me. You said you were a friend of Maggie's."

"Yeah, what of it."

Emerson sucks on her lip. "Well, if you were a friend of his, you would have called him Maggie. Not DiMaggio."

"I was being formal, so there were no misunderstandings."

"If you said Maggie, I think I would have understood."

"I feel like you're getting at something."

"I don't think you're a friend of his."

Kevin sighs heavily. Tightens his grip on the steering wheel. "It's a figure of speech."

"Do you even know him?"

"I met him." Kevin takes a left. "I've known him or known of him for a while. We've run in the same circles for some time. I'm closer with some of his other associates, which is who I'm taking you to. So I guess you could say, I'm a friend of a friend. There, that make you happier?"

"Friend of a friend?"

"You don't have friends of friends?" Kevin sniffs and rubs the back of his hand across the underside of his nose.

"I have friends of friends, but I don't break into other people's homes and say I'm their friend when I'm not really their friend. A friend of a friend. That's more like an acquaintance. Are you an acquaintance? Work buddy? Something like that... hey, that was you wasn't it?"

"Who?"

"You shit and didn't flush it."

Kevin smiles, a lipless clenched smile, showing his teeth but keeping the toothpick in place. "Just be lucky it wasn't the living room."

"What's wrong with you?"

"It's my thing. I like breaking into people's houses."

"And that makes you want to take a shit?"

Kevin shrugs. "When you gotta go, you gotta go, but forget about that. I was nice to you; I chose your toilet, not your rug. I didn't know how long you were going to be. You were in your room a long damn time. What were you doing in there? Working out? You know what, it doesn't matter. I don't really care or wanna know. What I want you to know is we're going to meet a guy who is a friend of ... *Maggie* ... and this guy's known him a long time."

Emerson doesn't like the face Kevin makes. "Like who?"

They stop at a red light. Kevin turns in the seat to look at her. "Guy's name Wilson. You know about Wilson? Your friend Maggie mention him?"

She shakes her head.

"Wilson and Maggie go way back," Kevin chuckles like he's remembering an inside joke. "Wilson's in charge right now. You could say they were like brothers, more like step-brothers. I get the impression Wilson never cared much for Maggie, and Maggie didn't care much for Wilson." The light changes. Kevin looks back at the road as he waits for the line of cars to start moving. "Course, all that was before my time. I came around a little later."

"In charge *right* now," Emerson says, "as opposed to not being in charge before, or it's subject to change?"

Kevin glances at her again, this time longer. Traffic starts moving steadily, so his eyes go back to the road. He doesn't say a word.

They drive for a bit longer, going toward a suburb of Tulsa, a dirty old part of the city, where the setting sun in the west casts long shadows over industrial-like buildings.

After a time, Kevin says, "I'm a good friend of Wilson."

"But not of Maggie?"

"I know him."

"Did you know he used to play baseball? Like, do you or this Wilson go that far back?"

"I heard something."

"But you didn't know he played ball."

"Heard something about it the other day."

"But didn't see him play?"

"No, I didn't see him play," Kevin admits. "What'd he play? Where?"

"He played for the Dodgers. Did you know I knew that? Did you know that? I saw him play when I was younger. Both my pops and I did."

"He played for the Dodgers?" Kevin says, it like he doesn't believe it.

"Well for the Drillers. They're a farm team for the Dodgers"

Kevin whistles. "Why'd he quit? What'd he play?" He flicks the right blinker on to turn into the parking lot of a Waffle House. Emerson sees the half dozen people seated at the narrow booths or the counter.

"He was a pitcher." Emerson turns to look at Kevin. "He was pretty good, but he never made it to the majors."

"So why's he not playing anymore?" Kevin not looking back at her is focused on making the turn. "He get hurt or something?"

Emerson stares at him. "You really don't know him, do you?"

"No, I don't know him. I don't care about him." Kevin removes the toothpick from his mouth. "I'm a helper. I help Wilson. Like I said, a friend of a friend. Wilson's my friend, not Maggie." Kevin navigates the Toyota through the parking lot and down an adjoining drive, circling behind an empty tire shop.

Kevin brings the Toyota to a stop. On the opposite side of the lot, nestled up against the building is an old, black Chrysler 300 with two men inside. Neither moves to get out.

Kevin stops the car and parks. His eyes check the side mirror like he's waiting for someone. "If he was so good, why'd he stop playing?"

Emerson thinks this guy really doesn't know Maggie.

She says, "He had a problem with control."

CHAPTER TWENTY-THREE: PABLO JIMENEZ

"BE LIKE A LION," SIRIANO SAYS. HE SITS NEXT TO Pablo in the Chrysler 300 parked in the back lot of a tire shop in a rundown part of the city. Industrial buildings and old restaurants that have stood here for thirty years surround them. The location is not too far from the automotive shop. Pablo kept a bag on Siriano's head while he drove around for an hour to confuse the guy. He stayed within the same mile section of Alejandro's shop—no not Alejandro's, not anymore. Pablo figures it was easier this way. The whole time Pablo had the old man, the old man didn't know where he was, no idea, not a clue, and even if he did, no one knows about the automotive shop and forgets about the abandoned drive-in theater being out here, obscured by neighborhoods, overgrown trees, and a couple of empty lots. Once parked, Pablo removed Siriano's hood but left the duct tape binding Siriano's wrists.

They are waiting for the meeting to start, the deal. The hand-off. The trade. Pablo really doesn't want anything in return. When he called to set it up, the old man's son, Wilson, asked what he wanted. Pablo hesitated. Wilson said, "What, you don't want anything?" Siriano suggested Pablo ask for money just so things seem above board, not like a kidnapping's going to seem above anything. Pablo hesitated and stuttered, "How about some money?" Without missing a beat, Wilson said, "How much money?" Pablo thought, *Damn what's with this guy. Just fucking set up the time, confirm, and be done. Why's it got to be so difficult?* It's like when he orders at a fast-food place drive-thru, he knows what he wants, but the attendant won't shut their mouth long enough for him to get it out. Yes, I'd like a number one—would you like fries with that? What size? Anything else? Spewing the questions before he has a chance to get his order out. The kid was like that. "How much money?" Wilson asked for like the tenth time, repeating himself, which just showed how desperate he sounded, how desperate he is like he just wants to get his *father* back to make the world right. "Five hundred thousand," Pablo said, "How's that sound?" Course, Wilson didn't seem too bright either. "*Dollars*?" he asked. Pablo said, "No, pesos. Yes, five-hundred thousand dollars. Can you make that happen? Bring it to the meet." Pablo gave the location and time, didn't wait for an argument. All Wilson said was, "Jesus, that's a lot of fucking money." And the last thing Pablo said before he hung up was, "Be glad I didn't ask for an even million." When he said that, Siriano smiled at him and raised a thumb, even if both wrists were tied together at this point.

Staring out the window now, Pablo spots the yellow and black square sign for the Waffle House off in the distance, looming over a paint spraying place, or is it an automotive repair shop, he's not sure. Its fabricated metal sides, with a metal roof, looks like a tin box, brick façade for the front. When he thinks of this place, he remembers it used to be soccer fields. He remembers the Waffle House too because it's a local staple—although he's never been to this location. To his left are several industrial buildings, manufacturing, a granite place, and another paint spraying place. So maybe that's the automotive collision repair place in front of him.

Pablo asks, "Why a lion?"

"To show you don't take shit from no one." Siriano lifts his bound wrists. "Kinda like you've shown me."

"Maybe I should have told him how to bring me the money," Pablo says, not looking at Siriano. "Like, maybe I should have said how I want it, like in a briefcase or something. Maybe in a duffel bag. Might be a lot of money to carry. Might not. I'm not too sure. Five hundred thousand, maybe that's too much?"

"Nah, you did it like you shoulda. Told him how much you wanted. It's a respectable amount."

"Not too much?"

Pablo feels like it's too much. Maybe he should have asked for less or just said what he really wanted, which was for no one to get hurt. Say something like, take your father back, it was a misunderstanding. We've worked things out. But no, that wouldn't work either. Pablo's committed to this action now. He can work out whatever he's worked out with Siriano, but he shouldn't tell anyone else. Not Omar. Not Flavia. Not Vega. Hell, he didn't even tell Vega about the money. Vega left after shooting the kid and only called to say he'd be at the meet when Pablo sent him a message telling him when and where. Vega said he'd bring Flavia with him. He said they've come to an understanding. So either he's threatened her, or she likes him. Either way, Pablo needs to be careful about her. She turned Alejandro against him, and she'll do the same to Vega if she gets half the chance.

Pablo says, "I feel like it's too much money."

Siriano rolls his neck on his shoulders. "Not for this, no." He's wearing the same suit he's been wearing the whole time, except Pablo let him get dressed and washed properly to come to the meet because Siriano said he couldn't be out in public looking like he'd not showered in days. He asked what type of message that would send. "It's respectable. It shows how serious you are about things but not unreasonable. Unreasonable would have been that million dollars you threatened. And the way you said it lifted my ticker, to hear you speak that way. When you and I first talked, I thought, here's this guy who's here because of who he is and not what he did... that means something to guys like us... guys we're around all the time, the people who look to us to lead them. So hearing you then, talking to my boy the way you did, makes me think I've had some influence on you. You just gave it to him the way it needed to be said. Clear. No argument. No debate. Telling him 'Give me this reasonable amount, and you figure everything else out.' I like that. I like how you played that. And I'd like to think I've had some bearing on how you talked to him.

"My boy's not the brightest," Siriano says, "but he's a good son. He's my only one—only one I know about—and I've not been in his life the whole time. I liked his mother—don't know if I loved her, so I won't say I did, but liked her, sure. I kept tabs on her and her family. She had all these girls with all these other men—or maybe it was with me, I don't know—I don't claim them like I claimed him. He's the one I claim. The others, they never wanted anything from me, not that I didn't provide when I could. Cash here. Cash there. Envelopes for Christmas and their birthdays. Kept a whole list of them." Siriano laughs to himself. "My wife found it; she thought I was keeping a stable of side girls—I was—but it wasn't them. I told her don't worry about it and then slapped her for looking through my shit. But back in the day, in my prime, I didn't think about fatherhood, especially when she had him, Wilson. I thought about myself. But then thirteen or so years go by and all of a sudden, I get this longing for a legacy. You ever felt that?"

Pablo says, "Alejandro was all about legacy. Renaldo was supposed to be his legacy, but we saw how well that worked out for him. He went to work for you. I'm concerned about my legacy just not about having a kid."

Siriano jerks his head. "That's not legacy; that's how people *perceive* you," he says. "You can't do anything about that. You can do what you can do. People, they like to make these stories about themselves to make them feel better. People aren't honest with themselves about how they feel about other people, making people into villains, making people into heroes, putting people on pedestals while discounting others they shouldn't be discounting. That's not legacy; that's perception. No, I'm talking about, you ever want to have someone carry on your name, have a kid, settle down some. When you have kids—at least kids you claim—your life changes some. Think about all those cops who are hard-ass dicks, bulls if you prefer but I don't, they're dicks. You see them chasing some neighborhood kid their rookie year—like some fucking baseball player or something; people should print up these little cards so regular folk like you and me know who to stay the fuck away from. Hard-charging, black and white motherfuckers who like to fight. Then, when that rookie starts settling down, has a family, they become a little easier to deal with. And when I say deal, I mean bribe, but that comes later. These are life lessons; you paying attention?"

Pablo tells him he is. He glances over at Siriano to sell it. In reality, his mind's running all over the place, including wondering when Vega and Flavia will roll-up. He doesn't want to do this deal alone. What if something happens, like a double-cross? He's just going to have to trust Vega will show up.

"Good, because contrary to popular belief," Siriano says, going on, "I don't talk just to hear myself. I want to impart some life wisdom to you. Having a kid makes you see the world differently. Although, I suppose, just having a mouth to feed, some other living creature depending on you, changes your world. When I say that I get to thinking about doggies, and it ain't the same thing no matter how much some pumpkin-spice-loving suburbanite woman talks about having fur babies." Siriano holds up his bound wrists and counts off, lifting one finger. "First off, fuck them. Secondly, a doggie isn't a kid. So what I'm asking is, do your balls ever ache with the idea of planting a seed in a woman just to get something that's part you out into the world?"

Pablo hasn't thought about having kids, he's been too busy living—surviving—getting by in a world that's been cruel to him. How could he bring someone into this world? Besides, he doesn't deserve a kid. He is a coward. He doesn't view himself that way, but that's how he feels. He should have killed Renaldo for killing Alejandro, and he couldn't because greed took over. Renaldo helped him see a different life, see more. Suddenly, he could reach for something, reach for more.

Pablo shakes his head.

Siriano asks his second question without paying any attention to Pablo's answer to the first. "Want to carry on your name?"

Pablo shakes his head again. "No."

"I didn't think so." Siriano shifts in the seat to get a look at Pablo as he speaks. "I think that's something you feel when you get older, and it becomes more and more like it's not going to happen, and death becomes more and more like a thing that *is going* to happen. I had that feeling, that worry. I don't know, I wasn't a young man at that time. I could've had one, a kid, with the woman I was married to, but she was like a fucking desert, nothing in there but dust blowing all about, dunes shifting, if you get what I mean. I couldn't get her wet if I sprayed her down with a firehose. She just never had the desire, and then when she did, there's nothing flowering down there for my little swimmers to latch on to. But then I think, hey, I have this kid. I already did all the hard work. Maybe I can reach out to him, his mother. I mean it wasn't difficult. I'd been fucking her on the side for a while now, a whole stable of girls, she'd come and go, and when she was around, I'd cum. She'd cum. Then, she'd go." Siriano smiles to himself. "It was a good thing. I thought, maybe I should get to know this kid. He's what thirteenish? So I did. You telling him five-hundred thousand is all right. Not too much. I've seen a man kill another man over thirty-eight bucks. Course, that man was me and the news said it was like two hundred. But it was thirty-eight bucks. Did it with Wilson, too. Made him go with me, a pop his cherry sorta thing. We were going to put some fear in this old geezer who wouldn't blink, you know the type,

Mr. Hardass." Siriano pauses. "Pay my money, or don't, but don't stare me down, dare me to do something, because I'll do it. You know what, it wasn't just the geezer, it was his muscle too, so I guess you could say, I've seen two men die over thirty-eight bucks."

"How'd Wilson react?"

"He did what he needed to do, which is pretty much how I figure he'll act today. He'll bring you the money. It's a good amount of money. Consider it a gift from me, alright. No hard feelings on this end. But if I had to leave you with some advice, I'd say you need to be in control of your people. I get the feeling, especially considering what happened in that room, you're not in control of your fucking people. Am I wrong?"

Pablo thinks about it for a second. About Flavia. Omar. "You're not wrong."

Siriano gives him a satisfied grin. "Look, I could take this whole thing personally, be upset, but I'm not. I figure you got me out of having to testify in the Grand Jury, and that's a good thing. But what you're doing, working with Vega's people in this manner, it opens a door I've kept shut for a long time, so I hope you know what you are doing."

Pablo knows what he is doing. Vega's his cousin.

"What do you mean?"

"The people that your attack dog—yes, he's a dog, not a lion; he follows orders— these fucking people... the people that own him, they aren't like us. They're ruthless in ways that make us civilized people squirm, cutting people's heads off and chopping them up with machetes and other bullshit. I mean, I've done some wicked shit in my life but nothing like what I've seen them do. I see a whole house of people roped like this," he holds up his hands to make his point, "and I was made to watch as these fuckers cut this broad's head off for not wanting to fuck no more. She didn't want to have sex for money anymore. She was a prostitute. I don't think she needed to die over it, but it wasn't my show. Sometimes I can hear the chainsaw starting up. Fucking nightmares you know, but it's their world, was their meeting, and so I had to sit there and share drinks with the guy who was watching them do all this shit like some Victorian socialite watching some horsies play polo on the pitch. You know, in the old days we might do something like that, but it was to make a point and it was to someone who generally deserved it. If a guy had to die, then the guy should just die. There's no point in making him suffer unless you needed to extract information. And if you have to take out his family, well you didn't do that, but raping and pillaging like we've just gone back to Roman times? That shit's fucking evil.

"I guess what I'm saying is you better be careful how much you trust your man and his people. They could come in on this deal and really mess things up for you. He killed that kid like it was nothing. Shot him. Would you have done that? And if I got this figured correctly, that kid was the brother of one of your people. In my experience, when the family gets involved, things tend to go badly. You kill one, you have to kill them all. Or you don't make it to where they know it was you. Do it like a car crash, an accident, or something. If you can't do that, blame it on your enemy. Or kill them during a robbery or something."

Killing Gabino was going to happen sooner or later. Omar needs to be brought under control. Flavia too. It was always a possibility. Would Pablo have ordered it? No, but having Vega do it surprised even him. Kind of like if Siriano is telling the truth and for some reason, Renaldo decided to kill Alejandro without running it by his boss. "You didn't send Renaldo."

Siriano shakes his head. "I'm not saying I would tell you if I did. One of my rules is to stick to your story... no matter what. You give nothing. Why do you think the feds are so out for me? I gave them nothing. And how the fuck do you think they could keep me in prison for taking money from my own businesses? It's my business. I can do what I want with my money no matter what a dick-sucking weasel accountant says. It's my money."

"Truth be told, Renaldo did me a favor," Pablo admits. "He could have killed me."

"But he didn't because he knew the difference between doing things smart and doing them stupid. Doing things out of emotion and doing them with an idea of what's going to happen."

"Who killed him?"

"That's a good question." Siriano looks away, thoughts painted on his face, and judging by him scrunching his nose and narrowing his eyes, he must be thinking hard. "One I'd like answered. You know after he disappeared, my son tells me he heard Renaldo was fucking some cop's wife and this cop just so happen to be *the cop* my third-party dealers killed during a bad deal that Renaldo's man set up. God, when I heard that, I about lost it."

"So what are you saying?"

"It's about perception and my perception is Renaldo set up the deal, while fucking the cop's wife, that ended up being with the cops—don't care one of them died—makes me think he's awfully cozy with those fuckers, like he's an informant or something. So would he have died eventually? Yeah. Did I kill him? I didn't order it is what I can tell you. Sure as hell didn't tell him to kill Alejandro. That guy knew how to keep your people down south in check, didn't like that medieval bullshit making its way up here. He ran things with logic, not emotion."

A Toyota rounds the building. Parks opposite of them in the lot.

Pablo says, "Look alive."

Siriano says, "I am alive."

He's looking through the glass too. Both of them try to peer across the parking lot and make out who's in the Toyota: a woman and a man, neither Pablo knows.

"Who the fuck are these guys?"

Not that Pablo expects Siriano to know. Another car comes around the corner, joining the first, almost at the same time Vega's shitty truck parks next to Pablo's Chrysler.

Siriano looks at him. "Now that things are about to heat up, I'll leave you with this," he says. "You have to be careful how you treat the people under you, especially the ones you betray."

"Oh yeah," Pablo says, "why's that?"

"Because, speaking from experience, it can come back to bite you in the ass."

CHAPTER TWENTY-FOUR: FLAVIA SANCHEZ

VEGA'S RUSTED PIECE OF JUNK TRUCK PULLS UP TO the meeting, parking next to Pablo. Flavia sees he's still talking to the old man in the passenger seat—you'd think after a few days they'd run out of things to talk about. Vega tells Flavia, "Get out," demanding it like she needs to be ordered around and didn't just make a deal to get her husband out of police custody, or the fact that they're on the same level now. She's going to be in charge, with Omar as her second. Husband and wife, working together to reclaim this town, carry on Alejandro's legacy, accomplish what he couldn't, and be rid of Siriano once and for all.

Alejandro would say it's about time. He always hated the old man, and after spending a few days in his orbit, Flavia tends to agree with Alejandro's assessment of Siriano. The guy likes to talk, talk his fucking balls off, but he never says anything of any use. Alejandro would say, "You can't trust someone who doesn't know how to shut up."

But Alejandro's gone. Renaldo too. What's left is Pablo, who won't be a problem after this meeting, and she and Omar. She'll take care of Vega. She may not know a lot of things, not what Iris King really hopes to accomplish, but she knows she can't let Vega remain a factor in whatever is going on here.

Flavia opens the passenger door and exits the truck.

A third car joins the other two across the parking lot, which is hemmed in by a field on one side with industrial buildings beyond that, and the garage doors of the tire shop.

She says, "These people can't all come at once?"

Vega tells her to shut up as he studies himself in the rearview mirror and slips the straw hat on his head, fingertips twisting the brim to the left, bringing it low over his eyes. He checks the look in the mirror, smiles a wicked smile, makes sure everything's set on his head the right way. Omar would say he's putting a smart turn to the brim or wearing the hat smartly. Omar would say that's what his books say is the right way to wear a hat like his. But Vega isn't a cowboy, nor is he an Indian; he's something different, a throwback, a savage. He's a barbarian dressed in a Mexican's clothing, dressed like a lawn care technician. That's what Gabino said he was called when he got his first job at fifteen: a lawn care technician. Omar asked him what that was, and Gabby shrugged saying he didn't know, but it sounded better than a gardener.

As she slams Vega's truck door, Pablo is getting out of his vehicle, looking at her. He nods and crosses around the front of the Chrysler. He helps Siriano get out of the car, treating the man with kindness. Subservience. He's fawning over the guy like he's falling in love with him.

Flavia can't stand it. She swallows, trying to keep the bile, building in the back of her throat, down. She stares at Pablo as he walks Siriano, who's dressed in his suit, showered, and cleaned up, around to the front of the car. "Let's get this over with."

Vega gets out, shuts his door, and pauses to stuff a revolver he pulled from the truck's door pocket, in the back of his pants. What's he need with another gun? Was that thing in there the whole time? She could have used it to shoot him. Must be why he zip-tied her, so she couldn't go for it.

Vega steps to the front of the truck, hand checking the handle of his big 1911 shoved in the front of his pants, tight against the belt. Gun to his left side because of the big round belt buckle that looks like something a rodeo star would wear.

The whole time, Flavia watches him from the corner of her eyes, acting like she's not looking.

A car door, then a series of car doors, open and shut across the parking lot. The others from the other cars across the parking lot get out. There's a man who looks like Siriano who takes the lead at the tip of the triangle.

Hands held behind his back, patient-like. He must be Wilson Notaro, the old man's son. His hair is well-kept, swept back, like in the movies from the 50s. He's wearing a simple black polo over dark blue jeans. He's trim, fit, and good-looking.

The others, a girl and a guy get out of the Toyota, the girl acting like she doesn't want to be there. Flavia notes she's not wearing a bra. She looks like she's wearing clothes she just threw on. Like she had no time to get dressed after taking a shower, hair still wet. That's typically how Flavia looks, her hair wet and stringy when she shows up to work at the restaurant. No reason to get all dolled up when she's going to sweat in the kitchen. Omar's never complained. He likes when she looks like that. He said he'd prefer that over someone that takes hours to put on a face.

One of the girl's sandals folds under her foot as the guy who is wearing a Bull's hat tugs on her arm. The girl stumbles, tripping over the sandal. The guy tugs harder. Either the sandal broke, or she kicks it lose, but she leaves it behind and kicks the other off. Now she's standing in the parking lot barefoot, looking uncomfortable.

The guy tugging on her wears a sweatshirt that goes with his hat and he looks serious. He says something to Wilson. Wilson looks back at him over his shoulder. The guy motions with the revolver, from this distance it looks like a .38, at whatever Wilson holds behind his back. Wilson doesn't seem to want to tell the guy what it is. Wilson tosses his head to the side, which must be the signal for the guy in the ball cap to bring the girl forward.

There's another man, a serious man, distraught and in a rush, who's getting out of his car. His eyes are locked on the girl. He rushes over to the man in the ball cap with the girl. The guy in the hat shakes the .38 revolver at the charging man, stopping him in his tracks. He's put together, has dark hair with some hints of gray at the edges. He looks like a man of action, who's rendered helpless. The girl struggles, pulling away, but the guy in the hat holds on to her. The guy in the hat flicks the gun toward the charging man a few times, motioning for him to back up. The serious man backs up. He looks like a seething bull, snorting and huffing, shoulders up and down.

They exchange a few words, but Flavia can't hear them.

After a moment, now that everyone seems to be in place, Pablo pushes Siriano forward. Vega follows, off to Pablo's left. Flavia follows behind them. The other group, the seething bull, the guy in the ball cap, and the girl all keep their places behind Wilson.

Wilson steps forward.

"You brought the money?" Pablo asks, holding onto Siriano's elbow, gripping it tight so the old man can't run away.

Flavia glances at Pablo; she sees a change in the man. Pablo doesn't sound like the Pablo she knows. He's more confident. Sounds like he's in charge. Like he's got this figured out. This Pablo isn't a coward. This Pablo is in charge or thinks he is and is comfortable with the power.

Flavia glances to the butt of the revolver shoved in the back of Vega's pants. He's not looking at her. She could reach for the gun and grab it. She could shoot him. She bets she could get to it before he knows what's happening. His back is turned to her because he thinks he can trust her. He can't trust her. He should know better.

Flavia knows the field now. She could shoot him and work out a deal with Iris, whatever it is that woman wants, and everything would be okay. Iris doesn't care about Vega. She cares about the people who control Vega. Vega's just a piece. A piece that's not needed anymore.

The other group steps forward behind Wilson.

Wilson speaks loud enough for Flavia to hear him. "It's here." He produces a small gym bag, blue with black straps, from behind his back. Wilson tosses the bag forward. It lands at Pablo's feet.

Pablo gives the bag a look and focuses on the three standing behind Wilson. "Who are these people?"

Without turning to look at them, Wilson says, "Kevin's my man." The man with the ball cap nods. "The girl's with him."

"And the other guy?" Pablo's eyes shift to the seething bull.

Wilson, dismissively, says, "That's Maggie."

To which Siriano exclaims, "My boys!" Like he's happy to see them both. Flavia doesn't know who Maggie is. She thought Siriano only had one bastard.

Maggie, the seething bull, shifts his body toward Flavia. He's looking at Siriano now, but the look isn't one of affection. There's something dark there. Pain. Flavia sees it. Something is going on here, on the other side.

Pablo shoves Siriano forward again looking like a parent about to let go of the kid learning to ride a bicycle. Pablo lets go of Siriano's arm, freeing him. Siriano staggers forward, almost stumbling to the ground, half-turning to look back at Pablo. He rushes into his boy's arms.

Flavia watches as the two men embrace. Wilson hugs Siriano tight and whispers something in his ear, wrapping a hand around the back of Siriano's greasy head, pulling him closer, tighter, bringing him in.

Then, with his hands around his father, Wilson nods toward Vega. It dawns on Flavia that these two know each other, but before she can question it, Vega reaches into the front of his pants and withdraws the 1911. He brings the gun up and shoots Pablo in the back of the head. Pablo drops to the dirt never knowing what happened. Vega takes two more steps. Now he's standing over Pablo, and he shoots him again, two more times. Insurance shots. The first gunshot surprises Flavia. She blinks once. Then the follow-ups come so quickly she barely has time to process it. Her mind flashes back to Vega killing Gabino. The man looks the same. Uncaring. Cold. Emotionless. This is just another day at the office for him. Not for her. Today means something. Right now means something.

She looks at Siriano and his boy. Wilson nudges his father to the side to step forward toward the gym bag, reaching for the handles. Vega transitions the gun from Pablo's body, arm straight, to Wilson. And before Wilson can understand what's happening, Vega settles the gun on him.

Flavia lunges forward. Her hand wraps around the pistol grip and rips the revolver from Vega's back waistband, shoving him as he pulls the trigger. Vega lumbers forward a few steps and his first bullet misses the mark, tearing into Wilson's cheek, turning the man. The second one takes Wilson high in the chest. The good-looking younger Siriano collapses near the gym bag.

Vega starts twisting around to face her, but Flavia is ready for him. She shoots him in the kidney, the right one, three times, yelling at him, "That's for Gabby," a bullet for each word.

Silence descends on the scene in the parking lot so quickly that the reports of the gunshots echoing off the industrial buildings make Flavia question if any of this happened. For a moment, Flavia isn't even sure she actually shot Vega. He half-steps forward, rigid, and then drops the 1911 to the ground. He finishes turning around, one hand grabbing at his kidney, face a mask of confusion like he can't believe what just happened.

That's when Maggie, the seething bull, charges the guy in the Bulls' baseball hat. Maggie throws a haymaker into Kevin, connecting full-on with the guy's cheek, knocking him to the side, throwing the hat off, turning him. The Bulls hat blows away. The guy releases the girl's arm and drops the revolver, which tumbles off his foot, kicking it across the ground toward Siriano. The braless girl takes a step back as Maggie tackles Kevin. Maggie slams the man's head against the pavement, hand gripping the guy's hair. Slamming his head into the ground until the guy stops moving. Flavia doesn't think he killed him, but he certainly took out whatever frustration he brought to the meeting.

Siriano stands frozen, watching the whole thing. He says something to Maggie that Flavia doesn't hear. Maggie shoots him a murderous look and says, "I know about my father."

Siriano turns toward Flavia and Vega, eyes beseeching them both for some help. "It wasn't supposed to go like this," he says. "We had a deal." His face says he doesn't know what's happening here. Flavia ignores Siriano; she'll deal with him in a minute. She brings her revolver up and lines it up with the brim of Vega's hat. Vega smiles, showing off his rotted teeth, playing like her shooting him isn't a big deal.

She shoots him in the face. The hat stays on his head as his body crumples to the ground.

As the gun goes off, Siriano drops into a squat on the ground, hands still bound with duct tape. His fingers grope at the concrete, searching for the dropped .38. He finds it, both hands latching on to it, and then he is up and running off to the side around the tire shop building. He points the gun at Flavia, shifting from her to Maggie and then back to her. Flavia doesn't respond to him. She steps over Vega and shoots him a few more times.

Then she drops the gun on Vega's body.

Maggie stares at her. He's crouched over Kevin, still with the guy's wispy hair in his hand. Maggie drops the guy's head. It falls limp to the ground. Maggie stands up. His blue eyes are on Flavia the whole time. He keeps his hands out to the side, shaking his head, telling her she doesn't have anything to worry about from him. He's not in this. Maybe he's right; it doesn't matter to her.

She shrugs one shoulder and nods, closing her eyes.

When she opens her eyes again, Maggie is taking a hesitant step backward and then another, and it's not long before he's gripping the girl's arm, telling her to come with him, saying, "We gotta get out of here. We gotta get out of this place. Come on. Let's go," and pulls her with him as he makes for his vehicle.

Flavia doesn't watch them go because she can hear the sirens blaring in the distance, coming from Alejandro's automotive shop, which means the cops knew where Siriano was. They figured it out or someone told them, but she can't worry about it now. They and everyone and their dog must've heard the shots, all of them. She needs to leave.

Flavia steps toward Vega's truck, but then she reconsiders. She turns and scoops up the gym bag. She tosses the bag in the back of the truck without looking where it lands, and she opens the door. The keys are still in the ignition. She climbs inside and slips the truck in gear. Flavia doesn't bother going in reverse. She drives over both Pablo and Vega, and then Wilson on her way out of the parking lot.

Siriano is nowhere to be seen.

Maggie and the girl pass her going the other way. Maggie doesn't run over the bodies. His tires squeal as he maneuvers around them and the corner of the building.

Rounding the tire shop building in front of her, she yanks the wheel to the right, the truck hopping the median, a curbed island separating the tire shop from the Waffle House. She drives the truck through the Waffle House parking lot, almost hitting a black woman in a business suit who's walking toward the restaurant. She exits on the main road, making for the nearby highway.

CHAPTER TWENTY-FIVE: SONNY ROWAN

SONNY SITS WEDGED IN HIS EDITOR'S LITTLE corner office. His elbows nearly touching two of the four walls is how cramped he feels. He tells Jimmy, his editor and best friend of many years, how he was at the Waffle House, watching a fat trucker wearing a blue ball cap eat a plate of chicken fried steak and eggs when it happened. He explains to Jimmy how half the guy hung off the seat to every side like a melting glob of goo just like the runny yolk that slid off the guy's fork before he slurped it up.

"The whole thing grossed me out," Sonny says, "so I looked somewhere else. Noticed how it was a nice day outside. Clear skies. Not sunny, but not gloomy either."

With his hand jammed under his chin and his boney legs crossed, leaning comfortably back in his chair, Jimmy patiently listens. His white hair brushes his forehead. Tulsa skyline outside the window behind him. Jimmy's only perk for all the head, heart, and ache that comes with being in charge.

"It's the setting, I got it." Jimmy's way of telling Sonny to hurry up with it. "You going to get to the good part, or not?"

"I'll get there. I just wanted you to know what I was doing."

"You were working on your novel, right?" Jimmy says. "That's what you're usually doing when you're supposed to be working for me."

Sonny shakes his head. "No, I was just telling you how I like the Waffle House. Emerson and I have eaten there so many times, I've lost count. That place—"

"The Waffle House?" Jimmy asks, interrupting.

"Yes, the Waffle House." Sonny annoyed he's had to stop the story. "That place is my place, always open, and always inviting, comfortable. The cliché, I guess, would be to tell you it's my home away from home, but it is. It really is. When I'm suffering from a block on a story, I like to gather up all my notes, go there, and work everything out by hand."

Jimmy smiles a closed mouth smile. "Old school-like," he says. "Like how I want you to turn in copy, not serenade me with local flavor, which is nothing but B-roll, forgive me for borrowing a phrase from our broadcast section."

"It's more than that," Sonny adds, "and I'll forgive you… besides, I do work on *your* copy. Once I've got an idea, I pull out this little rinky-dink laptop you gave me ten years ago—a new one would be nice, especially after capturing this exclusive for you, by the way—and I pound out a story."

"I'll buy you a laptop if you can tell me you weren't fucking the source."

Sonny can't tell him that, so he says, "When I'm done with the story, so what if I enjoy myself? Watch others. That's what I really like to do, and that's the best thing about the place, the other people who come there: all walks of life and socioeconomic levels. Rich people. Poor People. Sober People. Drunk People. It doesn't matter; when they're in there, they're my people. Everyone has a story, and I love telling their stories. Sure, sometimes people get upset, don't like how I quote them, don't like how I describe them, but what I say to them about that is, 'What, you don't like looking in the mirror? I can't hide all the mirrors of the world.' You know, tell them to deal with it."

"I know, I've fielded the complaints."

"Is it selfish?" Sonny asks. "Yeah, sure."

Jimmy says, "No, not… yeah sure, it is."

Sonny smiles. "It's flippant, yes. Also caused some problems as I've gone through things. But as you know, people began to see what I'm really saying, actually read my words. So that it also becomes something of a declaration of my determination. A promise delivered sort of thing."

"You think so?"

"I think so," Sonny adds. "I tell the truth."

"The way you see it," Jimmy cuts in.

" I tell the damn truth, and I'll never betray the truth. I think that comes through in my writing."

"Maybe that's what this Kelly sees in you, a fellow truth-teller."

"Maybe." Sonny tugs on the collar of his gray shirt, flattening it and fixing it.

"What happened next?"

"So, I'm waiting for Kelly. Earlier, I texted her suggesting we could catch an early dinner, suggested breakfast for dinner because I thought it would be cute."

"What kid doesn't want pancakes for dinner?"

"Emerson sure did."

"I assume Kelly texted back taking you up on your shitty food offer?"

"Texted: 'You take me to all the nice places.'"

"And you did what?" Jimmy drops his hand from his chin. "Say something like, 'Is that a yes?' And add a few emojis just for fun."

Sonny didn't add the emojis. "I don't understand how people communicate like that."

"The Egyptians did it," Jimmy spouts off, "communicate in pictures that is. Not smiley faces."

Jimmy retrieves his coffee cup from the desk. Sonny's first sign that he's settling in for the long story, which is why Sonny started the way he did. He likes to torture the man, make him slow down.

"First a bar. Then a Waffle House. What's next, skid row? Ask her to come hang out in the locker room with you after the next local sporting event, whatever that might be, baseball? Basketball? Football? Whatever."

"Football won't be until the fall," Sonny says. "If I were to do that, it'd have to be a Drillers spring training camp."

Jimmy lifts his eyebrow, showing he wasn't serious. "Would she go for that?"

"She seems to enjoy my company, and we've been texting back and forth like a bunch of kids."

"Spring training for the big leagues is an interesting thing to watch. Sometimes these kids who are on the way up, come down to Tulsa. These kids are going to be something."

"Not all of them, but some of them."

"You could regale her with trivia like how Sammy Sosa played for the Drillers. You could mention a lot of other guys too: like Dexter Fowler,

Matt Holliday, Nolan Arenado, that kid is still tearing it up in the big leagues, but she might not know any of them."

"I could tell her about meeting Maggie. Tell her about that day at the ballpark with Emerson again. Tell her how special it was to me... to us both... and how meeting him was coming full circle. Actually explain to her how we've both held on to that memory, which was pleasant for us. There are not many, especially after I threw myself into my work, ignoring Emerson and driving her away as soon as she could leave."

Jimmy nods along. He knows a lot about Sonny and his relationship with Emerson. They've talked about this a lot. "I figure if you do that, you'll have to talk about your late wife, but you don't like talking about her."

Or thinking about her, but Sonny doesn't say that. He once wrote a novel about it, something like the *Notebook*, something Nicholas Sparks would mine for every emotion it's worth, like he's digging for the gold that shoots out that guy's ass, but Sonny's not much for romance novels. He figures maybe when he retires, maybe he'll be the next Jimmy Breslin. That's the guy he looks up to, a regular Joe who went out there and did his thing, writing sentences fun to read and bringing people to life. Sharing his world, or the way he sees it, with other people.

Sonny can't imagine a day of not writing, so he'll probably shift his attention to the novel when Jimmy finally throws him out on his ass. Maybe he could transition to features for some of the bigger magazines, a retirement gig worth something, but then Sonny thinks about guys like Bob Costas and how that guy's been working for freaking forever. Madden, some of the others, Charles Barkley. What's he going to do when his time comes?

"If I did get Kelly to go on a date, watch guys whack some balls around and play grab-ass, I could mention how the guy, Maggie, worked for Siriano, say something like, 'Isn't that a small world?'"

"It is a small world," Jimmy says, "Which is why I want to hear about what happened at the Waffle House, but you're doing that thing where you waste my time. You like doing that."

"It seems unbelievable."

"What?" Jimmy says. "People connected through unlikely events. That's a story, right? I mean, that's what you like to write about in your column. Isn't that what Malcolm Gladwell does: take unlikely stories and events and put them together, mash them up, see the connections between them? Your connection just happens to be Russell Siriano."

Sonny agrees. "The thread that brought us together."

"A powerful figure, looming over your story."

"Not just *my* story."

"Alright, United States Deputy Marshal Kelly Chambers's story too."."

"After her story ran something seemed to shift in Kelly," Sonny says. "She didn't feel so defensive like she's got to explain herself to people, and I would like to think it's because I told her story, gave a face to go with a name. Helped her go beyond being just a sound bite or some viral video people laughed at. Now people know a little bit about her. Know the real her."

Jimmy sips his coffee. "Like how losing Siriano wasn't her fault?"

Sonny nods. "She did what she had to do to keep others safe."

"Or she didn't," Jimmy says.

"Jim, you know as well as I do, people aren't heartless, not in my opinion. They care. They understand. They will try to think about others and maybe, just maybe, if we do our jobs correctly, if I write it correctly, they will put themselves in someone else's shoes. See the world from their point of view."

"Oh, that's what you do, is it? Not just waste my time?"

"That's what I did with Maggie. I told you about it. I had to stop seeing the guy, frozen in his moment of triumph, hitting that cycle, throwing that game. I had to see the guy for who he was. Someone whose father's early death haunted him. Christ, hearing the guy talk about how he felt like it was his fault. It wasn't his fault. He was just a kid. A teenager going on being a man, sleeping late is what teenagers do. It wasn't his fault. That's the last thing I said to the guy before we parted. It's not your fault."

"How'd he take it?" Jimmy asks.

"He just gave me this blank look," Sonny says. "Emerson may like it, but I don't. It scares me. It's like there's all this emotion, summoned up into this guy's blue eyes that coalesces into nothing. It's cold. There's something heartless about the man that makes me uncomfortable. But even with him, when you put yourself in his shoes, you start to see why he's made the decisions he's made, where the anger and lack of control... where all that came from."

"Emerson could do worse than someone like him." Jimmy licks the edges of his mustache as he tries to wipe away the coffee without actually wiping away the coffee. "You can't do any better than someone like Kelly." He gives up and runs a hand across the mustache.

Sonny figures he's right and nods and goes back to his story as his memory takes him back to the Waffle House. "She was supposed to be there by then, so I checked my watch, glanced out the window, noticed a few cars rounding the corner of the closed tire shop next door."

"Did you wonder what they were doing there?"

"At the time, I don't know," Sonny says. "I don't know if I paid much attention to what was going on. My mind was somewhere else."

"It was in the clouds," Jimmy smiles, "because you are in *love*." Nearly sings the last word like they're in middle school and on a playground.

Sonny shakes his head to the side, closes his eyes. "Then the waitress came over to my table, distracted me some more so I don't remember what happened after noticing the cars go around the building."

Sonny pauses as he reads Jimmy's face, seeing the man's features shift as he starts to interject a question.

"I don't know how much time passed," Sonny says, stopping Jimmy. "The waitress refilled my coffee, and we shared a few moments of polite conversation."

"Mr. Nice Guy." Jimmy grins.

"I felt good. It had been a good day. Been a good week, with meeting Kelly and finally getting somewhere with Emerson. Maybe not as far as either one of us had hoped, but it was something, especially when I thought we were at the edge and there'd be nothing."

Jimmy finishes Sonny's thought, "But then Maggie came into your lives."

"Yes, reminded us we both had something special happen that still connected us and, you know what, that's alright with me."

"Okay, enough." Jimmy places both feet on the floor and squares up with Sonny in the chair. "Tell me what happened at the damn Waffle House—words I never thought I'd utter."

Sonny laughs. "I was just taking a sip of coffee, blowing on it, nursing it kinda like you're doing yours now, when the first gunshots rang out, tightly grouped. They faded off before my brain could put the pieces together and figure out what the pops were."

"How many?"

"What?"

"How many pops did you hear first?" Jimmy retrieves Sonny's write-up off his desk. Sonny notices how Jimmy holds it, where his thumb is, and how he holds the paper to look at it, but he is pretending to read it because Jimmy needs reading glasses, and they are sitting on his desk. Sonny spots the red circle on the paper. "You weren't clear. I want to know how many pops you heard first."

"Three," Sonny says. "First one and then silence and then two more."

Jimmy places the paper on the desk. "Go on."

"Just as I was thinking to myself, were those firecrackers or gunshots—"

"Like every Fourth of July. You ever listen to the police scanner sitting over by Judy's desk on the Fourth of July, people calling in saying they heard gunshots? Callers saying something like, 'I know guns; I was in the military,' or 'I hunt,' or 'My father taught me about guns, and I think those were gunshots.' I don't know how the dispatchers don't scream at them, it's freaking fireworks. It's Independence Day."

"Yeah, but dogs don't like the loud bangs."

"So they have to call and annoy everyone? I'm just listening for any big stories and even I'm annoyed... kinda like I'm annoyed with you."

Sonny grins. "Listen, I don't know how much time passed between the first set of pops and the second. Yes, I see you circled that too, but it wasn't long, and the second set came a lot closer together, three pops, then a hesitation, and then more."

"How many more?"

"I don't remember."

"You're a shitty reporter if you don't remember."

"You want to hear some shooting next door and go investigate, be my guess."

"Then, the cars get out of there."

"This truck, with this lady, she pops the curb, nearly runs Kelly over in the parking lot."

"Where was Kelly before this?"

"Helping Tulsa Police Department—"

"Not the Marshals?"

"Not the Marshals," Sonny confirms. "Helping TPD serve a search warrant at this abandoned drive-in and automotive place where Siriano was supposed to be held, but they came up empty."

"So she made her meeting with you?"

"It was a date, and it just so happened to be close by, like within a mile. And she nearly gets run over in the parking lot for her trouble."

"Funny how things work out like that."

"She's looking at me through the window, and I'm looking at her through the window, both of us with the idea of what the fuck was that?"

"And then she comes inside."

"Yes, she comes inside. How do you go on a date with someone if you stay in the parking lot?"

"Ask your daughter. I'm sure she still remembers her high school years and can answer that question."

Sonny dips his head down and narrows his eyes.

Jimmy holds up a hand. "Low blow. I'm sorry. Go on."

"Anyways, she's inside the Waffle House now, walking down the aisle, coming toward me."

"How'd she look?"

"Good, like she was happy to be there, wearing her business suit with a yellow shirt, all the colors made her shine," Sonny continues. "She's walking toward me, smiling, happy to be there, and then the little bell hanging above the door, dings. I look beyond her, and she instinctively—police instincts before you say anything."

"I have a problem with words like instinctively. How do you know what she was thinking at that time?"

"I asked her. That's what reporters do."

"Having sex with her sure helps you get *inside* her head."

Sonny ignores him and continues. "She looks over her shoulder, and there he is."

Jimmy acts surprised, even though he's read the story that'll go out in tomorrow's paper, a big spread, double-page thing. "Siriano?"

"Siriano, with duct tape around his wrists, holding a revolver. I can't see from where I'm sitting what type of revolver. He's still wearing the suit he wore when he was kidnapped. He rushes inside, a dirty mess, and asks to use a phone. He grips the gun but not like he wants to use it. But the server with the coffee pot, all she sees is the gun. She ignores his plea and screams bloody murder. He realizes why she's screaming, looks down at the gun, thinks about throwing it down."

"How do you know what he was thinking?"

"Fine, that's an embellishment. You caught me," Sonny says. "You want to hear the rest of the story or not?"

Jimmy motions at him to go on.

"Kelly turns around, throwing the folds of her sport coat to the side, yells out at Siriano, announces herself, gives the whole title: Deputy United States Marshal Kelly Chambers."

"Just like that?"

"Just like that," Sonny echoes.

"This is really her story, funny how she loses the guy, and then after she's done looking for him, he appears."

"Siriano gives her this look, a glare, and he shifts his attention down to the gun in his hands. All Kelly does is say, 'Not a good idea' and Siriano looks back at her, but this time, not a glare."

"He say anything?"

"Yeah," Sonny laughs. "He said, 'Shit, it's you.'"

BIO:

MARK ATLEY WRITES CRIME STORIES. THE CHARacters he met on the streets meet those he drew in his head. They interact with exhilarating results. The ride is wild and entertaining, and the dialog bounces like an old pickup in a pothole-ridden back alley. Mark's first novel *The Olympian* was positively received. *A Bright Young Man* will be published by Close to the Bone in 2022. His short fiction appeared in *Punk Noir Magazine*, *Bristol Noir*, and others. Mark works as a detective for a suburb of Tulsa, Oklahoma. He graduated from Oklahoma State University with two degrees in journalism. Follow Mark on Twitter @markatley.

More books from 4 Horsemen Publications

Anthologies & Collections

4HP Anthologies
Teen Angst: Mix Vol. 1
Teen Angst: Mix Vol. 2
My Wedding Date
The Offices of Supernatural Being
The Sentient Space

Demonic Anthologies
Demonic Wildlife
Demonic Household
Demonic Carnival
Demonic Classics
Demonic Vacations
Demonic Medicine
Demonic Workplace
& more to follow!

Cozy Mysteries

Ann Shepphird
Destination: Maui
Destination: Monterey

Crime, Detective, and Noir

Joe Davison
Journey to Hell

Mark Atley
Too Late to Say Goodbye
Trouble Weighs a Ton

Horror, Thriller, & Suspense

Alan Berkshire
Jungle

Amanda Byrd
Trapped
Moratorium
Medicate

Maria DeVivo
Witch of the Black Circle
Witch of the Red Thorn

Erika Lance
Jimmy
Illusions of Happiness
No Place for Happiness
I Hunt You

Mark Tarrant
The Mighty Hook
The Death Riders
Howl of the Windigo
Guts and Garter Belts

www.ingramcontent.com/pod-product-compliance
Lightning Source LLC
Chambersburg PA
CBHW020250030826
48979CB00030B/2775/J

* 9 7 8 1 6 4 4 5 0 7 4 3 8 *